Return to the Outer Banks House

A novel by
Diann Ducharme

ISBN: 0692312927
ISBN 13: 9780692312926
Library of Congress Control Number: 2014919006
Kill Devil Publishing, Kill Devil Hills, NC

TO NORMAN AND PATRICIA--

FOR BRINGING ME TO THE BEACH

CHAPTER ONE

WHALES HEAD, NORTH CAROLINA, ON THE OUTER BANKS
NOVEMBER 5, 1875
ELIZA DICKENS

Ship ahoy! Have ye seen the White Whale?

–*CAPTAIN AHAB*, **MOBY-DICK**

MY ARM BURNED HOT, LIKE I'D LEFT IT TOO LONG OVER THE cook fire. I had a notion to let fly with the man's case, titter as it two-stepped down the stairs.

What was in the damned case, bricks of gold? Might be so. Just a look at the Yanks and I knew they were the richest men I ever laid eyes on. Up here in Whales Head, on the northern parts of the Outer Banks, I was hard pressed to find a man who owned a decent pair of boots.

I'd caught sight of their shiny black shoes when they'd stepped from the skiff to the docks. The sunlight made their footwear hard to miss.

There I'd stood gawking at their finery. They'd traveled by rail, sail, ferry and buggy to get here, but you'd not know it by the slick looks of them. I gnawed at the nubs of my fingernails, no better'n a monkey.

They stood to face their diggings.

"My stars" was what they said. They looked pleased in general. Amos looked to piss himself he was so chirked. After a while one of them smiled at me, in that way men do when they ain't really looking at you. He'd handed his case to me, and I took it from him quick too, heavy as it was. I didn't care to cow-tow to him, shiny shoes or no.

I knew I had a job to do. I'd been hired for the post of housekeep for the newest hunting club on the Currituck Sound, and carrying cases up a flight of stairs seemed a natural part of the job.

At the top of the stairs I took the air like a heifer about to foal. The air still smelled strong of paint and wood. I dragged the case into one of the bedrooms, then heaved it onto a fancy stand looking too needle-legged to hold all that heft. I shook my arm out, fit to cry.

Down below I heard the men talking loud. I heard the clink of a bottle on the lips of glasses. About the time when I reckoned they were swallowing their liquor, I heard the calls of the snow geese. Nigh on a week ago they showed up in droves to winter on the Currituck waters. Now I heard them all night long, sounded just like a gale a-screeching.

Amos Pickerson—he's my friend Iola's man—built up the clubhouse last year with a crew of Currituckers. The heart pine lumber was cut afore it even sailed and sent down on barges straight from New York. I've never seen a thing like it in my life. Amos said it was harder to put together than a house made of flotsam, on account each piece of wood had to fit its proper place, no varying.

Shingles over every bit of it, and a porch wrapped around the sound side. It wasn't a grand abode, but it's sure to be one of the finest buildings in Currituck by a long shot. Even counting the new brick lighthouse. Seemed to me a waste the Yanks'd only be staying here five weeks of a winter. But I reckoned with pockets full of rocks men could do as they pleased.

Once the clubhouse was up, the furniture got sent down. Me and Iola worked as if in a dream those days, our eyes popping over every crate got carried off the barge. We had the say of where each piece would set on account the crew hadn't a notion, hardly even knowing the sight of a bona fide brass bedstead or a coal-burning cook stove. But I will say that we'd never seen so many tables, nor tried to figure their uses. Seemed like they needed a table for every possibility. Set a jug there, set a candlestick there, set a gold brick there.

A thousand acres of land the men owned outright. It was still a hot summer back then but Amos had himself a long list of things needed doing before the wildfowl season started up. Him and his crew cut corn sedge with sling blades for the blinds, then strung 'em together and stuck them all over the coves and shoals. They carved up 200 new decoys, then went through all the jars of paint. They bought new everything with the Yanks' money, save the shotguns the men brung themselves. They built a real fine hunting boat too.

Iola and me brought firewood from the mainland, for Whales Head was nothing but a desert of sand, no trees to be found. Digging the well and stocking preserves and pickling vegetables and unpacking the what-nots the wives sent. Linens, dishes, silver, pots and pans and cookware, and more liquor bottles than I'd ever pictured.

I was afraid to even touch some of the finery. My hands had a grey sheen to 'em, even when scrubbed clean. I snickered good at their foolishness forbye, sending such fine things to the Banks. Everything warped out here so close to the sea.

I couldn't picture the grandfather clock rotting though. It looked built to last 'til the end of time itself. I heard its ticking all over the place, even in the garden. I could stand for hours watching the skinny gold lines tickle those feather numbers. When it called the time I stopped to listen to the dinging and wondered over how small the bell in its innards must be. But mostly the clock pleased me on account it stood up straight and did its own work, unlike the silver that called for polishing all the time.

I didn't reckon the men cared about the niceties. The hunting and none other had lured them here from New York City, not the chance to use their silver punch bowl. And they ain't the first group of Yanks to buy up sound side land from the locals to build their clubhouses. There's Currituck Shooting Club, Palmer Island Shooting Club, Swan Island Club, and more to come I'm sure. All atop one another.

Amos told me they called this new club the "Golden Feather," but I figured the "Bloody Feather" was a more likely name. I'd never afore seen such rafts of wildfowl as I'd seen on the northern Currituck Sound. If a man wanted a duck dinner, all he needed do was venture outside with a shotgun.

I went back down the stairs and stood there watching the men strut in the firelight. They were so busy with themselves they didn't notice me.

So I piped up. "I'm Eliza Dickens, the housekeep here. If something's puckering you, and it's got something to do with keeping house, you can let me know about it."

Afore I could clear the door frame, a man said, "A moment please, Miss Dickens?"

Didn't take long for them to find a thing amiss. I turned back, put my hands on my hips. "What?"

"I can see you're not one for conversation, but at least let us introduce ourselves. I'm Mr. Langston Parrish, and this is Mr. Odell Sexton and Mr. Percy Sanders."

His words carried what I knew to be a Yankee accent. His black hair was slicked back and sliced down the middle of his square head. I pegged him for a man in the middle of his life, yet not gone to pasture.

"Pleased to meet your acquaintance, Miss Dickens. Everything looks in fine order," said Mr. Sexton. His jelly-belly quivered though he stood in place. Skinny Mr. Sanders just offered me a wink.

Mr. Parrish kept on. "I'm sorry you ended up with that particular case. I meant to give you the lighter one back on the docks. The one you carried was packed full of books."

The other men put their noses into their glasses. I reckoned he was pulling my leg.

"We've already told him they're going to gather dust here. Should have left your library alone, Langston," said Mr. Sexton.

Mr. Parrish sat in a cushioned chair and crossed his legs at the knee. "My companions only find time to read the financial reports in the *The New York Times.*"

I cut eyes at him. "They *were* books in your case?"

He shrugged. "A man cannot live without books."

"Thomas Jefferson," said Mr. Sanders. He raised his glass up and drank.

I had no notion a-tall about a man named Thomas Jefferson or why they'd drink to him and his queer notion of books. I reckoned a man could live without books, but would have a harder go of it without food and water, plenty of other things.

I left them mulling over things of such mystery to me they might have been talking a different language than American.

In the kitchen house Iola stood over the brand new step-top cook stove. Her wood spoon dipped into a pot of turtle a-stewing.

"Alright then, let's have it."

"Ain't nothing to tell, Iola. It's just as we suspected. Bunch of blue-noses, raring for the frolic of a lifetime."

Iola gave me the spoon and sat down on the stool. "Any of 'em good looking?"

"One of 'em is, I'll wager. And married to boot." I stirred Iola's famous stew.

"That don't mean nothing. Nothing at all!" She liked to poke fun on marriage, but I knew Iola's union with Amos was a happy one, on account I stayed in the same one-room cabin with 'em.

"Get on up, Iola. You're the cook here, ain't you?" I handed her back her spoon, but not before I licked some sauce off it. "Needs salt."

"Consarn you, Eliza Dickens!" She ran to wash the spoon off in the washing bucket. "You are some disgusting. You need some manners about you, 'specially round men like these ones. You say they got fancy clothes?"

"And then some. You'll get an eyeful when you help me serve the supper."

Iola's mouth flopped ajar. "Now, I'm happy to cook, but serving 'em too? No thank you, Eliza. I'm not proper! Just look at me!" She held out her apron for me, good and smeared with turtle meat drippings.

I rolled my eyes. "What, and I'm all slicked up? I believe I spun the wool for this dress when I first grew my chest! Least you can light their cigars after supper."

"I reckon they can light their own cigars. They ain't younguns." She wrapped her hand in a rag afore taking the biscuits from the oven. "I hope we get some leftovers tonight."

"Me too. There's nary a bun at the cabin."

"There ain't. I ate the last one yesterday."

"You pig, Iola."

But I knew whatever came about this winter me and Iola and Amos would not go hungry. In all likelihood we'd get fatter than brood sows, which had me worried. At the pace I was moving I'd end up a old maid for certain.

The cabin where we stayed was nothing more than a lean-to of unhewn logs daubed with clay. But it was only a couple hundred yards north from the hunting club so's we could come and go lickety-split. Amos and Iola were used to living here and there wherever Amos got work. So it wasn't a circumstance to have me sharing their roof. And anyhow Amos had promised Iola a house of their own in Whales Head, soon as they got paid what they planned to earn this season.

The night was bitter cold with a hard breeze, and I was glad of the short walk home. I foretold a spell of weather coming.

Iola's gabble eased the sting on my cheeks. "Law almighty they're rich, ain't they? I never seen such dandies in my life."

I recalled snippets of the supper talk. The men went on about railroads, steel, oil and even Mr. President Grant, seeming like a dear friend to them.

"But they ain't at all uppity. They seem right natural. Don't you think so? That Mr. Sexton even talked with me when I was lighting up their cigars."

Iola had not been able to keep from the dining room after all, but she did see fit to take off her apron aforehand.

"He asked me if I'd lived in Currituck all my life, in just the most nicest way. And praised my turtle stew as the best he'd ever eaten."

I snorted loud. The hardness of my life had taught me not to look kindly on rich folk. I grew up down south in Nags Head, had one too many dealings with the mainlanders that spent their summers there. My own mama still ran a market that sold them their perishables. No sooner did I learn to put one foot in front of the other, and mama had me cow-towing to those people. Course I grew to despise all their neediness. It's no different with these Yankee men, mannerly as they seem. They got needs a-plenty.

Time we got to the cabin, Amos was already asleep.

"He's been so tuckered of late, poor thing," Iola said.

Last fortnight had Amos working night and day to get ready for the Yanks—working with the tollers, finishing up the game barn, outfitting the new skiff. He was a good guide, but woodworking and boat-building in particular were his specialties. Folks came from all over the state to get him to build them their boats. Yes, Big Amos did alright for himself. Iola had seen his worth long ago and had latched onto him tight as a tick.

I took down my bun and started to undo the buttons along the front of my dress. But my fingers felt stiff as bucket handles so I gave it up. I stretched out on my own tick and fell straight to sleep.

When I woke, it was dark and cold as ice in the cabin. I heard the wind whistle low through the cracks of the logs. I pulled my blankets up to my chin, but then my legs started to cramping. I switched around a bit on the tick, rubbing at 'em and falling to sleep once more. But a loud bark from Amos made me jump. I turned over and in the shadows I saw Iola huddled over Amos with a tin cup, trying to get him to drink. A rag stretched across his forehead.

"What is it?"

Iola moaned. "He's got a terrible ague."

Amos let loose with a torrent of hacks.

"He ain't fit for work today," said Iola.

"I got to go, Iola." Amos tried sitting up, but flopped back down, the rag on his forehead askew.

"It's fixing to storm bad," Iola said. "If you go out in that weather today, you'll die for sure. And I ain't ready to be a widow."

Up I got, wrapped in a blanket, and opened the door. Sand blew across the dirt floor of the cabin afore I banged the door shut. I could already picture the skies full of waterfowl, already hear the shooting of the rifles.

"Those men need a guide today," I said.

Amos's coughing answered me. It went on and on. Iola and me waited him out.

"I could do it. Until Amos is better," I said.

Iola let out a breath like she'd been holding it for days. "I'll tend to your housekeep chores," she said. She squared the rag on Amos's forehead.

My mind turned over jobs to do. "I'll need Old Skelly."

Old Skelly was Amos's toller, a fat, mean-tempered old snow goose trained by Amos from a gosling to call for other geese. There had never been a toller as good as Skelly, but she was spoiled as a animal could get and Amos kept her close.

Amos shook his head on the roll of homespun under it. "Skelly won't mind you."

"Sure she will. All you do is feed her bits of corn and she goes out callin'. I've seen it dozens of times."

He coughed hard for a full minute, then said, "You'll want the black ducks."

"You spoil that goose, Amos. You worried she's gonna catch cold? Let me just bring her on the skiff, see how she does."

Amos started making sounds akin to snoring, so I took that for a yes. Iola lay down next to him, a arm over his belly.

I fumbled around in the cold dirt for my hair pins and stuck them in willy-nilly. Once I got my dress off, I pulled on a pair of Amos's thick work britches over top my drawers, cinched them tight across with a old apron string from the sewing basket. I added two of his woolen shirts, a coon fur hat, and two pairs of his yarn socks under his big rubber boots. I topped it all off with my coat, a blue Union army coat I found umpteen years ago, waterlogged on the sand and a musket hole in the back.

I peeked through a crack in the logs and saw nothing but black. But I knew dawn would arrive in just a couple hours.

"We best get on over."

I watched Iola tuck Amos inside his blanket. She whispered into his neck, kissed both his cheeks. He kicked a leg out from the blanket, showing us a gray sock with more holes than wool. Iola huffed and tried to stick his leg back under the blanket.

"Quit your fussing," I said.

I lit the lantern, and we pushed out into the dark and the wind, scarves wrapped tight about our faces. In the game barn I held the lantern up to the rack to find my own shotgun. I slung her over my back, then spotted that fat pile of white feathers in the toller pen. First I dipped my hand into the bag of corn and poured handfuls into my coat pockets. Then I picked Skelly up careful, staying far away from her beak. Skelly was known to bite anyone that wasn't Amos, 'specially Iola, who called the goose jealous. The meanest dogs gave Skelly a wide berth.

At the docks the new boat bucked high in the rough waters of the sound. I pulled it toward me with the rope and put Old Skelly in the hull with Amos's wood box full of gear: paper shells charged with shot, oil, wiping sticks and wads. The bags of decoys were already stashed in the dinghy, for Amos was always at the ready.

Even out on the docks I heard the grandfather clock chime five times from the parlor.

"Don't forget their night jars now," I told Iola.

She sucked her tongue at me. "You just worry about your own self. You'll be lucky to get out to the blinds before the weather starts up."

Back at the clubhouse Iola lit the fire in the dining room grate and was soon serving eggs and bacon to the men on the china, pouring Yankee coffee into the matching cups. They ate it all up fast, talking of nothing but ducks and swans and geese. They looked up from their plates. I saw 'em take notice of the men's britches and coon hat.

"Amos is poorly this morning and won't be up for guiding you today. We thought it best if I took you out. Until he gets better."

The men looked at each other, forks and cups froze in the air. They looked out the windows, the light just enough to see bits of marsh grass blowing fast by the glass.

Mr. Parrish said, "You?"

Mr. Sexton chuckled nervous. "Pardon me, Miss Dickens, but I find it hard to believe a young woman such as yourself would know the first thing about waterfowl hunting. You can't tell me you've shot a gun before."

"Course I have! What do you take me for?"

They all stared at me, words stuck in their throats for likely the first time in their lives.

"Well, you're the housekeeper. Isn't that right?" said Mr. Sexton. He looked at his fellows, all shrugging and nodding in their nice corduroy suits.

Iola tittered from the other side of the table. The men turned to her.

"I declare Eliza can ride, fish and shoot better than most men on the Banks, and that's a fact. She can name a duck a mile away just by watching it circle the sky, and she can cry like any bird—duck, jay, goose or crow. Course, she ain't got nothing on my Amos," she said, with a sorry look for me. "But you won't go wrong with her today, I promise you."

"What seems to be ailing Amos?" said Mr. Parrish.

"Oh, just a cold in his chest," said Iola. "He'll be back to his old self again in no time. That one's strong as a ox."

The men sized me up all over again. They ate their meals and made ready for the day's hunt, and I reckoned that was that. Iola handed me a lit lantern and a basket of cornbread and ham, and the men fetched their fancy guns, donned their caps and buttoned their long rubber coats.

"You think you can row all of us, Miss Dickens?" asked Mr. Sexton at the docks. He patted his belly. "Some of us are heavier than others."

"Won't be rowing so much as poling," says I. "And yes, I can pole all of you and then some."

"There's a goose in the boat," said Mr. Parrish.

Mr. Sexton and Mr. Sanders bent to look. Mr. Sexton said, "Shouldn't he wake?"

"He's a she. Name's Old Skelly. She'll wake when she's ready."

Mr. Parrish stepped into the skiff real soft and derned if he didn't reach over and cover up Skelly with a blanket. He pulled it up to her twisted neck like she was a babe in the cradle. I figured there was something about Old Skelly that made men want to spoil her, but I couldn't feature what trait that might be. I myself had a good bit of orneriness, but I didn't see any men pulling blankets over me.

I untied the skiff and we set off into the dark, the lantern perched on the corner of the stern. I stood in the middle of the men as I guided the boat north with the long pole. The men and dinghy *were* right heavy, 'specially with the wind in front of us. And the black foamy water made it hard to see the bars, ready to ground a boat in a second. The wind tore out my tears when I faced full forwards. Day like today fowl would keep away from open water and head straight for the coves and inlets for shelter and food.

"Best hold two feet ahead of your fowl today. They'll be flying slower and lower 'gainst the wind," I called.

We soon reached the point, a marshy bar jutting out into the sound. Amos had set up two blinds in the cove, knowing it for a canvasback feeding spot. I stepped into the shallows to spread the decoys. Soon about 100 wooden ducks and geese bobbed on the water, and the dawn was putting out a little light.

I took the blanket off Skelly and lifted her to my chest, ready for her to flap to the water like she'd been trained. But Skelly blinked her eyes, her body heavy as a anchor. I put her on the floor of the skiff in the hopes of rousing her up a bit, but Skelly just poked her head into her wing.

The men looked on right curious. I drew my hand into my pocket and held out a palm full of dry corn.

"Skelly, I've got some treats for you," I said, in the sweetest voice I could muster. "Look here."

Skelly took out her head and waddled over to me. She ate the corn up like she was starved. I thought she'd jump into the water, all set to call. But Skelly just stood there, watching my corn hand.

I huffed at her. Amos really had spoiled the goose.

"Skelly, it's time to get wet," I said, nice voice gone for good.

I clapped my hands loud, but still the goose stood her ground. So I grabbed her good around her fat middle, and she let out a honk. I threw her over the side of the boat, and she landed in the water, wings a-flapping. The men grinned as Skelly floated about, looking as unlikely as a goose can look.

I guided the boat into a blind, and Mr. Sexton and Mr. Sanders walked around to crouch in the other. We all hunkered down and watched the skies. The wind grew louder in the quiet. I could hear Mr. Parrish taking the air, we were so close.

All the moving about had warmed me up, but after setting in the blind for a few minutes, and the sweat cooling in the wind, I shivered from my scalp to my toes. I didn't have a ounce of extra fat on me, if I wasn't counting my tiny breasts, and it felt to me like I was setting there naked. As if I didn't have on umpteen layers of wool at all.

I groped around in Amos's britches and found what I reckoned was already stashed in the pocket—a plug of tobacco wrapped in paper. I cut a large piece with my knife and stuck it in my jaw. My mouth worked it over, and my arms and legs started to warm.

Mr. Parrish watched me. "I've never seen a woman enjoy chewing tobacco so well."

"Now you have."

He stretched out his legs, rubber boots squeaking. "It's not very lady-like."

I spat juice into the water and wiped my mouth with the back of my mitt. "As you can see, I ain't worried about being called a lady."

"No, I suppose not," he said. "Where on earth did you come by that coat?"

"Found it."

"And it suits you, wearing a Union soldier's desecrated uniform?"

"Well, whose army it fought for ain't a circumstance to me," I said. "It's a coat."

And I did like the fancy brass buttons down the front of it. And breathing in its old salty tobacco smell made me feel I was close to a man again.

"There goes your goose," Mr. Sanders called. I looked to the land, and sure enough, there was that blasted Old Skelly a-waddling up the banks.

"Skelly, get back here!" I hollered, and the plug of tobacco came loose. "You shit-bird!"

Skelly just kept on strutting, wind blowing at her feathers. She never had no intention of minding me. The men guffawed so loud it drowned out the wind, but my face burned hot. I reckoned I wanted the men to trust me with the job, but Skelly had turned me into a fool. I'd hunted waterfowl for the family table off and on since I was able to lift a firearm. Nothing but hunger had honed my skills to the point I was now one of the sharpest shots on the Banks.

"Now what?" said Mr. Parrish.

I spit the plug of tobacco into the water and sucked in the cold air. "I'm gonna go get me some new tollers, is what. Birds that can tolerate a leash!"

I'd show these men I didn't need Old Skelly to give them a grand day of shooting. I climbed over the side of the skiff into the water and plunked Amos's boots through the cold shallows and marsh grass to the land. In no time I caught up with Skelly. I reached down and plucked her up and derned if that goose didn't turn and hiss at me. I clamped a stiff hand over her beak and tucked her backwards under my arm. We went on that way clear back to the clubhouse, a shorter walk than boat ride.

At the game barn I dropped Skelly into her nest of straw and picked two black ducks that Amos favored. On the way back to the cove with the cage, it started to sleet on me so's I had to look out at the world through slices of eyes. Even so I heard the steady rush of canvasback feathers straining against wind. Though the sleet stuck to my eyelashes, I saw the sky was full of food, the prettiest sight I've ever seen.

Canvasbacks were skittish of decoys. But I knew they'd come to their feeding spot and felt at their ease. When their wings bent downward in a soar, my hands held steady a invisible gun. On their turn I heard the men's ten-gauges explode from the blinds. Easy volleys, splashes and smoke. Only a few ducks drew away.

I splashed into the cove, knowing the men would be pleased with the feisty canvasbacks. I could already hear their hollering. I grabbed a net and my shotgun from the dinghy and waded into the water to scoop up the dead and shoot the crippled afore they could dive. I counted 23 canvasbacks and three redheads. I tethered the two black ducks to a stake, and they rode the choppy water. *That'll learn me to choose fancy over plain*, I thought.

The sleet quit time I climbed back into the skiff. Mr. Parrish opened up his coat enough to pull out a small book. Mr. Sanders and Mr. Sexton started talking low to one another and eating on the ham and cornbread. I cut another plug and sat chewing.

After a while Mr. Parrish looked up at me from the book. I squirmed on the seat. I wasn't used to men staring at me. I didn't have what was called good looks like Iola. I lacked a ample backside, and my face was thin and brown and sagged in a downward direction, even as a youngun.

"Do you like to read, Miss Dickens?"

"No."

"I don't suppose you have a lot of time for the exercise."

"That's right," I said. "And anyways, there ain't no schools out here."

Not a soul in my family ever could read or write, but mama knew how to add sums in her head. She was always the sharpest of the family by a long shot.

"You never learned?"

"I don't need that kind of learning, and I never wished for it neither."

The sedge of the blind liked to close in on me and smother me. The air left to me smelled of bird death and wet marsh grass. I blew my nose into the water, then wiped it with my mitt.

"Look here," I said. "I once knew a man—he was a decent man too, a real good fisherman and hunter and...just a good man."

I stopped talking, my chest tight like I had the consumption. I licked my chapped lips, over and over.

"Well, he just wasn't satisfied with himself. Wanted all kinds of things he didn't have. Didn't see that he was happy nonetheless. Well, he went and met himself a pretty teacher gal and got himself learned. And then he became the worst man that ever lived and forgot who he was. Now, *that* ain't something I'm striving for. You catch my meaning? I like myself just as I am. And reading folks shouldn't go and think themselves better than me, neither."

Mr. Parrish took on a sorry look. Hot tears came from the depths of me. I tried to blink the water away without rubbing my eyes dry. A boat was no place for a woman's tears.

I hadn't even said Ben's name in such a long time, much less mulled over the mess with a stranger. I tried hard not to even think about him, but it was near impossible not to. He was the reason I moved so far north up the Banks, away from my very own family.

Back yonder in Nags Head, Ben and his wife popped up out of nowhere, paying visits to their little house. They'd fixed up a school over on Roanoke Island. Heard black and white alike went to the school, rain or shine. But still they found the need to cavort around Nags Head on Sundays, shoving their love in my face.

I couldn't take it no longer. Me and Iola took the housekeep and cook jobs at the hunting club, Amos already signed on as caretaker and guide, his crew as the builders. The pay was more'n good for a job that only called for a few months of work a year. That's a rare thing out here, and we all counted ourselves as lucky.

But miles away from Ben I still couldn't shake the feeling I'd been lugging around with me for seven years—the notion I'd lost my whole life somehow, that someone had snuck up on me and stolen it. I might even say the feeling had grown worse, away from the only home I ever knew, though I knew I'd go back again in a few weeks.

Back to no one and nothing, save mama, I thought.

Above me the sky went dark like it was the dead of night. I looked up to see nothing but Canada geese traveling with the wind. The tollers hadn't a care the birds weren't kin. They started to quacking loud as they could, calling to the strangers. Soon some of the flock were so close I could hear their feathers flipping.

The men creaked the boards of the skiff as they crouched. And Mr. Parrish grabbed my gun, handed it over to me. I never shot Canada geese, not since I was a youngun with a fowling piece. But even so, I raised the gun to my shoulder, eyed the big birds as they crossed the water of the cove, and began to fire with the men. When the smoke cleared, dead geese floated all over the water, and the guns smoked around us like a pig barbeque. I thought to myself, *I used to feel things.*

Mr. Parrish said, "I think Iola was right about you, Miss Dickens."

It was almost dark time we poled back to the club-house. The windows were lit up pretty. The men helped me carry the bags of ducks to the game barn, they were so chirked with themselves. Didn't even need to pack them in ice tonight, cold as it was in the barn, but we did take some time to string 'em up to dry.

I was in a fine temper when I took off my icy things and hung them in the mud room. I made my way to the kitchen house, smelling of steamy fish and fresh baked bread.

Iola set a tray of buns on a sideboard and turned to me with a pinchy look on her red face. "I was get-ting worried, you all were out so long. Everything go alright?"

"More than alright. Must be over 100 birds in the game barn tonight, no thanks to Skelly. Hardly room to string 'em all up. Haven't ever seen a day like this one."

I reckoned Iola would be glad of our good for-tune. But her face soured, and she turned back to the pot.

Staring at Iola's hunched back, my good temper faded fast.

"How's Amos tonight?"

Iola turned half a face to me. "I guess you *would* want to know."

"What's that supposed to mean?"

Her bony elbows cut through the air as she stirred the stew. "Over a hundred birds. Law me. Those men sure like to wallow in excess."

She knew well as I did that the buyers would be along to check out the leftover birds, once the men picked the ones they wanted sent to a New York commission house. Those birds would feed many a hungry mouth.

"Well, you'll be happy to know Amos is even worse off than he was. Can't even get up to piss."

"I'm sorry to hear it." I reached out a hand to her arm, but she scooted away.

"Don't do this now. I was helping you out, and here you are acting like a wild hog's been cornered. What, you hoping I'd come back empty-handed?"

Iola cut her eyes to me and said, "If you want to know the truth, I was. I don't think it was right, what you did, after all. That job is Amos's. You're going to take it right out from under him, and with him being sick as dog to do a thing about it!"

"Great Jehoshaphat, Iola. I think all this cookin' is souring your brain. You may need to take the air."

I stomped out of the kitchen, come to find the men wanted me to take my supper with them at the long dining table. But I was still wearing Amos's wool socks and three layers of shirts, and I felt terrible awkward on the embroidered chair cushion. I stared at the china and silver and linens in front of me. I recalled unloading it all from the boxes and ironing and polishing it. And now here it was waiting for me to sup on it. I looked about at the men, their faces chapped red from the weather. They didn't seem all that amazed with the spread before them, so I reckoned I shouldn't be either.

Iola didn't look anywhere near me when she came from the kitchen. Her head looked like a squashed tomato, and she still wore her dirty apron. Even on the thick rug I heard her boots stomping as she moved from place to place, sloshing the stew into the bowls.

"Miss Dickens certainly was everything you described her to be," Mr. Sexton said to her. "I'm glad I saw it with my own two eyes, or I'd never have believed it. This woman knows her way around a 12-gauge."

Iola's face jerked into a lopsided smile. "One hundred birds, ain't that right?"

"At least," he said. "I've never seen anything like it, and that's the truth."

"Well, it ain't a circumstance to what my Amos could have brung in on a day like today. Too bad he's layed up sick."

"How is Amos this evening, Mrs. Pickerson? Any better?" asked Mr. Sanders.

Iola bit her lip. "No, he ain't any better. But it should be any day now, and he'll be ready for guiding you men."

"Sounds like he could use a doctor," said Mr. Parrish.

"Yessir," she said. "I was planning to hang the towel up tomorrow morning."

Mr. Parrish squinted at her. "Pardon?"

"We all hang a white towel on a pitchfork, so Doc Warbush can see it over on the mainland," she said. "He comes day or night."

They all shifted round on their seats. "And this Doctor Warbush is the only qualified man available?" said Mr. Parrish.

"Him and the witch over yonder in the marshes."

"The witch?"

"She's got healing powers," Iola said. "For Bankers only though."

Mr. Sexton's mustache wiggled with a smile. "My, my. We'd best not get sick out here then."

"Well, give Amos our best, would you?" said Mr. Parrish.

"Oh, yes. I surely will do that," said Iola. "That will please him no end."

After shooting me a hateful look, Iola swept out of the room with the pot of stew. My bowl was only half full, I saw. And Iola hadn't given me a bun neither.

After supper the men stepped to the parlor, where the fire burned high on the grate. I tried to skedaddle, but Mr. Sexton grabbed my arm and steered me to a chair. He plopped me down and pulled up a footstool for me.

Then Mr. Parrish poured some brandy into the crystal glasses. He held out one of the glasses. I had the urge to titter at him, for I ain't never took brandy afore. But I shrugged and reached out for the glass.

The men raised their glasses in the air. "To Miss Dickens!" they called. They looked at me like I was a long lost sister.

I scooted about in my chair like a youngun. I sure hoped Iola couldn't hear us in here. I heard her in the kitchen house, banging the pots as she scraped them clean, a job I always helped her with.

"And to Old Skelly! May she rest in peace, the old goose!" Mr. Sexton hollered.

I sipped at the brandy real careful. I found that I liked it, much better than the anti-fogmatic Amos passed round the cabin. I went on to swallow the whole of it in four big gulps. I felt the stuff make its way through my arms and legs like flames licking wood. I tried hard to keep my eyes open. The men leaned back sloppy in the armchairs, full of whiskey and brandy and stew. They lit some cigars and started puffing away and talking about the state of a world where I didn't live. Saying words like "shares" and "profit" and "trusts."

I hardly took note of Mr. Sanders filling up my glass again. I lost count of how many times I sipped at it, how many times he'd filled it. I did hear the back door slam, and featured Iola hurrying home to Amos. I felt the wind blowing on the clubhouse, hard as a harem of horses running. It was fixing to storm but good.

Mr. Parrish'd pulled out his book.

"There you are reading again," I thought I heard myself say.

I couldn't figure how he could read like that with the liquor running through him. It brought to mind something that I saw Ben do, seven years ago, soon after he'd quit me. I'd trailed him after watching him from mama's market. He'd rowed his skiff up to the Nags Head docks, then sold a crate full of his fish to the hotel. Then he took off through the sand toward Nags Head Woods. My heart hurt bad just seeing him. I figured I'd try to just kiss him, instead of talking at him.

But when I saw him through the trees, all I could do was stare, for there he sat in a duff of leaves, reading a book in a bit of sunlight. Now, I'd seen Ben do many things. He was real good with his hands and had a knack for figuring things out. He fished and hunted so good, like the fish and the fowl waited only for Ben to catch 'em.

But I'd never seen him do something so queer as read. He held the book in one hand and the finger of the other hand moved along the page real slow. His face looked happier than I'd ever seen it look.

I knew it was that Abigail Sinclair up in his head. I'd thought up until then that I still had a chance to get him back fair and square, since that uppity schoolmarm was due to leave for home at the end of the season anyway.

But I knew then that I'd lost him forever, for watching him read was like watching him move from me to her, from a life of reading the calls of nature to a life of reading words. I felt I didn't even know him anymore, and I'd grown up following him around like I was paid to.

I'd left him sitting there with such a ache in my chest I thought I was gonna keel over and die, right there in Nags Head Woods. I tried not to cry out until

I got to the market. I still recalled the smell of that crate of ripe tomatoes that was privy to the saddest sounds I ever made.

Mama'd rushed over in a panic. "What, is it that danged snake? Did he get you, girl?"

I just shook my head, snot and spittle eeking out of the holes in my face.

"He's gone."

Mama's dirty bare feet shifted on the wood, looking for the snake. After a while, she said, "You mean Ben?"

I couldn't hardly breathe. "He's really gone for good."

"How do you know all that, now? I told you he's just going through a spell. All men do."

I looked up to mama's bony brown face. "He can read."

After a bit she said, "Well, now."

She hauled me to my feet and drew a hanky from her pocket, wiped at my nose with her apron like I was a youngun again. Then she walked on back to the front of the market, where a customer waited. Mama knew as good as me that Ben had changed, and there was nothing more to do or say.

And now dead anger rushed through me, the kind of anger that's caused by the drink itself. I wanted sorely to holler at someone, but the Yanks didn't quite deserve it. Mr. Sexton was snoring away on the chair, two chins tucked under him. Mr. Sanders was staring cockeyed at the fire, a tiny pucker on his chicken lips. Soon enough, the angry thoughts fell away from me, and I saw I had nothing to say. Not much a-tall.

I stood up on my jelly legs and said my farewells, but the words came out backwards. Mr. Parrish got up and rummaged round in his pocket. He yanked out a roll of money, counted out some bills and handed 'em to me.

"We wanted to give you a bonus for your good work today."

All I could do was stare down at the paper money in my hand. I thought of Amos and Iola and wondered if I should share with them.

He walked me to the door, helped me pull on my coat. I lit the lantern and opened the door. The cold wind took my breath away, but I couldn't talk anyhow.

"Get some rest, Miss Dickens," he said. "You're going to guide for us tomorrow morning."

Back at the cabin I lay down on the tick and fell fast into a brandy-slopped sleep, still holding onto the roll of bills. I almost didn't hear Amos hacking away, all through the night.

CHAPTER TWO

NOVEMBER 5, 1875
ABIGAIL SINCLAIR WHIMBLE

*"Swim away from me, do ye?" murmured Ahab, gazing
over into the water. There seemed but little in the words,
but the tone conveyed more of deep helpless sadness than
the insane old man had ever before evinced.*

–ISHMAEL, **MOBY-DICK**

IN THE COLD SCHOOLHOUSE, EVERYTHING IN FRONT OF ME—
except the forty or so eager students themselves—
looked more downtrodden than usual.

"When you think I'll be able to start on the next
reader, Miz Abby?" Luella asked, distracting me from
the fire, gasping its last in the woodstove. "The one
with the stories in it."

Luella put forth that same question every day, but we both knew she had a difficult time stringing more than a few words together.

"Pretty soon, Luella. You just need a bit more practice."

"I already done practiced," she said. Her beautiful face never rested; it constantly showed strain, distress. She pointed to her slate, where I'd written ten easy words for her to sound out. She read them all as fast as she could, then glared at me, her brown eyes tinged red with indignation. Of course, I knew that she'd memorized their order after going over and over them at least 50 times.

"I'm talking about reading long sentences. Paragraphs."

"I can read those too," she said, rolling her eyes.

"It takes practice," I said again. "Remember what Mr. Africa always said."

At that, Luella squeezed her eyes shut. Even though she was nearly fourteen years old, she still hadn't forgotten the night of Elijah Africa's murder. Her mama Ruth told me Luella still had nightmares about it, the same way that she'd had nightmares about her daddy getting shot when they tried to escape from the plantation, back during the war. But instead of wetting the tick as she used to, Luella would wake up naked, her nightdress thrown off, covered in sweat and screaming. Other than her mother, she trusted no one, not even me.

I supposed it didn't help that we still conducted classes in the "Elijah Africa Freedmen School" where the reverend was finally found by my daddy and his disguised men. Even I fought the memories that haunted the place.

In spite of its history, the schoolhouse was a source of pride for the students. It boasted a slick black door and shutters that Ben had painted, in the late winter of 1869. Ben had also constructed log benches along the walls of the building for seating and had installed four more windows, for a total of six, for extra light and air in the summers. He'd made shelves for every inch of wall space, and they now teemed with all manner of things we'd scouted out and written about: turtle shells, arrowheads, osprey feathers, pine cones, otter and raccoon skulls.

The students had worked to scrub every corner of the room, and before she'd passed away, mama had sent the professionally painted placard, just as she said she would. She'd also sent an old woodstove, several lamps and boxes of candles, and countless crates of our own books, a few at a time over four or five months so the packages wouldn't draw too much suspicion en route from Sinclair House.

I'm not sure where she found the money, but she'd also ordered dozens of first, second, third and fourth McGuffey Eclectic Readers, which spanned several different levels of ability; there were so many of the instructional books that often one student was not required to share with another. With bindings already worn and pages ripped and smudged, the books now lined four long shelves along the back wall of the school. The supplies had called even some of the white children of the island to the schoolhouse.

And now, faces black and white stared up me, the conversation with Luella more interesting than mathematics.

I sighed. I didn't feel like forcing anyone to my will today, especially Luella. I hadn't slept well for almost a month, since Ben had left for the Jones's Hill Lifesaving Station in Whales Head, and my mind felt like a dead fish, frozen for a time in a bucket of ice.

"Ain't we got some more wood for that stove?" asked Leo, rubbing his palms together as he turned a mean eye to the old woodstove in the center of the room. "We all gonna catch our death in here."

An elderly black woman near the front coughed softly into a handkerchief.

"No, that's the last of it." I wore my coat over my homespun dress, and most of the students were bundled into every item of clothing they owned. "Perhaps we should end class. The lamps are almost out of oil, and we're running low on candles."

The class sighed as one, loath to cut precious learning time short. But it wasn't my fault that we couldn't even afford to buy candles or oil for the lamps, much less a set of mathematics books, chalk, slates, desks and chairs. And in the aftermath of the war, wood on Roanoke Island was still scarce. Most of the trees in the vicinity had been used for the freedmen's houses and Union barracks; wood for the islanders was still brought over from the mainland across the Croatan Sound.

"You all act like you ain't never been cold before," snapped Asha, the book only an inch from her eyes. In the years since she'd been coming to the schoolhouse, Asha had made remarkable progress; she even taught lessons here during the evenings. But lately she'd begun to complain about her eyesight. She needed spectacles, but she couldn't afford them on her laundress's pay, no matter how many sheets and tablecloths she took in.

"I swear, you all is just plain lazy," she scolded.

Despite Asha's admonition, the class got to their feet and made for the door. Wearily I gathered my things and headed into the gray afternoon with them. A stiff breeze wrestled with the scarf I was knotting around my neck.

As I locked up, Leo called, "I'll bring some more wood for you next time, Miz Whimble."

"Thank you, Leo," I said, my voice making barely a sound. Leo came to class when he could, but sometimes weeks would go by and I wouldn't see him, due to the demands of his work as a boat pilot. The schoolhouse might be cold for a good while.

I rested my forehead on the black door, my eyelids inching down like slugs.

"You alright?" asked Asha, her words now laced with motherly concern.

"I'm just tired. Someone was snoring like a broken clarinet last night…"

"Ain't no body snoring like that," she sniffed.

I'd been living with Asha in her pitch-pine cabin on Roanoke Island since Ben had left for Whales Head. Even though the autumn wind blew straight through the cracks between the crooked logs, and she huddled into her few blankets and quilts when the fire in the mud-plastered hearth died out, the home had become a part of her, so that when I thought of Asha, I thought of those roughly split logs as well. She'd taken ownership over it when her good friend Pearl Jefferson passed away. They'd lived in the house together for several years, building up a laundering business until Pearl had gotten sick.

It was four houses down from the house in which Ben and I had lived since I'd decided to stay on the Outer Banks. I walked by our boarded-up house every day to get to the schoolhouse, and I still hated the sight of the place, with its peeling white clapboard and seven rotten stumps in the front yard. It was more spacious than the Nags Head house that Ben had built, being a story-and-a-half, and it boasted a down-stuffed tick on a four-poster bed, but the place smelled of old wood and stale smoke instead of sea and salt. Still owned by the Freedmen's Bureau, it had been a temporary home of the previous missionary teachers, I was told, and the Bureau thought it was only right that we live there.

Ben and I had agreed. Working as a teacher at the schoolhouse required me to live close by, so the house in Nags Head had been boarded up. In the early years, Ben and I had still managed to visit the little house every so often, but only on the Sabbath when the weather was pleasant. Yet our visits had dwindled with time; we hadn't visited the house together in a long while.

After Ben had left for Whales Head, I had some-how convinced Asha that the house in Nags Head needed me to check on it sometimes. Ben *had* left me his own skiff, after all. I'd already returned twice in the month he'd been gone, but both times I'd ended up pacing the empty house for a couple of minutes, then going outside to walk the deserted strands of beach, wondering why I'd come over in the first place.

I turned to Asha and said, "I'm heading over to Nags Head."

"No, you surely ain't," she laughed. "Let's head on back, and I'll fix you a chicken supper. If you eat like a good girl, I'll give you the last of the pie. Then you can lie down and rest."

She took my arm to guide me toward the road. But after a few paces, I wrenched my arm from her grip.

"I'm a grown woman, not a girl," I said.

Asha sighed. "It's your own business. But act quick, you hear? There's a wind blowing."

She hugged me to her, and in the folds of neck and scarf, I gulped her scent of laundry flakes and cooking spices. She reached into her pack and pulled out a biscuit, wrapped in a clean, white rag. I smelled the jam soaking its innards, but before I could unwrap it, Asha pushed me in the direction of the docks.

"Get on now, before the dark comes on."

Through the years Ben had instructed me in all things nautical, and I had done all I could to impress him with my meager abilities. After no fewer than seven years of instruction, he had declared me fit to sail the skiff on my own. But my most recent trips showed me that I should have practiced more. I should have taught myself to survive on the Outer Banks without him.

In our Roanoke Island home, Ben did everything for us. He'd rise before the sun to prepare a meal, which involved gathering eggs from the coop and milking the cow and starting a fire in the hearth. He'd wake me with a kiss and I'd dress for a day of teaching as he cooked food over the fire. In warm weather we'd sit on the steps of the front porch, tin plates in our laps, and eat as the sun colored the drabness. Then he'd walk me to the schoolhouse before spending the rest of the day fishing with his daddy and trading what they'd caught.

Ben would come home in the evenings smelling of fish guts and sweat, while I put my feet up after a long day of standing. He always wanted me to read *Robinson Crusoe* to him while he got started on our supper. He'd rekindle the fire in the hearth, skin the fish he'd caught and fry it with some lard and vegetables from our garden. After supper he'd heat a big boiler of water over the fire and pour it all into two barrels. Outside, he'd wash the dishes and pans and sometimes our clothing in the barrels. He'd hang his shirt and britches up on the line to dry overnight. Then we'd read a bit more by candlelight, if we had it, and go to bed, the smell of ash lye and firewood all around us.

He told me he didn't *want* me to help him with the chores, and I'd stopped even offering.

And yet he did believe that I needed to learn to use a boat. Every woman on the Banks knew how to sail a skiff, as did most children over the age of ten. I would have much preferred to wash clothing and cook food, for maneuvering a spritsail skiff, even straight across the narrow sound, always taxed my strength, what little I had before Ben left.

Without him, I was doing chores I'd never had to do. After teaching, I spent the afternoons with Asha, helping her wash, hang and fold laundry on her numerous clotheslines, tending to her garden and the stock, assisting her with supper preparations, and discussing literature with her on the crooked front stoop while the daylight still held. Then Asha would head back to the schoolhouse to teach the adults who hadn't been able to attend the day lessons. I was asleep when she returned, usually around midnight. Then we'd rise before the dawn to tend to tasks too numerous and exhausting to detail. And yesterday, we'd cleansed the house of chinches by taking all of our possessions outside, then pouring buckets of scalding water over the floors and walls.

Now, as I stood at the protected northern cove where I'd beached Ben's skiff, I thought of going back to Asha's cold cabin, where the wind blew straight through the cracks of the logs. I thought of all that I would have to do there, just to put a meal on the table. I balled my mittened hands, now calloused and raw underneath the wool. They were rougher than I ever imagined hands could be, with the constant barrage of warm water and soap and friction that Asha's laundry service required. My back ached from bending and stretching sideways, my legs ached from standing. I never wanted to see a washboard and washtub again.

I placed my bag into the stern of the skiff and untied the rope that tethered the skiff to a pole. I then pushed the boat hard toward the water, hopped inside and used the oars to pole out deeper. Once I hit open water, I raised the sprit sail, which quickly billowed out. The skiff skimmed over the surface of the disturbed water, too fast for my own comfort, and I forced myself to conjure Ben's steady hands on my own, his whispers in my ear, as he told me exactly what to do.

The wind took me clear across the sound before I'd even realized it. I had an urge to cry out in triumph, but I soon found that I recognized not one bit of the island in front of me. I'd ended up too far south; the familiar docks near the two hotels were nowhere in sight.

In a panic, I lowered the sail and rowed about in the shallow grasses, tree branches scraping at my head and pulling at my bonnet. I finally spotted a long, sturdy oak tree branch that I could tie the rope to. But as I took in the conditions, I realized that I would have to step through the sludgy, wet marshes to get to land. I heard Asha's scolding:

"Now look what you've gone and done, and here you could be nice and dry and settin' by the fire, a meal in your belly."

I took a deep breath, lifted my skirts and stepped. In a few seconds, the cold water had soaked my old leather shoes and the wool stockings under them.

The cold stole up my legs, into my chest, making it hard for me to even breathe. On land I squelched stiffly northward, through the blowing sand and swaying pine and cedar trees. A branch cracked over my head, and I looked up expecting to see a crooked shadow falling on me. But all was cloudy twilight. My teeth clattered of their own will, and in my attempt to wrap the ends of my scarf around my face, I tripped over my own cold feet.

With my forehead in the sand, I huddled into myself, knees to chest. *Ben,* I pleaded in my mind. *I need you.* I reached out a hand to the air, could almost feel his large hand enclose my own with warmth. But the sensation was gone before I could take comfort from it.

I got myself up, grabbed my bag, and trudged on. It was the very edge of night now. I walked for what seemed like an hour through nothing but blowing sand, scrub brush and live oak trees before coming upon a handful of darkened homes built on stilts along the sound, the homes of Nags Headers I didn't care to know. Nags Headers, I'd found, were a rough, clannish sort, and isolated from society like they were, their minds had grown closed and lazy. They kept to themselves, and always made an effort to go the long way around me.

But their homes gave me an indication of where I now was, so I adjusted my path eastward, toward the sea. The foliage grew thicker still, and I soon tripped over what felt to my frozen big toe to be a substantial rock. For a brief moment I wondered what a rock was doing in the middle of the island, but then, looking down, I realized I'd tripped over the grave stone. And to my right, standing solid within the doomsday shadows and noise, was the house.

All I had to do was turn the wooden knob, push the door open and latch it closed, for I'd already pried away the planks that Ben had nailed across it the first time I'd come back to the house. I dropped down to a thin wool blanket I'd left behind and breathed in the smells of wood smoke and salt and long absence. The wind raged at the shutters, battened down over the house's four windows. The interior of the cottage was darker than the angry night outside.

I believed I was too tired to take off my shoes, but a prickling island sense told me to use all of my remaining strength to wrench them off my deadened feet and start a fire in the hearth, an oftentimes difficult trick. Once I got my shoes and stockings off and wiggled my frozen toes, I crawled over to the hearth and threw onto the grate the last two logs, old deadwood from Nags Head Woods. I fumbled on the dusty floor for the box of wooden matches and held one to the wood. The fire was slow to start, and slow to grow, beneath the cold wood, but finally satisfied it wouldn't go out, I wrapped myself into the blanket and pulled the slowly warming air into my lungs. My feet tingled as they thawed, and my eyes rested on the shelves of shells, lit like relics by the stirring flames.

The collection had begun in the early years, when we'd still visited the house from time to time. I'd told Ben that the house needed some decoration. I'd learned their names: lion's paws, scallops, cockles, whelks, clams. The collection amused Ben—shells weren't overly special to native Bankers—but he'd constructed the shelves to display them for me. I must have collected over five hundred shells, and many specimens told a story from our brief visits to the house.

My mind began winding through the old conversations we'd had while walking the beaches. So much had happened since those pleasant and rambling talks, and too much had been left unsaid. And now, even Ben's letters were few and far between.

I rummaged through the books and papers in my bag and found the second of his two letters, buried at the bottom. I held the thin paper up to the firelight, comforted by the childlike sticks and circles I knew so well. (He'd never learned to read or write cursive.)

I remembered how happy I'd been to fetch this particular letter from the new Manteo post office. As I'd read it though, I'd been disappointed with the impersonally itemized details of his days. I thought if I heard any more descriptions of the crew's daily drills, I'd apply for a job as a surfman myself.

For lack of a new letter, I unfolded it and began to read it through once more.

My dearest wife,

The first few days of training have gone right fast. Today we pulled the beach apparatus cart through the sand as good as mules, us harnessed to the cart with long rope. That cart has all manner of equipment in it and is heavy as the dickens.

In the space below this sentence was a carefully drawn picture of a two-wheeled cart, pulled by a creature with a man's head and a mule's body.

Then Captain Gale called a halt and we started to taking all the equipment out. The men are supposed to have ideas of how to use the equipment by now, specially the firing of the shot line and how to use the breeches buoy. But they don't seem to have the first notion of it all, though they all worked here last year.

Here he drew a picture of a rope stretching from the beach to a shipwreck in a wild sea. Halfway down the rope was what appeared to be a life preserver attached to a pair of little trousers, which I knew now to be the "breeches buoy" in which the rescued sailors sat as they were pulled to safety by the surfmen. The surfmen, in turn, were rendered as stick figures bunched together on land, and a large question mark was inked over their oval heads.

I'm a good shot with the cannon so Captain Gale has me do it all the time instead of getting the other men used to it. And it seems to me the captain seems overly attached to the surfboat and steering oar. He hollers out instructions from the stern all day long, and now I hear him in my sleep, what little I get.

I still can't figure how the men got their jobs in the first place. It is just like it is at the Nags Head station, how we couldn't understand how such men ended up working a lifesaving station when they couldn't even man a oar. Same story here. Only now I'm stuck in the middle of it.

They're all good men I'll wager. And they can row the surfboat pretty good on account they're all

right strong limbed. But big farmers shouldn't be the end all in qualifications for surfmen, in my view. No offense to you Abby but talking to them about tides and currents is much the same as talking to you of such things.

I wish I could write more to you tonight, but I'm tuckered out from carrying the weight of five other men. I'll write more tomorrow I promise.

(I hope Asha is feeding you good.)

Your loving husband,

Ben

I ran a finger over his signature, three capital letters that leaned far to the right. His penmanship was neat and careful, a challenge for hands that were used to hard labor instead of the rigors of academia. And his words were friendly as always, yet in the deliberate spaces between them I felt a disturbance, bubbles from an unseen bottom dweller.

He was frustrated, I could tell. Two years ago, Ben had helped to construct the Nags Head Lifesaving Station, a sturdy, two-storied building on the vacant seascape of Nags Head. But last year, when it came time to assign surfman positions, Ben and a number of local men had been overlooked by the superintendent of the district, who'd instead filled the station with what most locals considered to be politically connected mainland men and even brothers of the keeper. Ben had been disappointed, but it hadn't stopped him from coming around the station in his spare time, offering his services.

Last summer, Ben had met a man named John Gale at the station house, a man with a great knowledge of boats and the sea. Ben had had no idea who he was, but they'd shared stories while playing cards one evening. Two months later, Ben had received a letter from the service superintendent, Charles Guirkin, informing him that there was a position as a surfman at the Jones's Hill Lifesaving Station in desolate Whales Head, on the northern shores of the Currituck Banks. John Gale, it turned out, was the keeper at the Jones's Hill station, and had apparently recommended Ben to the superintendent to fill an open position.

Ben had looked up from that letter with eyes as bright as beacons. *I'd never have been able to refuse him.* A letter from daddy had dismissed Ben from the paying job at the Cape Hatteras lighthouse site all those years ago, and he'd gone back to his life as a fisherman and guide without complaint. But I knew how disappointed he'd been. We'd traveled down to see the lighthouse when it was completed, and Ben had declared it to be very grand, likely the finest lighthouse in the world. I'd seen a longing in his face when its bright, white light revolved across land and sea.

He'd wanted to be a part of something important.

The plan, said Ben, was to live and work at the lifesaving station from November through March, a requirement of the service. Then he would return to Roanoke Island with currency, a rare item on the Banks. Ben and I, as well as most Bankers, still traded for everything we didn't grow, catch or raise ourselves. As a lifesaver, he would earn forty dollars a month, plus three dollars for every wreck he attended. He would start the job again the following November.

Five months out of the year didn't seem so bad at first, not where money was concerned. That much money would enable us to acquire a cook stove, to invest in more livestock, some new fishing implements for Ben.

But when I'd given him my consent, I didn't realize he would have to leave in October to begin his training, or that he would be too busy drilling and patrolling to even sail a skiff south for a short visit with his wife.

I hadn't realized the power of my words when I'd said, "Maybe it's for the best."

I had a hard time calling up Ben's face at its happiest, but the vision of his face when I said those few words to him trailed me like a shadow.

I ran my hand down the thin cloth of my dress, feeling my shrunken breasts, my protruding hip bones, the washboard of my ribs. I thought of Asha's biscuit in my bag but I was too tired to get up and fetch it. I didn't even feel hungry.

The night birthed a fretful storm. I barely slept, with the sound of the rain and wind prying at the gaps in the shutters.

In and out of sleep, I thought of Ben, and how he slept with his arm draped over me, heavy as a goose on my belly. In the winters I'd welcomed the constant steam that seeped from his skin. But in the summers

I'd push his sweaty arm away and strain to catch a breeze from the windows.

In better times, we'd gone swimming in the Croatan Sound on summer evenings. I saw us as we used to be, bare arms slipping with small splashes through the dozing water. Ben stayed underwater for minutes at a time. Childlike, he often grabbed my feet or tickled my thighs. He dunked me, shrugging if I came up with hair covering my face.

But the night that I told him I was with child, he didn't pull any tricks. We stretched out on our backs, the water rising and falling over our naked torsos, our fingers laced at the tips on the surface of the sound. The moon wasn't quite full that night, and I'd wished out loud for a round, full circle overhead.

But Ben had said, "Sometimes we have to wait patient for things to round up."

The black sky above us was vast, overflowing from God's enormous hands. The stars collected my prayers of gratitude, nautilus shells in a golden pail.

That's it, I thought. Sleep wasn't offering herself to me tonight. I rose from the floor and stepped to lift the latch. Daylight was a blurred black line on the eastern horizon, but the wind still bawled and kicked. The possibility of a timely return to Roanoke Island was remote. I hoped Asha wouldn't worry too much over me.

In the half-light I saw that the high tide had flowed right up to the porch steps during the night, a rare occurrence given that the house was nearer the soundside woods than the sea. The sea had left some torn-up seaweed and a few dead fish as a calling card.

The house had withstood the assault well; it was strong because Ben had built it. A picture of Ben rowing a surfboat of unknown construction through white-capped waves with the five unqualified surfmen flashed in my mind as if lit by a lightning bolt, then was gone into darkness.

The night before he'd left for Whales Head I had asked Ben why the job of surfman appealed to him so much, and he'd looked at me in the blinking candlelight like I'd suddenly shifted into a stranger.

"A ways back this New England bark—the Orline St. John—wrecked off Hatteras. Sea swept clean through the cabin and trapped the captain's wife. Crew pulled her out alright and strapped her to a spar for her safety. But they couldn't fight the sea for long. Next day she died in her husband's arms. And a Negro sailor perished, still hanging in the rigging. One sailor drank sea water to slake his thirst and grew delirious, never to be seen again. For a week the crew hung tight to the ship, hungry, thirsty, cold and soaked to the skins. Vessels coming and going tried to help but couldn't reach 'em for the weather. To live, they had to eat the body of the dead Negro. Then, ten days after they wrecked, a bark got close enough to help and took them back to Boston, all in a bad way. Had to cut off one of the sailor's feet on account of the frostbite."

The candle had guttered out with the conclusion of his story, but I'd hoisted myself up from the bed and turned to him in the darkness.

"Why would you tell me such a story?"

He'd sighed. "I grew up hearing these stories. I was only a youngun when that wreck came to pass, and stories of it made their way to my ears soon enough. What sort of tall tales did you hear as a youngun? Tom Thumb? Cindyrella?"

"Certainly not true stories of dead women and cannibalism and amputations."

"Well, it sounds to me like you don't get why I'm going to Whales Head, and here I am set to leave in the morning!"

He'd sat up on the bed, closing the space between us. "I know why you show up at that school every morning."

"Why, then?"

"Because you want to help. You feel a better person for it. For the good you're doing."

He'd reached out to smooth the hair from my face, but I'd shifted away. We hadn't touched one another in a long time.

"I'm not that naïve. I see that it's dangerous," I said, my voice raised. "*I'm* the one that's going to be waiting for you to come back alive."

"You think I'm not scared, Abby? Course I am. But it makes me brave to know that *someone*'s got to do it. Might as well be a man who knows what he's doing."

I had always known that Ben needed to feel useful and productive. He took a lot of pride in a good catch of fish or a string of ducks. It seemed like everyone in Roanoke Island and Nags Head needed him for something, and he was always glad to lend a hand.

But to him, nothing compared to the job of surf-man. The job had become his reason for waking in the morning, for pulling on his trousers, wool shirt and old coat, for running a comb through his salty blond hair. The job had pulled his true essence from him, had given him his pride.

I tried not to think about the danger. I had seen Ben try to save a stranded sailor during a bad storm, eight years ago. I had watched, completely captivated by a local man's bravery, the wish to risk his own life to save a stranger's. He'd worn a life belt, had a makeshift surfboat. I hadn't even known the man was Ben until he'd swum ashore with the dead man. I think I began to love him, in that moment.

I arrived at the cottage steps, my circle of the house complete. It was only when I'd stepped back inside that I noticed I hadn't worn a coat, nor even my shoes, when I'd ventured outside. My stockinged feet were numb, my body bent double against the fright of freezing.

CHAPTER THREE

NOVEMBER 5, 1875
BENJAMIN WHIMBLE

*Think not, is my eleventh commandment; and sleep when
you can, is my twelfth.*

–ISHMAEL, *MOBY-DICK*

I HAD GOOSEFLESH ALL OVER THIS FIRST NIGHT ON PATROL,
even in my patched wool coat. Might look to a passerby
that perhaps the man walking along was a homeless
bummer smoking a pipe, not knowing it was just a surfman's warm breath all around him, gone cloudy in the
frozen air.

I was now a long way from hobo, being a bona
fide member of the Jones's Hill Lifesaving Station
crew, which was itself a part of the great United States
Lifesaving District Number Six, seven North Carolina
stations and three in Virginia. Only six men given

surfman positions—in this, the station's second winter—and I was one of them.

It wasn't too fancy a job at that. Patrol just called for walking and walking, ten miles and four hours of a night, looking through the darkness for signs of peril on the sea. This particular night I was obliged to walk south for the midnight to four shift. It was five miles straight to a outpost—a halfway mark to the Caffey's Inlet station—where I'd turn around and make for the station again.

Anybody with two legs working could do this part of the job, except for the fact there were no stars out, no moon neither, and winds coming in steady from the northeast. It confounded the mind, knowing that the nearest lifesaving stations were ten whole miles away from ours, and there was no way a man could patrol on foot the entire coastline between them.

No, the job of surfman wasn't high-falutin', but it called for able legs and a strong heart. These days, I could vouch for just one of those, and like I said, I'm walking pretty good these days.

Weather or no, it was dark as a tinker's pot out here on the edge of the world. In just a few weeks, the Currituck Beach Lighthouse would shine its light for us to see by. The brick tower was all finished now and standing over 160 feet tall. Even that high up in the air, those lighthouse keeps would still feel the weight of the world on their shoulders, knowing they kept the sole light for a forty-mile stretch of the most treacherous coast in the world.

And that's where men like me came in, on account no on-and-off lighthouse light was going to save the poor souls already wrecked on the shoals of the Banks. On nights like this, disasters tended to happen. And surfmen were the ones heading straight into the sea with nothing but their courage and a life belt of cork, guiding a boat up and down the black waters of death. That lighthouse could blink and blink all night, while folks clinging to the masts of a broken ship could do nothing but groan at the irony of it all.

Lucky for us surfmen, we carried a brass lantern with us, but it hardly made a dent in the bottomless well of darkness. My eyes slid over to the angry sea, moving left then right then left again. I watched the black sky too, right above the water, for any shine or shadow that might show me a ship inching along the horizon.

The sandy wind sucked all the wetness from my face so that my eyelids stuck to my eyeballs and my lips stuck to my teeth corpse-like. My hair was blasted back from my head, of a mind to stay that way for eternity.

I figured it was fixing to storm on Roanoke Island too. I hoped Abby was tucked in tight on her tick, Asha sleeping close by.

"Abby Whimble! You hear me?"

My words sunk into air so meaty you could slice it up for supper. Abby couldn't hear me anyway, even if I was talking right at her. I missed the way we used to be.

I'd never got used to it, waking up next to her every morning. Even seven years married and living in the schoolmarm house, I'd wake up feeling to the right of me to see if I wasn't dreaming. I'd feel her there, all covered up in her night dress, but I could still feel those hot little freckles beneath, burning me like flecks of fire.

I didn't want to wake her, course I didn't. But I used to pull that lacy nightgown up and just barely touched the lamb skin of her thighs, and soon I'd see those green eyes peek out and roll in their sockets, knowing what I was up to.

"The sunshine," I'd say, real soft. I called her that all the time, back in those days. And she'd run her hand along my arm, smoothing all the white hairs down, making them all run in the same direction, nice and neat. Then she'd run that hand down my arm, squeezing it hard as she did so. I'd felt that her palm was a bit rougher than it was at the start, but it still spread like butter on me when she touched me with all that love.

In the months past though, I started to think I might break her if I tried to hug her the wrong way. Her rib bones stuck out, tight little ripples under her pale skin. I was scared to think of the storm, brewing just beneath those currents. And her shoulders and knees and even her ankles poked out like a starving mare's. She never complained of being hungry though. She just didn't feel like eating much, she'd said, like food was something she could take or leave.

Seeing her like that took the gumption right out of me. It was like my manhood was broke, wouldn't rise to do my bidding. Yes, the act of love brought us more pain and fear than it should have, so we stopped the act altogether nigh on a year ago. I still recalled the last time I was inside her, and wondering on the dryness of her, and seeing more than enough wet streaming out of her eyes.

I thought instead on the money I'd make from the new job. Money was easier to hope to, a lot easier than mending a broken love. More money could fix us, make us better. *The world*, I thought. That's what I wanted for her. I saw myself spreading my arms wide for Abby at something I couldn't yet see.

A few years ago my friends Jimmy Juniper and Harley Stickle left the Banks for the big city of Norfolk, Virginia. They got jobs loading and unloading the boats that came in and out of the port there, good money paid regular. But I couldn't ever picture leaving the Banks, and I felt kind of sorry for 'em in secret.

Sometimes in my head I see Abby and me with a house full of younguns, grand-younguns too. And it's a big house, for all that we're used to, with water to see and land to farm. And we're holding hands, wrinkled skin bunching up over the bones, and when we turn to each other, we see past the spots and lines to the younger people we used to be. And we're happy in that big house, content with our lot in life.

I reckon it's the station house where I now live that's giving me my grand ideas. I drew Abby a picture of it, when I wrote her my first-ever letter. Standing there in the October sun that first day, with nothing but sand to sight, I thought the Jones's Hill Lifesaving Station gleamed like Blackbeard's lost treasure.

The boat room holds the surfboat and its cart, plus all the gear: mortar, life car, breeches buoy, sand anchor, crotch, faking box, hawser, whip lines, shovels, life jackets and signal flares. In the back of that room is the tiny day-room where we eat and play cards. We all sleep upstairs, in a little room with cots all side by side. Captain Gale sleeps in a skinny iron bed in his own small room in back of us. A desk holds all of his log books and papers he's always writing on for the service, and shelves hold his sighting glass, compass, and barometer. A ladder in the middle of the room goes up to the lookout tower, and two tall windows, side by side, peer out on the ocean.

I can still smell the pine and oak used in its building. The paint is still fresh, no sign of peeling. And the curlicue woodwork on the corners of the roof add some fancy. But as nice a place as it is, it'll never feel like a home to us. Once you get to the top of the lookout tower, you see for once and all you're in the middle of nowhere, on a awful skinny strip of treeless sand hemmed in by water. By rights, Whales Head shouldn't be a home for anybody.

Surfman Spencer Gray stood waiting on me outside the station house to pick up the southbound patrol. "Coffee for you," he said with the wind.

Spencer was a little thin with hair up top, and he stooped a bit at his broad shoulders. But he wasn't much older than me. He'd left his pregnant wife Molly and two other younguns back on Church's Island.

In the light of the lantern it looked like he was pouring smoke from a flask into a tin cup. The steam of it melted my face. The coffee itself burned my whole pie hole, but I slurped at the gritty stuff anyway.

"Good, ain't it?"

"Well, it's hot," I said, and he laughed.

"I can't see a thing out there," he said. "Looks like the devil's play yard."

"Ain't a good night to be on a ship." I finished the coffee in two more hot slurps, then took the flask from him as I gave him the case of flares and lantern.

"Hope you're not afeared of the dark," I called after him. "Might as well be carrying a brass tuba around, for all the light that lantern's throwing off tonight."

Sure enough, the man was swallowed down the gizzard of the darkness before I turned for the boat room, gave me a layer of gooseflesh no amount of hot coffee could get rid of.

Sleep had turned on me since I'd become a surfman. I guessed the men must spend the entire spring just catching up on lost shut-eye. Night shifts aside, sleeping on a cot for only a few hours at a time in a room usually half-full of dirty surfmen is no treat. I tried my best to count sheep, but I'd never seen such a springy stampede of animals in my life.

I reached under the cot and drew out the box that held my pen, paper and ink, and propped my elbow up on the cot. I bore down on a rolled newspaper to write.

Dearest wife,

Well, it's done. My first night on patrol duty. Four hour midnight shift and in a nor'easter no less. I should be sleeping now but I wanted to tell you about it.

It was dark. And cold.

That's about all I can say.

I dipped my pen in some ink and thought. *I wish I were in bed with you, naked and not wearing a full set of clothes,* I wanted to write. But I didn't, on account it didn't seem right to use the word "naked" the way things stood with us. I decided to stick with the weather.

The sea was covered in fog. I wouldn't have seen a ship if it had wrecked in front of my face.

I chewed the end of my pen.

There's some women here that come by to help us out. They mend clothes, put linseed oil on our coats to keep out the water, knit us woolens. They're also making clothes for shipwreck folks, if we ever save any. One is a girl no more than thirteen or so, her name is Jennie Blount. She puts me in mind of you. She's real pretty with freckles and lots of yellow hair and she grins a lot. She knit me a long, thick scarf and dyed it indigo.

I stopped writing. *Why on earth did I tell her about the women up here?* That wasn't right. I didn't know why talking to her was so hard to do now, where once it was so easy, like petting a dog's head. I looked out the dark windows on a cold and rolling ocean so close I could reach out and touch it. *Forlorn* was the word that came to mind, but I couldn't recall ever learning it. My hand was ice cold and not of a mind to write. I decided I'd written plenty for the night.

I signed my name and told her I loved her. And I did still love her, I could feel it in my heart when it beat fast whenever I thought her name inside my head. *Abigail Sinclair Whimble.*

But I think we both knew it when I left, that our life together wasn't going the way we'd wanted. And that my leaving her alone was the end of something between us.

When I told her goodbye, she'd said, "Maybe it's for the best." She'd *wanted* me gone; she'd as good as said it. And because of everything we'd been through, I'd wanted to be gone too. Lord God, but those thoughts hurt more than a thousand nights of such cold and dark patrol.

I crumbled the letter up and laid back on the cot, my mind aswirl even more than it was before I'd put pen to paper. Used to be a time when I'd read *Robinson Crusoe* at night, the act sending me to sleep better than lovemaking. But I hadn't lay eyes on our copy of *Crusoe* for years, and there had been a time when I didn't go a day without cracking it open to read the odd paragraph.

Lately I was feeling like Crusoe himself, so lonely that a little footprint in the sand could set off a thousand different thoughts in my head. So lonely that I'd welcome a boat-full of cannibals to my island and set down with them to supper.

Next morning I woke to find the nor'easter squatting smack on the Banks. The sky looked to be wearing a grey sweater, only it was old and stretched and held no warmth.

After a night of hard patrols, I wasn't all that surprised to find three of my fellow surfmen still out cold. But the door to Captain Gale's room was open, so I ventured up the ladder to the tower first thing.

He stood knee-knocked with his back to me, there being nowhere to sit up here on account men got lazy and watched the tops of their boots propped atop the rail instead of the sea. The bitter wind blew his pipe smoke in a northeasterly direction.

"Anything to see this morning?" I hardly heard the sound of my own voice over the ruckus of the sea.

He didn't take his eyes from the mismatched waves. "Schooner way out, heading north. Couple of barks too."

"The ocean is running mighty high." The inshore waters usually held at least one fishing boat, but the sea had scared off all life, even the sea birds.

"You figure we should walk patrols this morning?"

He shook his head. "Not yet. There's cleaning to do. And that tholepin needs mending where the oar gets loose."

I reckoned he knew best, but I figured the cleaning and tholepin could wait a while.

In the cook house I stripped my clothes and washed up best I could with a bucket of cold water, for the stove had yet to be lit. I grabbed some stale cornbread before heading out to the shed to fetch a cleaning bucket and rag.

Jerry Munden was already in the boat room scrubbing salt from the steering oar. He was the only Negro surfman in these parts, and some of the local folks thought such amalgamation strange. But I'd heard that some crews on the Virginia coast had all kinds of black men working as surfmen right alongside whites. "Checkerboard" crews is what they called them.

"Sing me a song, Jerry. Make the time go faster."

Jerry had himself the deepest voice I ever heard in a man, like a ship's fog horn. When he called out on the beach or in the drilling boat, you just had to grin, even if your clothes were soaked and your body was numb. And he did like to sing.

He looked askance at me. "I your singing slave?"

But he started up with "Swing Low Sweet Chariot," a shine to his eye.

And the men came and went for a few hours, working lookout and running soapy rags over the equipment. A local man George Wilson even stopped by to fry up some blue fish for us while the wind threw sleet against the windows. The tholepin got fixed, and Malachi played his banjo and sang some tunes. When he ran out of songs, most men drifted off for better things to do, in warmer quarters.

Around noon, Lewis White came into the boat room with a bottle of whiskey. The men popped thirsty from all directions.

Lewis waved the bottle around in the air. "Lookie what I found," he sang. Lewis was the youngest of the crew—a day away from his twenty-second birthday—and had gotten a basket of goods from his ma and sister last week.

"I wondered where you were hiding that at," said Malachi. "I'll get the cards."

Everyone, even Captain Gale, dropped their rags.

"We ain't near to done with the cleaning," I said. "Look at the throwing line. It's all knotted and sandy."

"Heavens! We ain't done with the cleaning," said Lewis in a girlish timbre. "Well, why don't you coil up the throwing line for us, Benny, if'n it bothers you so?"

"Can't promise we'll save you any whiskey though," said Malachi, already out the door. "My belly's dry as a lime-kiln."

I looked to Captain Gale, who just shrugged. I wasn't sure what I expected of the man, since when we'd met, we'd both been drinking whiskey and playing cards. Captain Gale got bored on cleaning day, just like the rest of us.

He pulled a timepiece from his pocket. "Lemuel's on lookout for another hour," he said. "Then it's Spencer's shift."

I threw my rag into the bucket and followed the men into the day-room behind the boat room, where a rough-hewn table sat. We used seashells for counters, but no coins to speak of. Even so, our gambling was no joke, for losers got stuck with the next day's cook house duty. Spencer started to dealing out the cards, already sticky with finger-grub.

"How's the wagon coming?" he asked me.

"Ready afore Christmas," I said. In my spare time I'd started a little four-wheeled cart with a seat for his son's pet goat Wally to pull. "You sure old Wally's going to like getting tethered to a wagon?"

"Junior's got him trained up good. Hand-raised him from a kid."

"Ain't that something," I said. "Goats can be ornery."

"You and your wife got kids, Ben?" asked Malachi, squaring his cards.

"No." My hand was right good, so I threw in two big clam shells.

"I didn't know you were hitched," said Lewis. He tossed out half a mussel shell.

"You ain't seen me writing?"

He thought a bit, then said, "I guess I did, at that. But I figured you were writing to your ma. You never mentioned your wife a-tall."

"I didn't mention my ma neither," I said. "She's dead these twenty-odd years."

"He told me about his wife," said Captain Gale, tossing two clams onto the pile. "Her name is Abigail. She's down on Roanoke Island, teaching school."

Malachi said, "My own schoolmarm was old and almost blind. No teeth neither, but mean as the dickens."

I looked hard at my cards; the queen of hearts frowned up at me, red lips apucker. "Abigail's the most beautiful woman I've ever seen," I said. "I mean it."

The men whistled. "Well, when are you going to bring her around?" asked Lewis, the only unhitched man in the crew.

I snorted. "I'm not so addle-minded as to bring her around here."

Surfmen were only given time off from sunrise to sunset one day a week, the liberty getting shifted about through the crew. Most of the men's mothers, wives, and children had already been to the station house for a visit so the men didn't have to leave. By way of excuse I told myself their families were close by—most were a couple of hours away at the most.

But it wasn't close enough. There had already been talk of building some little cottages near the station house where all the families could stay during the season. Yet I doubted Abby would want to live up here. If Roanoke Island was a backwards spot of land compared to Edenton, then Whales Head was as uncivilized as the moon. I'd always counted us as lucky to have decent marketing on the soundside, well-worn roads, good-sized dwellings, and the schoolhouse. Whales Head was nothing but sand, a dozen houses near the soundside in the shadows of moving dunes.

"We'll behave ourselves," said Spencer, throwing down his cards like they threw up a stink. "I'll allow this is the worst hand I've ever had. I fold."

He stood up, saluted us, and made for the stairs to the lookout tower.

My eyes were steady on my cards, but I knew Captain Gale still stared at me. I'd gotten right corned when I'd met him last year, but I could recall going on and on about Abby.

"Abby's mighty busy at the schoolhouse on Roanoke Island. She can hardly take a day off when she's sick with a fever, much less travel up here for a visit," I said.

"How does she keep house for you then?" asked Lemuel, taking Spencer's empty chair. His wife Polly had passed eight years back, so the keeping of a house was always on his mind.

"She doesn't," I said. The men all stared at me.

"She must make money," put in Spencer.

"Not a jugful," I said. "She teaches the students of the old Freedmen's Colony, and her students can't afford to pay her. She gets good things in trade though. All kinds of food, hens, quilts and such."

"Why she teaching at a school for Negroes?" asked Lewis. He seemed truly puzzled.

"She's the best teacher North Carolina's got, and the Negroes need her the most, in my view."

They all eyed Jerry, then nodded and said a bunch of "I reckons."

Malachi tossed his cards to the table. "Fold," he sighed, giving wind to his long, black mustache. He took up his banjo again, plucked out some sad notes.

Captain Gale leaned back in his chair. "What about Christmas?" he asked. "I might allow a visit."

I threw down two more shells. "We'll see."

Lewis started pouring whiskey into glasses, but I put a hand atop mine. "We got patrol tonight!"

"He's right," said Captain Gale. "Go easy on the combustible. I don't care if it *is* your birthday."

Lewis sat back down, grinning. "I fold too."

Captain Gale leaned forward, showing us his cards. "I got a straight flush."

Jerry groaned and put down his full house. My belly tussled with the liquor as I laid my cards on the table.

Lewis leaned over. "He's only got a straight," he crowed. "He lost again!"

"Should have just stayed in the boat room in the first place," I said.

As we made our way out of the room, Captain Gale said, "You all could learn a thing or two from Ben, you know."

"Like what?" laughed Lewis. "How to lose at poker?"

Still feeling the whiskey in my blood, even after two hours of coiling rope and scrubbing wood, I pulled on my hat, coat and Jennie's scarf and ventured out for the sunset patrol. Daylight was fading fast by the time I set out north, a more fearsome stretch of land I'd never seen.

Great breakers of foggy swell pounded the beach, the racket so terrible I had a notion to put my hands over my ears. Sea mist reached up my nose holes, stung my eyeballs. The sand rose up with the wind to batter my cheeks. The sleet started up too, so I wrapped my head up in the scarf and watched the ocean just like a cooter in a shell.

I was almost to the outpost when I spotted a shape through the mist in front of me, looked like a boat washed ashore. When I reached it, I saw it was a broken up pilot skiff—maybe twelve, thirteen feet long—stuck in the wet sand. It was empty of men and equipment, with its oars gone too, and its center-board was broken clean in half, though the rudder still stuck out the back. A barrel was tied down and stuck hard in between the struts.

I got my hands around the bow and pulled the boat up to dry sand. It was only when I dropped it down that I saw a body in the wash a couple hundred yards up the shore.

"Hey there!" I hollered, and tore through the breakers to him, my scarf flying off into the dunes. But the body—more a boy than a man—didn't budge. I grabbed him under his arms and pulled him up the beach.

Looking at him upside down, I saw his eyes were closed, skin so white I could see blue veins in his forehead and temples. He was no more than 13, with red hair slicked to his scalp. Nothing more than wet rags hung on him.

On my hands and knees next to him, I leaned over to see if he had any breath left, not expecting to see signs of life. And yet, I felt the point of a knife on my bare throat.

"It's m-m-mine," he whispered.

His white lips quivered; his blue eyes rolled like a slaughtered cow's.

"What's yours?"

"The b-barrel," he said, breathing too fast now, where three seconds before he'd had no breath a-tall. "You hear?"

"Alright," I said. "It's yours. I don't want it anyhow."

Still he kept that knife point on my neck, his shaking hand making the thing dig a little deeper than I felt easy with. I felt warm liquid mix with the cold sea water dripping down my throat.

"Don't let 'em take't…"

A few drops of my blood fell on his forehead as the knife dropped from his grip. His eyes were still open, but I knew they weren't seeing a thing. A look at his chest told me his lungs weren't working either.

"It's alright now," I said. I closed his eyelids with my thumb.

In a daze, I fired up a Coston flare, then placed the wooden holder of the flare in the sand. I picked up the knife he'd stuck me with, one made special to clean fish; I'd sharpened more than a few on a whetstone in my time, and the one he had was a good one.

"Alright now," I said again.

I stepped to the barrel with the knife and sawed through the ropes that bound it to the boat. Then I spent a good amount of time working the barrel from the skiff. At last I felt it give way, along with the two struts it was wedged between, and I heaved it over the side of the boat.

Then I rolled the barrel up the dunes, kept rolling 'til I saw a wind-scoured wedge in a dune, covered with a growth of sea oats. I buried it in there best I could, then found a hunk of driftwood to mark its place. I went back down and pawed through the boy's soggy britches, trying to find anything that told of him or where he came from. But there was nothing in his pockets save sand and seaweed.

I sat beside him, slid his knife back into the sheath on his belt and wiped my blood from his forehead. The sleet had turned to snow, and in the light of the flare I watched the flakes dance in the wind, never landing. In a little while I heard the creak of the cart's wheels moving up the beach. The men appeared in the red-lit dark like horned demons, yet when they came close, I saw their shoulders and heads were dusted with snow, angels of a sort.

"No need to hurry," I said.

The men dropped their ropes, and their eyes swept the scene of body and chewed up skiff.

"Jesus have mercy, he ain't but a boy," said Jerry.

"I didn't see a shipwreck from the lookout tower," Captain Gale huffed.

"Can't see a thing out there," I said.

He looked around the beach. "There's just this one body?"

"Far as I know," I said. "He was alive when I pulled him from the wash, but he passed on soon after."

"That boat's too big for him to handle alone."

"If he did, he can't have come far, 'specially in this weather."

Captain Gale looked down at the boy. "He say anything before he passed?"

"Nothing in particular." I figured I should tell them about the barrel, but it seemed my mind and mouth had been unhooked from one another, cast free. The boy's last thoughts had dwelled on the barrel, and I would keep it safe for him, long as I could.

"What happened to your neck?" asked Spencer.

I put a hand to the bloody wound on my throat. "Oh. He held a fishing knife to my throat."

"Why in hell did he do that?" barked Captain Gale.

I shrugged my shoulders. "You know how a man will lose his wits when he's dying? Try to drown the man that's saving him? He was beside himself."

Captain Gale gazed down at the boy once more, shaking his head.

He took up the lantern and walked over to the busted skiff, ran a finger along the prow. Then he drew himself up and looked out to sea with his hand shading his eyes, as if the sun troubled him and not the dusky mist.

"We'd best keep an eye out for more bodies coming ashore," he said.

We gathered around the sailor, and Captain Gale led us in saying the Lord's Prayer. I stumbled over the words, for it had been some time since Abby'd taught me. When we were done, I put a hand to the cut at my throat, stinging like a bee bite in the salty wind. I found Jennie's scarf, stuck like a jellyfish in the wet sand, and laid it atop the boy's face when we loaded him in the cart.

CHAPTER FOUR

November 6, 1875
Abigail Sinclair Whimble

Our souls are like those orphans whose unwedded mothers
die in bearing them: the secret of our paternity lies in their
grave, and we must there to learn it.

–Ishmael, Moby-Dick

It started to snow as I edged my way through the beach heather and cottonbush along Jockeys Ridge. In no time at all, the brambles were frosted with white so thick it appeared a fungus. Down around my sinking boots, the white flakes mixed with the sand at times, so that it was hard to tell mineral from condensation. The wind still faced me down like a dog, but I kept up my northwesterly pace through the thickening woods.

I'd been granted permission, rather grudgingly by my drunken father-in-law at the wedding, to call him Oscar, a name I'd never heard anyone call him and at times even doubted was his real name, although Ben had assured me that it was. Most of his friends called him Tremblin', T.W. for short. Even Ben wasn't sure of the nickname's origin. But after seven years of marriage, I still had a hard time calling him anything other than Mr. Whimble. The man and I had never been on a first name basis, much less a nickname one.

In his absence, Ben had arranged for Jacob Craft and his wife Ruby to see to his daddy's needs: bringing him food, feeding him, changing his clothing and bed linens, keeping his home and garden in order. He'd offered to pay them in the spring, but they had turned the money down. They lived right next door, they'd claimed, so it was hardly any trouble at all. A few local women helped out here and there as well. I hadn't seen Oscar in months.

I'd told myself that I'd been living on Roanoke Island, that I was busy and didn't have a good opportunity to visit. But deep down, I knew that visiting was nothing more than another unpleasant chore.

Ben's daddy had suffered a paralyzing fit three years ago. His mind had gone soon afterward, so that he didn't even recognize Ben any more. He was a man laid flat, as crusty and immobile as a starfish in the sand. Dr. Collins from the mainland had told us that death was often not far off in these kinds of cases. But Oscar had so far outlived all of the expectations.

In the heart of Nags Head Woods, I came upon a smattering of little houses surrounded by loblolly pine, juniper, red cedar and live oak, with sandy yards. One of them was Ben's daddy's house, the house where Ben had lived his entire life until we'd married. It had been constructed of mostly washed-up planks and weatherboarding, but the wood had dropped from its fastenings, giving the whole house a tumble-down appearance. The crooked roof was already frosted with snow.

I knocked on the door, more to alert Duffy of my presence than Oscar, and heard a trembling bark. I turned the knob—a discarded spool in a previous life—and pushed the door open into the small room, where Duffy circled me, sniffing and wagging.

I made out a lump of dog-haired blankets atop the tick and when I leaned over, Oscar's glassy, blue eyes fastened on me in the dimness. I fought the urge to run from the house, and sat down in a lopsided chair. Duffy curled up creakily beside him.

"Hello, Mr. Whimble," I said, my voice too cheery for a room that smelled of sour dog's breath, of fouled linens, of death waiting in the corners. "I wanted to check on you this morning. We're having quite a nor'easter."

The wind keened through the cracks between the old boards, yet it didn't disguise the sound of the man's ragged breathing. His face sagged on one side, skin like crumpled paper and covered with gray stubble. What was left of his hair stuck up like ghost's fingers from his head. I wanted to reach out and smooth it down for him, but touching him discomfited me.

I had to keep talking. "It's even snowing. Can you believe it?"

I glanced to the salt-grimed window in the back of the house, where nothing whatsoever was visible. His runny eyes still watched me, and in them I saw disgust, even hatred. I don't believe that he ever liked me. *What was I doing here,* I wondered suddenly? *Why had I even come?*

I took in a breath that sounded as uneven as his. "I suppose you're wondering why I'm here." *Had I just said that?*

I giggled, and Duffy's ears pricked up. "I…I was worried, I suppose. About you."

Saliva crawled from the corners of his blue lips, and still he stared. My eyes combed the numerous wall shelves, crowded with items. Nothing had ever been discarded, it seemed. I saw numerous feathers, a rusty gardening spade, a pot with a handle broken off the side, bits of rope, big shards of crockery, jugs with cork stoppers, two or three old lanterns, a candlestick with a melted nub of wax, a silent mantel clock, a bundle of dried seaweed. And now man and dog contributed their own brand of tossed-aside uselessness.

I concluded that no one had been to see to him yet. It was still early in the morning after all, and the storm had likely delayed the Crafts' coming a bit. I knew that the man should probably eat something, but I hadn't a morsel to give him.

I pulled my coat closer around my body. I figured I should start a fire in the hearth, but I didn't see any wood in the grate.

"I'm worried about Ben too. If he weathered the storm alright in Whales Head. I won't know anything until he writes me."

The bare room closed in on me then, and I imagined that this was what it was like to lie dead in a coffin. My eyes lingered on the old tick that Ben had once used. The reeds and seaweed inside the burlap were likely black with rot.

"The two letters he's written to me are so very short, with no feeling to them at all," I blurted, my voice almost accusatory. "And I can't seem to think of anything to write to him either. You'd suppose that I could think of at least something to write in a letter to my own husband."

Oscar's head rolled off the pillow, giving me a glimpse of a crusty scab on his scalp, covered with stringy hair. His purple-spotted hands were curled into rigid fists.

At last I heard the squeak of wagon tires, then footsteps on the porch and murmuring between a man and a woman. Jacob pushed open the door, holding a string of firewood in his hand. He eyed me curiously while tipping his hat, and Duffy notched herself up and hurried to the porch, where a bowl of scraps now waited.

When Ruby appeared at the door, lugging a large laundry basket, she cried, "What on earth! Miz Whimble, what you doing here, and in this storm too? Just about blew off our roof! Apple tree done fell over, busted the fence."

"We ain't seen the last of it neither," said Jacob, placing some wood on the grate. "When'd you get here?"

"I...I came here—yesterday— to check on the house, so I thought...while I was in Nags Head..."

Jacob shook his head, likely at my island ignorance. He'd never quite understood our marriage.

"You don't need to trouble yourself with the
house, Miz Whimble," said Ruby. She put her basket
down. "We looking in on it twice a week."

Soon Jacob had a small fire burning, and the
warmth of it quickly filled the room. He lifted Ben's
daddy beneath his arms and maneuvered him into
the chair. The smell of urine soured the air, but Ruby
just balled up the soiled linens, opened the door and
threw them outside onto the porch. Then she flipped
the mattress over, unfolded the clean linens she'd
brought and tucked them around the tick.

"Miz Whimble, we gonna change his clothes now,
wash him down. You probably want to get on." She
patted my arm.

"Yes, alright. I'm outlining some new lessons 'til
the weather breaks. I really should go."

But I couldn't make my feet move toward the
door.

"He be fine, now. You go on." She walked me to
the door. "It was nice of you to peek in on him. Do
him a world of good, seeing faces he know."

"He doesn't know who I am," I said.

"Sure he do," said Ruby. "I know *something* getting
through up there."

There was no trace of anything but sincerity in
her face. "Family important to him. Yes ma'am. He a
good man, your daddy."

My daddy. "Yes. Yes he is. Well, thank you. Both.
For your help. Ben and I…well, we don't know what
we'd do without you."

The gray clouds were as thick and imposing as castle stones, the wind still punishing. I stepped off the porch and into the snowy sand, a ghost of myself. I left no shadow on the pale ground, either before or behind me. Even Duffy cocked her head uncertainly and watched me go.

I slumped through the woods, but after a while my walk turned to a gallop, and I found myself dodging branches, no control over my legs at all. Through sand drifts and snow-covered greens, I ran right up to the spot where the grave stone rested, breath smoking around me.

I shoved the snow from the brown stone with a wet boot. Ben had chosen a smooth, flat stone about a foot wide, discovered at the bottom of a fresh pond. It remained unadorned. I had never once laid eyes upon it, though Ben had placed the grave within shouting distance of the Nags Head house.

I reached out and placed my gloved hand on it, rubbing it with stiff fingers. *Just a rock, a rock in the woods.* I took off a glove and placed my palm on the chilled stone, colder than the air, its skin worn smooth from the wind and rain and sand. Pressing down, I felt the bones of it, the innate hardness, full of life's sad truth. It could sit there a thousand years, a stubborn signifier of life gone before its time.

Ben had swum down through the pond's cool water that summer. Had he already known the stone was there? Or had the swim been the beginning of his escape—a trip through the old, familiar waters? I could imagine his strong arms stroking him further from the light toward the dark detritus on the pond's floor. He must have felt the terrible burden of it as he struggled to bring the stone to the surface. Then he'd wrapped his daughter's small body in a blanket and sailed her and the stone to Nags Head, where he'd buried her himself. I had been too ill to travel.

And now I put my hand to my gray and empty womb, where once there was a handful of bursting blue sky, and I wept.

Ben and I had been excited to fill the teacher's house with new life. We talked for days about what it would be like to have a baby in the bed with us, between us, like a pearl in the clasped halves of an oyster. We planned to read to the baby; Ben had wanted to start with *Robinson Crusoe*, of course. He'd wanted to sail with the baby in his skiff. In my mind, I saw him holding a bundle in his arms and pointing out the sun on the water and the shadows of clouds moving across the sea, counting dolphins and pelicans.

Inside me, bird's wings had turned to rabbit's feet, and Ben lay so close to my belly that he could feel the thumps. I remember feeling peace, the way the woods settle when the wind dies.

Soon after we buried the baby girl, I became pregnant again. We were cautious with our joy. We spooned it out here and there, instead of gulping it down every chance we got. We thought such small portions would make the pregnancy last. We had paid our dues.

But I lost the second baby quite early. I almost died from the blood loss. No stone marked the death.

The babies, while still in my womb, had been proof that Ben and I were meant for each other, that our lives together weren't lies, missteps.

The loss of life foretold a future for us.

The cold and barren Nags Head house offered no comfort other than protection from the elements. I collapsed onto the blanket once again. My eyes stung, but they refused to close. Mama would have told me how God had helped her through the deaths of her babies. Daily readings of the Bible, prayers, church attendance. When I'd taken up residence on Roanoke Island, I hadn't felt comfortable attending the nearby church for whites, nor the churches for Negroes, and I'd slowly fallen out of the habit of worship.

And now I wished to ask mama how she could have turned to the very one who'd forsaken her? Who'd watched her heart crack like a shell, its soft, living innards dry and shrivel in the heat? God was the sun, hidden in storm clouds. God was a mighty ship, swallowed by the sea. I couldn't pray a single word any more. I couldn't even conjure His name on my lips.

I'd endured a long first labor, and a procession of island women—including some of my students—had come and gone throughout the day and night trying to help, but I'd hardly noticed one from the other. In a haze of pain I'd begun to realize that I was doing something wrong, that I was birthing the shadow of the sun. My womb grasped it, afraid to release.

Our baby had come into the world with open eyes—big, blue Ben eyes with nothing behind them. Blue as a bored summer sky. No birds soaring. No clouds to roam the surface, just endless swaths of simmering nothing.

She'd had red hair. I'd run my fingers along the strands, matted with my blood. Fully formed, ten fingers, ten toes. A bump of a raspberry nose on a pale face—a face primed for freckles. I'd held her rigid body in my trembling arms while she struggled to breathe—a handful of raspy hiccups—and then the breaths had stopped. In Asha's eyes I'd gleaned the truth. She had seen it all before.

Ben had appeared and kneeled beside me. But I'd seen nothing except the baby. Asha had tried to take her from me with her still-bloodied hands. I wouldn't let go of her, though her eyelids had closed over the blue like the thinnest of shrouds, her spine gone loose as rope.

Ben had kissed my perspiring face. But all I could see in his searching eyes was sadness. I'd turned away from those haunting eyes. I fell asleep at nights after grasping the empty canvas of my belly, a sail for a life going nowhere. And I would wake in the darkness, crying and shaking, my arms still heavy with an imaginary baby, the front of my nightdress soaked through with milk. I'd begun to think of death in friendlier terms.

The second loss brought us to our knees, though neither of us would speak of it. I hadn't conceived again, because we never made love.

I knew now why it was difficult for me to write to Ben. I knew why the barnacles of words were stuck to the wooden insides of my mind. I was dead inside, and had been for a long time.

I looked up at the array of shells gazing benignly down at me from their shelves. Whitely empty, they mocked me now. I drew the chair over and began collecting the shells into the old blanket. I ventured outside, and at the ocean's edge, I tossed the lot into the wet sand. I watched as the water rushed for them, then walked back to the house to gather some more.

When the dusty shelves were bare, I gathered up my bag and closed the door on the empty house.

Monday morning silver breath poured from my lungs as I recited sums with the class. Leo had indeed brought in some damp firewood that morning, but the storm had brought with it a bitter cold, and the students still wore their wool sweaters and hats. Only a few of the children wore coats, too large for their thin bodies.

I was standing over Luella's long back observing her computations when an unusual rapping resounded on the door of the schoolhouse. My only rule about entering the schoolhouse was to enter quietly. Students were constantly coming and going, depending on their work schedules, and knocking on the door was more disruptive than merely walking inside.

Faces turned to me, wariness in their expressions. Most remembered, or had been told of, the events that had led to the death of Elijah Africa seven years ago. Luella reached up and grabbed my upper arm, pinching the fleshy underside. I peeled away her fingers and placed her hand in her lap. With measured steps I walked to the door and opened it.

There stood a tall man, clad in a fine gray topcoat with shiny gold buttons and a black top hat, clothing I hadn't seen on a man in a long time. He carried a brown, leather case with him. His fair cheeks were flushed with cold, his hazel eyes bright.

He removed his hat, revealing hair a deep auburn, carefully combed toward the back of his head. Strands of grey threaded through the thinning mane. And yet, his face showed all the signs of aging indoors.

"Good morning, ma'am!" His confident Yankee voice assaulted my ears in the cold air. "My name is Mr. Graham Wharton. I don't wish to keep you from your teaching, but perhaps you have a small moment to spare?"

I knew that men and women and sometimes children would wander Roanoke Island, selling any kind of ware imaginable. They weren't usually Yankees though, nor were they this well-dressed. I concluded he'd been very successful.

"I'm sorry. We have no money to buy anything from you," I said, closing the door to the cold.

"I'm not a salesman, ma'am," he said through the wood. "My business here is education-related."

I opened the door to find him still amiable. "Oh," I said. "I do apologize."

I turned and said, "Asha, would you please continue to lead the class in the recitation of their sums?"

Asha's enthusiasm brought her barrel over with a clatter. Her loud voice reached us on the steps.

"Five and eight is…."

"Thirteen," recited the class, save one loud, male voice that bellowed, "Twelve!"

I shut the door on Asha's scolding.

"I'm here on behalf of the Peabody Education Fund, regarding a letter sent to the trustees. A letter explaining an unusual situation at one Elijah Africa School, one of the only legitimate schools on the Outer Banks of North Carolina. We—the trustees, that is—were quite taken with the picture of it. We agreed that a visit to the school was in order."

The schoolhouse happenings faded from my mind. "Someone wrote a letter to the Peabody Foundation? About the school?"

"Oh yes. It cast the school in the best possible light, and spoke highly of the young, female teacher. Much innate ability and energy, perseverance and faculty, not to mention graceful manners and an attractive face," he said, bowing his head a bit. "I take it that the author was referring to you?"

"Who was the author?"

"The author is anonymous," he said, with a small smile.

And the trustee, Mr. Wharton, had put enough stock in the letter to come to the Outer Banks. It must have been well written, to say the least. From what I'd read in the newspapers, the Peabody Foundation was one of the few foundations set up to assist the South with their educational shortcomings, primarily by strengthening existing schools, not by founding new ones.

"If it's not an imposition, I'd like to observe your teaching," he said. "And observe the students as well."

"Observe? For what purpose?"

"There are both Negro and white students attending this school, is that correct?"

"They are mostly Negro, but I do have about ten white students, all children."

"That's a typical ratio, I've found," he said. "You see, I'm currently researching such schools throughout the South for a book I'm writing. I observe the classrooms for a period of a week or so, examining the teacher's methods and student responses and interactions with one another. This schoolhouse would be the thirty-fifth school I've observed in the seven years of my research. The book is almost complete."

"A book," I repeated, running a hand over the untidy bun of my hair. "And you'd like to observe the class *now*?"

I ran over the conditions of the schoolhouse. Cold room, only a couple of oil lamps, hardly any decent chairs or desks or chalk.

"I do apologize, but you can see that an impromptu visit would afford me a more accurate picture of a school's elements than a planned one," he said. "Most of the teachers have been more than pleased to accommodate me."

I stared at him, my breath circling in thought.

"I'll be here for several days," he said calmly. "If today doesn't suit you, I can certainly come back tomorrow."

"No, no," I said, drawing myself up. "Today is fine. But you'll have to keep your coat on, I'm afraid."

He leaned backward, his eyes traveling over the placard above our heads. "I'd also like to know who this Elijah Africa is."

I inhaled, my mouth opened, but no sound came out. He studied my face in the silence and said no more.

"Come inside, Mr. Wharton," I said instead, standing back so that he could enter. Unnatural silence descended on the room as Asha made her way to her overturned barrel. "Students, this is Mr. Wharton. From…"

"Dover, New Hampshire."

"He's going to observe our class for a while."

Luella mouthed, "Why?"

"Try to forget that I'm here," Mr. Wharton said.

"You'll probably be most comfortable at my desk," I said, indicating the sturdy oak desk and chair that Ben had crafted for me.

"Oh no, my policy is to remain unobtrusive. I'll make do in the back of the room."

Despite his kind tone, the students eyed him as he picked his way through the crowded barrels and boxes to the bench at the back of the classroom. Leo jumped up and offered him his seat. After some gesturing back and forth, Mr. Wharton bowed his head to Leo and sat, and the log bench gave a great crack.

The class snickered, and sweat formed under my arms despite the chill in the room.

"Let's continue with your sums," I called. A few of the students faced me, but most of them continued to stare at the man in the back of the room as he opened his case and removed a tablet of paper, a pen and bottle of ink.

Mr. Wharton looked up expectantly, ignoring the class's lack of focus. I decided to move on to the literature lesson. I told the class to retrieve the 15 battered copies of *Uncle Tom's Cabin* from the shelf in the front of the room. I took up my own copy and began reading where I'd left off the previous day. The students followed along, most sharing with two or three students close by.

Every year I read Harriet Beecher Stowe's novel to the class, and some of the students must have heard the story at least six times. But they all enjoyed it so much that I created other lessons from the reading of it. It served as a vehicle for discussions of plot, character and theme and provided vocabulary and spelling words. More important were the discussions we'd had after the reading and lessons were complete.

I knew their attention was riveted because we had come to the part where Mr. Shelby, the kindly plantation owner, has decided to sell his favorite slave, Tom. But Leo soon raised his hand. "Can we play act the parts, Miz Whimble?"

The students assigned the parts. Faith, a Negro girl about Luella's age but a much better reader, got the part of Mrs. Shelby.

"Why not make a pecuniary sacrifice?" she drawled, stumbling a bit on "pecuniary." I wrote the word on the blackboard.

"...O, Mr. Shelby, I have tried—tried most faithfully, as a Christian woman should—to do my duty to these poor, simple, dependent creatures. I have cared for them, instructed them, watched over them, and know all their little cares and joys, for years; and how can I ever hold up my head again among them, if, for the sake of a little paltry gain, we sell such a faithful, excellent, confiding creature as poor Tom, and tear from him in a moment all we have taught him to love and value?"

The class applauded her smooth rendition of the Mrs. Shelby's dilemma. Then it was Jamie's turn, a ten-year-old boy with bright red hair, to read the party of Mr. Shelby.

"I'm sorry you feel so about it, indeed I am," read Jamie, and the class laughed at Jamie's puffed chest and high chin. *"And I respect your feelings, too, though I don't pretend to share them to their full extent; but I tell you now, solemnly, it's of no use—I can't help myself. I didn't mean to tell you this Emily; but, in plain words, there is no choice between selling these two and selling everything. Either they must go, or all must."*

Faith continued. *"This is God's curse on slavery! A bitter, bitter, most accursed thing! A curse to the master and a curse to the slave! I was a fool to think I could make anything good out of such a deadly evil. It is a sin to hold a slave under laws like ours, I always felt it was, I always thought so when I was a girl, I thought so still more after I joined the church; but I thought I could gild it over, I thought, by kindness, and care, and instruction, I could make the condition of mine better than freedom—fool that I was!"*

"*Why, wife, you are getting to be an abolitionist, quite,*" read Jamie, and the class chuckled again. After reading through the chapter in that manner, the class read the following chapter to themselves as I walked about offering assistance. With Asha's help, the younger children worked in their readers.

I wrote more vocabulary and spelling words on the blackboard, and the older students copied them onto their easels. Mr. Wharton's hand flew over his paper for several minutes. The students eventually departed for the afternoon, leaving us alone. After a while he raised his head, noting the shelf full of turtle skulls and butterfly wings, feathers and eggshells.

"We occasionally walk along the soundside, discovering items to write about," I explained. His eyes lit up, and he went back to scribbling.

At long last, he put his pen in the inkstand and looked up. "It appears that the exterior and interior of the schoolhouse were painted somewhat recently."

"Yes, my husband and some of the students painted it," I said. "That was almost seven years ago though."

"It's kept up well," he noted. "Some schools I've seen are thoroughly filthy. Rats strutting around."

"Some of the women and children arrive early in the mornings to sweep and scrub the floors. And the men make repairs when necessary, bring wood for the stove."

He took up a few readers from the shelf and flipped through them. "And the books, supplies," he said. "They are in relatively good condition."

"My mother…" I began. "She sent books, easels and chalk for the school. This blackboard. She also purchased the placard. The one you saw above the door."

"And where does she live?"

"Edenton," I said. "She's passed on."

He squared his papers. "I'm sorry to hear that. Your mother must have been a very kind woman."

I stifled a laugh. "No one ever used the word 'kind' in reference to my mother."

He turned to the rows of books beside him. "Well, she must have cared about education at least."

"Learning was perhaps the *only* thing she cared about."

"You must have gotten your ability to teach from her," he ventured.

"She tutored me off-and-on during the war," I said. "But teaching didn't come naturally to her."

"No?"

I always found that words failed me when it came to mama. "She was…an intelligent woman."

At that, he laughed loudly. "Are you saying that a *lack* of intelligence makes for a good teacher?"

"Not at all," I said. "It's only…she had a hard time emerging from the library."

"Ah. I've known a great many of those kinds of men in my time. Pedagogy before people."

He stood up, and stowing his things in his case, made for the door. "I'm staying at the boarding house down the street. Perhaps you know the proprietor, Mrs. Ida Dunley? She seems a…true Southern lady."

I suppressed laughter at that assessment. Ruth and Luella worked as cooks and maids at the inn, and Ruth complained about Ida Dunley almost every day. Ida's only son had been killed in the war, and she seemed to consider Ruth and Luella responsible for his death. Both her son and her husband were buried in a family cemetery in back of the house, and Ida insisted that Ruth tend the plots. Every month she placed fresh Confederate flags and seasonal flowers on the graves and picked the weeds and grasses that sprouted along the head stones.

"Oh yes, her employees attend school here. Ruth and Luella Washington. They'll make sure you're well fed. Ask for the rhubarb pie."

I locked the schoolhouse door and began walking with him down Roanoke Avenue. The sagging homes of the old Freedmen's Colony loomed left and right, the overhanging iron of the sky casting them in a penitentiary light.

"Do you live close by?" he asked.

"I do. But my husband is away for a few months for work, so I'm living at Asha's house."

I pointed out the house where Ben and I had lived, weathered planks nailed over the windows and weeds growing in the dirt. In less than five minutes, we reached Asha's cabin. The unpainted, one-story house rested crookedly on its foundation. Clotheslines laden with linens of every variation cobwebbed the yard.

"Was Asha the woman who took over for you today?"

"Yes," I said. "She was also my nurse, once upon a time. Back in Edenton. She quit working for my parents seven years ago and took up residence here. She adopted a surname common to the area, and started a laundry business with another woman. She learned enough at the school to become a teacher herself. In fact, she teaches the evening class of adults at the schoolhouse."

"That's a testament to your own skill, I imagine."

"Maybe," I allowed. I thought of her white head scarf in the dark window of the cottage, how determined she'd been to learn to read and write. "But she's also bright. A hard worker."

He glanced back at the schoolhouse, still visible at the end of the street. "I'm impressed with the school, Mrs. Whimble."

"Thank you." I was surprised how good it felt to share the schoolhouse with an outsider, a man of education.

"Would you care to join me for supper at the boarding house this evening? I've a few things to discuss with you, for my research."

My face warmed in the cold air at the thought of dining with a man that wasn't my husband, a man that was now looking at me like I had something of value to tell him. Ben had looked at me like that once.

Just down the street, I saw tentative fingers of smoke beckoning from the inn's two chimneys.

Two hours later, I found myself pulling up my skirts and running to the boarding house through sudden sleet. Mr. Wharton stood from a porch rocker at my fast approach.

"I've not seen a woman run so fast before," he said, as I brushed the icy pellets from the shoulders of my coat. "Or run, for that matter."

"We *do* have the capacity for it, you know," I said, still catching my breath.

"So I see," he said, holding the door open for me. "You certainly could outrun me, if it came to a footrace."

Luella stood in the foyer with a small curtsy for me, and I smiled at her. She had pulled her mass of curls into a neatly rolled bun at the back of her head, and her smooth, brown skin shone from a recent scrubbing. She smelled of soap and butter.

Ida Dunley lurked in the parlor, watching as Luella took our coats and hung them by the door. Luella led us to one of four square tables in the empty dining room, where a fire nosed about the hearth. Mr. Wharton pulled back a chair for me, and I sat down, aware of my homespun wool dress and old shoes, warped from their recent foray into the sound. I smoothed down wily strands of hair. It had been a long time since I'd been served food in a restaurant's dining room.

"What you want to drink?" asked Luella, then added, "Water's free."

Mr. Wharton ordered a brandy and looked to me.

"I'll have a glass of scuppernong wine." I knew from Ruth that Mrs. Dunley had a small vineyard of the local varietal on her property.

"You sure?" Luella asked. "Miz Dunley say ladies ain't to take no…"

"She's sure," Mr. Wharton answered.

He grinned at me as Luella walked to the kitchen. "She's a beautiful young woman," said Mr. Wharton. "Tall, it seems, if she wouldn't hunch so much."

I agreed. "She's also my hardest student to teach. She's stubborn, and sometimes lazy and disrespectful. But I think it all stems from a type of learning disability. I'm just not sure." I sighed. "I wish that there was something more I could do for her. She wants so badly to learn."

The door to the kitchen opened, and we turned to see Luella walking slowly toward us bearing a tray laden with drinks. The liquid sloshed to the rims with each timid step. Mr. Wharton made to help her by taking his glass off the tray, but she snapped, "No sir. Don't do that! I got it."

But the force of her objection tipped the tray, and the wine splashed onto my bodice. Luella gasped and hurried to the kitchen, returning with a rag. She wiped hard at the stain, craning around to watch for Mrs. Dunley.

"It was his fault," she said. "He made me spill it."

"Luella!" I scolded. I grabbed for her hand, mindlessly rubbing my chest.

"She's quite right," said Mr. Wharton. "I shouldn't have reached out like that."

Luella nodded violently, still scrubbing away.

"Don't fuss, Luella. It was only white wine. And this is an old dress."

"Don't I know it. You worn it every winter the past five years," she said. "If'n it's ruined, you fixin' to learn us in your underthings?"

Mr. Wharton feigned great interest in adjusting his napkin. Ruth, with a sweaty face and a dirty apron, came out of the kitchen with another glass of scuppernong wine and set it down firmly in front of me. With a scathing look at Luella, she took her daughter's arm mid-scrub and steered her to the kitchen.

I swallowed several sips of the sweet wine, then blotted my lips with a napkin while trying to ignore the sucking damp of my chest. Mr. Wharton took a sip of his brandy and calmly began to butter a yeast roll, as if Luella and Ruth weren't shouting behind the closed door of the kitchen. I figured that Ida Dunley was now upstairs in her own quarters; I also guessed that she had grown hard of hearing.

"So your father…what does he do for a living?"

With the wine, speech had become an easier task. "He is a former plantation owner."

"Former?"

"He lives in Texas now."

"Oh?"

"It suits him," I said. Texas was just now endeavoring to recraft its Reconstruction-era constitution to better reflect its current ideals, which included an emphasis on a small, populist government, agrarian interests, segregated schools, a tight budget, and of course, white superiority.

Mr. Wharton sipped his brandy but kept curious eyes on me.

I barreled on. "After my mother died, he just couldn't...he never could adapt himself. But mostly he was burdened with debt. He sold the plantation to the highest bidder and moved to a small home in the city. When my sister married, he sold again and moved to Texas, taking my brother with him. I...I haven't heard from either of them in a long time."

I hadn't noticed Luella, standing by the table again. "We got chicken, pork and fish, however you like it," she enunciated.

"What's the cook's specialty?" asked Mr. Wharton.

"For sure the *poisson a la crème*," she said, mispronouncing the French, so that the dish came out sounding something like "poisonous cream."

Mr. Wharton smiled. "Ah, my favorite. We'll take two plates?"

I nodded, hardly hungry.

When Luella had retreated to the kitchen, Mr. Wharton said, "I wonder how it was that you came to teach at an integrated school on Roanoke Island?"

"It wasn't without some difficulty."

"Was it the school that beckoned you here from Edenton?"

"No," I said, thinking back to that summer of 1868. "Not at first. My family was staying in our summer cottage in Nags Head a few years ago, and I found the school, and the Freedmen's colony, that summer. But I really stayed on the Outer Banks to be with my husband, Ben. A fisherman. That is to say, he wasn't my husband when I decided to stay on the Banks. But I stayed. For him."

"I can't imagine the decision went over well with your parents."

"No," I said. I found myself telling him the story of how Ben had brought me to the school, and how I'd ended up coming back every evening to teach there. I briefly touched on Elijah Africa, but omitted the fact of his murder. I took from Mr. Wharton's silence surprise at my recklessness and scolded myself for revealing so much of my personal history.

At last he said, "I must say that your teaching methods are quite different. Revolutionary."

"How do you mean?"

"Most every teacher begins the day with a Bible passage and a prayer. Then there is singing and the recitation of the alphabet, followed by drill work—tables, spelling, and so on. And finally, if there is time, they accomplish some actual reading. But you, Mrs. Whimble, prefer *reading*, both yours and the students'. Followed by discussion led by the class. Followed by the students' writing. Perhaps a little impromptu singing and play-acting. Then there are drills, for of course we must have drills. But they are not the primary focus of your teaching."

He leaned toward me. "The primary focus is literature. And this is where the revolution lies," he said. "You are unlike any teacher I've ever seen."

"Thank you?" I still wasn't sure he was favorably affected.

"What happened to Mr. Africa?" he asked. "Does he still live on the island?"

The wine was a puddle of poison in my belly. I tore a chunk off the roll, chewed for a long time, then swallowed hard.

"The Ku Klux Klan murdered him."

I watched as the implication of my words made its way across his face, a diseased vine of horror.

"You're sure of that?"

"I was teaching there when the Klan men came into the schoolhouse, looking for him. It seems that he'd been a wanted man in Bertie County for many years, and…" I broke off, recalling the events of that night for the first time in a long while. The night had marked the end of my childhood and torn apart my family. Ben and I had barely survived it.

"Was the crime ever reported?" he asked, doubt in his voice.

"No," I said. "Most believed he'd gotten his justice. He'd admitted to murdering his master and mistress with an ax, after all."

Scuppernong nausea rolled over me. "Excuse me," I said, my hand over my mouth. I lurched up and ran for the front door.

The night air smelled of fallen ice, and leaning over the porch railing I breathed it in, calming as the cold slowed my blood. I soon heard the door open and turned to see Mr. Wharton, my coat over his arm.

"I apologize, Mrs. Whimble," he said, helping me into the sleeves. "What a terrible thing to have lived through."

He had no idea. Daddy's voice, muffled from behind his hideous costume, sounded clear in my memory, not dulled by time.

"Mr. Africa's buried beneath some dogwood trees near the schoolhouse. We can see the wooden cross from a window."

"And yet, the students still come. And you've continued to teach there." His voice was as gentle as the drizzle on the bushes below. "I believe that most young women would have run for the hills after witnessing such an ordeal."

I shook my head. Leaving those students had never occurred to me.

"I've read reports of people burning down Negro schoolhouses, assaulting teachers of Negroes, refusing to serve teachers food at restaurants or sell them provisions at markets," he said. "Have you been threatened, teaching at the Elijah Africa School?"

I lowered my voice to a whisper. "I'm surprised Ida Dunley allowed me inside her house."

He smiled. "She doesn't much care for Northerners either," he said. "But as I'm her only tenant at the moment, she can't be too choosy."

"Some families avoid me—some men on the island fought for the Confederacy—but I've not been outwardly threatened," I said. "It's a bit different on the Outer Banks. Slavery never took hold out here, and it's so isolated."

"And yet the integration of black and white in education is rare—and becoming rarer—throughout the South," he said. "There is too great a divide among the races, it seems, for blacks and whites to work together in a schoolhouse."

"I suppose a good education is rare as well. All of the students here want to learn," I said. "There have never been schools on the Outer Banks, for blacks *or* whites. Most people here—adults and children—are illiterate."

He was silent for a while. I watched his soft hands stroke the peeling porch railing, and wondered if he ever hurried or raised his voice.

"I gather you've heard of normal schools," he said. "Schools for the instruction of teachers."

I nodded. "A bit."

"I'm on the board of one such normal school, the Peabody Normal School. It will be part of the University of Nashville campus, when it opens for classes December the first. At least, I hope it will," he said. "It's gotten off to an inauspicious start. The buildings are in considerable disrepair, and books and supplies are lacking. On the campus, weeds grow instead of grass, and the lawns are entirely destitute of trees and shrubs. Not to mention we've only 13 students signed on to attend."

He waved a hand about. "We'll soon get it all sorted out. Dr. Stearns is the best man for the job, no doubt of it. We coaxed him away from a prosperous New Hampshire female academy, and alas, the poor man found a hotbed of indifference, ignorance and mistrust in Nashville. But he is a man to overlook these obstacles and plow ahead with his mission. In fact, he and the trustees have a vision of developing the school into the model normal school for the entire South. It will train the best and brightest men and women for the teaching profession, to meet the needs of our growing country."

He turned to face me formally, as if ready to lead me in a waltz. "I can see you there, Mrs. Whimble, as a teacher. President Stearns would very much appreciate your methods, I'm sure. He's already chosen two women to assist him on the faculty, and I imagine you would get on very well with them, especially Miss Julia Stearns. You see, he is a very forward-thinking man."

I opened my mouth to protest, but no words came out.

"Pardon me for asking, but you don't have children of your own?"

I took in a long, icy breath. "No."

"It would be an ideal time to come," he said. "Children are terrible distractions. My wife is quite pleased our three sons are fully grown men."

I shook my head. "I would...leave the Outer Banks?"

"You could at least consider the *possibility*," he said. "You recall the difficulties that Luella is experiencing with reading? You may be interested to know that I have discussed such cases with colleagues from time to time. There are now theories about such individuals, studies being conducted. At the normal school, you could learn how to confront those difficulties with instructional strategies, shared from the faculty. From time to time, you could return to the schoolhouse and help Luella."

"Help Luella..." I repeated. Her face appeared in my mind, joyful at finally cracking the code of reading.

A teacher of teachers...

He smiled at me then. "I've given you enough to think about for one evening. Pardon me if I overtaxed you."

He offered me his arm.

"Brave enough to try your poisonous cream? And perhaps some of that famous rhubarb pie."

Back in Asha's cabin, my racing mind refused to slow into sleep. Asha had returned from teaching long ago, but I'd pretended to be asleep.

I dug at a burning itch on my ankle, only to feel a similar tug on my thigh. I sat up and threw off the blankets. I couldn't see a thing in the darkness, but I knew the cabin was still infested with chinches. There was nothing to do but wait until the morning to replace the seaweed and straw in our bed ticks, the only step we'd left out of our first attempt.

"Why not?" I said aloud, and Asha bolted up on her tick.

"What? Who?"

"Go back to sleep," I said softly. "I was just talking to myself."

She said irritably, "Scare me to death." She lay back down, scratching at her neck. Soon she began to snore.

Then it was as if every chinch in the world had found me. I stood up and pulled on my shoes and coat, still emanating *poisson a la crème* and scuppernong wine. I opened the back door and drawing my coat about me, sat on the back step. I watched the clouds move past an almost full moon, heard the soft clucking of the chickens in their roosting boxes, the grunting of the pigs in their pen.

I fought them every day and night, but at last I gave my mind up to thoughts of Ben.

"Hi, Ben," I said.

He shaded his eyes with a brown hand. "Hi there, sunshine."

I wouldn't cry. I scratched hard at a spot on my arm. "I could do it," I told him.

He kept smiling at me, and I spotted the dark hole where he'd pulled an infected upper tooth not too long ago.

"Would you be angry with me?" I asked after a while.

"I doubt it," he winked. "For what?"

"For leaving."

"You already left," he said. His sad voice rasped like tangles of sea grass.

"I know. I'm sorry."

I wanted to keep talking with him. To keep going, further than we ever had. But he wasn't there, after all. He had left me too finally.

The early years with Ben came back to me, full and rich as sponge cake. I wanted nothing more than to be with him, to share in his simple life. The sight of his sea-carved face at the end of a long day would often take my breath. The days had been too long and hard to sustain us though.

I saw myself now, how my mind had slowly shrunk and closed, how I'd begun to live life like a mental hunchback. I didn't expect good things to happen to me. I expected things to slip away from me and die.

I looked to the moon and thought that it looked more like a cannon hole in the black sky, instead of something precious, heavy to hold. I imagined jumping through that hole to see what I might find in the gaping white.

CHAPTER FIVE

NOVEMBER 7, 1875
BENJAMIN WHIMBLE

*And all the time numberless fowls were diving, and ducking,
and screaming, and yelling, and fighting around them. Stubb
was beginning to look disappointed, especially as the hor-
rible nosegay increased, when suddenly from out of the very
heart of this plague, there stole a faint stream of perfume,
which flowed through the tide of bad smells without being
absorbed by it, as one river will flow into and then along
with another, without at all blending with it for a time.*

–ISHMAEL, **MOBY-DICK**

I CRACKED MY EYES APART AND SAW THE TWO WINDOWS
of the station house beside me, full of gray. The first
thought I had was of Abby, same as every morning:
Abby's not here.

The cut on my neck burned like I'd rubbed it with sand, and my head was wrapped in tentacles of pain. It had been a long night, and I'd tossed and turned for the duration, dreaming on the lost boy, his skinny bones.

It was so cold we'd left the boy's body laid out on the floor of the shed. Captain Gale aimed to let people know about the boy at church service today, then head over to the lighthouse to ask the folks there. Sooner or later someone would come for their kin.

Being as today was Sunday, it was our one day to rest, excepting lookout. A peek out a window showed a sea as gray as the sky. Seaweed was strewn about the shore like the guts of soldiers. I pulled on my britches and shirt, still sandy from the night.

In the day-room sat Malachi and Lewis, eating fried eggs and toast. They were all slicked up for visits from their families. Lewis's hair was plastered to his head with pomatum, and both men wore their dark Sunday suits.

"You look like the devil," Lewis said. "You could at least comb your hair afore my mama gets here."

"Least my hair ain't set to explode if I step too close to a flame," I said.

Lewis reached up and patted his head. "Mama likes me to look nice."

Malachi leaned over to look at my neck. "That wound looks to be festering."

"Feels like it too," I said, touching it tender. I was lucky the boy didn't stick my jugular.

I piled a plateful of eggs and ham from the platter and pulled a chair to the table. Got one forkful of food into my mouth when I heard the hollering and whining of younguns outside.

Malachi jumped up and opened the side door. "Jessie, Perry! Get on in here!"

His boy and girl scampered into the day-room, bringing with them cold air and tittering.

"Where's mama at?" said Malachi.

"Outhouse, daddy," she said behind her hand.

I broke the yolks over my toast and watched out the corner of my eye as Malachi scrubbed their curly heads, making them squeal. I tried hard not to think on the boy laid out in the shed.

"We brung you some apple cider and four whole apple cobblers and a bushel of apples we gathered all by ourselves," said Jessie. She looked up at Malachi like she'd never seen a better sight than her pap's long mustache.

"Sounds like the whole orchard. It's a good thing the men here like apples," said Malachi. The younguns stole looks at me and Lewis.

Lewis patted his stomach. "I could eat one of those cobblers all by myself."

Perry's peepers opened wide. "Mama says you all got to share."

"Oh, well," sighed Lewis. "Mamas do know best."

"You all set to go to church?" I said.

They nodded. "I brung my fishing rod too, so's we can fish after," said Perry.

I stood up to clean my plate and fork in the washing bucket. "Catch one for me then. I'll be back for lookout this afternoon."

"Ain't you going to church?" asked Lewis. The men attended church in the parlor of a Whales Head widow's house, where the preacher was said to stay rent-free. He was a traveling preacher, hopping about the Banks to bring the branch of Methodist Christianity to the heathens out here. Being from the mainland, the men were used to going to church, but myself, I'd never been to a service in my life.

I opened the door, ready to pull foot. "Not today."

"What you got better to do?"

"Climbing sand dunes."

Wide eyes all around at my Sunday sacrilege.

"Sand dunes? What for?" asked Lewis.

Even the younguns had their yellow heads cocked at me, akin to a couple of retrievers. To most folks, the Outer Banks dunes were nothing but a hindrance.

I shrugged. "Sand dunes are good for looking."

"Looking for what?"

Not hard to tell these younguns lived on a farm. "Well, I'll tell you. Way back when, folks here used to climb those big dunes to look for whales. Then they'd get in their boats and kill the whales with harpoons, bring 'em in, boil their blubber for oil. Use all parts of the sperm whale, 'specially the oil from their heads. You see, that's why they call these parts Whales Head. Either that, or on account of a long ago whale that came ashore. 'Twas so big a man drove horse and buggy clear through its mouth."

The younguns' mouths popped wide. "You ever see any whales from up there?" asked Jessie.

"No ma'am, sad to say I haven't. They're all fished out, I heard."

"Then what are you looking for, if there ain't any whales?" asked Perry.

"He's looking for the love of Jesus Christ," said Malachi. "And he'd be better off going to church service than setting on that heap o' sand."

Jones's Hill wasn't as tall as Jockeys Ridge, but close enough. And just like Jockeys Ridge its sands were on the move, thirsty for the waters of the sound. Mayhaps 100 years ago a nearby dune called Penny's Hill was so parched it swallowed a whole inlet and closed it up for good. It's only a little creek now, where it used to cut clean and wide through the island, ocean to sound.

At the top I pulled the crow bar from my britches and sat down to survey the stew of sea and sky and ocean, the way I used to like to do in Nags Head. When we chanced to visit the house on a Sunday, Abby and me used to climb Jockeys Ridge, no matter the weather. We liked the surprise of a different kind of view—the sea never looked the same way twice. But after our losses we never could find it in ourselves to climb anymore. We just got stuck in the earth, afraid to even look up.

We went up once, after we lost the baby girl, just to see what we'd find of ourselves. And too it was

Abby's birthday, so Asha had made her a picnic lunch of her favorites. Course, it wasn't the kind of fare she'd called her favorites back when we'd first met. It seemed the Sinclair folks couldn't be trifled with ordinary fare on their fancy plates. They'd had their servants fixing food that needed a French dictionary to learn how to say proper. One dish dealt in duck liver and queer little mushrooms. I'd take Asha's fried chicken any day over such a concoction, which is just what she'd made. She'd fried its juicy parts in a heavy coating of flour and spices, then did the same with some green tomatoes. So we kind of felt like we *had* to go somewhere, faced with all that goodwill.

I'd sailed us to Nags Head, the chicken steam making my mouth water all the way over. But once we reached the top of the dune, we sat stiff as planks, not even holding hands, not saying a word, and the wind did the talking for us. It whipped and pushed and blew us cold to the bone, even though the sun was out, nice and warm on a September day. We vamoosed not too long after we sat down, our picnic spoilt.

It was around that time that she'd started reading like there was no tomorrow. If Abby wasn't at home of an afternoon, I knew where to find her—in the bookshop in town, trading what little we had with Rodney Gillikin. In about three months, she'd read just about every book ever written in the world. I'd picked up one or two and tried to read them, but it was like the words were all written backwards for all the sense they made. I could just feel our own words getting buried under the stacks of books around us.

We'd built up a love from reading, there was no denying it. From the first day we met, *Robinson Crusoe* was a part of us, like a youngun almost, or a pet, with its way of bringing out our true natures. She had me believing what she did—that there wasn't a single word sounded better'n "book."

Abby had wanted to move on. But reading *Robinson Crusoe* was like taking in the sights from the dunes; I always got a new view of things. I never wanted to read a thing else. Fact, I learned how to write by copying out sentences from *Robinson Crusoe* itself.

Abby had pulled away at some point, stopped the sharing. She'd stopped laughing too, and I hadn't noticed the slowing of it. Put me in mind of the way the sun slips away to the west while I was still atop the strut with my nets out.

I knew that the sight of my face and the touch of my hand turned her hard and cold, where once she'd smiled and burned, warm and soft as a candle dripping wax.

For a while there, I tried to be easy around her, not push her to love me, on account I saw how it was with her when our baby girl had died. She'd felt the baby grow big in her belly, had felt her wiggle, had gone through the sickness. And I'd seen how the surprise of growing something inside her gave her a joy she'd never had before. She said it was like reading a good book, how it grew on you slow, how you found yourself thinking of it all the time, mulling over possibilities.

A few months after the second loss pap had had his paralyzing fit, and then it was just me on the skiff, doing the work of two men and coming home to a wife sunk deep in the cold waters of sadness. My days started to drag by so slow, where once they had flown like geese on the wing. For too long I'd felt like Crusoe, marking time on his cave wall. I knew there was nothing I could do to help her, except maybe to leave her.

I stood up in the sucking drifts of dune, tried to get my bearings. I figured I'd go see what was in the boy's barrel, something I could mayhaps put to rights.

Couple of miles up the foamy shore I spotted the driftwood marker. I dug through the sand to pull the barrel up, then pried the lid off with the crowbar.

The smell hit me all at once, the smell of old fish. I tipped the barrel to the gray light, and halfway down I saw what looked to be a big white-grey rock. I was dumbfounded, wondering why the boy had died for a rock. But then there a different kind of smell that made its way through the stink of fish, a warmish sweet and salty smell. I reached a finger to the rock to rub it, then stuck it in my mouth and tasted.

And then I knew.

It was ambergris, otherwise known as the dung of a sperm whale. I'd seen and tasted it just once, but once was plenty. I grabbed the barrel and breathed deep.

I'd heard tell that the stuff started out as nothing but reeking, watery, black grime, the kind of stuff that one would expect a whale to spit up or shit out. But after so many years floating on the sea, this whale dung turned into the sweet-smelling, spongy stuff that now abided in the barrel. Perfumes, folks made with it, the best kinds in the world, and just a little bit of ambergris sold for hundreds of dollars. Ambergris was that rare. More precious than gold to most.

No wonder the boy held a knife to my throat, I thought. I tipped the barrel back and forth, gauging its weight—nigh on 50 pounds. It was enough of the stuff to make a man rich.

The ocean pounded the sand nearby, matching the hard beat of my heart. It was such a scenario no one would believe me, even if I showed up at that church service and swore on the Bible.

But it wasn't mine, I told myself. The boy had wanted to keep the ambergris safe from somebody. But whoever they were, they were likely good and sore right about now missing such a fortune. I doubted we'd have to spread the word about the boy. Somebody would come hunting that skiff before I could say whale dung.

It couldn't be worked out in a morning, I decided. I placed the barrel back in its hiding spot and covered it up. Then I crowned the spot with the driftwood again, its sandy limbs reaching for the heavens, and I thought on the boy, if he was watching me from above, making sure I did what he wanted.

A look at the sun told me I could still get to the widow's parlor for church, but it seemed I didn't want to be parted from the spot. I looked down shore, told my limbs to start walking, the way they'd become accustomed. Once I got going I was alright.

Most of my fellow surfmen and their kin stood in the back of the widow's parlor. They all grinned and pointed at me, and the preacher took a break from his sermoning to nod at me as I made my way along the parlor's edge. The sandy floorboards groaned and cracked as I walked.

"She'll soon touch bottom," declared Mrs. Della Blount, Jennie's ma. She and Jennie waved to me from the midst of the locals, all bunched up in the warm, smoky room. All held prayer books, but most were shut. I reckoned the preacher should have started with a reading lesson instead of a Bible one.

I *was* a bit curious about the goings-on at a church service. When I was a youngun, there was a tiny wooden chapel in Nags Head near the old hotel, used to serve the vacationers during the summer times. Preachers from Elizabeth City and up yonder would come to sermon for them. Natives didn't visit, but we could hear the sermoning and singing through the open windows.

I did recall walking under live oak branches so I could peek inside the chapel, it having the aura of mystery. It didn't have a ceiling, but the weatherboards and joists were whitewashed, looked as if angels had come down and breathed all over it. I worked up a feeling of jealousy on those visits, for it seemed a special place, full of peace, and I didn't see why the Bankers wouldn't use the chapel too. But those feelings didn't last long, for the Yankees tore the whole thing down during the war, used the wood for freedmen houses on Roanoke Island.

The spider webs in the corners of the widow's ceiling looked fit to catch a shoat, and I got no fit of jealousy, standing here in the musky crowd. The preacher himself looked spiderish, with a face like he'd walked smack into one of those webs, and his long, skinny arms and legs poking from his black Sunday preaching suit. As soon as he started reading from the Bible in his Judgment Day tenor, my mind drifted back to the barrel of ambergris, ripe for the selling. Smelling of gold.

"And Jesus answering said unto them, Suppose ye that these Galilaeans were sinners above all the Galilaeans, because they suffered such things? I tell you, Nay: but, except ye repent, ye shall all likewise perish."

I reckoned the folks around me had their minds on their repentance, or wondering who in tarnation the Galilaeans were, yet nothing but the picture of the barrel started to burn like a flame inside me, warming me like a shot of whiskey instead of the righteousness of religion.

"You alright, Ben?" Lemuel whispered. "Your face is all red."

I wiped my brow with the sleeve of my coat. "I reckon it's the close air in here. I can smell Lewis's pomatum from here."

That set Lemuel to sniggering, and the preacher ratcheted up his volume so that the spiders could hear him. It seemed to work though, for the devil-thought of the barrel had gone.

The service ended with one last song and the folks all piled out, taking in big gulps of fresh air like a crop of landed fish. We milled about in the yard for a while, talking with the preacher. Soon enough the men circled, and talk started on the boy who'd washed ashore. We talked around and around it for a while, but not a one of them could put a name to him until we told of the color of his hair. Eyebrows shot up and looks got made, and the men wanted to see the boy for themselves. Even the preacher said he'd come back with us.

In a hurry for Sunday dinner, the women and younguns had already climbed atop the wagon and made for the station house. They should've waited for the poor old preacher though, for he walked slow through the sand like a man made of sticks and we were obliged to match our pace with his. He didn't wear out, much to my surprise, and with the stew still another hour to cook we all walked straight to the shed. The boy looked even whiter and skinnier than before, and his sandy clothes had dried frozen to his body. My scarf had been pulled down to his chin, the blue of it matching the boy's parted lips.

One man started to shaking his head. "That there is the youngest of the Spruel boys. Livy," he said. "I knew it. You all said red hair, and I knew."

"I know him," the preacher said, putting his knobbed hand on the boy's chest. "He attended a good many of my sermons. I never saw his kin. He came on his own."

"I saw him there too. Standing with the Blounts. I reckoned he was sweet on Jennie. He was a good boy," said the other man. "For that clan of folk."

Others started to nodding.

"That clan?" I said.

Boot shuffled on the sandy floorboards. The man said, "The Spruels keep to themselves. Fish and farm, as little of both as they can."

"They won't do a thing for nobody 'less there's something in it for them," said another man.

"You said the boy came to your services?" Captain Gale asked the preacher.

"Once a month, going on a year or so. He always skedaddled before I could reach him."

"Did him some good, I reckon," said Malachi.

"He came ashore in this?" asked a man with a long, gray beard, pointing to the cracked-up pilot skiff. "That skiff is too big for a boy like him to handle on his own."

"We thought the same. He didn't come ashore with anybody else, far as we know," said Captain Gale.

The men stared down at the boy like they were waiting on him to sit up and answer for his actions. The preacher rubbed a hand along the side of the boat and proclaimed over the power of the sea as nothing to the power of God. We bowed our heads, hats in hand, for his words had the sound of a prayer. He talked of the queer way the boy had died, wondering on the omen of it all. He concluded that God works in mysterious ways, but I figured we could all agree to that prophecy. Didn't have to be a preacher to conclude that living life was one puzzlement after another.

The folks were real proud to have the preacher at dinner. The women called him Reverend Washburn, and all the younguns minded themselves. The men even held back on the cussing. Reverend Washburn said the blessing and stood in the boat room to eat the fish stew with the rest of the men. Soon Spencer pulled out his mouth organ, and Malachi strummed his banjo, and Lewis let himself out in a jig. The Reverend Washburn tapped his boot-clad feet to the tune, even sang along in a trembly tone.

Must be nice to be a preacher, I thought. With God to point fingers at, a man could explain anything sad and terrible that happened along and still find it in himself to sing.

Late that afternoon the women and children made to leave for the soundside docks, and folks were hugging goodbye. I pulled on my hat and coat and headed up the ladder to the lookout tower where Jerry stood watch. The sight of me caused him to recall a letter he held for me in his coat pocket.

Seeing Abby's writing on the envelope made me turn my back on Jerry, grin on my face. But when I pulled out the letter and saw she'd only written a few lines worth—and a *poem*, at that—I all of a sudden felt the sting of the wind.

Dearest husband, she began. Then it was word for word a poem called "Lines Written While Sailing In A Boat At Evening." She'd written out the author's name—William Wordsworth. Then she'd signed it: *Your wife, Abigail.* I read the poem over and over again, my nose going numb.

How richly glows the water's breast
Before us, tinged with evening hues,

While, facing thus the crimson west,
The boat her silent course pursues!
And see how dark the backward stream!
A little moment past so smiling!
And still, perhaps, with faithless gleam,
Some other loiterers beguiling.

Such views the youthful Bard allure;
But, heedless of the following gloom,
He deems their colours shall endure
Till peace go with him to the tomb.
– And let him nurse his fond deceit,
And what if he must die in sorrow!
Who would not cherish dreams so sweet,
Though grief and pain may come to-morrow?

I could read it just fine, but I had no notion what Wordsworth meant. What the devil were loiterers beguiling? Faithless gleam? I needed Abby to tell me, go over it line by line the way she liked to do, all those years ago.

At first, Abby was always saying lines of poetry to me. Then she got so she'd recite an entire poem to me and ask me what it was about. She'd fire one off while I was rowing the boat, or milking the cow, or walking beside her on the road, take me by surprise and set my mind to aching. Let's just say it wasn't my favorite game. We hadn't played it in years though, and I hadn't thought of it neither.

I pictured her writing down the poem in Asha's little house, sitting by the hearth with a quilt on her lap, smelling of smoke and oyster stew. She likely knew the poem by heart, didn't even need to copy it out of her ratty old book. She stored poems in her mind the way some folks stored potatoes in root cellars.

She likely chose the poem because it spoke of a boat, something I could grasp ahold of. I recalled a poem about a gallnipper she'd told to me after getting set upon by a swarm one day on Run Hill. I had a hard time believing a poem could be so amusing. I made her tell it to me over and over, but I couldn't conjure up a word of it now if my very life depended on it.

I looked down at the boat poem again. I almost could hear Abby, trying to explain, but her words got drowned out by the ocean noise. I was left with nothing but another man's words.

CHAPTER SIX

NOVEMBER 14, 1875
ELIZA DICKENS

*There are certain queer times and occasions in this strange
mixed affair we call life when a man takes this whole uni-
verse for a vast practical joke, though the wit thereof he
but dimly discerns, and more than suspects that the joke is
at nobody's expense but his own.*

-*ISHMAEL*, MOBY-DICK

JUST UNDER A WEEK AFTER HE TOOK SICK, AMOS DIED.

His blood must have boiled him to death I
reckon. At the end he was hotter than the point of a
fire poker. He'd stopped his hacking, and that turn
was even worse than the fever.

We could hear the flim-flam in his lungs rattling
round like bone buttons, but Amos was too tired to
even breathe. Iola was so upset by the sounds that she

lifted him up and pounded on his back, looked like a mama trying to burp a giant baby. Then she started to coughing her own self.

"You ain't catching sick, are you?"

"No," said she. And I knew she wasn't. She and I seemed to outrun sickness of any kind. Except heartsick.

We'd run out of wood for Amos's old stove, so we had ourselves a room full of winter, wouldn't have been a circumstance to see icicles hanging from the rooftops. The remedy from Doc Warbush had run out, but it hadn't done a lick of good anyhow. I'd watched Iola lay what must've been a mighty cold hand on Amos's cheek, and he seemed to get some relief from it.

"I could leave you two alone," I'd said.

"Don't you leave me," she'd said to Amos.

Not much later, when she realized Amos had really gone, she cried so much blood started mixing with her snot. She lay up next to him for hours that night, quiet as a mouse. Next day I'd gone out guiding for the Yanks, but that night I sat up with her while she moaned and carried on fit to wake him from his death. I was beside myself, no sleep to be had and wading about in Iola's misery. She wouldn't speak to me, wouldn't eat nor drink.

I'd got it out of her where she thought he'd be buried—somewhere in Wash Woods, where Amos was reared up. But she declared Wash Woods a terrible place to spend eternity, for some of the coffins in the sand boneyard there were washing into the sea. Iola said she once saw shiny things through the rotten wood of the coffins, thought they were jewels or the like. Turned out on closer look it was rows of toads roosting amongst the bones. Not to mention the stumps of long dead trees still stuck from the sandy shores, more reminders of life gone by. 'Twas a haunted place full of evil enchantments where lost spirits roamed, she said. A place unfit for a soul as good as Amos's. She decided she wouldn't bury him a-tall but just keep him there in the cabin with her forever.

By morning I'd got it in my head to find Abner when he came with the post that afternoon. He had himself one of the Outer Banks routes. He came up here about once a week with post from parts further south, like Roanoke Island and Nags Head. He took the mail over to the post office on Knotts Island and then over to the mainland and started back the way he came. I reckoned he was on a boat most of the days of his life now, which suited him perfect with his bad leg.

I was stringing up the day's fowl when at last I spotted Abner's skiff come creeping along the edges of the sound. I hurried down to the docks, all the while hearing him whistle a tune as he poled along.

"Abner!" I hollered. "Quit your dilly-dallying and get over here."

He almost toppled from the boat at the sound of me. I fought the urge to guffaw. I never was very sweet to Abner, but that ain't my fault. See, Abner always had an eye for me, even when I was Ben's. As a youngun he'd do anything I said, even if it went against his better nature. I'd been waiting a long time to watch him blow his stack, but it ain't happened yet.

He poled the boat lickety-split over to where I stood and looked up at me like he was about to get a whooping.

"What's wrong, Eliza?"

"It's Amos. He's passed."

His lazy eye spun round in a panic. "Oh. Well now." His bare hands rubbed back and forth on the boat pole. "I can't rightly believe it. That quinine of Doc Warbush's didn't help none?"

"That bitter stuff? Not a lick," I said. "And the sea-weed remedy from the midwife neither."

"Well, folks is gonna be real sad to hear that," he said. "Big Amos gone, it's right hard to believe. There he was, strong as a ox."

"Uh-huh. I know." I wasn't sure what else to say about Amos. He was Iola's man, after all. "I need you to tell folks back in Nags Head that Amos has passed. Iola needs her family here. She's beside herself, and I can't help her like she needs right now. You think you can manage to do that? Soon as you get back to Nags Head?"

He started to nodding his head even before I'd done talking. "Sure I can. I'd be happy to. Well, you know, not happy. But I'd be real...proud to help you all out."

"Well, get on then." My words crawled tired from my mouth.

"You doing alright there, Eliza?" He put down his pole and made to tie the boat up.

"Don't you dare tie that boat up, Abner Miller. Get on, now."

I made to leave him, but he called, "Wait! The post!"

He grabbed some letters from his mailbag, looked 'em over and handed them up to me. I turned around and walked quick as I could down the docks.

Three days later I found myself in that Wash Woods boneyard, north of the lighthouse. God-awful sandy spot of land, only about nine wooden posts still standing. Amos's post stood well back from the sea and was carved up fresh from a block of heart pine. I could smell it from where I stood, nothing like death.

Along with a good many of the Whales Head folk, there was a little crowd of Nags Headers there. Must've taken 'em a whole day to get here the way the sound was running. Even the Yanks came, drove me and Iola over in their horse and buggy. They stood out like three teeth in a row of empty gums.

A few folks were still straggling in, some on boats and some on foot and some on horseback. Mama was there, hugging on Iola. It was so good to see her that I just about ran over.

"We'll catch up after," she said to me. But her eyes had stuck on the Yanks.

"That them?"

I nodded, and she grunted. She'd seen all their slick nonsense before. Mama's hair looked grayer than I recalled. And it seemed she'd tried to bustle her dress with some sea grass or some such, for her dress was jumped up in back and showed an eyeful of her yarn stockings. I tried to yank it down, but she smacked my hand away, eyes still on the Yanks.

Abner came shuffling up to us, smelling of too much pomatum.

"A grist of Nags Head folks came up," he said. I reckoned he wanted a pat on his shiny head for his help, but I was in no right mind to give him one.

"Go stand over yonder," I said. "Iola doesn't need your stink making her eyes water any more than they have been."

He sniffed the inside pits of his coat, then scooted a couple paces off.

I moved to stand near Iola and her kin, all sniffling into their sleeves. She wore her only dress that she'd dyed black, and the color washed her out good. But there was something pretty about her, something to do with being so sad yet still standing on her own two feet. Plus she was the prettiest woman on the Banks anyway. She reached for my hand without looking at me, and I squeezed it tight.

I'd sat with Iola and dead Amos every night, us wrapped up in blankets and quilts on account the cabin door was open to let out the smell of him. Iola had seemed not to notice neither the cold nor the stink. But it was all I could do to sit there. That's what best friends do though. Amos's friend Tommy came over to the cabin to shave his face while Iola combed out his hair. Tommy told her flat-out that Amos would want to be buried with his kin, so she'd come around to the notion.

Amos's uncle started up talking about Amos as a youngun. Folks always thought he was older than his years, he said, on account of his size, and took to giving him more work than a boy his age would do. But Amos didn't complain none, was chirked getting to work with grown men. And the work just made him stronger.

I stood there, having the devil of a time trying to picture a little boy Amos, and my eyes found a face in the crowd. I stopped breathing, my hand in Iola's going limp.

The sky above was all cloud, but even so it was like someone had shined a sunbeam on this face, just for me. I tried not to stare his way, but I couldn't help myself. A brass band and gypsy parade could have marched us by, and I wouldn't have even looked away from him.

He stood there, Ben did, and I hadn't even seen him come. His face had thinned out since I'd seen him last, but he wore a coat I remembered from the old days. His britches were finely made, the collar of his wool shirt under the coat clean. He had on some leather boots too, not the shiny ilk that the Yanks wore, but nice enough. His yellow hair was combed back off his clean shaven face, and I reckoned he was more handsome than even before. But more than that, he stood so straight now, black slouch hat in his hands. He was a man full grown.

No sign of his wife, I saw.

Had he seen me too? I lowered the ugly black shawl from my head and smoothed out my hair. I knew my cheeks were red from the cold so I wouldn't have to pinch 'em. I licked my chapped lips good, then looked down at my beat-up boots and Union coat and homespun dress. He'd see I hadn't changed a lick, be bored with me and we hadn't even said two words to one another.

Then, as the uncle kept on, I saw those blue eyes meet up with my brown ones. I saw that he saw it was me. He made me a smile, kind of a sad smile for Ben, and tipped his head to me. I kept my face flat though. Didn't want him to think I was happy to see him.

Which I was.

And it dawned on me that I shouldn't be so happy when here Iola was, burying her man. I looked over to her, found her staring at the hole in the sandy ground where Amos's coffin already sat. Tears wet her face. I reached up with my hand and swiped the wet away with my mitt.

I'd known Iola even longer than I'd known Ben, ever since we were knee-babies. Me and Iola would ride along with Iola's daddy while he fished and shot. I reckon it was where I learned about those things 'cause it wasn't from my own daddy, the lazy piss-maker who was only too happy to stick me with Iola's daddy for the day so he could loll about mama's market and beg from the customers.

Iola and me did most everything together, us living so close in the flats the way we did. She learned to fish and shoot too, but never near as good as me. She just liked to sew and keep house and garden. Her favorite thing to do was visit mama and me at the market and help us stock food. She was better at ordering things just so than I ever was.

Once I took up with Ben though, Iola took to the wayside. Oh, she'd try to tag along, but I'd holler at her to go on home, play with her filthy, button-eyed dolly Ermaline. We went back and forth like that for years 'til she got sweet on Amos, a great big boy-man born with more brawn than bone.

He was always down our way helping build boats and fishing or hunting for weeks at a time. All the gals on the Banks wanted him, but Iola tried the hardest to get him, in spite of the fact that Amos always favored traveling about, even as pretty as Iola was with her shiny yellow hair and rosy skin and big blue eyes. He'd come crawling around when he got over-hungry for sustenance other than fried fish or needed some socks darned. Iola was more than glad to do for him—cooking, baking, mending, rubbing on his shoulders. But she'd only do so much. She stopped at the hand-job, she'd said, and she wouldn't let him go up her skirts too far, 'cause she knew how puckered he'd get when she slapped him away. I reckon he proposed at last on account pretty Iola wouldn't give him the goods until they were hitched.

It was clever doing, you ask me. She made him a good wife, the year they'd been married. And there I was, always thinking I had it better than Iola, with Ben as my beau. Little did I know.

One thing I remember about Ben is I liked him from the first time I met him, though some folks did say as how he was a bit different from other boys. I learned what they meant by that when Ben fussed at me for lugging home a Canada goose I'd shot with my daddy's old fowling piece.

"They mate for life," he'd said. "What in tarnation's wrong with you?"

He'd told me the story of a Canada goose he knew. She and her mate always picked Ben's yard as home when they came back to the Banks, year after year. One year they brought back two goslings, tame as could be when Ben's daddy trained 'em as tollers. But one day mama goose left the yard, went round and round the skies, day after day, night after night, honking her awful honks. Ben's daddy reckoned she was calling for her lost mate. She finally died, said Ben, wore herself out with looking.

I'd laughed, knowing that everyone on the Banks shot Canada goose, and didn't give a care about lost mates. But the sight of Ben's long face straightened me out. We never shot Canada geese, though they crowded the sounds in untold numbers in fall and winter.

Even as a youngun he worked so hard, and he always had a grin on his face. And before he was even old enough to dip, he was a bona fide expert on the moon phases and tides, ocean currents, sky and weather omens, bird and whale travels. He always talked of things that never'd crossed my mind if it weren't for him. Things he'd learned about the building of boats and houses and docks, things he'd heard about outsiders and their opinions and cares. He talked so much about so many things that folks kind of sidestepped him when they saw him coming. But I listened to him. Me and his pap.

It was hard to believe, but Ben and his pap had even less than my family. He didn't have a mama, which always made me want to cook and clean for him. I thought he liked it, until he took up with that Abigail, who looked like she never cleaned nor cooked a day in her life.

When I saw her up close that night of the July Fourth party all those years ago, my heart closed on itself like a fish mouth. Even in the firelight, she was pretty as a summer duck, with a long pretty neck and wild colors. Her clothes…well, let's just say she wore on herself more money than I'd ever earned in my life, all added up. She was the kind of woman didn't know where her food came from. I just couldn't feature why Ben was so taken with her. I worried on it every second of every day. I truly believed Ben to be a different kind of man entirely, one who wouldn't be blown over by such things as clothes and prettiness. Could she feed herself, if it all went to shit? Clothe herself? I doubted it wholeheartedly.

But gone he was over her and her rich life, and I soon learned there was no coming back for him. Folks told me to look elsewhere.

"Plenty of unhitched men out here on the Banks," they'd said. "Looking for a wife to tend 'em." I looked around and saw nothing but nothing, all around me. No one could measure up to Ben. I reckon I was the goose that had lost her mate.

And course, standing in a busted up boneyard no less, I felt all our history there in the cold space between us. Might as well have dug a hole and dumped it all in there, along with Amos's eternity box. Because it always did feel like a death to me, his leaving me like that. I thought we were to marry, the fool that I was. I even dreamed on the babies we'd have together, no better'n Iola. They all looked like tiny Bens. They all grinned happy at me, their sour-puss mama.

I felt mixed up—kind of happy and sad both—when I heard that Abigail lost a baby fresh from the womb. I couldn't help thinking the house Ben built was never meant for her, that their baby was never meant to be, that it was really my baby with Ben, still inside me, that was waiting to be born.

When the uncle stopped his talking, Iola took up the shovel and started to filling in the hole over Amos's coffin. The whole boodle snuffled and snotted, and I myself wanted to bawl watching Iola wield the shovel. But Ben's standing there, not far away, helped to shore me up.

When all was said and done, the crowd broke up into bits and pieces and I stood my ground. Soon enough though, I heard his voice behind me.

"Hey Eliza," he said. Like we were just out walking on the north Banks and happened to bump into each other. Like a everyday happening.

"Hey yourself, Ben." My voice came out too loud for the day. I looked down, saw he fiddled at his hat with hands so clean I didn't know them.

"Heard you were working up here at the new crack club. With A...you know, with him and Iola." He cricked his neck toward where the men stood, smoking pipes. "Those are them over yonder, I reckon."

I bobbed my head up and down. "Uh-huh."

It was all this time without each other just hanging there between us like dead ducks strung up in the game barn. Turned me to a simpleton.

Ben whistled in outright wonder. "Bunch of dandies."

"Dandy as it gets." I took in a long and deep pull of cold air. "So, you take the boats up this morning with the rest of them?"

"No," he said. "I'm working at the lifesaving station. Jones's Hill. I just walked on up here. Abner told me, you know."

It was like my nose holes forgot how to take the air. "You're working up here. At the Jones's Hill station." Just to make sure those were the words he'd said. "The one up here. In Whales Head."

"The very one."

I laughed then. Right out loud. And he looked me over real queer too. Here I stood, taking a paying job in Whales Head, just to get away from Ben and all our ghosts. And now here he stood, taking a paying job in Whales Head. I reckoned for sure that God was out to get me then, and I really did wonder what-all it was I'd done.

Then I recalled hearing the station's news the other day. "You must have attended that poor boy," I said. "We heard all about it, couple days past. Local boy, they said."

"Yeah," he said. "I found him."

"*You* found him." I felt my hand itching to touch him, so I made it into a fist. "I ain't the slightest surprised."

"I didn't do a thing. He passed on soon after I found him."

"Mercy. What do you reckon he was doing, going out in such rough waters?"

He shrugged. "Two of his kin came by the station house couple of days back to fetch up his body and the skiff," he said. "They didn't say a word."

"That's sad. Truly." I chewed at my lip. "So...your wife up here?"

He looked down at his boots then, started shaking sand off the tops of them. "She's back on Roanoke Island. Teaching at the school, you know."

I was glad of all the clothing I had on, so he couldn't see my heart jumping. "How long you fixing to stay up here working?"

"It's a four month shift. I go home end of March."

"And...and she ain't gonna live up here with you?"

"Wives aren't allowed to live at the station."

"Oh." I tried to play like I cared about dear, sweet Abigail. "But she could move up here, live close by. Only for a little while, anyways."

"Well, she's got her teaching, and she'd be hard pressed to leave those students of hers." He sounded like he'd said that to lots of folks.

Some folks from Nags Head—Mary and Edgar Anderson—came over and hugged on Ben for a while, talked with him about being a surfman. I listened too, happy to know what all he'd been up to without asking him myself. Mary gave me a wink behind Ben's back when they left us.

"How are those men faring without a guide?" he asked. He nodded to the Yanks.

"Well, as to that... I guided for them when Amos got sick. And they seem to think of me as their guide now. Least for this season. Then they'll like to find a man to replace me."

Ben looked at me long and hard. Then he grinned. "Remember how I always said you should be a guide? It pays a lot better than seamstress or house-keep, I'll wager."

"And I always said there ain't no such thing as woman guides."

"And now there is."

"We'll see."

"Make sure they pay you good now. As much as they would Amos."

"Alright, Ben."

He wagged a finger at me. "If you have any trou-ble with them, now, you let me know."

I clean forgot about ever feeling lonesome. "Hard to believe, I know, but they're good men," I said. "And they already done paid me good for the guiding I did for them while Amos was sick. They pay *too* good, you ask me."

"Take it all and run," he said. "And tell 'em not to shoot Canada geese."

"Too late for that."

I looked around and saw mama's eyes watching me none too kind. Even Iola was laying a pair of wide, red eyes on us. Fact it seemed like the entire Nags Head boodle was quiet, milling around us.

"Well, it was good to see an old friend, Eliza. Whales Head ain't so big. I'm sure I'll be running into you some."

"You think so?"

He shrugged, shook his head. "I don't know."

His shuffling nature set my heart to pounding. "Well, if you ever need some ducks or geese to feed those men of yours at the station, come on over to the clubhouse. We have more than we need, all iced up or salted. I'm sure they won't care none."

"That's real nice of you. I just might do that. We got fish aplenty we could offer you in trade. I go out in the station rowboat fishing when I got the time."

"I see you ain't changed much, Ben Whimble."

"Oh, I've changed," he said. And he looked so sad that I almost opened my arms for him, like the old days.

I watched him leave me then, and damned if the picture of his back wasn't the exact same as when he left me on my own porch steps in Nags Head, after he told me he was leaving me for Abigail. It made all those terrible feelings come back to me, and I had the sense to pull my shawl over my head, hide my face.

But calling to mind his ease just now, a quick smile split my cracked up lips deep enough to draw the blood. I didn't care. On the inside I felt like I'd drunk at least two cups full of the Yanks' best brandy.

"You got to stop waving your arms about like that."

I scolded Mr. Sexton for the third time. He and Mr. Parrish shared a blind with me, and he couldn't stop his chatter for a split second. "You're gonna scare the birds away."

He looked up to the sky. "Where are all these birds you keep speaking of?"

He winked at me and kept up his talking. They had schemes a-plenty, but as for me I moved through my days in a haze of gun smoke.

After the burying, Iola took to running a broom across the porch any chance she got, though there wasn't a bit of sand or marsh grass on it to be found. And I wasn't right in the head neither. It was like a fire had started deep in the wood of it, knowing Ben was so close and without his wife around. I pictured him alone in some bed, the covers pulled over that brown body, his arms cocked behind his head and him staring at nothing above him. Him thinking of nothing. Not even that wife of his.

I'd seen Ben look that way, at peace, right before sleep took him from me. I knew that face full of happy tired well, for the fact was that Ben took my maidenhead. We weren't more than 12 or 13 years of age when he took me on the shores of Roanoke Island, where we used to go when we wanted to get away from things for a while. When Ben rescued me from waking in the morning to find mama's eye swollen shut and daddy passed out drunk on the bare floor, clothes soaking in his own piss.

I was raised up in a cabin not much bigger than Ben's. Full up with cats and dogs I'd found, pigs and goats, mama and daddy, two little brothers, granny and grandpap, and at times auntie and uncle. It got so close in there, 'specially during the winters, I just had to stay away most days. And Ben saved me the way I saved the critters.

I could sleep so natural with Ben next to me. No sounds to wake me but gull's cries, water noise. I sometimes thought maybe I shouldn't have let him take me so quick, or so much after that. But we both couldn't help ourselves I reckon. I thought those times would go on forever. I thought I'd just keep counting the days of my bleeding 'til I didn't have to no more. Until Ben chose to make a honest woman out of me.

I shouldn't have thought that way, I reckon. I shouldn't be thinking of him now. But old habits die hard, if they ever do.

"Listen," said Mr. Parrish, and shouldered his gun. I heard the flap of wings and looked up into the sun to see widgeon making for our decoys in a draft of wind. It was all shooting and smoke for a while. Then I caught the dead ones up in the net and piled them into the skiff. The men lit their pipes and picked up their talk like they never stopped.

I cut a plug of tobacco and stuck it in my cheek. By now I'd heard too much about their lives in New York, and it sounded to me the wives didn't do one bit of cleaning nor cooking nor child-minding, having hired help stashed in every corner of their houses.

I'd tried hard to picture what a woman would do in a big house if she didn't have to clean or cook or work in the garden or do for younguns. I'd seen women with money in Nags Head. I saw how they pranced about the hotel and the docks and the boardwalk in their fancy skirts and hats and little umbrellas. They all looked bored as sea sponges to me, not even a ride along the shore in a horse-drawn cart could keep their interest for long. I heard their voices when they came to mama's market with their help, calling out what-all they wanted even if it was clean out of season. Mama had seen Abigail at the market too once upon a time, said her silky skirts had splayed out like money itself, just downright rude.

"I didn't grow up wealthy," said Mr. Parrish. I reckoned he was talking at *me* now.

"I didn't say you did." I spat juice out the corner of my mouth.

"You've been silently denunciating our Christmas plans over there."

"Whatever that means."

I heard him slide around on the boat, closer to me. "Can I give you a word of advice, Miss Dickens?"

"If you have hankering to."

"I do."

"Go on, then."

"You should try looking people in the eye more often. Especially when they're speaking to you."

"And here I was thinking you were gonna tell me something of use," I said, spitting out juice again. "The only thing I need to look in the eye is a duck on the wing."

"You deal with *men* first and foremost though." Out of the corner of my eye I saw his teeth flash, a row of pearls all lined up on a necklace. "I'm only trying to help you, as I would my own daughter. My father was a farmer, and he couldn't teach me the importance of certain things. I had to learn about the world from others."

I snorted. "Ain't nothing wrong with farming."

He stretched his gloved hands out in front of him and looked at them like they'd done him a wrong. "It was a struggle for him, every day of his life. I wanted to earn more money for my sweat."

"Sweat, you say?"

"Of the mental sort." He tapped his head with a finger.

I reckoned he'd gotten himself some learning along the way, just as Ben had. I saw Mr. Parrish as a youngun in overalls, sitting in a schoolhouse like the one Abigail learned the Negroes in. He must have had a real good schoolmarm, or else he was the smartest youngun in the entire world, brains lined with gold.

I'd started to wondering on the innards of my own skull after that. Were they cut out for such shenanigans as reading and writing? I looked at my bare hands, scarred and roughed up with work. Could they even hold such a thing as a writing pen without busting it after one stroke?

Next day the Yanks went off to another crack club for some visiting, left me to piddle about the game barn cleaning and fixing. After a while I went into what they called "the library." Their brown leather book was setting on the desk. One or the other of them wrote in the book every day, things like the day and time of their outings, kill scores, weather, whatever perked their fancy that day. I opened it up and saw their scratching in lines up and down the pages. I didn't have to read it all to know what was said: they were having the shooting of their lives.

I found the pen they used, kept in a satiny box such as a woman would use for her baubles. Little tools for writing lay inside. I took 'em all out and laid 'em before me like parts of a shotgun. Looked easy enough to me. I unscrewed the lid from the bottle of ink, picked up the pen, and dipped its golden nib in the ink. I put my left hand down on a nice sheet of paper, then ran the pen along the edges of my wrist, my fingers, my thumb.

I took my hand away, to see the look of it on the paper. There were dirty smudges where I'd set it down hardest, and the hand looked wide, like a man's hand, fingers short and thick.

But I knew that dirty hand could do anything, like snap a writing pen in half, if it wanted to. But it didn't want to. Not yet, at the least.

No surprise, I found Iola rocking to eternity on the porch, not even actual leaves on the wood to keep her upright and sweeping. I joined her in the other rocker, feeling I'd rather be working than setting with Iola with naught to do. Yet just as I started up rocking, I caught sight of Abner tying the skiff up at the docks. His bony wrists poked through the ends of his coat as he fumbled with the rope.

I clenched my jaws, watching him clamber out his boat and limp up the docks. He made his way up the porch steps, a big grin on his face.

"Afternoon ladies," he said. He tipped his cap to us.

"Abner," I said.

"You ladies enjoying this nice weather?"

I sucked my teeth. "You think we don't have a thing else to do but set here and take in the weather?"

I sound just like mama, I thought. Nagging and hen-pecking even in her sleep.

"Oh, well, that's not…." He looked down at his pigeon toes. "I know you all work hard. Heard you been guiding, Eliza."

He eyed Amos britches that I'd cut and hemmed to fit. "I must say, britches do look good on you."

"Enough about my britches!" I stood up, hands to hips. "Why didn't you *tell* me that Ben was working at the lifesaving station?"

"Say what? I…I…I didn't think you'd…well, you and him are…"

"Eliza Dickens," said Iola, her voice gone rusty as a door hinge. "Don't you dare start on *him*!"

"On who, Ben or Abner?"

"Either one! I'm in no mood for one of your conniption fits."

I crossed my arms across my chest real tight, grit my teeth.

"You could have at least told me," I said to Abner. "I ain't going to run over there and moon all over him or anything of that nature."

"Well, I know that, Eliza. I didn't think you cared anymore is all."

I opened up my mouth to holler some more, but all the gumption had petered out of me. "I saw him at the…" I said, then looked over to Iola, who turned from me quick. "He told me what he was up to."

"I know. I saw you two talking," he said.

"It was…a surprise to me is all. And I sure as hell looked the fool. It would have been nice to know he was…so close."

I sat and started to rocking so hard the back of the chair banged the window frame behind me.

Abner pulled out the post from his bag and handed it all to Iola.

"Well, best be getting on now," he said careful, backing away. "Seeing ladies such as yourselves makes the day go a little faster. Gets kinda lonely on that boat all day."

Iola cut her eyes at me, so I got up and started to walking down the docks with Abner. He looked over at me like he thought I was going to push him into the sound.

"I'll allow you got a pretty good government job for a cripple like yourself."

"It ain't too bad," he said. He still watched me wary. "My leg does start to aching when I sleep in the boat though."

"You do that a lot?"

"Just about every other night."

"Must be downright awful being you."

He lifted his leg by his pants sleeve and made it dance a jig on the wood. "I'm lucky to be alive, says mama. She says she is too, for that matter. I got stuck coming out, and it was hell on us both."

"You do alright though," I said. "Even if it does drag like dead meat."

He laughed then. "Well thanks Eliza. You're full of kind words, as always."

I eyed the mailbag on his back. "I reckon you know how to read," I said. "Being a post man and all."

"I sure do."

"Who was it that learned you?"

"Mama," he said. "She has a little learning from her pap. And I went to Mr. Mosby's for lessons during the summer times when I got past the point of mama's learning."

His mama, the widow Miller, was always real nice to everybody, even knowing how much we poked fun at Abner.

"Your mama doing alright? It's been a coon's age since I saw her."

"She is. Though I don't see her too much these days neither."

He threw his mail bag into the skiff, then grabbed the rope to untie the boat.

"Say Abner," I said. He stopped fiddling with the rope to look at me. "I believe you should learn me my letters sometime."

He reared back, eyes boggled, like I'd just cussed him up and down. "Learn you your letters?"

"I don't have too many other options. It's either you or Abigail Whimble."

He let out a loud bark at that. Then he started to stroking his chin like he was thinking hard about it, like he could ever tell me no.

"I reckoned you were going home to Nags Head when the Yanks took their leave," he said. "That ain't much longer, am I right?"

"I was, but..." I turned my head from him. "I think I'll stick around for a bit. See to the clubhouse and whatnot for the winter. Amos and Iola were set to stay on up here, but now there's just her."

"Hmm. Well then. I see, I see." More chin strokes, more agitatin'. I groaned aloud.

"Might only be once a week, when I come up here with the post. And it couldn't be too much time.

Maybe an hour or so. I'd have to get on over to the mainland."

"Fine by me."

I didn't think I could take more than a hour once a week with Abner anyhow.

CHAPTER SEVEN

NOVEMBER 19, 1875
BENJAMIN WHIMBLE

Dry heat upon my brow? Oh! time was, when as the sunrise nobly spurred me, so the sunset soothed. No more. This lovely light, it lights not me; all loveliness is anguish to me, since I can ne'er enjoy.

–*CAPTAIN AHAB*, **MOBY-DICK**

I DIDN'T KNOW WHAT ABBY WAS DOING ON THE SURFBOAT with me, nor where the other men were. But it was just like in that poem she sent me.

She was all done up in a fancy dress and bonnet. She held the steering oar, but lacked a life belt. I rowed for the sunset, the sky behind us already dark with night and following us like a pack of shadows. It was gaining on us, and the ocean took a turn for the worse. The waves rocked the boat, knocking Abby clean into the water. She splashed about, forgot how to swim. She called my name before going under, and when I looked over the side of the boat, I saw her sinking down into the sea, her hair spread out like blood all around her white face. As I stood there crying over her, her arm reached up and grabbed my shoulder, and I hollered out. But her cold hand pulled hard at my bone, shaking it, shaking me awake.

I cracked my eyes to see Jerry Munden standing over me. I saw that I was in the lifesaving station.

"Jerry?"

"It's your wife!" he said.

"What?" I sat up quick on my cot, but the dream of Abby sinking into the water still weighed me down. "What about her?"

"She's come to visit! Get up!"

I smacked my feet to the cold floor, not knowing what to do first. I stood there staring at him like a simpleton.

"Get dressed, fool!" he said. "She's waiting in the cook house for you. She's brung us geese and ducks too."

"Geese and ducks?"

My head spun with the thought of my Abby, down in the cook house this very minute. I pulled off my night shirt and stepped into my britches, the seams ripping when a foot missed its hole. Malachi and Spencer had woken to the news too and were donning clothes beside me. I led the way down the stairs.

Her back was to me when I busted into the cook house, but even so I knew she wasn't Abby. The woman turned at the sound of me, and her face cracked into a smile.

"Ben," said Eliza.

My big smiling face drooped like a flag with no wind to move it. Abby would be teaching today anyway; it was the middle of the week after all.

Malachi and Spencer and Jerry all crowded behind me. They grinned at me and her, waiting on me to make the introductions.

"This is Eliza Dickens," I told them.

They all looked like students caught with no answers.

"I thought you said your wife's name was Abigail," said Jerry.

"It is," I said.

Still they stared from me to her.

"This ain't my wife," I said slowly. "She's a friend of mine, Eliza Dickens, from Nags Head. She's working at the new crack club on the sound."

Jerry's mouth hung open. "Dad blame it. I thought she was your wife."

"I never told you I was his wife," said Eliza in that way of hers.

She looked at me then, and her face brightened up, making her look a different woman entirely. "I brung you all a barrel full of fowl from yesterday's shoot. They're out on the back steps."

The men whistled at the notion of so much food.

I tried to act happy for her. "It won't go amiss."

The men behind me shuffled around us, jollification over and hunger coming on.

"I'll help you stow the birds in the shed," she said to me.

I stepped out the cook house door with her and saw a horse and wagon stopped next to the shed. I lifted the barrel down, and we carried it inside the shed, head to head. Once that was done we just stood on the threshold.

Not counting Amos's funeral, Eliza and I hadn't spoken a good word to one another in over seven years, ever since I'd broken with her to court Abby. I'd seen her about, here and there in Nags Head through the years, but we just nodded to each other and went about our business.

I knew she'd never found another beau though, which always had me worried. She never did care for anybody else but me, other than her mama and some-times Iola. She didn't like people as a general rule.

When I'd seen her at Amos's funeral, I couldn't not go speak with her. I'd heard a while back she was living in a cabin near the crack club with Amos and Iola, heard she and Iola were there when Amos died. And when I talked with her I'd felt that block of lone-some in my chest start to melt a bit. I reckoned it was just talking with a old friend that did it. But it had also put me in mind of how close we once were to one another, how I missed that particular feeling.

"Figured you'd be out guiding this morning," I said.

"Couple of the Yanks are feeling poorly in their bowels," she said. "Could've been Iola's chittlins. They ate at 'em 'til they were fit to bust. We'll likely go out this afternoon."

"You want me to show you around the station?"

"Why not," she said.

The men were shoving down breakfast in the day room when I came through with Eliza. I grabbed two chunks of hot cornbread and offered one to her, but she turned her head away.

"I've had enough of the stuff to last me eternity. Iola fixes cornbread for every meal."

I showed her the boat room first, then brought her all the way up to the lookout tower where Lemuel stood watch. The day was a no-account cloudy one, one of those kinds of days you forget soon as you close your eyes at night. We stood there looking out to sea, not saying a word. The sandy land reached out in all directions, so empty as to break your heart in half.

Eliza said, "Well then." Then she turned and headed back down the stairs. She never was one for words.

We stopped off in the bedroom, quilts still lop-sided on the cots.

"So which one is yours?"

It felt queer to point out my cot to her. She stepped over to it and pulled the quilt up to the pillow, smoothed it out with two hands. Then she straightened up and looked at me.

"How's your pap these days? Any better?"

"Worse than ever. Mind's gone. Fed naught but broth with a little spoon."

"I'd heard he was bad off." Her cheeks sucked in, made her look a hundred years old. "I was sorry to hear it."

Eliza used to go fishing and hunting with us every so often, when her mama didn't need her at the market. Pap talked to Eliza more than he did to anybody, told her things surprised even me. He'd called her "Lyzee."

"He always liked you," I said.

"Course he did. Folks looking in on him for you?"

"I got Jacob and Ruby Skinner caring for him regular. The Weeks stop in too, and the widow Miller," I said. "He sure does need the care."

My voice cracked on the last word, and she reached out a hand to pat my arm, quick as a cat's paw.

"So how's the guiding coming along?"

"Right good," she said.

"You know, you were almost as good a shot as me when we were growing up."

"*Almost?*"

"Your timing was a little off. Nothing you could help, bein' a gal and all."

She wholloped me hard in the arm, and I started to laughing. It had been a long time since I'd been anointed by a woman.

"Shut your bone box. You know I was just as good as you," she said, hands on her hips. "I just didn't want to upstage you, you bein' my beau."

"Do tell," I said. I saw her fist coming again, so I ran ahead of her down the steps. But I soon tripped over myself, and when I tried to straighten up, I felt Eliza's boot kick me hard in the ass.

"I see you ain't lost any of your strength," I said, straightening up and rubbing my backside. "Women tend to lose that with age."

She breathed in hard, and I shimmied through the day room and out the door. I felt to be in as fine a temper as I'd been in a long time. Eliza came out, shaking her head at me.

"And you told me you'd changed," she said.

I quit grinning, for what I'd told her *was* true. I felt to be a different person altogether from the one that used to call Eliza my girl.

I looked her over then. She hadn't changed much, with her tough brown skin and dark hair. Her brown eyes still blinked darkly at me, with their black eyelashes like spider's legs and thick, black brows always throwing off a angry look. She was still thin as a arrow, but with a back wider than her frame should allow, like the letter Y. Eliza was never what one would call pretty, but I'd cared for her because she was brave, loyal, as good as family. She'd been Friday to my Crusoe.

"What?" she said, touching all over her face. "I got something on me? Is it wagon grease?"

"No," I laughed.

I'd been dilly-dallying like I had all the time in the world, but drills and lookout were waiting.

"Thanks for the fowl. And…" I wasn't a-tall sure what I wanted to say to her. "Just thanks. For coming around."

"I'll see you soon," she said, matter-of-fact. And I reached back to that feeling of sadness I'd felt upon seeing Eliza standing there in the cook house instead of Abby. It was right queer, but that sadness was now turned on its head, a happy feeling in its place.

I had the devil of a time sleeping that night, my belly over-full of fried duck meat and sweet potatoes and men coming and going for patrol. But turning from side to side brought on thoughts of the barrel of ambergris, resting in its sandy spot. Seemed like I made the whole thing up.

My mind turned to counting imaginary sperm whales, making their way up the east coast in the early spring. Whalers had worked the area near Capes Lookout and Hatteras for untold years, them being the best places to catch sight of blowholes busting. Pap and me would venture down to the cruising grounds some Februaries when we'd needed the work, and I'd served as lookout when I was too little to go on the pilot boat. I'd hated sitting atop that lookout tower, nothing to do but watch a crew fish with seine nets on the ocean. But spotting those big whales not too far off shore made up for the lost time. I'd helped women tend the fires while pap and crew launched the boat from the beach, harpooned and lanced the whale and towed it bleeding to shore. Then I'd help butcher it and boil the blubber down for its oil. But before we did a thing, we always searched the whale's innards for ambergris. Course, we found naught but belly juice.

But there was the time when pap's friend Rasmus Rollins found a grey and waxy ball big as a melon in his seine net, softer than the rock in Livy's barrel. Rasmus called me and pap to his hut that night, and we all stared down at it, glowing mysterious in the firelight. Pap tasted a bit off his little finger.

"You reckon it is what I think it is?" he'd asked pap.

"I do," said pap. "Men say the best kind is hard as a rock. But this'll suit."

I'd stuck my finger in the sponge too, the way pap had done. And I found it didn't taste a thing like food, but more like a bunch of good smells all put together that made you want to eat it, smear it on your skin, sleep with it beside you. I'd tasted tobacco, old leaves, driftwood, salt spray.

Pap reached out and clapped his shoulder, Rasmus smiling for the first time in his life. And we left him there, never saw him again. Word had it that he sold the lardy ball to a perfume maker up north and bought a poultry farm near New Bern.

The sound of footsteps in the bedroom pulled my eyelids open. I saw it was Lewis coming in from patrol, holding a candlestick to light his way. I'd been lying here awake when he'd left for his shift, four hours ago.

It was cold in the room, the woodstove long since out of driftwood. I could see my breath coming out of my mouth in the light from Lewis's candle. The wind made a racket like a cat in heat, bawling and carrying on in the night.

Lewis blew out the candle and settled onto the cot next to me.

"Ben," he said, loud as ever. "Where'd you learn all your boat rescue skills?"

"Just growing up on the Banks," I whispered. "Used to run a boat out to shipwrecks down in Nags Head."

"You save some lives then?"

"A few. Lost some too."

"You'll be a keeper someday soon, I'll wager."

I said nothing to that, and Lewis wrestled around with his blankets and piped down. But after a while, he said, "Ben?"

Malachi grumbled and turned about on his cot. Spencer coughed up what sounded like wet sand.

"What?"

"You ever get…well, you know, afeared out there on the water?"

"Depends on the sea of a day," I said. "Do you?"

"I'll allow I do get a trifle…well, not afeared as such," said Lewis. "More like froze up. Limbs don't work right."

"You all are land-lubbers. Farmers. Carpenters. Why did you all want a surfman job in the first place?"

It was Spencer that answered. "It's good money."

Then he started to hacking again. When he quit, I ventured to say, "Word has it that you all knew the man did the hiring for these jobs."

None said a word to agree or refute.

"Word has it that's the case all around the Banks," I said.

"You knew John Gale. If you hadn't, you'd never have gotten this job," said Spencer.

"I'll agree to that," I said. "But Captain Gale hired me on account of what I knew about the job already. He didn't have to train me up."

"We know everything we need to know," said Malachi.

"Take it from me, Malachi, you don't," I said.

"Well, tell us what you think we need to know, if you're so damn smart."

"We ain't done one capsize drill since I got here, for starters."

The men groaned like planks in a heavy sea.

"Here he goes again," Lewis said.

"It's too cold for that," said Spencer. "We'll have to practice that when the water's warmed up."

I snorted. "Shame on you, Spencer. You got flesh aplenty to keep you warm. And anyways, we don't work in the summer time."

"Those drills are dangerous to boot. I heard that many's the surfman got drowned from getting hit on the head by a capsizing surfboat," said Lewis.

"That happens in a heavy sea," I said. "We can try it in a calm one. It would behoove us to know how to right the damn boat if we need to."

I heard Spencer pound the pillow under his head and lay back hard. Well, I didn't care if I sounded on a soapbox. These surfmen were my fellow soldiers. We were obliged to go out on the battlefield of the sea, bring fallen comrades to safety. Only the men around me didn't know how to fight.

I lay there fuming. No wonder Captain Gale wanted me to come work here, I thought. His pack of boot-licking farmers weren't up to snuff, and he'd end up taking the fall if things went wrong. He'd needed somebody with some bona fide experience on the sea. Well, I had half a mind to quit, then. Just up and leave and go on home. *But home to who? Home to where?*

Just like that, my thoughts took a turn from mad to sad, and at last my mind dragged into its den like a old retriever. And in settling, I made a decision. *I'll keep that barrel for myself. For Abby. It's mine now, fair and square. 'Twas Banker law...whatever was found floating or washed onto the land was yours, unless someone could prove it wasn't.*

I fell into sleep hard after that thought. But I woke at the dawn with the same thought wiggling through my brain, like I never slept a wink.

The thought of the barrel had stewed inside me and filled my head like a cloud of burning pitch. It burned so hot I couldn't speak at breakfast, couldn't even think how to raise a fork to my mouth. I washed the dishes and pans, I worked lookout, and all the while that thought smoked in my head.

Round about noon, I put in for my day off, told Captain Gale I planned to go visiting down south. But how far down south, I didn't let on.

Sunday morning I got up before dawn and set out north up the shore. The sun still hadn't risen over the horizon, but the light was gray enough for me to see the driftwood marker. I dug around for a bit until my hands hit wood. I pulled the barrel from the sand and started rolling it toward the sound side. When my back started to aching, I used my feet to kick it through the sand, the rock banging about inside. It was almost daylight by the time I got to the light-house docks, but not a soul was astir. I found *Tessa* in the sand where I'd beached her, then turned her over, pushed her into the shallows and heaved the barrel into her.

I set off south through the Currituck Sound, pol-ing through the shoals. There wasn't much wind, but soon as the old boat moved beneath my feet, I felt all my worries falling off my back, could almost hear them plopping into the water like fishing weights. I stood taller, breathed the air easier, was even sung to by the birds in the marsh grass.

I was heading by the new crack club when I heard the call of a voice I'd known almost as long as I'd been sailing on this skiff.

"Where you heading so early?" Eliza called from land.

"Down to Nags Head," I called back. I worked the pole hard in the sand to hurry the skiff along. I didn't want to get mired in talk. I shrank down in the seat when I heard her quick steps on the docks, but I could only see her dirty boot toes and tops of her britches through the grasses.

"Going visiting?"

"I thought I might."

She was quiet for a measure. "Your pap?"

"That's right."

"Long trip."

"Yes ma'am. Weather's fair. Shouldn't be too bad."

"What's in the barrel?" she asked. Nothing ever got by her.

"Some fish for the Skinners," I called, telling the tale I'd practiced in my head.

"What kind?"

"Red drum." I pushed hard on the pole and damned the sluggish air.

"When you gonna bring *me* some fish?" she called. "You owe me, you know."

"Soon as I catch 'em."

I didn't hear a thing else from her. Soon I maneuvered into the middle of the sound, found a bit of breeze and raised the spritsail. I hung out a net from the back of the skiff and sat back to watch the day grow.

It being late on a November Sunday, not many folks were out and about the Nags Head pier. I lifted the barrel from the skiff and started rolling it toward the ocean side. I figured I'd have to wait 'til spring before I could set sail for New York, where I knew I could fetch a good price for the ambergris. I'd have to pay money for a schooner trip north, but I'd have money a-plenty when I sold it.

I was nearly hunched over double from rolling, but at the sight of the house through the stooping trees, I stood up straight, my heart settling. I rolled the barrel up to the house and lifted it up the four porch steps.

Just there, I thought, *was where Abby and me'd sat one summer night, her reading poems by the light of the moon.* She wore naught but a shift, and her white skin had shone dark like thousands of oyster shells melted together. I took her there on the steps, book tossed to the sand below.

That was poetry enough for me.

As I reached for the claw hammer in my coat pocket, I saw the planks I'd nailed to the door had been taken down and stacked on the porch. My ire rose, figuring some wayward fishermen had camped out in the house, might even still be around. I pushed open the door hard but the house was empty save for a blanket and a balled up paper on the floor.

I picked up the ball, smoothed it out, saw it was my own letter to Abby, the one with the little pictures I'd made. Then I saw the shelves, empty of their shells. I stood there staring at them for a time before I could think sense.

I stepped to the shelves and ran my hand along the smoothed pine wood of the middle shelf, picking up dust and sand on my palm where once there had sat hundreds of pretty little seashells. I'd gotten used to seeing them there, seemed like a bunch of old folks setting in rockers watching the world go by. Now it seemed to me like every single one of them had up and died, and I'd somehow missed their funerals.

It must've been Abby, I thought. She'd gotten rid of them, all of those shells that'd once been special to her. And to me too. She'd read one of my letters here and had crushed it up and left it. Hadn't even bothered to board the house up when she left, caring so little for what was ours.

I looked about the little house, recalled how I'd built it fast and hard. I'd had splinters and cuts and bruises on myself for days. I'd hoped to fill up this house with Abby, our children, friends and family. Every board I put in place brought me one step closer to that notion. I'd looked out the windows on the live oaks and scrub pine and sand and saw years and years of happy days. I'd heard the shouts of our younguns and Abby's laughter and the sea. But now all I heard was the scouring of the sand on the wood, the rattling of the shutters, the sound of my own breath in the empty house.

I stepped to the porch, kicked the barrel inside and slammed the door on it. I picked up the planks and nailed them into the door, shaking the house on its pilings.

When Duffy saw it was me at the door of my old abode, she squealed high as a sow and snuffed about my feet. We had our big reunion, then she headed outside. Jacob and Ruby'd taken Duffy to their cabin when I left for Whales Head, but Duff had stole back here first chance she got. She'd die her own self before she'd be moved from pap's side.

I lit the oil lamp by the door and saw pap laying there on his tick. He didn't even crack his eyes open at the noise of boots on the floor boards. I sat down on the chair beside him for a long while, looking at him in the orange light of the lamp.

The blankets were pulled down a bit, so I could see his nightshirt was laundered and his skin was shaved clean. But he was downright starved under those blankets, where once he'd been a great hunk of a man. He couldn't get a thing down his gullet 'cept spoonfuls of soup, for he'd lost the notion (and the teeth) to chew. I could see the skeleton of him, just under his yellow skin, seeming to be normal-size bones instead of the bear-clubs I always reckoned him to have. It was no great matter to picture those bones joined by stringy tendons like turkey legs, barely holding the whole job together.

All the dust and dog hairs gave me no choice but to cough, and pap opened his eyes a little, looked at me for a second or two. But the eyelids soon wiggled over the watering eyeballs and slid down again, the sight of me not near enough to keep him in the world.

He must've been in the midst of a dream, for his good hand raised itself up, waggling here and there before making like it was casting a line into the water. Down shot his arm so fast, I thought sure he'd wake up. But he went on dozing.

Even when pap was awake, he couldn't talk. His tongue was all twisted from the fit. And I'd grown up to the sound of his voice. I still heard him the way he used to sound, somewhere in the dark pits of my ears.

But if he *could* speak, he wouldn't know me from Jacob. Doc later told us he wasn't in the least bit confounded by the deficit, said it was right common in these kinds of fits. The losing of his mind came on slow it seemed, on account we couldn't be sure what-all he knew or didn't due to his lacking of speech. But I recalled the day I was sure he didn't know me anymore. His blue eyes stared through me. I talked at him for a while, but he didn't even grunt or spit. His chin dropped to his chest, and he just closed his eyes and slept. I left that day feeling like he'd just died on me. I'd had things to say to him, knowing that he still heard me for the son he raised. I wasn't ready to lose him to the fog.

"Found me some ambergris, pap," I said, like we were having us a real good talk. "Big old white rock. The best kind there is. Better then Rasmus Rollins' even."

He didn't budge a eyelid. Just one look at his face and most folks might think he'd already passed on.

"I'm thinking of selling it," I said louder. Nary a twitch.

I bade myself to shut my pie hole then. I sat by his side, listening to him breathe in and out. *Least he was still living*, I told myself. I could still look on his face. I tried to carve it into my memory, so that when I closed my eyes I could still picture him. I didn't want to forget his face, like I had with ma's.

Pap taught me everything he knew about fishing, piloting, hunting, didn't hold a thing back from me. He gave me *his* life. Made a good day's work in the open air seem a thing to marvel over.

Thinking on all pap had done for me, I started to see what Abby might have felt when her Uncle Jack died, him like a pap to *her*. Abby never did get over losing her uncle. Then her ma died, along with her unborn baby sister, and that set her back too, even though she didn't have the same kind of love for her ma as she did for her uncle.

She lost her brother and sister too, in a way. She didn't miss her son-of-a bitch pap none, but she sure did miss Charlie and Martha. They never did come back to that house by the sea. Her mama died birthing that winter. Then a couple years later the house caught fire, burned to the sand from a lightning strike. I went over there with her after we heard to see the house nothing but ashes. The barn and privy house were alright so I took them apart, used the wood for our own barn in back of the schoolmarm house. She found a few things in the ashes that had been spared in the sand under the china cabinet: pewter tea service, silver knives and forks, some crystal. We sold it all and bought the milk cow, brood sow, shoat and chickens.

Soon after, I saw her standing in the yard, looking over everything we had, our little farm. Her shoulders drooped so far forward I thought she was gonna topple over into the cabbage. I think it finally dawned on her all she'd given up, marrying me.

And then our own babies died a couple years later, and she started to thinking that all of her sadness inside her was killing them. That she couldn't grow a baby because all was black and hard in her body, where it should be softly pink, like a field of roses.

I figured that was all gum. I'd watched her too many times learning those students of hers, and I tell you I've never seen a more kind-hearted person in my life. She treated each person like they mattered to the world at large, not just to her. They bloomed under her hand, every one. But trying to talk her out of her sadness was like walking through quicksand bound by ankle irons. By then she was mired in her doubt, visited one too many times by death and loss in too short a time.

And now, sitting by my pap who I reckoned to be dying, I saw how it happened.

I knew I'd mourn pap's dying. I knew it would hurt bad, all of my love left inside me, nowhere to go. But it was more than that, I figured. We mourn because we see how much *we* were loved in turn. And that thought hurts more—that our dumb-assed selves were loved by a person, and now that person is dead. We know for damned sure no one will ever love us that much again.

I reached out a hand to my pap then, squeezed his shoulder soft so as not to wake him again. He was fishing, and I liked not to disturb the joy of it for him.

I got back to the station late on Monday morning. When I opened the door to the day-room, ready with apology, I jumped to see the room and the boat room crowded with strange men, women and younguns and even a baby, all redheaded, grey-eyed and pale-skinned as corpses. The whole house smelled power-ful of gutted mullet and unwashed clothes. I knew the smell well enough, but I could hardly breathe for the stench and stayed by the open door.

All heads were turned to me, and not even my surfmen looked pleased to see me.

"This is him," said Captain Gale. "Ben Whimble. He found Livy."

A tall, broad-chested man stepped to me like he was ready to snatch the head off my neck, but Captain Gale put a hand on his arm before he could reach me.

"Hold your horses, now," Lewis spoke out. "Let him speak."

Captain Gale looked white as a ghost beneath his dark beard. "Ben, this here is the Spruel family. From up in Wash Woods."

The man stepped toward me again, but Captain Gale still had ahold of his dirty shirt sleeve.

"And this here is Jonas, Livy's older brother. And there is his ma and pa, aunt and uncle, sisters, brothers, cousins, what have you. They've buried Livy, and now they've come up here to put things to rights."

"To rights?"

"They say the boy made off with some of the family's valuables the night he took the skiff."

Jonas leaned his head toward me, for he couldn't get closer with Captain Gale's grip on him. "You see a barrel aboard that boat when you happened across Livy?"

His breath smelled as if he'd eaten something rotten, washed down with the worst of liquors.

I stared at crumbs, stuck in his greasy, red beard. "I didn't find a barrel," I said. The lie hung heavy in the air same as the nasty stench.

"What was the way of it then?"

Jerry reached around behind me to close the door, shutting me inside. "Set 'em straight, Ben," he said to my ear.

"I was walking patrol at dusk and came up on the boat, all busted up. Then I spotted the boy, not too far away. I pulled him up to shore. He was near dead then."

The women whimpered, and Jonas squinted at me. "I heard told Livy stuck you with his knife." He pointed to my neck, where the wound still refused to scab. "Right there in your gizzard."

"Like I told Captain Gale, he was fixing to die. He was full of nonsense."

"That so?" His mouth fashioned itself into a ornery grin. "I picture it another way."

"What way is that?"

The man looked about the room to see if everyone was hearing him. "He stuck you on account he come ashore with our barrel. 'Twas setting there in the boat, and with him froze cold head to toe, all he could do was stick you."

"No, that's not the way…"

"I ain't done yet, by thunder! Livy's one to hold tight to the nets, see. He never let go. Bloody hands warn't a circumstance."

He showed me his own cut-up hands, big as dinner plates. "His foolishness—taking our good fishing skiff and our barrel full of goods—a boy's mistake is all. But he paid for it with his life. Our mama and daddy are just about broke to splinters over it."

A red-headed woman and man bowed their heads.

"But I know that barrel he took is all of a piece, and I opine you know where."

I opened my mouth to say no once again, but Captain Gale spoke up. "The skiff, Ben. We all saw there'd been some rope *cut*." His hands made the sawing motion of cutting a rope with a knife. "Looked like the rope had tied something down between the struts at some point. The struts, too, they looked as if they'd been pulled apart. Like they'd been forced up."

I felt all of the folks in the room move closer to me. The baby started to bawl.

The man blew out air from his nose like a cornered boar. He flexed his dirty hands out in front of him, and knuckles popped in all directions.

"He could've used Livy's knife," Jonas said.

My face was slick as summer now. I saw the barrel, turned on its side in my own house. I saw myself leaving the rope on the sides of the boat. It had been dark, and too cold, and a boy had died in front of me after asking me to keep his barrel safe.

"Let's fix the flint right now," I said. "I ain't seen your barrel. And in my view, I reckon you should've kept a better hold on it, if it was so dear to you."

At that, the man shot from Captain Gale's grasp and whacked me hard upside the head with the flat of his hand. I would've gone down if it weren't for Jerry holding me up.

I saw nothing but stars, but I heard boots scuffling on the floorboards and men grunting and women and younguns hollering. At last I made out Spencer and Malachi holding the long arms of Jonas. They dragged him to the door, and Lemuel opened it so they could push him out.

Then Captain Gale started to waving his steering oar about, almost set me to laughing. "Get on now. All of you. You heard him. Ben never saw the barrel."

Jonas loomed in the doorway, and Captain Gale aimed the oar in his direction. "Go on now. Get out of here."

The family filed out the door, all giving me the evil eye, even the baby.

Spencer closed the door and bolted it shut. "You all right, Ben?"

"I reckon so," I said. I rubbed at the goose egg on my head.

"Must've been gold in that barrel, for them to come over here and act like that," said Lewis. "Pirate treasure, full to the brim."

CHAPTER EIGHT

NOVEMBER 23, 1875
Abigail Sinclair Whimble

Now, from this peculiar sideway position of the whale's eyes, it is plain that he can never see an object which is exactly ahead, no more than he can one exactly astern. In a word, the position of the whale's eyes corresponds to that of a man's ears; and you may fancy, for yourself, how it would fare with you, did you sideways survey objects through your ears...The whale, therefore, must see one distinct picture on this side, and another distinct picture on that side; while all between must be profound darkness and nothingness to him.

–Ishmael, **Moby Dick**

I DANGLED MY LEGS OFF THE EDGE OF DOCKS ON THE Croatan Sound. I tossed the last of the stale bread crumbs to the ducks in the shallows and showed them the empty bowl, yet they still refused to leave, paddling about in hopeful ovals.

Weary of stalling, I removed Ben's most recent letter from my bag and ripped the envelope open. Unfolding the thin paper, I saw his blocky script amidst blotches of ink.

Dearest wife,

I see you started up the poem game again. I thought we'd pulled anchor on that game a long time ago, though I reckon my mind could use a bit of shining up these days, too much time watching the ocean coats it with rust. So I'm sorry to say I can't make heads nor tails of that poem. Your dictionary would come in handy I'll wager. But even then I don't think I could grasp the meaning too good. I do like sunsets though. The ones I get to see up here while walking the beaches are right pretty on a cold evening.

The light house up here is fixing to get lit in a few days time and folks are getting stirred up as bees in a hive. I plan to go see it if I can work the shifts just so. I will say it's just as nice as the Hatteras light, only not as fancy on account its bricks are to be left unpainted.

I do hope you're well. And your students, and Asha too.
Your loving husband,
Ben

My face rose up from the letter as my heart sank to my belly. I crumpled the paper and tossed it into the sound where the ducks hurried over to inspect it. Feeling foolish, they at last swam away, and I watched

Ben's words take on water and float down to the darkness.

The poem hadn't even been that difficult to understand. I'd first read the Wordsworth poem years ago during the war and had been struck by the image of someone leaving the dark past behind and moving toward a dream-filled future, though misery and death always waited. It had resonated with me once again, for different reasons. It spoke of head-strong resiliency, in spite of dead children, lost love. Ben had only seen the sunset.

After the storm, I'd waited impatiently on word from Ben. Finally a letter from him had arrived, and I'd read it while standing at the counter of the sound-side market, relief puddling into my ankles. But the letter was an almanac of weather conditions and surf-man activity. I could just about feel the cold ocean winds blowing over the page as he labored away with the pen. Nothing but another duty.

I'd pictured an endless succession of those kinds of letters through the long months of winter. I saw us to be strangers at the end of it all.

When it had come time for me to respond to him, I couldn't think of a thing to write. Even the excitement of Mr. Wharton's arrival and the men-tion of possible employment at the Peabody Normal School had waned when I was faced with a blank leaf of paper. I thought, *how will we ever move beyond this impasse?* I'd sent him the poem.

Ben had always groaned when I'd pulled out my book of poetry, but he'd played along. At first he hadn't been able to grasp anything but the simplest of poems. He'd mumble things like "the author liked daffodils" or the poet "was down and out." But soon he'd begun to understand metaphors, learn unfamiliar vocabulary. I almost heard his mind stretching inside his skull.

I supposed without practice his mind had resumed its previous shape. I feared his heart had taken on a smaller stature as well.

My legs were numb from sitting on the old Union docks for so long, but I couldn't seem to rouse myself. Mr. Wharton had departed yesterday, taking a skiff from Roanoke Island to Nags Head, then a ferry from Nags Head down to New Bern.

I'd ridden along with him on a buggy to the docks at Shallowbag Bay when I should have been teaching. Asha was more than happy to help me, though she declared she didn't care for the notion of me and Mr. Wharton on a buggy together.

"What would Mr. Benjamin say, you wheeling around town with another man?" she'd asked. I'd just shrugged, for we both knew Mr. Wharton was a happily married man. He spoke of his wife Anna as though he considered her his intellectual equal, often mentioning their lengthy discussions and heated debates.

Mr. Wharton had taken over two weeks to complete his research, appearing every morning for classes and staying for the duration of the day. He'd also attended the classes taught by Asha, fascinated with her journey from slave to student to teacher. He'd revealed that he was devoting an entire chapter to her.

We hadn't dined together after that first night, but we did eat luncheon together during breaks in classes. Over Ida Dunley's corn bread with baked ham, he'd spoken of the Peabody Normal School in Nashville and how much promise it held for the state of education in the South.

He'd told me about the possibility of higher education for women, described colleges specifically for women that were forming this very day, with female faculty.

Yesterday, when Mr. Wharton departed, I'd felt unaccountably bereft. I'd watched his skiff making for Nags Head, imagining myself making the long trip to Tennessee with him. When I'd caught sight of his ferry moving south through the Roanoke Sound, I'd never been so reminded of how my life had stalled here on the Outer Banks, like a ship stuck forever in the shoals.

The wedding had taken place seven years ago. Ben had proposed marriage two days after I'd decided to stay with him. He'd taken me for a sail on the Roanoke Sound on a warm September morning. He'd laid his forehead on my knees, then looked up and asked me to marry him. I'd said yes with no hesitation.

The ceremony had been held in a clearing of Nags Head Woods, close to the Fresh Pond where he'd taught me to swim.

The imported reverend from Hertford had said, "I'm not accustomed to wedding a man and a woman out of doors."

And Ben had said, "What better way to get hitched than surrounded by God's own creation?" And the reverend had agreed, even though it had started to rain.

The drops were as light as ashes drifting from the branches above us; they landed apologetically on the long veil spread over me. Somehow, in her confinement, mama had sent me a gown to wear, an ivory one to signify that I did indeed come from a well-off family, albeit an absent one. The silk satin creation spilled out around me from a high waist, heavy with crinolines and trimmed with needle lace.

In addition to the thirty or so students of mine, a smattering of Bankers—old friends of Ben's and his family's—had attended the October wedding. I heard them comment on the bad omen of rain, felt them eyeing my impractical dress. A Banker, I knew even then, would never be caught dead in a get-up that could only be worn once. A bloom of some sort tucked in a woman's hair was sufficient decoration for a wedding day; my own hair boasted a heavy arrangement of roses that Asha had woven through a towering bun of thick, red hair. I didn't dare look up to the clouds to search for signs of the sun.

Ben had worn a black sack suit borrowed from Abner—it had been his own daddy's. His blonde hair had been slicked back with a bit of pomatum, revealing his handsome face. He'd searched awkwardly for my gloved hand through the long veil. Our vows echoed off the trees as the rain fell around us.

I'd no wedding ring, no bridesmaids. Eye-rolling panic had shuddered through me, until an osprey flew through the clearing to its nest in a tree over-looking the Roanoke Sound. It dropped a fish into its circular thicket, and a smaller osprey raised its head in thanks. Joy, just a slender ribbon of it, rippled through me.

Ben lifted the veil from my face to kiss me so hard that I felt my ponderous hair shift. Just as we turned to present ourselves to the little crowd, the rain stopped, and Asha stepped over and kissed me on my cheek and hugged me to her. The crowd applauded lightly, and as we ate from the rain-spattered fare spread on the back of a wagon, Ben never left my side.

As dusk came on, a keg of beer was rolled out, Ben's daddy's wedding gift. Almost everyone slurped the warm beer as if they were dying of thirst, as if it hadn't just rained and lowered the temperature in the woods by fifteen degrees. Ben's friends played music, and Oscar got so drunk that he fell asleep in the wagon bed atop the leftovers.

That evening Ben and I wore our wedding garb when we rested in the hammock in back of the Nags Head house and watched the live oak leaves dance for us, listened to the gulls call. My dress belled out around my legs in protest, and the crushed roses in my hair dropped white petals onto the ground around us. We stayed in each other's arms until dark.

He'd led me inside by the hand and lit a candle. He fumbled with the satiny buttons that lined my back, and removed the crinolines, the stockings, the underthings, with the same quiet attention that he gave fishing or carpentry, until I stood before him naked. He looked and looked at me, and without a word he'd lay me down on the tick, then removed his own clothing, folding the suit across a stool. Then he'd lain down next to me in the watery glow of the candle.

"You know, those Bible words were nice and all," he'd said, running a shy finger down the outside of my breast. "But they didn't really say what I felt. About you."

His finger traced the circle of my navel, stopped to rest in the shallow hole. Then he brought up his hand to turn my face toward his.

"I'll never leave you," he said. "I'll never stop loving you. I...I'll...until the day I die..."

Then he'd sucked his teeth and shaken his head. "I sure ain't a poet."

I'd just looked at him, my husband. But his eyes had strayed to my bosom. His mouth came down and surrounded the nipple, his tongue just barely rubbing the tip of it. I'd rolled on top of him then, white petals and hair pins falling atop his chest.

Words had failed us both that night, and I'd welcomed the silence. Words had escaped me the next morning as well but in a different way, when I came to realize that I was married to a fisherman for the rest of my days.

Now, watching the water bounce along beneath my swinging feet, I wanted to jump inside it, join with it, follow it where it would go. A new life, as colorful and promising as the poem's sunset, beckoned me forward. It pulled me along like water to land, an inevitable meeting. I saw myself rise up from the water to walk once more on the solid land.

On Sunday, after a laborious skiff ride across the sound, I found myself in Nags Head Woods once again. I knocked on Oscar's door and pushed it open slowly, my hand at Duffy's level with a bit of cornbread.

Oscar was lying on his side, but his eyes were open, staring at the wall next to him.

"Hello, Oscar," I said. "It's Abigail."

He continued to regard the wall. I set the basket on the table.

"I've brought you some broth," I said. "You won't believe it, but I made it myself." It was Asha's recipe, the same broth that she fed me when I was sick as a child.

I added two more logs to the dying fire and lit the oil lamp. I walked over to his tick and stood over him, Duffy following me with hungry eyes.

"I'm going to sit you up so you can eat."

I took hold of Oscar's shoulder to turn him to face me, but he strained against me. Duffy yipped at me, and I released his shoulder. Now we all stared at the wall, Duffy included.

"Maybe you're not hungry," I said.

I sat down in the chair near his tick. Drops of rain began to crawl down the dirty windows of his cabin. Soon I heard it falling roughly off the eaves and filling the barrels beneath. *It was going to be a long, wet sail back to Roanoke Island*, I thought, but before I could get up from the chair, a drop of rain landed on my forehead. Duffy looked up to the ceiling as a drop landed on her nose.

I smelled mold then, where before I'd only smelled wood smoke and body odors. The drops continued to fall in random spots throughout the cabin, leaving small puddles of water all over the warped floorboards.

"Your roof is rotten," I said. "The rain's coming in everywhere."

I found some cracked crockery bowls on a shelf and placed them under the more serious leaks. But I couldn't very well put bowls atop Oscar to catch the periodic drips onto the quilts. I would have to move his tick, but after several hard yanks I only managed to budge him a few inches. He was still getting wet.

And out of the corner of my eye, I saw something large and grey scurry along the edge of the wall where Oscar's tick had just been. Duffy had seen it and was now bounding around the cabin after it, barking and knocking her tail against the table and chair legs.

My heart pounded in my throat as I watched Duffy sniff and pounce, but Oscar lay motionless on the tick. Duffy quit her bounding and looked to me, her grey-streaked forehead wrinkled in frustration. I took up the lamp and forced myself to walk around the cabin, searching the walls for a sign of the rat as Duffy followed at my ankles.

The buckets and bowls played a sad kind of music as we plunked our way around. Duffy sighed as we came to end of the route. The rat had escaped.

I turned to the matter at hand, figuring Oscar would need something over him to keep the rain from soaking his bed linens. Seeing nothing along the many shelves that would suffice, I tied my bonnet on and ventured out to the shed. In the cramped and musky enclosure I found more shelves, full of mostly fishing implements and tools. I finally found a discarded piece of old sailing canvas. I lugged it back inside the cabin and laid it over Oscar. The rain hit the heavy canvas, rolled to the sides and puddled on the floorboards.

It would have to do.

The afternoon light was turning swiftly to darkness when I heard steps on the porch and the creak of the door. Jacob's face poked around the door frame, and Duffy strode over to him, her tail wagging low.

"Here you is again," he said, eyes wide as he took in the scene. "What you doing with your poor ole pappy?"

"I came to visit," I said, too defensively. "I brought him some soup."

"Ain't that nice, and in this here rain," said Ruby, stepping into the cabin behind Jacob with her large basket.

Jacob leaned over Oscar, grinning. "You gettin' wet again?"

"So you're aware his roof is rotten?"

"I got some shingles left from the last time Ben and me fixed the roof, but I ain't had time to get to it."

"The leaking's been going on a while, from the smell of the mold."

"Sure enough," he said. "House been leaking for years now. Here and there, you know. Oscar don't mind."

"He's going to catch his death in here."

"Well, he used to gettin' wet."

"There's a rat in here too," I said, spanning my hands apart to show how large it was. "I tried to find it, but..."

"What you gonna do if'n you find it?" asked Jacob.

"You know about the rat too?"

"Just one?" laughed Ruby. "We all got rats, winter time and all. Duffy a prime rat-catcher. But she getting too old to catch 'em all. If Jacob see one in here, well, he'll get rid of it. But won't be long 'fore its kin shows up."

Ben had taken care of traps and exterminations and never bothered me with the details. Asha kept a cat fed for the purpose of rat-catching, but we did have a raccoon that had burrowed its way under the house and made a racket at night, shuffling under the floorboards.

"I just...don't like leaving a man like Oscar....in this...condition," I mumbled. "Alone."

Ruby nodded her head and went over to Oscar, removing the sail and damp quilts and blankets from his wasted body.

"You hearing this?" she asked him. "Your daughter, she worried about you."

Jacob hooked his hands under Oscar's arms and hoisted his torso into the air, while Ruby pulled the tick out from under him, turned it over and moved it a couple of feet away from the roof leaks.

I busied myself tidying the hodge-podge of items on the shelves as they stripped, sponged and redressed Oscar. Then they propped Oscar onto the tick and settled fresh blankets over him. Jacob spread the sail on the floor under the worst of the leaks.

Ruby lifted the lid on my pot of soup. "He get any down for you?"

"No," I said. "I figured you'd given him breakfast."

"I wouldn't call it that," she said. "Bit o' cold tea."

She fixed a large napkin around the grizzled wattles of his neck and nodded her head at the pot. "Go on and fetch your spoon."

I filled the bowl with broth and slowly brought a half-full spoon to the corner of Oscar's mouth. I squeezed his cheeks the way that Jacob had done and snuck the spoon into a corner of his mouth. A few drops dribbled out, but I heard him swallow the rest.

"Lookie there," said Ruby, patting his lips with the napkin.

I continued to spoon the broth into Oscar's mouth as Ruby pulled a loaf of bread from her basket. She gave me a large chunk, declaring I could stand to put on some weight.

"Don't be thinking I can't see your shoulder bones poking through that dress," she said. "Like joints on drumsticks."

It was almost dark by the time Ruby piled the soiled linens in the basket. "You come back with us for the night now," said Ruby.

In the shadows, Oscar looked just like Ben.

"Thank you," I said. "But I think I'll stay here tonight."

Jacob and Ruby turned to one another with raised brows.

"Well then, you better take one of these here blankets," Ruby said, handing me one of the drier blankets that Oscar had recently used. "It gets right cold in here tonight, you smoor that fire."

I took the blanket from her. "I'll be fine."

Jacob opened the door and Duffy ran in. She shook the rain off her dark coat, then went to lay beside Oscar, his veined eyelids not quite closed.

"You know where we at," said Jacob, then closed the door.

Duffy stared at me, her ears perched high on her head.

"It's just us now," I said. "Is that alright?"

I set about removing the pins from my hair and running my fingers along my dry and itching scalp, then pulled Ben's old tick toward the fireplace. I smelled the musty reeds and seaweed inside the tick, but it was comforting, knowing that Ben had once slept on it.

Duffy at last laid her head down, but still watched me through narrowed eyes.

Oscar's chest rose up and down in a somewhat regular pattern, so I put the lamp out and laid back on the tick. I could still see his outline in the flickering of the fire. I figured Oscar had resembled Ben, in his day; he'd lived here his entire life, had always been a fisherman. I'd seen them together on the skiff countless times, father and son, making a living together. Ben would in time look like Oscar, wrinkled and whiskered and almost toothless, a product of the sea. I fancied that if I put an ear to Oscar's chest, I'd hear the sound of the ocean, the slap of water on a boat.

Would Ben succumb to a paralyzing fit as well? Would I feed him, the same way I fed Oscar tonight? Would I change his bed linens, his underthings? Would his eyes still spark with hope, or would they peer out dully at the world like Oscar's?

Feeling terribly traitorous, I wondered if Ben would even make it to Oscar's age, especially if he remained a surfman. I remembered him that first day of his tutoring: his eagerness, his summer stink, his bare feet. His innate ability breaching through his surface like the broad back of a whale. I missed that man, the man he'd been that summer.

I crackled around on the tick and listened to the babble of the buckets and bowls, the snoring of dog and man. The house groaned as it settled, and the fire died slowly in the grate. It was so dark I wouldn't see a rat if it came close enough to steal a strand of my hair. The blanket reeked of wet dog and mold and urine, but I didn't care about smells or the cold or rat-watching or caretaking as much as I thought I would.

I wasn't sure if this was progress toward enlightenment or evidence of my sensory deterioration over the years. But when I ran my hands over my stomach, I felt not the usual emptiness there, but a fullness, an opening bloom. I attributed it to the bread, almost an entire loaf puffing out the edges of my belly, a sensation I never thought to welcome again. Sleep came surprisingly easy when I closed my eyes.

CHAPTER NINE

NOVEMBER 24, 1875
ELIZA DICKENS

*But how? Genius in the Sperm Whale? Has the Sperm
Whale ever written a book, spoken a speech? No, his great
genius is declared in his doing nothing particular to prove it.*

–*ISHMAEL*, **MOBY-DICK**

I MADE MY WAY DOWN CENTER STREET, CHOCK FULL
of city folk. It wasn't my first visit to Elizabeth City. Me
and mama came here plenty of times afore on buying trips. Mama liked to buy hard-to-find items here
like coffee beans and sugar, then charge the summer
folk a powerful grist more than what she herself paid.
They paid it too, no complaints.

But all nature hustling on the streets made me
skittish. I figured it was on account mama wasn't with
me. We always walked quick down the streets with our

full baskets pinching our arms. We didn't lollygag about.

But I had me the day off and I meant to take my ease.

I came upon a man selling paper cones of fried fish so I bought one and made myself sit on a bench to eat. I blew, then took a nibble as I watched a lady step out a black buggy, all slicked up. She strolled from shop to shop, her Negro woman tagging along behind with arms full of packages. They hopped back into the buggy and galloped away. I'd wager Elizabeth City'd been named for a woman just like her. Time and money aplenty.

I squeezed the roll of paper money in my coat pocket, thicker than a turkey's neck. I wasn't used to the feel of so much money, knowing it for mine. I'd held bits of mama's paper money before, for mama was the rare Nags Header who dealt with summer folks who didn't trade. Mama kept the coins and paper under lock and key, though most Bankers would find it handy for wiping their hind parts and not much else.

I licked my fingers clean, then walked into the dry goods store, making for the bolts. I thought to buy me some material for a new dress for the lighthouse lighting. I walked up to the row of dresses hanging on a pole on the wall and aimed to give them a look-see. But before I could even touch 'em a voice like a gallnipper talked right into my ear.

"Can I help you with something?" it said.

I cut an eye at her, saw by her skin she was younger than me. Her skirts moved about her like she was hiding twelve litters of kittens under 'em.

"I reckon not."

She didn't budge a hooter. She reached out a tiny hand and stroked one of the dresses like it was her very own.

"These are very nice dresses, aren't they?" Sounded like she was scolding a scummy youngun caught touching the wares. I cocked my chin to her.

"I'm looking to buy me a new dress today. One of these ones here."

I hadn't a notion for buying one of the ready-mades, but I knew I could've.

She grinned at me, but it wasn't a pleasing look. "We have some fabric that might interest you, just over there." She flung her arm out at the bolts.

I curled my hands into fists. I could knock her into a cocked hat in a second. "I said I want one of these ones here."

She snuck a look at my boots, and I was glad I hadn't worn the britches too. "Hm," she said. "You're sure you have enough money to buy a *ready-made* dress?"

"I ain't been more sure about anything. What's your name, now?"

"Penny." She puckered like she just sucked at a lemon.

"Well, Penny. Why don't you pull that blue one down for me and help me put it on, see if it suits me?"

Penny looked to the shopkeeper for answers to her current pickle. But he was holding the door open for a customer, nodding and grinning like a simpleton. Penny huffed and yanked the hangar off the pole. Then she stomped back to the dressing room with the dress.

"I reckon I'm going to need some underthings, Penny. A corset, and some petticoats and what-not."

Penny laughed like that just beat all. "You'll have to go to a dressmaker's for all that."

I stripped off my clothes while Penny stared at the ceiling. Then I stepped into the dress and pulled it up. Penny stretched it about me and buttoned it up, and I'll allow I was good and hot by the time she quit me. I turned to the long looking-glass and saw a trussed-up woman in it. The fabric sure was fine, and the dress was made good enough. The cut of it seemed to say that a great round hind part was something worth having.

But it was my face that didn't play along. It was too brown and saggy, and it poked out of the dress like a wolf's head in grandma's nightdress. It just wouldn't do.

Penny stood there in the doorway, arms cocked out like I was set to run out of the store with the dress still on.

"I don't think it suits me after all."

"I thought the same thing." The shopkeep came too near for Penny's comfort. "Perhaps another color?"

"No. Just get this thing off me now."

I couldn't step out of the dress quick enough. I watched as Penny hung the dress back up on the rack, smoothed it out and fluffed it up.

"You have a nice day now," she said.

"Just because I ain't buying a dress don't mean I'm yet done with my marketing."

Penny squinted her eyes at me, then walked along with me through the store while I played at putting on bonnets and pulling on gloves. I looked through the bolts of fabric. I picked out some silky material the color of Mr. Parrish's brandy, then found a pattern featuring the latest style. I piled on buttons, lace, ribbons and even a fancy bonnet with fat ribbons. I'd stitch up a dress gooder than those ready-mades, faster than I could spit.

I stopped cold at the shoe rack though. Thin suede, they were, set to wear out after one day on the Banks.

"I reckon I need some shoes, Penny."

She snorted. "I reckon you do. I'm sure I couldn't begin to imagine what-all it is you do in those old boots."

She took a tape from her skirt pocket and bent down to measure my left foot, careful not to touch it. "Well, which ones do you want?"

"I seem to like those ones."

"They're awful expensive," she sang. But she pulled a box from the cabinet anyhow.

At the counter I picked out a new snuff box for Iola, plus some snuff and chewing tobacco. Penny rang up the total and told it to me, all smug.

"That all?" I said.

I pulled out the roll of money from my pocket and counted out the bills I needed, right before her wide open eyes. Sweat started to prick at my temples, for I hated to give that money over to a prize ninny like Penny. But some things just needed buying.

At the cabin I put away my wares—including a petticoat I bought at the dressmaker. Then I hurried to the clubhouse to help Iola tend to the garden and pick feathers from the fowl. We reckoned by the end of the winter we'd have 100 pounds of feathers to sell, all at our own profit.

I was fixing to head into the kitchen house with a basket full of greens when I saw Abner Miller poling up to the docks.

"You ready for some learning?" he hollered.

"Took your time, didn't you?" I hollered back.

He'd showed up a couple of times to drop off the men's post, him yakking it up with the Yanks like he was somebody. The coot always came straight up to the main door, it never dawning on him to use the back door me and Iola and everyone else doing business here used. But then he'd turn to go and wouldn't say a word about learning me.

He slung himself up the docks toward the clubhouse. When he reached me, he said, "It's only been a couple of weeks since you asked."

"That's what I mean now, ain't it?" I said. "Two whole weeks I been waiting on you."

"I've been real busy," he said. He hung his head down.

"Ain't no excuse. If you don't want to learn me, then I'll get someone else."

"No, no," he said, eyes wide. "I'll do it. I want to, Eliza."

I bit my lip. Scolding him just came too natural.

In the house we pulled out two dining chairs and sat at the table. Abner pulled out a paper book he had in his coat pocket.

"I brung this here book."

He put it on the table between us and smiled at it. "This is the book mama used when she learned me to read."

It had skinny, black writing on the yellowed front. "I can't read no book, Abner."

He wiped at his nose with a hand. "Well, I know. This book teaches you *how* to read."

I thought on that. "I don't see how a *book* can teach a person doesn't know *how* to read a book, how to read."

He laughed like I'd said something funny. "That's where the school master comes in."

He opened the book up to the first page. "You know these things here?" He pointed to a bunch of black lines and circles and dots.

"I reckon they're letters."

"Yes ma'am, they're letters!" He smacked a hand on his thigh.

"Bully for me."

"This here is the alphybet," he said. "You got you 26 letters here."

"That all?" Twenty-six letters didn't sound so bad.

"That's all. But you'll be surprised how many words those letters can make."

He set about calling out the letters as he pointed to them in the book. Then he covered up a letter with a finger and had me try to recall what it was. Took me the rest of the time he'd set aside for me to remember all 26 of 'em, but I did it.

I sat back tuckered like I'd spent all day working in the sun. I reckoned Mr. Parrish was right. Using your brain made you sweat, but on the inside.

"You see these small letters here?" He pointed to the next page. "These here are the small ones of the letters you just learned. See, the big'uns are called 'upper case' and little'uns are 'lower case.'"

"Do I have to learn both?" Mayhaps we could just skip those.

He guffawed good at that. "Most words are written with lower case letters."

"Well, why did you learn me the big ones then?" I had to holler at him for that.

"You got to know both," he said.

He patted his pockets, then looked about the room. "You got you some ink and a pen of some sort?"

"The Yanks do."

I fetched their satiny writing box from the library, carried it out to Abner like it was a box of dynamite, but he'd seen such a contraption before. In no time he'd wet the golden nib and started writing on the inside of the paper book. He turned the book to show me what he'd written.

I saw **ELIZA DICKENS** written there, all "upper case" letters.

"Is that my name?"

"It is," he said. "Pretty, ain't it? Why don't you learn to write it out yourself?"

I counted twelve letters in all. "What's the gap between the letters there?"

"There's spaces between words, so folks can tell where one word ends and the other begins." He touched the space between **ELIZA** and **DICKENS**, real soft like.

He told me how a reader would go about sounding out the words by taking each letter in turn and making its sound.

"When I learn you the sounds of the letters, then we can start on short words. Like "me" and "my" and "she." He clapped his hand with each word. "Sea" and "sky" and "duck" got one clap apiece.

"And …Ben," I said. It was hard not to clap when I said his name.

Abner dropped his hands to his lap.

"Do…?" Then, he said, "Do you…?"

"Do I what?" I asked. "Spit it out."

"Nothing."

In the quiet I heard the sound of ponies whickering, the stable door squeaking open.

"They're back," I said. I shoved the pen and ink back into the box and hid it on my lap under the table. We listened to the back door open, the men's talk.

They walked past the dining room toward the parlor, likely with cigars and brandy on their minds. But Mr. Parrish saw us through the doorway and doubled back. They all stepped into the room, their faces red and chapped. They looked from me to Abner to the learning book.

"Shootin' good?" I said.

"Only fair," said Mr. Sexton. "The guide didn't know half as much as you do. We told them about you, but they thought we were pulling their legs."

Abner pulled up his mail bag. He drew out a grist of envelopes and handed them over to Mr. Parrish. The grandfather clock rang five times. But still they stared.

"Abner is learning me my letters," I said.

The men grinned at me like I was a blue-ribbon hoss.

"Was it something I said?" Mr. Parrish said.

"No." I was ashamed somehow, like I'd been caught carving decoys out of the dining room table. The satiny box burned a hole in my skirts, clear down to the skin of my legs.

"I wasn't aware that teaching was one of your hobbies, Abner," said Mr. Sexton.

"It ain't, really," he said. "But I'd do most anything for Eliza here."

Steam poured from my ears. "No, he wouldn't," I said.

They grinned some more, then shuffled out the door for the parlor. I got up and stole into the library, put the box back nice and straight on the desk and hurried out the door to the porch. I took a big pull of cold air into my lungs, over and over. Abner came out and hobbled over to me.

"This don't feel right after all," I said.

"You ain't thinking of quitting when you've just now started?"

He handed the paper book to me. "This is yours now. Got your name in it and all."

The book seemed right heavy for such a little thing. "Well, ain't that…I never had no…"

"You're welcome."

I rolled my eyes. "Thank you. But you *better* not wait two more weeks for—"

He tweaked my nose between his thumb and forefinger, and none too gently. Then he loped off to the docks with his mailbag, jerky as a three-legged dog and humming a tune.

I worked myself into a tizzy getting ready for the lighthouse lighting. In a few days I'd cut out and sewed up a new dress, all by lantern light. It did look a bit rough on account it was hand-sewn, but it'd suit the Banks just fine. At last the 3rd of December came around, but Iola didn't want to come to the party, thought it better use of her time to sit around and sulk.

"I'll never love another," she said, sunup to sundown.

But I told her folks were coming from all around to see the light get lit, that as a old maid and a widow, we had no choice but to go. Course, I didn't care to see anybody but Ben.

We each took turns at the other's head of hair, tying braids with ribbons and such. Iola looked nice enough with just some simple twists. But I thought I ended up looking like a May Day nanny goat so I took the whole mess down, wore my hair like I always did with a part down the middle and a bun at my neck. I was just gonna fix the new bonnet atop my head anyhow.

Iola and me and the Yanks hitched the horse to the buggy and rode on over to the lighthouse. It was cold with the sun heading west, but there was already a big boodle gathered around the bottom of the lighthouse time we got there. I smelled a pig roasting, and folks were serving themselves from fare laid out on tables.

The Yanks helped Iola climb down from the buggy and hitch the horse to a post, but I sat solid on the buggy seat craning my neck for a sign of Ben through the crowd. No luck; it seemed there was nothing but old folks, rich Yanks and younguns here.

"Are you coming or not?" Iola said.

I gathered up my skirts and stepped down into the sand. The new shoes were already starting to rub my toes raw. But they did please me when I saw them poke out my skirts like doe feet.

Heads turned as we all walked toward the crowd. Behind our backs I heard a woman in her homespun make comment on my dress and bonnet, wondering where in tarnation I came about such fabric. I heard another say that I worked for those rich Yanks, and didn't she hear how much they paid me. Then another said something about paying me to do what, and I was about to turn around when Iola grabbed for my arm and squeezed.

"You're just going to stand there and let those biddies make ugly talk of me?"

She just shook her head at me, lips shut tight together. Amos's dying had taken the gumption right out of her, I swear. I turned about anyway and cut my eyes at the ladies, but they'd already wandered off. The Yanks went off toward the other slicked up men like ducks to decoys.

Me and Iola started to piling our plates with collards, potatoes, sweetbreads and salted pork. We each took a cup full of hard apple cider, then made for some chairs. The band struck up and soon folks started to jigging in the sand.

"Ain't you glad I made you come?" I said. She grunted.

Sparks from a cook fire danced in the breeze and the hot cider warmed my throat. Iola and me commenced to dipping after the meal. We set back in our chairs, chewing and spitting. I thought, *all I needed now was Ben.*

I saw Iola had her eye on a couple of men across the way, both with bright red hair. They looked like a couple of peckerwoods, with their raggedy clothes and grizzly beards. They were scarfing down food like they hadn't ate decent in weeks. The tall one stood out, looked like a poor man's Amos. I reckoned he was the one she had her eye on.

"You should go on up and say hey," I told her.

She picked up a handful of black skirt to show me. "I can't. Why don't you go?"

"I can't neither."

She huffed loud at me. "Ben's not your beau anymore," she said. "He's a married man."

"So?"

She spit out her plug too close to my new shoes, and I kicked her shin.

Before we knew it, the peckerwoods had planted themselves before us, looking a bit corned and smelling of pork and onions.

The tall one whistled at us. "Evening, ladies," he said. "You're setting there pretty as can be, ain't you."

His teeth had a gappiness to them, and his nose had been broke one too many times. Amos'd been better looking. But up close I decided he was even bigger than Amos had been, and younger to boot.

"We like to keep up appearances," I said. "Which is more than I can say for some. You kin?"

"We are, at that," he said. "Cousins."

"Do tell."

"We ain't danced in a coon's age," he said. "You up for it?"

He took notice of Iola's black dress before reaching his big hand out to me, but I shook my head.

"Iola might be," I said, cocking my head at her. "That black dress used to be light blue, you know."

His hand shifted left to Iola. "Iola, let's have at it. I'm mourning a death as well, and a dance won't come amiss."

To my surprise, Iola tittered at him. Then she got to her feet and went off to dance with him without a word or a look.

"You hitched or something?" asked the other one, his tight red mop not even blowing in the breeze.

"No, I ain't," I said. "But I'm waiting on somebody."

He looked about as if to find the man that kept me waiting and beat him senseless. But finding no such man, he started to drift off toward the food tables again. I watched Iola and the big man dance. She was about as spritely as my old granny out there, but at least she was up and moving.

At candle-lighting folks started for the lighthouse. A man named Burris was to be the keeper. He stepped up in front to talk at us. Two other men in uniform stood next to him, and I figured they were set to be his helpers. They had wives too, and younguns looking on. I saw the hunting men up front, where all the rich Yanks figured they should stand. I reckoned the folks directly behind those top hats were good and mad about their view.

It was quick getting dark, it being a moonless night, but no sign of Ben. I tightened the bonnet ribbon under my chin and smoothed the skirts of my dress anyway.

Burris told us that his first assistant keep was named Lewis Simmons and the second keep was named Thomas Everton. They all shook hands for us, like they were acting in a play. Then Burris told us he was sure glad the lighthouse had finally gotten built, on account it'd been planned for way back in the 1860s to help with the dark spot between the Cape Henry light and the Bodie Island light, 60-some miles apart. But the war had gotten in the way of the money, and they'd had to wait.

He told us he had to rotate the big lenses that made the light flash. He did such a thing by cranking on some weights under the lantern every two and a half hours—a lot like the workings of a grandfather clock, I was happy to hear. It would be calm and steady as the tides. The thing ran on lard oil, and he said he had to carry up three gallons a night, clear up the 214 stairs. I figured the job would get old in short time, but a man would do a lot more than that for a government job out here.

Burris finished up, and the men made their way to the door at the bottom of the lighthouse tower. Folks talked loud now and started to crowding one another. I turned, looking to find Iola and the big man, which wasn't hard to do. But the man was fit to bust, I saw. It took me a while to realize he was hollering at Ben, standing a good six inches shorter than he, even with his slouch hat on.

I spat out my plug and pushed my way through the crowd to find a whole boodle of red-head folk getting in on the ruckus too. Every single one of them—even the younguns and women—were hollering at Ben. Just as the big man was set to poke Ben in the chest, I gave his sleeve a yank. He drew back and stared at the person who dared to pull on him.

"Who do you think you are, coming here and causing trouble?" I said. "This here man is a surfman at the lifesaving station. He's *respected*, if you catch my meaning. I reckon you all ain't used to proper company, but let me tell you we don't care for your trashy shenanigans. You best get on back to the sorry-assed huts you came from, drink what's left of your corn liquor. Leave your betters to their party."

The folks opened their mouths wide as bottom feeders. The big man grinned at me. "Ain't you a spitfire."

Ben said, "She's right. I've done said all I'm going to say to you, and you best be off."

Other folks had turned from the lighthouse to look on the ruckus. The big man saw this, started to nodding his head. He cocked his head to the brawlers, and they all grunted and spat before leaving us.

The big man called over his shoulder. "Thankee for the dance, Iola. I'll be seeing you soon."

Iola gave a little wave, and I turned to Ben. "Who in hell were those corn-crackers?"

He put his hands over his face for a bit. "The Spruels, kin of the boy I found on the beach that night. Seems the boy'd taken something of value to the family before he took off in the skiff, and now they're looking for it," he said. "They've been out every day in their boats, dragging their seine nets, looking for a barrel. Have to walk right by them on our patrols every day and night."

"What's in the barrel?"

"They didn't say."

"And why are they put out with you?" said Iola.

"They reckon since I'm the one that found the skiff, then I must've made off with the barrel too."

"That ain't fair," I said. But my thoughts snagged on a picture of Ben just the other week, poling south with a barrel in a boat. How he wouldn't slow down to speak with me.

"That big one was a good enough dancer," said Iola. "He paid me nothing but compliments."

I snorted. "That whapper's full of more than compliments, I'll wager."

"And you just about threw me at him!" She huffed and stalked off to the grub.

Ben wrapped a blue scarf tight about his neck, fought down a shiver.

"You drilling in the ocean today?"

"Yeah. Water's cold as the devil's backside lately," he said. "Any colder and it'll be ice."

"I wouldn't think a surfman would whine about the temperature of the sea water."

"I don't mind it so much," he said. "But the others do. Matter fact, it's why we ain't done one capsize drill."

"You're telling me they're all a bunch of ninnies?" I said. "Didn't *look* the case when I saw them that day, but I guess you never can tell."

"So you thought they looked right brawny?"

"So what if I did?" I said. "I ain't hitched, you know. I can look."

He took his hat off and ran a hand through his hair. "They're all married men, save Lewis."

"Well, you make the introductions then," I said. I poked him, then looked straight at him to see what answer he'd give.

He rubbed his nose, then picked up a stalk of sea oat from the sand at his feet and started chewing at it.

"I don't think he'd be right for you," he said.

And the power of our lost love washed over me hard then, so that I wanted to fall down on my knees and cry. I recalled a time when Ben and me were loving on each other, loving so hard on the sands of the sound that we lost track of where we were at and ended up half in the cold water. We didn't even stop, just kept grinding at each other. I didn't know the half of how much I missed that feeling, the wanting of him. It would build up in me during a day, and by the time I laid eyes on him at night I'd be ready to rip his clothes right off. I'd scratch his back and bite at his chest and neck and leave marks that lasted for days, but he never complained.

Now when I looked over to him, him with his face turned up to the night sky, it seemed like we could have it all again.

There was a commotion at the top of the light-house then, and the heat that I was putting out started to flow away into the cold night. It was too dark to see a thing, but I reckoned any minute now, and the light was fixing to come on.

"Recall when we took Iola's pap's old rowboat out?"

"How could I forget?" he said, rubbing at his backside. "I still got scars from that whooping."

He'd made me row an oar fast as I could out to the middle of the sound to a pretend shipwreck. He'd hollered, "Women and children first!"

Then he made me say the shipwrecked lady's parts, like "Help me, oh mercy me, help me and my little baby girl!"

And he'd pretended to pull the lady aboard, and I got jealous he was touching on some lady, even if she was only a shade.

"You always wanted to save lives," I said.

"Iola's pap thought we were more like pirates," he said. "I didn't think he'd miss such a sorry piece of wood. Fact, I thought he'd shake my hand for getting it into the water."

Iola's pap told Ben's pap, and Ben's pap gave him a whooping. It was a lesson, he'd said, on vamoosing with another man's boat, the most prized property a Banks man can own. Ben had wanted to point out that Iola's pap owned three other skiffs, but figured that saying as much would have gotten him killed outright. Ben's pap used a sanded up piece of driftwood for a paddle, and one smack on bare skin peeled it right off.

It was such a night, I figured I'd go ahead and tell him the news. "Abner's learning me my letters."

It was pitch dark, but I could feel him looking over at me. "Well, now," he said. My whole body hurt waiting for him to touch me. But he didn't.

"He ain't but come one time so far. I'll be dead and underground afore I'm able to read the words they might sketch onto my marker."

He laughed, said something about it taking a lot of time to learn proper. And I saw in my mind a picture of Ben and Abigail on her porch together. Friends had told me of it during that long, awful summer, said they'd held a book with both of their hands, that the book seemed to weave a spell about them, good as black magic. It seemed it hadn't taken him any time at all for him to learn to read.

I'd laughed at the stories and said, "A love built on book-words won't last." I'd said, "Those two are about as alike as a heifer and a horseshoe crab." And my friends had thought as much too.

"You ain't said one word about my dress," I said. I opened up my army coat and slid it down my back, to show him my handiwork. I was proud of the way the dark purple dress showed off the thinness of my belly, the way the bustle fattened the size of my backside. And I knew Abigail wore only homespun now. Us Nags Headers poked fun at the way she'd worn her one nice dress for two whole years until it just about turned to dust on her. I reckoned Ben found his wife a lot less pretty without those fine dresses draped over her.

I kept that coat open for him, the cold air blowing over me, hoping he'd recall what was *underneath* my dress.

"It's real nice, Eliza," he said. "You made it yourself?"

"Course I did," I said. "Did you see this lace here? And here?" I turned about to show him the backside, where ruffles and lace were sewn.

"It's nice," he said again. "You look real…pretty."

I was about to show him my shoes, when the lantern in the lighthouse tower lit up the dark sky. It shone out brighter than the sun, lit up our faces so as to burn our cheeks. There was a flash of cherry red, then it was gone, leaving just the white light brighter than the moon. We all waited a while until it flashed red again, and only then did folks cheer and holler.

"Would you look at that," said Ben. He gazed up at the light like he'd never seen a better sight. Poppers and sky-rockets went off nearby, but I only saw his face, close to me once more.

CHAPTER TEN

ELIZA DICKENS
DECEMBER 20, 1875

He seemed to take to me quite as naturally and unbiddenly as I to him…

–*ISHMAEL ON QUEEQUEG*, **MOBY-DICK**

IT WAS NIGH ON A WEEK AFTER THE LIGHTHOUSE LIGHTING when the Yanks left for home, leaving me and Iola to count the paper money we earned. We kept it all in a tin box under a rotten floorboard in the cabin. 'Twas as good as a dead possum under there, as much as we ever touched that box. Had to travel way off the Banks to spend money like that.

There wasn't much to be done at the clubhouse 'til we went back to Nags Head in the spring: tending to the stock, gardens and tollers, mending nets, cleaning the poles and skiff and oars and decoys. Keeping watch out for poachers and thieves was another job altogether, and we both kept shotguns at the ready.

Iola and me had taken a shine to cooking our food in the clubhouse cook stove and eating at the dining table. Seemed at times Iola was over Amos and then the next minute she'd fall to pieces, back where she'd started. She wasn't eating much, but she slept the day away sometimes. She'd wake and tell me about her dreams—wild dreams of color where she'd be flying in the sky, or swimming down deep in the ocean, or talking to cows and pigs and horses in a foreign tongue.

"Sounds downright tiring," I'd said, after one particular yarn about digging a hole in the sand so deep she found a way into the past. She'd met up with the Indians used to live on the Banks, let 'em tattoo her white body with inky spots.

"As if living your life wide awake ain't enough, you've got to live a whole 'nother life in sleeping."

"It ain't tiring," she'd said. Though dark shadows marked the pale skin beneath her eyes. "Sometimes I don't even want to wake up."

I shuddered, thinking of getting stuck forever in Iola's dreamland. "Good thing I don't dream."

She squinted at me like I'd told her a falsehood. "What?"

"I never dream." I'd thought about Ben plenty before falling into sleep, but I'd never once had a night story about him.

"You just can't recall what they were about."

"No. I sleep, I wake up."

Her blue eyes were big circles as she turned this fact over inside her head. "I just can't imagine. I reckon I'm a little worried about you."

"Worry about yourself, why don't you."

Next day Abner showed himself at the door. He had smudges under his eyes and a growth of beard. There were leaf bits in his hair, and his eyes were shot with blood. The knees of his britches were dirty and ripped. I reckoned he'd taken a bad spill not too long ago.

"You look like hell," I told him.

"I been sick as a dog." He started to hack. "But you see...here I am."

"Ain't I the lucky one."

But he was so sorry-looking, I fixed him some yaupon tea, and we sat down at the table with the book he gave me and some of the men's writing paper, pen and bottle of ink. But he just stared into the fire with the tea cup in his grubby hands.

"You seen the doc?"

"Don't have the time."

"You got the time to die? Amos was busier than a springtime jackrabbit too. Then he took himself a nice, long sand bath," I said. "You got someone to take over for you when you take sick?"

"No."

"Course you don't." His cheeks were red like someone'd slapped him raw. "There's a leaf in your hair."

He reached up and stretched his fingers through the mess on top of his head but came up empty. I reached over and plucked it out from him, taking along a few strands of hair with it. He sucked his breath and put his hand to his head.

I knew I shouldn't have pulled at him so hard. It put me in mind of how mean we all were to Abner when we were younguns. We used to throw cow pies at him. We tripped him, just so we could watch him try to get back up. We called him names so much we forgot what his real name was. He didn't cry or nothing, even when I knew he got hurt. He didn't tattle-tale neither.

It got so bad I started to sticking up for him. I couldn't say why, but one day I just decided enough was enough. Might have been the sight of him trying to hurry from us, for he'd use his hands to swing his bad leg while he hopped along on his good one. But folks soon learned I'd fight anyone that picked on Abner, no matter the age nor girth. Then we were friends of a sort. Even though he still made me cringe.

I recalled knocking on the door of his nice and neat house on the sound, so different from my own abode. His mama would come to the door to see me, offer me a thing to eat, usually cornbread and a pat of butter. She grew on me, but mama poked fun at her with the other Nags Head women folk on account she'd gave birth to a cripple yet doted on him like he was the future governor. I reckoned his mama's spoiling was why Abner felt he could come to front doors.

I picked up the pen and dipped it in the ink, then wrote my first and last name on the paper.

Abner said, "Lookie there."

"I've had enough time to practice at it," I said, an edge in my words. But we both stared at those letters, happy for a bit.

"That reminds me." He clapped a hand to his forehead. "You got a letter!"

He reached into his mail bag and pulled out a handful of letters, passed through some of them before getting to the one he wanted. He handed the letter over to me with a big smile like I'd won it.

I looked down at the envelope, saw the stamp and the proof of its mailing. "That's my name."

"And that there underneath is the address of this club house."

"But who'd write me a letter?"

Abner pointed at the chicken scratching along the back of the envelope. "It's from Mr. Parrish. Up in New York."

"They think I learn quick, I reckon."

"Course they do. I'll read it for you, if you want me to."

"I guess I don't have me a choice," I said, and handed the letter back to him.

He tore the envelope open and pulled out a sheet of paper, smoothed it out on the table before himself, and read Mr. Parrish's words to me, coughing every other word. And when he was done, we both sat back in our chairs, breathing hard.

"They invited six other Yankee men to join the crack club," I said. "They'll all be coming and going November through February next season?"

"More Yanks," said Abner, shaking his head. "More Yanks than not up here now."

"I'm to be the new caretaker. And the head guide too, though they'll need to hire one more guide for next season. And they're going to build me a house." My mind still spun round and round, messy as Mr. Parrish's scrawled out writing. "Right beside this clubhouse."

"That's something," said Abner, his cheeks still red with fever or gladness or maybe both. "You charmed those men good, girl."

"They want me to corral a crew of men to build it up. Same as they did this clubhouse. Going up in the summer, they said." I sat there, hardly believing it. "It ain't mine, though?"

Abner shook his head. "No, they'll own it," he said. "It's for the caretaker. But you'll live there and work for them, and as long as you do, it might as well be yours."

I thought of the house that Ben built for Abigail, how when I saw it for the first time and doubted Abby knew how lucky she was to have a house like that. A house that a man had built her out of love. But she hadn't even wanted to live there, and now that poor old house just sat empty.

I hardly noticed Abner leaning over. He kissed my cheek, real tender. Then he leaned back in his chair and looked at me hard. "I'm proud to call you my friend, Eliza Dickens."

I looked about me at the shiny dining table, the china cabinet, the thick rug.

"What has become of me?" I said, voice cracked. "I hardly know my own self."

"You're getting what's been coming to you," he said. He reached over and took my hand in his, hard and soft at the same time. "It's good, Eliza. Don't fret, now."

"Help me with the letter back to 'em."

He looked at me stern.

"Please," I said, and I didn't even mind saying it.

He laughed and let go my hand. "I'd be happy to."

"I can write out my name at the end, at the least."

We set to our work in the reading book then, though I couldn't make heads nor tails of anything new. I reckon I'd taken my fill for the day.

There was a hog butchering next day.

Me and Ben had agreed to help the lighthouse folks with butchering some hogs in return for some of the meat. Ben and his men were hankering for pork meat too, so he agreed to bring along a surfman to help.

Sun not risen, I woke up in a fine temper. I just about skipped through the cold sand to the place where the Burris family was living temporary, until their new diggings by the lighthouse got built.

Ben was already there, a tin cup in his hand. A big man stood next to him, looking strong enough to butcher 30 hogs singlehanded.

"Like old times, ain't it," Ben said to me.

"Looks that way," I said. I wanted to tell him the news from Mr. Parrish, but surfman Spencer was there watching us. Plus there was work to be done. The fire was burning hot, a big kettle set up over it. The table was laid with sharp knives and saws, and tubs of water stood nearby the fire. Mrs. Burris and the other women were serving up eggs and toast.

The men soon left off to kill and bleed the hogs at their pen while the women tended the fire and dipped fingers into the kettle to test its heat. A while later the men came back pulling the cart of dead hogs, looked to be about a dozen. We all worked to throw the carcasses into the kettle one by one, then took 'em out and scraped at the hairs. Then we hung 'em from poles for cleaning.

The men slit the hogs down their bellies, then slid hands inside to tell where to cut through the breasts. We all stood ready with tubs, for when the hands came out, they brung intestines and stomachs, bladders, livers, kidneys. With our tubs full of parts, the women made for the kitchen house to cook 'em or pack 'em in barrels of salt.

Mrs. Burris said, "Your husband is a quick hand at dressing."

I hated to tell her the truth about us. So I didn't.

"You should see him carve," was what I said, and kept walking, tub of bloody hearts in my hands.

Washing the hearts in a bucket of water, I caught sight of Ben through the window of the kitchen house. He had his hands deep in the belly of a hog, and I got gooseflesh all over, thinking of his hands doing that to me, reaching into my guts and touching on my insides. He'd pull out my heart, maybe, and see that his own name was carved on it. And he'd know what was what, ain't nothing had changed with me.

"I see what you're grinning at," said Mrs. Burris, peeking out the window over my shoulder.

"I never grin," I said, but my mouth pulled upward even so.

I kept cutting up the hearts and rolling them in herbs and spice. A woman next to me washed out intestines for chitlins. Another cut up onions and mushrooms. Over it all I smelled cornbread baking and collards cooking and homemade grape wine. The women around me wanted to chat about family and gardens and such things as we cooked. But the only thing I could keep my mind on was Ben, his bloodied arms and his shirt wet in its pits.

When we marched the trays out, the men put on their nose-bags in a hurry. I sat with Ben on a rotted stump and ate with him. I breathed in his pig blood-sweat smell, thinking it was the best scent I'd sniffed all day. Made my belly growl.

"Either I'm getting older, or the hogs are getting fatter, for I've never felt so whipped from hog butchering," he said. He stretched out his back and I heard his bones pop.

"Those hogs ain't so fat," I said. And he turned to me with a cocked eyebrow.

"I know I'm getting old," he said. "You don't have to rub my nose in it."

"Well, it's hard work, and that's a fact," I said. I took a swallow of the cold grape wine. "Your woman ever help you butcher a hog?"

"No," he laughed.

"I reckoned not."

"I'd never let her do such work."

"And why is that?"

He shrugged. "She's a teacher."

"Teachers don't eat?" I scoffed. "You still writing to one another?"

He didn't say anything for a bit. "Sure we are."

He put his knife and fork down and pulled a paper from his pocket, all crumpled from being in his britches. I figured it a letter from Abby, and it pained me a little to see that he carried it around with him like he did. He opened it up and smoothed it out, held it with two hands in front of him.

"She says she was paid a visit by a man from Nashville, Tennessee, few weeks back," he said, then stopped. I could tell whatever was in the letter puckered him, for he sat there reading it through again.

"The man came on account of a letter his foundation received about the school where Abby teaches. He wanted to use the school in his research for a book he's writing," he said, his eyes still moving over the scrawl. "She says there's a normal school starting up in Nashville, funded by the Peabody Foundation where the man serves on the board. Says he wants her to work at that school, he liked what he saw of her teaching that much."

That all sounded good enough to me, but I kept my mouth straight. "What's a normal school?"

"A school for the training of teachers," he said.

"Huh. Women work there?"

"Sounds like it."

"Lord-a-mercy," I said. "She say one way or the other she planning to go?"

"No." He crumpled up the paper quick and stuffed it back into his britches pocket.

"You gonna let her leave?"

"That ain't...I don't *let* her do anything."

"Don't I know it."

He laughed then. But he said, "It sounds to me like she wants to go."

Ben started carving at the pig's heart again. A few younguns ran by with a blowed-up pig's bladder. They threw it into the air and took turns catching at it before it hit the ground. Ben and me used to do the same thing, not too long ago.

"How's your lessons with Abner going?"

"Abner ain't a bad teacher," I said. "But he's sick as a dog, and no one to help him with his route."

"He won't give that job to no one, unless he's dead," said Ben. "Good job like that."

Good jobs, I thought. *Abby ain't the only one with offers.* I told him the news from Mr. Parrish, picking my brain for every little word Mr. Parrish wrote. Ben seemed right happy with the news, but he didn't kiss me the way Abner had. Even though I'd shoved my cheek so close to him I could like his ear lobe.

For our help with the butchering, Ben and me and surfman Spencer got invited to the Christmas party at the Burris abode. I put on my new clothes once more and told Iola I'd bring her some food. I got to the house in the early afternoon, but Ben wasn't yet there. Mrs. Burris pulled me over to a tin pail of punch, not nearly as high-falutin' as the Yankee's punch bowl. But no one cared about the brand of bowl, just the quantity of liquor inside it. Which was plenty.

In no time at all I was off my head. Spencer was there, and he'd nodded at me polite enough but hadn't come over to speak to me. He left after a while, then Ben showed up.

Mrs. Burris said, "Your husband's here!"

I started to titter at her confounded notions, but my eyes settled on Ben crossing the threshold and forgot about all else. He looked finer than I'd ever seen him, with his hair combed back and filling out his nice, clean clothes with his strong body.

"I'm sorry I'm late," he said to the room at large. "I had to finish up a cart for Spencer Junior's pet goat to pull him around in. Both boy and goat are coming for a visit tomorrow. Should be a sight to see."

"You all got to work on Christmas Day?" asked Mr. Burris.

"Don't you?" Ben answered, and Mr. Burris grinned and nodded. The lighthouse work would never end, but Ben and the other surfmen got to go home in March.

I watched Ben grab a cup and ladle some punch into it for himself, then came to greet me. My whole head burned, my whole body was afire.

"Ain't that schweet of you," I said. "A lil' goat cart."

He peeked inside my cup and shook his head at its emptiness. "I see you've already tried the punch."

"'S good."

He drained his cup and nodded. "It is, at that."

He took both our cups back to the punch bucket, and we drank those down too. But I soon started to sway on my feet, so Ben took me by my elbow to a couple of chairs by the fire.

We listened to some men bow at a fiddle and strum at a banjo for a time. Their younguns danced about for us, and the sun shone gold through the windows. I wanted to talk to Ben, but my tongue wouldn't work.

Soon the preacher showed up. He spoke of the new baby Jesus, laid in a manger, at home in a barn full of animals. When folks bowed their heads to pray, Ben leaned over to whisper he'd been to the widow's house a couple of times for church service.

"Never figured you for a happy clapper."

He looked at his boot toes. "I been feeling…sort of, well, I don't know. Homesick, I guess you'd say."

"And you reckoned churching would help you find your way back home?"

"I thought to try it."

At that he put his arm around me. It lay heavy on my shoulders, and I was afeared to even move. Mrs. Burris grinned at me when she raised her head from prayer.

And I felt maybe there was something to church service after all. I figured maybe Ben *had* found his way back home. Praying to a man easy with barn animals didn't seem too bad to me. Felt like I was praying to a man kind of like Ben, and I'd been doing that on and off my whole life, shouldn't be too hard.

CHAPTER ELEVEN

DECEMBER 24, 1875
ABIGAIL WHIMBLE

But in pursuit of those far mysteries we dream of, or in tormented chase of that demon phantom that, some or other, swims before all human hearts; while chasing such over this round globe, they either lead us on in barren mazes or midway leave us whelmed.

–*ISHMAEL*, MOBY-DICK

I HELD *MOBY-DICK* AND *THE AMERICAN DICTIONARY OF THE English Language* on my lap and watched Leo navigate the skiff through the shoals of the Currituck Sound. He was an experienced pilot now, instructed by Ben himself, and his easy, knowing movements through the shifting, shallow waters reminded me of my husband.

It had only been three months since I'd seen Ben, but it might as well have been three years, for all of the distance that was now between us. This journey to Whales Head had been Ruth and Luella's idea, and Leo had offered to sail me up on Christmas Eve to surprise Ben. At first I hadn't wanted to accept the offer. I'd only written to Ben once since I'd received his last letter, and I wasn't proud of my correspondence.

I'd elaborated on Mr. Wharton's visit and the Peabody Normal School and his offer of possible employment there. Instead of hedging my excitement, I had made it sound as if I'd already planned to go. I'd made Mr. Wharton out to be a god of sorts: a man of education, passion, culture. I'd rhapsodized over Nashville, how exciting it would be to travel from the Banks at last, to perhaps live in a boarding house with other female faculty, to share ideas with people of like mind.

And I cringed at the thought of Ben reading that letter, of assuming that I preferred a life without him. The more I considered Ruth's plan, the more necessary the idea had sounded. But the trip was a long 30 nautical miles north, and we'd left Roanoke Island way before dawn, expecting to arrive in Whales Head in the late afternoon. Leo was prepared to spend the night on a spare cot, but I wasn't quite sure where I would find myself for the evening. Wives weren't welcomed to stay the night at the lifesaving station, but perhaps they'd make an exception for me.

The morning sun surprised me with its heat, and I recalled the young woman I used to be, sailing through a warm Nags Head night to teach at the Elijah Africa schoolhouse, Ben at my side, and a proscribed thrill bright in my blood.

"It's been a long time since I've done anything like this," I said to Leo.

"Do you good," he said, not turning from his place at the bow.

For lack of other conversation, I read *Moby-Dick* aloud to Leo. It had been seven years since I'd read it last. I vaguely remembered packing the book along with numerous others for use at the schoolhouse. It hadn't gotten much use there either—its size discouraged students from even touching it—and soon I'd forgotten it was even there.

I stroked the blue leather, the gilt lettering, the publisher's circular device blindstamped on the cover. The edges were a bit frayed, and the pages didn't quite lay flush against one another, victims of the North Carolina heat and humidity.

It had been mama's copy, an original published in 1851. She had ordered the book at the request of the Edenton bookseller, Mr. Whitney. She'd told me that Mr. Whitney had found the book intriguing, with its many interpretations and unusual style, but that he hadn't liked it as well as the other Melville novels. *Moby-Dick* hadn't been nearly as well received by the literary critics either.

Throughout my childhood, mama would refer to the novel occasionally, or quote lines from it. But she never suggested I read it until the spring before our departure for Nags Head, declaring that the whaling adventure would fill my time. I'd been a quarter of the way through the weighty novel when I'd begun to tutor Ben. Then my progress had slowed to just a few pages a day.

It had taken me three more months to complete it, with our move to the Roanoke Island house and getting settled in my position at the schoolhouse. I recalled closing the book at last on a cold November day, and Ben, my new husband, eyeing it with desire.

I'd admired the book—seemingly more than the critics—but it had been complex. I'd put off the reading of it with Ben, and I wasn't proud of my reasoning: even though he'd impressed me with his pace of learning, I'd become more and more aware of his lack of education.

In our early years of marriage, I'd truly wanted to help him, to teach him. But there had been only so much time in our busy lives. I'd offered him books from the many that mama had sent to me, books that I'd read many years before—novels by Dickens, Thackeray, the Brownings, Eliot, Bronte, Balzac—or ordered books recommended by Mr. Whitney. Yet when we'd tried to read *Gulliver's Travels*, another travel adventure, Ben had found the various themes confusing and we'd given it up.

He'd circled back to *Robinson Crusoe* soon after, first reading it aloud and then silently to himself, still running his finger under the lines. Then he'd taken to copying out the novel on paper. I'd read on my own more and more. And after a while, I think we both lost interest in his education. Ben had never even learned how to read or write cursive.

And now, as I read *Moby-Dick*, Leo kept turning to look at me with a bunched forehead, but I kept reading, unable to stop.

It was mid-afternoon when we reached the docks at the lighthouse, and Leo whistled at the sight of the Currituck lighthouse looming over the trees. I handed him my bag, and he helped me out of the skiff onto the docks. I started walking east through the sand, Leo hurrying to keep up.

After seeing nothing but sand dunes and sky for several long minutes, both Leo and I pointed with outreached arms when we caught sight of the place of Ben's employment: the lifesaving station appeared in the afternoon sun to be as impressive a sight as Ben had described it to be. It looked just like the Nags Head Lifesaving Station, yet somehow more appealing.

A man stood watch on the tower atop the station. I didn't think it was Ben, but it was hard to tell with the sun at his back. I picked up my skirts and scampered around to the front of the station to peer up at the man on the tower.

"Good afternoon, sir," I called. I swayed a bit from the hard and fast walking, the excitement, the height of the tower, its gilded silhouette.

"Afternoon, ma'am," he called back. "Help you with something?"

"Yes," I breathed. "I'm Abigail Whimble, Ben's wife. I came up from Nags Head to surprise him this Christmas Eve."

He turned and disappeared from view, coming out a few moments later through the equipment room and down the big ramp. He strode up to me and took my hand in both of his. He was older and more barrel-chested than Ben, but he wore a patched-up coat and a slouch hat just like Ben's.

"I'm Spencer Gray, Mrs. Whimble."

"Oh, yes. Ben has written of you," I said. "This is Leopold Williams, a student of mine. He was kind enough to sail me here today."

"Long day of sailing, I'll wager," said Mr. Gray. Leo whistled low.

"It's quite a long trip," I agreed. "But we couldn't have gotten nicer weather. We made excellent time."

We all nodded and smiled at one another, and in the interval I heard the voices of men from inside the equipment room, the shifting of wood on sand. And I saw that a surfman had already replaced Mr. Gray top the lookout tower.

"Ben will sure be surprised to see you," he said.

"I'm counting on it."

I peered past Mr. Gray to see if I could spot Ben somewhere, but I could only see the lifeboat and cart in the dark room.

"He isn't here right now," Mr. Gray said. He scratched hard at his beard with his fingers. "Sorry to say."

"Oh. Where is he?"

"He's at a shindig of sorts," he said, his eyes straying to the ocean. "At the house where the lighthouse folks are staying. Ben and me went on account we helped them with the hog butchering."

I forced a smile. "I'm pleased that he could be of help."

On the boat ride here, I'd envisioned him to be somewhere in the station house, fed up with the hard work, lonely and dreaming of home. But instead I saw him to already be a part of this isolated community, his old home in the past.

"Whereabouts is this house?"

He widened his eyes. "You heading over there?"

"Of course."

"Well, he'll be back soon, I reckon. You can wait here 'til he comes back."

I laughed. "I've come all this way, Mr. Gray," I said. "I really do want to see him. As soon as possible."

He nodded briefly. He then gave us directions that took us back toward the sound, telling us the house wasn't but a few hundred yards from the lighthouse itself.

The sun was setting in the west when Leo and I began walking again, and my calves cramped in protest. But I kept striding forward, the image of Ben's face in my mind, delight inscribed on it like the golden publisher's seal on the cover of *Moby-Dick*. I'd offer him the book and the dictionary, and say, "Merry Christmas, Ben." And he would grin at me, maybe laugh, and kiss me hard on the mouth, marvel at my spirit, recovered at last. I had to stop myself from trying to run, as tired as my legs were.

It was almost dark by the time we reached the lighthouse. We then veered north along a path through scrubby pine and wax myrtle. Soon we came upon a handful of houses along the sound. The white clapboard house was set on a wide clearing of sand. The windows glowed with a golden light, and I heard music playing, people singing. I smelled fried pork and potatoes, some kind of pie.

I turned to Leo. "I'm sure you'll be welcome."

But he shook his head and handed the books to me. "I'll stay out here," he said. "You take your time now."

"Thank you, Leo. We'll bring you some food."

Breathing hard, I climbed the stairs to the porch and peered through one of the windows. The large room was lit with candles, oil lamps and a fire in the hearth and was crowded with people of all ages. Some were singing, some were dancing, and some were just sitting on chairs conversing, cups and plates in hand. I couldn't see the musicians from where I stood, but I heard a banjo and a fiddle playing a lively song.

I laughed at a young boy and girl tugging at each other in an imitation of a waltz, and as my eyes followed their spin through the room, I caught sight of Ben's profile. I exhaled slowly at the sight of him, looking so handsome in a clean beige shirt and leather boots, with his hair combed back neatly from his red-cheeked face. He was smiling big at a well-dressed woman seated next to him, and I saw that his arm was wrapped around her shoulders. The woman threw back her head and laughed at something he'd whispered in her ear, and I recognized her as Eliza Dickens.

I stepped back from the window a couple of paces, my body rigid, my heart silent in my chest. I couldn't look away from them. I watched them for what seemed a very a long time, but his arm never moved from her shoulders. His hand dangled close to her chest, his lips were only a few inches from her ear. She leaned into his shoulder and rested her head.

I heard Leo come up the porch steps. "Ain't you going in, Miz Whimble?"

Leo stared through the window with me, the smoke from his clay pipe drifting across our view.

"Who that woman he with?"

"Her name is Eliza."

"He seem…friendly with her."

"Yes, he does."

The music stopped, and I heard happy voices, the clink of cutlery on plates. He finally put a hand on my elbow. "You want to go back home?" he asked.

I shook my head and continued to stare at Ben, perfectly comfortable in that jolly room, and willed him to look to the window. But his eyes were on the children, still careening around the room despite the lack of music. Eliza looked over to him like a pup to its master, then turned to watch the children as well. She said a few words to him, and they both laughed.

"I could go in, fetch him out for you."

"No," I said at once. My jaw trembled from holding it firm. I looked down at the books in my arms.

The fiddle struck a few chords, which I made out to be "It Came Upon a Midnight Clear." I hadn't heard it in a long time, and the fiddle drew out the notes in a slow and sad cadence. Ben's arm still lay across Eliza's back when I finally looked away from him.

The boat ride back to Roanoke Island was the longest, darkest journey of my life. It was Christmas Day, but it felt like my entrance to the underworld. It seemed I really was dead, for I couldn't feel what I thought I'd feel at the sight of Ben with another woman.

"That woman he with, she ugly as a dog," Leo said, his mouth full of the surfmen's burned cornbread and cold ham. "But that don't matter when he missing his woman. *Any*body will do for him. I ain't trying to get him out of trouble or nothin', but those is the facts. He don't care for that woman no how."

"He and Eliza were together once, before he met me," I said into the dark. "They'd loved each other since they were children. But when he met me, he broke it off with her. She had a hard time getting over him."

He choked on a bite of biscuit. "Well now, why didn't you say so?"

The wind had picked up since the morning. The sail whipped out hard in the thick silence, and the vicious blow keened around the edges of the boat and smacked my face raw. Winter was the whole world, no room for speech or thought.

But Leo forced me into it headlong. "What that woman doin' all the way up here?"

"I don't know," I said. "But Ben does."

I stretched out as well as I could on the little skiff, my head propped on a blanket spread on the strut, and stared up into the holy night. The moon above me hung frosty as a ham pulled from an icebox, nothing the angels would sing about.

I remembered such an icy evening not too far into our marriage, when I'd told Ben that he seemed to know a great deal about my body, for the short amount of time that we'd been married. He knew even more than *I* did about it, what it could do and feel.

Under half a dozen blankets, he'd held me close but had pulled his head back so that we were eye to eye. "I need to tell you something."

I'd run a finger along his stubbled jaw line, ready for sleep.

"When we first made love, I'd already been with another."

I hadn't been surprised. "Eliza."

He tightened his hold on my lower back. "Yes ma'am. It was."

I'd still felt the warmth of his confident hands on my legs, my breasts, but my thoughts had turned as green and slippery as seaweed.

"More than once?"

"More than once." He buried his face in my neck, scratching it with his stubble, and mumbled, "I'm sorry, Abby. I maybe should have told you sooner."

I had known that the history that bound Ben and Eliza was never something I could compete with. Yet I'd thought he'd forgotten her through the years. He never mentioned her once since that day of his confession. But I often wondered if he ever thought of her, conjured her face when he made love to me.

Leo startled me when he spoke again. "You said *Moby-Dick* was about looking for a whale, but we ain't never got to the part about the whale."

"It's a long book," I said. "The whale eventually makes his appearance, believe me."

"You say so," he said, voice laced with doubt.

"I'm so cold, Leo," I tried to say, but he couldn't have heard me, for my icy words had shattered about me as soon as I'd uttered them. The morning's warmth had been nothing but a lie, the false hope of a fool.

The sun was coming up by the time Leo poled the skiff up to the old Union docks. Asha's house wasn't a far walk, but Leo insisted on accompanying me. He'd long since given up speaking to me, but he hummed a psalm that he likely believed would comfort me. He was mistaken.

Asha was already up and dressed, a few eggs slung in her apron skirt.

"Merry Christmas," I muttered.

"Back so soon?"

"Seems like I've been gone for days and days," I said, and made my way past her into the cabin.

I sat down in one of the two chairs beside the crackling fireplace, a frying pan on its grate. Asha came in and quietly went about making eggs and grits. She piled two tin plates full of food and set one on my lap. I centered my face over the food to warm it.

"Leo done told me," she said, settling on a chair. "You don't need to trouble yourself."

The steam from the food coated my cheeks with a moisture I couldn't yet feel. I had a childish urge to cry, now that Asha was near. But my body was still numb, either from cold or grief or discomfort from a long night on a skiff, and I couldn't work up even a sob.

"Go on and eat," she said, handing me a fork.

I ate the entire plate of food, but I didn't recall doing it. And when I leaned back, empty plate still on my lap, I didn't even feel the sustenance in my belly.

"Miz Martha done had her baby," said Asha. "Baby girl."

A proud smile lit up Asha's chapped face. I hadn't expected to feel a mirthful feeling so soon, so it took me a few moments to respond.

"Is she faring well? Is the baby alright?"

"This here is her letter," she said, pulling it from her apron pocket. I reached out for it, but forgot about the plate on my lap. It slipped from my skirts and clanged about our feet. I shuddered at the cacophony and squeezed my eyes shut.

Asha said, "Oh no." Then she reached over and hugged me hard to her, and the silent press of her body soothed me the way it always had. I could have sat there for days, if she'd have let me. But she gently pulled herself away and put the letter into my hand.

Asha always let me read Martha's letters, which came every couple of months or so. She felt badly that my sister and I had grown apart, and always asked me if I wanted to write a little something on one of her own letters before she sent it to Martha. But I never could.

I slid the letter from the envelope and opened it along the thick folds. Martha's handwriting was always neat and flowery, like mama's had been, and this letter was no exception. Martha told of the birth, which she felt had turned out to be rather easy compared to the things she'd already seen and heard. She said she was still recuperating—the birth had taken place almost a month ago—but the baby, named Sarah Capehart Newman, was feeding well with the wet nurse and already growing fatter. She begged Asha to come to Edenton for a visit.

"Are you going to go?"

She retrieved the plate from the floor. "I thought you might go instead."

"She doesn't want to see me."

Asha dunked the breakfast dishes into the wash tub and began to scrub them off. "I could stay here and teach for you."

"I don't have any money for traveling," I said, my cold skin now prickling with heat.

"Miz Martha sent me some paper money with that letter." She scrubbed the frying pan hard with the brush, and my heart began to race. "You use it."

"You know I haven't seen her since that summer," I said. "I...I don't even think I'd recognize her."

Martha was now 18 years old; she was 11 when I last saw her. After I'd agreed to stay on the Banks with him, Ben had accompanied me back to the cottage, and standing on the same porch where I'd taught him how to read and write, we'd told mama and daddy our news. Face blazing red with whiskey and heat, Daddy had heard us out, told me I was no longer his daughter, and stomped back into the house. Mama had held my face with firm hands before she too turned to pull back the screened door. Martha and

Charlie had poked their heads out of the bedroom window soon after that, and I'd kissed them both on wet cheeks and told them I'd seen them soon.

But that had turned out to be a lie that they had never forgiven me for.

"You always know your sister," Asha said. "Time don't change blood."

Married to Ben and cast from my family, I'd let the importance of my blood ties fade. But now Ben's betrayal leaped into my mind, calling out the futility of my forgetfulness. Last night I'd waited there on a different porch for him, waited for him to turn to me, hoped it would only be a matter of time before he felt the force that drew us together and turned to find me at the window.

The day after Christmas found me on the bow of a passage schooner, bound from Roanoke Island to Edenton and points beyond. I wore my old wool coat, but the wind still froze me through. I stared straight ahead of me, forcing my eyes wide in the face of it.

In my earnestness to forget Ben, memories of a different sort surfaced, and I recalled the trip from Edenton to Nags Head all those years ago, images of Charlie and Martha, scampering up and down the decks, and Hannah and Asha, mama and daddy, the way we'd all been. I'd been so excited to travel on the ferry boat, to leave Edenton behind. I'd no idea it would take so long to come back again.

I'd never felt homesick, unless I thought of Uncle Jack. Then I'd mourn the tobacco fields, the smell of the barn, tall trees and fresh dirt. And as my mind reached for the mainland, a feeling of homecoming rushed over me, surprising me with its force.

I made my way to the stern of the schooner and saw the very edge of the Outer Banks, a blurred gray line at first and then nothing at all, just a dark blue smudge. I let out my breath, then faced the setting sun once more. I'd been gone from civilization too long, isolated on a tiny island with few good friends and a man grown unfamiliar.

I thought, *I'm going home now.* But I wasn't sure of the truth of it. For the past seven years, the Outer Banks had become my home, the house where I lived with Ben, the school, and even Asha's house. But perhaps it wasn't. Perhaps the Outer Banks was only a resting point, a shoal in unknown waters.

CHAPTER TWELVE

DECEMBER 24, 1875
BENJAMIN WHIMBLE

There is no folly of the beast of the earth which is not infinitely outdone by the madness of man.

–ISHMAEL, MOBY-DICK

NO ONE SAID A WORD TO ME WHEN I CAME IN FROM THE party sometime before midnight. Captain Gale, Lewis and Jerry drank whiskey and played poker at the table, and I took from the queer looks on their faces concern over their cards.

I climbed the stairs, too tired to play a hand. My patrol shift wasn't until 4:00 in the morning and I planned to sleep off the liquor I'd drunk at the party.

I sat on my cot to take my boots off in the dark bedroom. But halfway through the first boot I felt something hard under my rump. I moved and saw what looked like two books there. I held one up to the moonlight and made it out to be none other than Abby's blue-cloth copy of *Moby-Dick*. The other was our old dictionary.

Abby'd been here, I thought. *For Christmas*. I started to sweating even in the cold of the bedroom. I looked about, wondering if she was hiding somewhere, waiting on me. But the skinny room was empty of life.

I ran down the steps.

"Was my wife here?" I hollered.

They didn't even look up from their game.

"She was," said Jerry.

Captain Gale took a drink from the bottle setting in the middle of the table. "She went looking for you at the party," he said. "Spencer said he gave her and a Negro man directions."

"I never saw her!" I had half a mind to turn that table over, watch the shells fly and land where they might.

Captain Gale nodded once. "She came on back here with some books."

I bent over at the waist and groaned loud. "I was there!"

The men kept at their game, throwing down shells and cards while I stood there in my agony.

"She's gone?"

"Negro and her are sailing south as we speak," said Captain Gale.

I raked my fingernails down my face, didn't feel a thing. "She wasn't planning to wait for me?"

"We offered her a cot in here, next to the stove, but she turned it down."

"She didn't look like she *wanted* to stay," said Lewis.

"What gave you that notion?" I swiped at a bead of sweat running down the side of my head.

"She was all red-eyed," Lewis said. "Sniffling into her hanky and what-not. She walked real calm-like up the stairs and I pointed her to your cot. She left the books and turned to go."

Course, then I knew. She'd seen me and Eliza together, sitting close. *Dear Lord, did I have my arm around her? And Eliza with her head on my shoulder? Us whispering with one another?* She must have seen us through the porch window. She must have jumped to her conclusions, and what jaw-crackers those must have been! I'd never even written Abby that Eliza was up here, much less that I'd a notion to sit with her close on Christmas Eve.

The world fell away from me then, the lifesaving station, the surfmen, the sand and sea.

"You were right, Ben," said Lewis. "She's a bona fide beauty. With a fair amount of grit too, I'll wager. I wouldn't have let that one alone, I was you."

I walked straight out the door then, into the moonless night. I ignored the calls of Lemuel on the lookout tower and started out down the shore like I was walking patrol, though it wasn't yet my shift and I didn't carry flares nor lantern.

Walking, that was all I was good for. Walking and watching, watching and walking. I didn't deserve the wife I had, that was for certain, a wife who'd brought me a forgotten book. The sea knew me for a devil too. It growled nasty next to me, reached out fast paws for my feet to pull me down. It told me the awful truth of the matter, even though I clapped my hands over my ears. *I'd have to come to terms with the ending of things*, it said.

"Shut pan," I said to it. *I could walk all the way back to Nags Head tonight, then sail for Roanoke Island,* my legs itching to turn around south at the notion. But I kept up my northerly motion, for I knew that I couldn't, if I wanted to keep my job. Even Spencer'd asked for a couple days off last week—his wife was powerful sick, with child too—but Captain Gale had said no, he couldn't spare him for longer than a day. He wouldn't spare me neither, just to go make nice with my wife.

I'd just keep walking tonight, no other choice, even though my limbs felt just like peg legs, no feeling to them a-tall. And I wondered on the miracle of it all, how it was that a man could still walk upright in all the chaos, when digging downward like a sand fiddler would have been a much better notion.

I'd likely pass Malachi or Spencer on my journey through the darkness, but I wouldn't speak. I was nothing but the bones of a man now, skins and meat cut off, leaving naught but a skeleton to boil.

The forward march seemed to wind up my brain, even so. Thoughts of Abby mixed with cobwebbed memories of Eliza, of friends long gone, of rusty memories of pap. I had no force over it, like my mind had a notion to kill me with dredging up my old life. I let the thoughts roll through my head, snake through the hidden cracks. Like a shuffling of sticky playing cards, I saw how the people in my life had gotten all mixed up, coming and going willy-nilly. Abby and the lost baby; pap and the Nags Head folks; Eliza and me all over again.

I'd thought I was being friendly with Eliza, no more than that. But the more I mulled it over, the more I saw it wasn't the whole truth. Sitting with her tonight in that parlor, drinking Christmas punch like I didn't have a care in the world, I'd truly felt to be my old self, the Nags Head self, with no high-mindedness, no hopes other than getting a meal in his belly, a good day of work behind him. With a woman to love him for who he was, not for what he could learn and store forever in his mind. I saw that I'd missed that self, the way I used to be before I'd met the Sinclairs.

But I *had* met the Sinclairs, and the doing of it had made me yearn for things I never thought I could have. Reading, and writing, and jobs other than fishing day in and day out. Along with all that came dressing proper, better manners, clean clothes and fingernails. I'd tried hard for her. But I'd lost Abby anyway.

She'd emptied the shelves of her shells, had balled up my letter and left it to rot in the house I'd built, the house she didn't care for. She wanted like the dickens to break away from me and head to that teacher school, I knew.

I stopped my progress and looked out to the dark sea, now so much a habit that I looked at such a sea even in my dreams. Looking for something, all the time losing the one thing that mattered the most to me.

I thought, *I did still have the ambergris*. I could *show* her how much I loved her. I'd firstly buy her a dozen new dresses and new pairs of shoes and gloves and hats and jewels and boxes full of books, all the things I'd never been able to give her. We could buy a big house, with a coal-burning stove, find a bona fide doc to tend her when she got with child again. Our lives wouldn't need be such drudgery, such sadness, after that. We'd have more time to know each other again.

And she'd laugh again, smile her love at me. And I'd touch her, the way I used to when I couldn't keep my hands off her. Even at night, her skin always glowed like the dawn light shone on her. *The sunshine*, I heard a lost memory whisper. I wouldn't even have to tell her how I came about finding the ambergris, about poor Livy Spruel. The way I saw it, it came from the sea, a thing that no man could ever rightly possess. Those fishermen couldn't claim it, any more than I could.

I'd heard tell the Outer Banks Indians of old had believed the gods sent them either good or bad fortune across the waves of water. The white folks who came later surely thought on the same terms. Whatever managed to end up on the sands was theirs for the taking, and whatever got washed away was their own bad fortune, nothing to be done.

Flotsam has always been deemed our rightful property. Bankers walked the shores every day, looking for treasures they could call their own. Bits of shipwrecks were always washing ashore, lending us wood for homes, firewood, boats. Through the years I'd seen Bankers trotting off with crates of bananas, casks of whiskey, soggy sacks of sugar and coffee beans. I'd seen them showing off gold coins, shoes, broken mirrors, strings of pearls, oil paintings, saddles for horses.

Fact, the house where pap and me lived was made mostly of shipwreck wood. Pap used to take a mule and wagon over to the beach every so often and come back with more wood for the house. We'd cut it to measure and nail it up the same day. Most of our dishes, pans and cutlery had washed ashore too.

Yes, sometimes the sea was a giver of gifts. I couldn't help but think the ambergris came from the same generous God.

It wasn't a circumstance to picture a lonesome sperm whale in the dark sea before me. A whale that'd lost all his friends and family on account of the hunting. He'd gone slow as he made one last run up the Banks. And when he finally died, he rid himself of the ambergris, all his love turned to gold inside him.

The ambergris had been meant for me, I figured, *a fellow lost soul.*

I wouldn't think about the Spruel family. It was their bad luck they'd lost it, even Livy'd figured they shouldn't have it. As I stood staring, the tarry dark lay easier on me. I turned south, back toward the station house.

Captain Gale was on lookout, the card game wrapped up. I could feel how tired my body was, but my mind was awake as ever. And I still had to walk the 4:00 a.m. patrol in two hours' time.

I climbed the stairs, but I hardly wanted to set foot in the bedroom, where Abby had stood just a few hours ago. Even so, I made myself pick up *Moby-Dick* again. I thought back to the first day I'd met Abby, and her holding onto this book tight with two white hands. I'd wanted to be able to read it so bad it hurt. I'd wanted to see the workings of her mind, see what she held dear.

But *Moby-Dick* had been out of my reach. She'd said I was still learning how to read, to be patient. She'd played the poem game with me, to help me learn new words, to help me with understanding what was called "analogy."

But after a while, I plum forgot about *Moby-Dick*. Life and its hardships had a way of taking over doings like reading. There didn't seem to be time for anything pleasurable a-tall. I figured I'd wake up an old man someday, life fallen by the wayside, with no hankering for anything but sleeping, no thoughts in my head but those concerning my lowest needs: *I need to piss, I'm thirsty, my nose needs blowing.*

The book's leather cover was frayed round the edges, the lettering chipped here and there. I thumbed the pages, feeling the thickness of them. They gave off a smell of wood smoke and damp, and the thought of reading through such a thing made my shoulders slump. I reckoned the book was more out of my reach than ever, but Abby'd wanted to offer it up to me. Even brought me the dictionary. Left them both on my cot like frankincense and myrrh, in spite of what she'd seen.

I took up the book and dictionary and headed down the stairs. I lit a half-burned candle and sat at the table, where cups coated with liquor still sat. I opened the book and turned to chapter one. I read until the candle guttered out— three chapters worth—then got up to walk my shift.

Christmas Day came and went, a parade of people in and out of the station house. I worked lookout all day, feeling a man sheared partly away by wind and sand. Folks would wave at me every now and then and call up to me, but I couldn't do a thing except nod my head at them. I didn't even come down when Spencer Junior showed up leading Wally on a rope, hitched him up to the cart I'd made and rode down the shore, easy as pie. At night I walked patrol, and no one stopped me. My eyeballs burned as if licked by flames.

With night patrol done, I sat up the rest of the night reading *Moby-Dick*. But the looking up of words I didn't know in the dictionary took more time and effort than the reading. After I'd read to chapter 10, I dug up my pen and ink and paper and began a letter to Abby. I wrote on and on and used up five sheets of my paper, front and back. I asked her questions and made comment on everything I found worthy of mention, which was right much for so early on in the book.

And when I put down the pen, I felt I'd really been talking to her. To me, it was a feeling better than the fullness of a belly, better than the act of love, better than sunshine on a cold day.

I rubbed some dried up salt from my eyes and slept at the table, my forehead pressed against the letter.

Day after the new year arrived, the men talked me into going to church service. They opined it would put me in a better frame of mind. They said their younguns were all afeared of me, on account of the rangy look on my face. And it seemed they were right, for when I said hello to Jessie and Perry, they grabbed their mama's skirt and held it to their faces.

But even when I'd shaved, dressed in clean clothes, shined my boots and slicked my hair with pomatum, the younguns scrambled for the wagon at the sight of me. The men walked to church service before and behind me and kept their voices low.

There was a boodle of mules, donkeys and horses hitched up outside the widow's house when we got there. I recognized one buggy to be Captain Burris's, and sure enough, when we went inside the house, I saw all of the lighthouse families standing together, even the clerk of the station, H. T. Halstead, and J. W. Lewis, the superintendent of construction. All were bedecked in suit coats.

When I shook hands with Captain Burris, his wife took one look at me and said, "Are you feeling poorly?"

I tried to grin, but the movement stretched my dry lips to the cracking point. "Just a bit tired. You all know how it goes. Night shifts and all."

I licked my lips and tasted blood.

"Least your wife is here to take care of you," she said.

My face flamed at mention of Abby, and I reached for my hanky in my britches pocket. "I don't take your meaning."

Mr. and Mrs. Burris looked to one another.

"Your wife," she said, and pointed out a person in the crowd. My heart hammered hard and I turned to see Eliza making her way through the crowd.

"That *ain't* my wife, for God's sakes!" At the looks on their faces I softened my voice up. "My wife lives down on Roanoke Island at present."

"No," said Mrs. Burris. She shook her head and smiled at me like I was nothing but a simpleton who didn't even know his own wife.

"We're real good friends," said Eliza, and patted my shoulder. "Who needs marriage anyhow?"

The Burrisses stared wide at the both of us, Mrs. Burris's mouth working silent, trying to find some words.

"Heavens me," she got out, and they both worked hard at putting some distance between us.

I looked to Eliza. "She thought we were married."

Eliza shrugged. "We do match up."

I wiped my face down hard with the hanky. "What are you doing here, Eliza?"

"You had such good things to say about church service I thought I'd come see it for myself," she said. "Course, Iola wouldn't come with me. Used up all her praying on Amos."

The room spun about me, hats and bonnets a-tilt.

"You alright?" she asked, her eyes gone squinty. "You don't look yourself."

I figured I should tell her about Abby and what she saw Christmas Eve. But it wasn't Eliza's fault I'd wrapped an arm about her and talked into her ear with a mouth full of punch. I couldn't burden her with the weight of my marriage anymore.

Reverend Washburn started up then, and his voice stilled tongues better than a slap in the face. All of the Christmas sermons must have sapped his capacity for kindness, for the day's sermon seemed written only to tell us of our likely failures on Judgment Day. Younguns hid in their mama's skirts, and men bowed their heads as they would on the deck of ship heading into a gale.

Finally his tone lightened and folks raised their heads a couple of notches. "I've taken great satisfaction in seeing the lighthouse construction completed," he said. Mr. and Mrs. Burris and all the lighthouse folks bowed and bobbed.

"A light in the darkness is most welcome, a symbol of the Lord's watchful eye. A symbol of safety, and yet of warning," he said. "A warning to be vigilant, for sinfulness comes upon us as quickly as a storm, capsizing the mightiest wills and thrashing the most devout in waves of wantonness."

Mrs. Burris turned to eye us.

"I am thankful for the lifesaving station as well," he said, and Eliza gave my cheek a pat. "Brave men fighting for the lives of God's own children, at peril on the sea. In the name of the Lord, our own savior, I thank you indeed."

He put his hands atop the nearby children's wide-eyed heads. "Such a community we now have. And today, we can *all* take part in Captain Burris's gift—dozens of snow geese that have struck the glass panes of the lighthouse chamber and fallen senseless to the gallery. Blinded by the light of the Lord."

All the folks laughed. "Please help yourselves from God's bounty in the barrel by the door."

Younguns rushed to leave the house, and mamas followed in their wakes, geese in hand. It was a surprise to see blue sky and sunshine.

Eliza trailed me out the door and along to the hitching post.

"What a grand start to the day," she huffed. "Now we can all go drown ourselves and save the Lord his trouble. How can you stand going to such a ass-tearing every Sunday?"

"I don't go every Sunday."

She sucked her tongue. "I'm amazed the man can pack the parlor like he does."

My belly growled its answer, so loud that a horse rolled an eye to me.

"You eat this morning?"

I shook my head.

"So that's what's got you down today." She rolled her eyes. "Bunch of men, up all hours. No wonder you all look so mangy."

She reached out and ran a finger down my jaw bone, and I turned quick away. "You've lost weight."

She hollered out to Captain Gale, walking back to the station with Spencer and Lemuel, their families already gone on the wagon with Captain Burris's geese.

"You need help with cooking and cleaning out there?"

They stopped in their tracks and came walking back to us, faces lit up with notions of cooked food.

"I can come cook and clean up a little for you every now and then, now that the Yanks are gone."

"That's kind of you to offer," Captain Gale said. "But we couldn't pay you."

"The men pay me plenty. I want to help you all."

Spencer started to shaking his head. "It wouldn't be proper."

"And why's that?" she asked.

"You know, a unmarried woman such as yourself," he said. "The wives wouldn't care for it. You catch my meaning."

"Well then," said Eliza. She wasn't used to being told no. "You can't stop me from bringing food *to* you though."

"I reckon not," said Captain Gale, his hunger still looming in his sunken eyes. Spencer rumbled his throat but said nothing.

"Good," she said. "I'll see you all tomorrow. Better have yourselves a appetite."

She winked at me as she mounted the horse and drew up the reins. A steaming trail of horse shit followed them away.

The next few days, all I did was write to Abby and read *Moby-Dick*, though each word was like a boot step through quicksand, each page like a day of fishing in the summer sun with nary a bite on the line. I read any chance I could get between drilling and lookout and patrols. Sleep was rare, and any time I put my head down to rest, my mind turned over words from the book.

Melville had himself a hankering for words of all kinds. Especially long words that most folks—folks other than Abby that is—never would care to know. Every few words read and I'd have to look a doozy up in the dictionary. Then he lined all the words up into the longest sentences I ever had the misfortune to read. They just went on and on and on like a long snake a-slithering, so that by the time I got to the end of one sentence I'd have to go clear back to the starting point to see if I could figure out what he'd meant by the ending of it.

The men were all right curious about my book, and every so often they'd come up on me reading at the table and pick up *Moby-Dick* and flip the pages about, pretend to throw it out the door. They looked up swear words and worse in the dictionary. They never made mention of my letters, but I reckon they knew who I was writing to.

Eliza was good as her word. She came by that Monday afternoon with wildfowl and fig stew for our supper. As the stew warmed on the stove in the cook house, she sat down close to me at the table. I ran my finger down the left side of the dictionary, trying to find the word *somnambulistic*.

"You gonna tell me what you're reading at?" She was so close I could smell figs on her fingers.

I showed her the cover of the book, still looking for the word. *Somatic, somber, somebody…*

She looked at the words, grinned when she saw she could read them. "What's a Moby Dick?"

"A whale."

"This clunker of a book is about *one whale?*"

I shook my head. "No, it's about the hunt for a white whale by a crazy sea captain named Ahab, written by a sailor called Ishmael."

I marked *somnambulistic* with my finger.

"That sounds god-awful," she said. "You like it?"

"I do."

She pulled the dictionary toward her, and my finger slipped its place. "What's this big old thing?" she scoffed. "You could kill a body with this."

"It's a dictionary," I said. "Book with all the words ever made up and their meanings."

She whistled. "What kinds of words you want to know?"

"I was just looking up *somnambulistic*, 'til you pulled the dictionary from me." I pulled it back to me again. *I should tell her to go*, I thought. *Starving would be better than seeing Eliza now.*

"Why in tarnation you want to know that tongue-flipper of a word?"

"It's used in the book, see," I said. "*Therefore, the tormented spirit that glared out of the bodily eyes, when what seemed Ahab rushed from his room, was for the time but a vacated thing, a formless* somnambulistic *being, a ray of living light, to be sure, but without an object to colour, and therefore a blankness in itself.*"

"I didn't get one word of that."

Eliza reached for the paper I'd been writing on, but I quick slapped my hand down on top, almost ripping it.

"That a letter?"

I squared the pages of the letter against the table. There were about five or six sheets written already, heavy with dried ink.

"You writing to her."

"I am."

She chewed her thumbnail hard. "You got that much to say to her?"

"I'm writing about the book."

"*The book*? Why?"

"It's hard to say."

She got up then and went to tend to the stew in the cook house. When she came back, she said, "Things bad enough you have to write about a book?"

I chewed my tongue 'til it hurt. "I see how you'd think that."

I started plowing hard through the field of Melville's words, and Eliza just stood there and watched so that I mauled the same long sentence over and over again.

"Recall that coon hunt? The one with the tree?" she asked.

I looked up agitated, and thought for a bit. Then I nodded. We'd hunted coon many a time in Nags Head Woods, but the time of which she spoke still lived high in my mind, though we hadn't been more than 10 years of age. Eliza never cared for coon hunting as much as me. She had a heart for the critters with fur. And coons, well, they were her very favorite.

Born fighters, she called them. She only hunted them to please me.

This particular coon hunt had us running after Eliza's hound dog and a coon in the dark woods. I'd tripped over a tree root and snuffed out my pine knot. But the hound sounded out ahead of us and we soon found him looking up a big oak tree. But we couldn't see a thing up there to shoot.

By then the dog had caught the scent of another coon and was straining to go, so we let him loose. He ran off and disappeared for a good while, and me and Eliza ran and ran and ran seemed like all night, a old vanilla bottle filled with powder swinging wild on a string about my neck and my pockets full of caps a-clinking. We changed course when we heard the hound sound out, and we ran up, not trusting our eyes.

"This is the same derned tree we started at," I'd said. I had scratches and bruises all over, and my hands were numb from cold. "We done ran in a circle."

Eliza started hee-hawing, until I started a fire with some brushwood. In the light we saw about ten raccoons up in the tree. With my old single-barrel muzzle loader I shot every one of 'em down, some of them still spitting and clawing. Eliza closed her eyes and whimpered. Even the dog stayed away from the ruckus. But it had been a record coon kill for us, and I'd thrown my arms about her and kissed her on the mouth for the very first time. I'd thought that in the light of the fire, in those dark woods, I'd never seen such a pretty girl in my life.

And there she stood before me now, older and taller and wiser too. Sometimes I couldn't rightly believe what I'd done to her, leaving her like that for Abby. Seemed like something only a wicked person would do, a man with no hope on Judgment Day. She sat there tittering about the coon hunt.

"You got a soft heart underneath that hard shell, Eliza Dickens," I said. "You'll find you a man yet."

"Oh, I ain't worried."

And I turned back to *Moby-Dick* as Eliza got up to serve the stew.

The night found me walking patrol once more. Maybe it was the food, but my legs stretched along strong as ever. I would have thought I'd have fallen down in the dunes by now, my chest broke open from a busted heart. But I kept at it, much as I did with the reading of *Moby-Dick*, though the meaning of it all was senseless.

"Howdy-ho, Ben," said a stranger's voice up ahead, and I about jumped from my skin. Then I heard more voices, all kinds, even a woman's.

I stood there looking about, my eyes about to pop from their sockets in searching.

"We been waiting on you," said the first voice.

I stepped slow to the sound, swinging the lantern out in front of me to guide my way.

"We ain't gonna bite," said the voice. "Come on close."

Took me a while to make out a bunch of folks sitting along the edge of the dunes. When I got close enough, I saw it was the Spruel family, white faces burning in the light of their own little lamp. Jonas sat in the midst of them.

"What are you up to now?" I said.

"We're back like bad pennies" he said. "Can't be rid of us."

"We ain't going nowhere," said a young woman. "Show him your surprise, brother."

Jonas pulled something from the sand beside him. "This here is Livy's knife, the one he used for gutting. You know the one."

He wiped the sand off on his britches, then held the blade up to his face to gaze upon it. "Mama wanted me to bury it with him, but I just couldn't do it. He traded hard for this knife. I figured he'd want me to keep it, put it to good use."

"Good use, he says," cackled a man.

The scab on my neck started to itch beneath the wool of my scarf, but I wouldn't scratch at it.

"Don't you all have anything better to do than sit here in the dark, waiting to bother the man who tried to save your boy?"

"Man who let him die, more like," cried a woman. "Damn lot of good you surfmen do, waste of money on the likes of you!"

"Now, now, mama. Settle down. I'm getting at the truth here, like we talked about," said Jonas.

He was quiet for a bit, hand stroking the handle of the knife. "Now Ben, you know we've been all over this beach with nets and shovels for weeks, nary a barrel to be found. We figured we'd just ask *you*—where is it at?"

"I haven't a notion," I said. "And I can't stay here mulling it all over with you. I've got to keep up with my patrol."

I turned to keep walking northward, but I soon felt a giant hand grab the back of my neck. Spruels hollered wild from the dunes. I swung the lantern, but Jonas dodged it and grabbed my coat to pull me close.

"You're full of gum," he grunted.

I pulled my coat from his grasp, and we now stood face to neck. I smelled chewing tobacco and liquor on his breath.

"Why's that?"

"Cut rope. Busted struts. And your eyes," he said, taking two of his long fingers and pointing them at my face. "You are one shitty liar."

I started walking again, but I heard boot steps in the sand beside me. Shadows of noisy Spruels followed along beside us; I wondered which one now held Livy's knife.

"You planning on selling it? You got to go up to Yankee land for that," he said. "New York, Boston, most like. Get the most money up there."

I started to walk even faster, but he kept pace with me easy.

"We could split it."

All I saw was Abby in front of me, a new kind of life that wrapped its arms about us.

"Half of nothing is nothing," I said.

And before I could step away from him, I felt his fist pop the side of my head. I stepped back a few steps, lantern swinging, and the cold wash swept over the bottoms of my legs. In the rocking light I saw his arm reach through the air, so I backed into the waves and tried to run. I heard him splashing after me, and soon he pushed me forward into the water, my grip on the lantern lost.

He kept his hand on the back of my head, and icy salt water rushed into my mouth and nose. I heard all of the Spruels hollering at me from under the water. I ripped my hair from his fingers and took a deep breath before he pushed me under again and just about sat on top of me. I pushed with my back, my legs, my arms, but he had me pinned good. My air was going fast, coming out in warm bubbles around my face, and still he held my head. He was strong, a fisherman's strength. He was fixing to drown me over that barrel, and I was fixing to let him.

But just when I thought it was over, he let up on me and pulled me up by the back of my coat. I could hardly stand in the rocky waves. I bent over and coughed salt water back into the ocean.

"We ain't splitting nothing with you now," he said.

Then he sloshed back to the sand to speak to his kin. They didn't want to leave me, and in my mind I saw the knife flashing in a white, freckled hand, closing in on my throat, finishing the job that Livy had started.

But Jonas said, "Why do I always have to be the man talking sense? That barrel is as good as gone if we kill him tonight."

I looked about in the wash for the lantern for a time before giving it up for gone. Then I stumbled from the sea up to the dunes and stretched myself out. The sand felt warm to me, cold as I was. I knew I needed to get up and head back to the station house. But I couldn't make myself move. I heard the Spruels carrying on, somewhere far off.

I laughed out loud, or least I thought I did. I was never giving them that barrel.

CHAPTER THIRTEEN

DECEMBER 27, 1875
ABIGAIL WHIMBLE

Round the world! There is much in that sound to inspire proud feelings; but whereto does all that circumnavigation conduct? Only through numberless perils to the very point whence we started, where those that we left behind secure, were all the time before us.

–*ISHMAEL*, **MOBY-DICK**

IT WASN'T A LONG COACH RIDE FROM THE PORT TO THE house on Eden Street, one of the few streets in the city with views of Edenton Bay. The large Newman house was two stories of pristine white clapboard and black shutters, bracketed by magnolia and crepe myrtle trees and surrounded by shrubs and gardens.

Hector had done well for himself, I thought, with no surprise.

The coachman helped me out of the carriage and followed me with my carpetbag. At the front door he set the bag next to me and straightened up.

"You kin to the doc?"

"I am." *I could have been his wife once*, I thought. "My sister is his wife."

I faced the white door and its shiny brass knocker.

"Well, ain't that something. I'll tell you, Doc Junior fixed my wife up some months back. Such nastiness coming from her eyes, couldn't hardly see. The stuff he gave her smell like a tail end of a hoss."

He pinched his nose and waved his hands about his face. "But it clear her right up and she say she see better'n she ever did."

"He's quite a miracle worker."

The man clapped his hands and hooted. "Everybody love Doc Junior."

I smiled at the nickname, suspecting that Hector detested it. I was still grinning slyly when the door flew open, revealing my sister Martha to me for the first time in seven years. Her face at first showed surprise, but as she stared from me to the coachman, it slowly sank downward into dismay.

I cleared my face of its prior amusement. "Hello, sister."

She had grown into a beautiful woman, tall, with dark red hair like mine and large green eyes, chinacup features. I wanted to reach out and embrace her, but her hands clutched each other tightly in front of her.

"Abigail," she said.

"I know you were expecting Asha," I said. "But she thought…she suggested I come in her stead."

The coachman tipped his hat to Martha and brought the carpetbag inside.

Martha didn't move from the doorway, so the Negro woman standing in the foyer gently took my elbow and guided me inside. Yet I nearly tripped over the threshold because I couldn't take my eyes from my sister, her long neck, the silk-covered buttons down the back of her bustled green silk dress. I breathed in the scent of floor polish and fresh laundry, and I detected another smell, with notes both sweet and sour: *the baby.*

The woman took my coat and hat and gloves, eyes flicking from me to Martha. "I'll fix you ladies some tea."

Yet in the drawing room, Martha and I stood behind opposite chairs, staring at the fire in the hearth before us. My old shoes sank into the thick rug that covered the floor, and in the silence I saw how tightly she gripped the back of the chair.

"I'm so happy for you, Martha," I said. "Your home is lovely. And you're so beautiful. And now… there's my niece."

Her eyes flashed. "Don't call her that." She shook her head. "She is your nothing. You were cast out from this family."

She spoke so loudly that the woman appeared in the doorway. "Miz Newman?" she ventured.

"The tea, Hettie," said Martha, and Hettie withdrew once again.

I turned to the hearth, prickling with humiliation. I saw now that we'd not be taking the tea that Hettie was now preparing. I saw that we would stand here in this room and argue until my bag was fetched again. I'd be seeing that coachman again sooner than I thought. It was no more than I deserved.

Even an oil portrait of a handsomely attired man with fire-bright hair gazed down at me in accusation. I knew it to be the likeness of our planter grandfather, John Withersham Sinclair.

"The painting from Sinclair House," I said.

"Grandfather John," Martha said, her words clipped. "Daddy sold all of the family portraits before he sold the plantation. But Hector bought them back for me. Most are in the dining room."

"I'm glad."

I heard the ticking of a grandfather clock in the silence, the creaking of the upstairs floorboards.

She sighed impatiently. "I can't imagine what you possibly have to say to me that will make any difference at all in my opinion of you."

"I miss you," I blurted. "And Charlie. Every day."

Her eyelids and lips shrunk into slashes. "You should never have abandoned us."

I shook my head at the word *abandoned*. "I wrote you and Charlie letters every week. Until you stopped writing back."

"Letters?" she spat. "Do you know what we were forced to endure during the years you were gone? Writing to you about it would have been a great waste of ink."

"Was it daddy?"

For a long time I'd worried about my brother and sister, living in a house with such a madman. And news was hard to come by. Daddy had forbidden any contact with me, so mama had instructed me, in one of her own illicit letters, to send all of my correspondence to Mr. Whitney at the book shop. But mama never mentioned daddy once.

After mama's death, Martha had continued to pick up my letters at the bookshop, but at some point in the year following mama's death, she'd stopped responding to me. Asha kept her up to date on my life, but not even the loss of my babies had convinced her to write or visit me.

"He tried his best," she said.

I doubted I could ever tell Martha the truth about him. "Did he?"

She breathed hard through her nose, as if exerting herself mightily. "Look at you. Are you so poor that you can't even afford to feed or clothe yourself?"

I looked at my hands, expecting to see delicate, white appendages in such a fine room, but instead saw brown and calloused mitts. "Yes," I admitted. "We are quite poor."

She followed my gaze. "Your skin," she said. "It's brown as a nut."

"It can't be helped."

"It was a bad decision you made, staying there," she said. "You weren't raised to be a fisherman's wife."

I remembered the syrup of feelings that had swirled inside me that day I'd decided to stay in Nags Head, my anger at daddy, my gratefulness to mama, my admiration for Asha, my love for Ben. I'd often thought afterward that I'd made the decision to stay too hastily.

"I *had* to stay."

She snorted at me. "You didn't have to do anything."

"It was a choice that *I* made," I said. "If I chose poverty over security, then it was my own doing."

"I still don't understand."

"I loved him, Martha."

She looked to me then, likely intrigued by the usage of the past tense, but the look of curiosity in her face reminded me of how fond of him she'd been, how that first summer she'd written Ben a love letter in cursive, only to find out later that he couldn't read it.

Hettie entered the room with a silver tray bearing a pot of tea, two cups, scones and fine white napkins. When she left, Martha poured the steaming tea into two cups. At last she seated herself, careful not to sit directly on her bustle.

"I prayed for you and Ben to suffer. Not at first. At first, I was truly happy for you both. I'd wanted to come to the wedding. But when mama died, and the baby with her, and when daddy sold the plantation, well, I didn't think what you'd done was romantic any longer. I—we—needed you here with us. We lived in a small house on the outskirts of the city, the four of us. We had a new mammy by then, did you know, her name was Mercy. But daddy drank and gambled the money away, and we were forced to let Mercy go. It was just me—no tutor, no maid. Until Hector came along."

She smiled into her tea as she sipped.

"He courted me quite extravagantly," she said. "Of course, he didn't stay for a month at the Nags Head Hotel and compete with a local fisherman for my hand. But he did shower me with gifts of all kinds and squire me—unescorted, I might add—to many a ball and concert and theater party. They were the best days of my life."

Asha had told me that Hector had begun sniffing around the little house after his wife had died during childbirth. They'd married after only four months of courtship in our own St. Paul's church, and daddy sold the house and moved to Texas with Charlie soon afterward.

"You should know, Abigail. I've known just as much sorrow and disappointment as you. *I* tended mama during her pregnancy, *I* watched as she died, even as my baby sister had already perished. *I* raised Charlie through most of his childhood. *I* suffered as our good family name was shamed by an eldest daughter's rebelliousness. We all were forced to make sacrifices for your selfishness."

My entire body seemed to ignite, as if I'd stepped right into the hearth. "But Hector, of all men..." I said. "Surely there were others."

"How dare you?" she hollered. She flung out her arm at the grand furnishings around us. "Hector is a good man, but you never took the time to discover it for yourself."

I shook my head. "Mama and daddy arranged the marriage. They never thought to ask me my own feelings on the matter."

"Poor Abigail, encouraged to marry a doctor," she scoffed. "Hector knew of my struggle, and wanted to ease my burdens. He is a good provider, which is much more than I can say for Ben. He wants to fill this house with our children."

"That's...wonderful," I said around a newly formed lump in my throat. "You've made a good start."

Her eyes found my belly for the slightest instant, then flicked away. We sat in a taut silence then, filled with Hettie's kitchen noises. I knew the visit had come to an end.

"I'd like to see her," I said. "Before I go."

I gulped the rest of my tea and stood up. "Asha won't be satisfied unless I bring back a good description of her."

"She also would not approve if I didn't at least offer you lodging for the night," she said, standing as well. "Take supper with us tonight, and leave on the morrow."

Her downcast eyes and sour tone betrayed the good intentions of her words.

"Sarah Capeheart Newman?"

"After Hector's mother." Hector's mother was an Edenton Civil War heroine; even though her husband was away at war, serving as an army surgeon, she'd turned their large home into a hospital of sorts and tended to wounded Confederate soldiers, with the help of just a few untrained women. She'd died before the war ended from an illness she'd contracted from one of the men, but Edenton would never forget her and her sacrifice.

"It's a good name," I said.

The rest of the afternoon I spent in the guest bed-room, sitting at the writing desk by a window and lis-tening to the cries of the baby and the soothing voice of the nurse, mingling occasionally with Martha's ministrations.

I longed to tip-toe down the hallway to peek into the nursery, but I hadn't been invited. I contented myself with listening to her cries. Martha might have disagreed with me, but I thought I'd never heard any-thing more joyful than the cries of a hungry baby. Life sang in her veins and lengthened her bones, even as I sat here.

The nurse began a lullaby, and the familiar mel-ancholy stole upon me then. I rose from the chair and paced—from brass bed to mahogany wardrobe to cherry chest of drawers, and then back to the writ-ing desk and silk-cushioned writing chair. I reached across the bed to trace my finger over the "N" of the delicately monogrammed bolster cover. I bent to smell the beeswax candle in the brass candlestick on the bedside table.

I recalled the having of such fine things, how it felt to open a drawer to extract silk and linen, to sit on a padded chair. I'd grown accustomed to the flattened feather tick and thinning quilts and blan-kets, the hard schoolhouse chair that Ben had made, bare walls, my ragged clothing, so that the sight of Martha's guest room was quite ostentatious.

I sat warily on the chair once more and picked up the pen on the desk. I figured I should use my time to write a letter to Asha, but I hardly knew what to write, other than I had arrived safely and had been offered a one-night's stay.

Instead, I lay down on the feather bed, rested my head on the bolster pillow and tumbled into sleep. When I woke to the sound of the baby wailing, the late afternoon sent gold-tipped shadows through the clean window panes. I smelled baking bread and roasted meat, heavy fare that I feared might be too much for my deprived belly.

I splashed some cold water from the ewer onto my face, then re-pinned my hair. But there was nothing I could do about my dress except run my hands down the length of it to smooth out the wrinkles.

I was descending the stairs for supper when the front door opened and Hector walked in. He jumped when he saw me, likely expecting Martha on the stairway but instead finding a familiar stranger. With the door still ajar, he stared at me while I stood frozen on the stairway, my hand on the rail. He looked just as he did the last time I'd seen him. Seven years had washed off him like water on oilskin.

Then he started to chuckle. "Good Lord, Abigail, I took you for the washer woman," he said. He placed his doctor's bag on the table and hung his fine overcoat on the stand. "Martha was expecting a visit from Asha. I imagine she's rather disappointed."

He sauntered into the drawing room, so I descended the remaining stairs and followed him. He'd poured himself a drink and seated himself on the sofa, facing the hearth.

"How are you, brother?" I said to the back of his head.

"Better than you, from the looks of it," he said, taking several kitten-sips in a row, the way he used to.

I walked around to face him, but he didn't get up.

"Congratulations on the birth of your daughter," I said, seating myself in the chair. "And on your marriage."

He flashed a white smile. "We do have much to be thankful for," he said. "My, my, you should have seen the wedding."

"I wasn't invited."

"So you weren't," he said, nodding.

He gazed openly at me then. "I do believe I got the better of the Sinclair sisters, in the end."

"I couldn't dispute the fact."

"I don't imagine you could. And my Martha is truly lovely," he said. "Tell me, does your husband *insist* you look like a fishwife? Or did it just happen over time?"

I opened my mouth to speak, but my wits had fled. I couldn't speak about Ben. I didn't know what he liked or didn't like any more.

"Don't be rude to our guest, my darling," said Martha, standing in the doorway. She walked over to Hector, her green dress whispering over the thick rug.

"I was only jesting with her," said Hector, taking Martha's hand and kissing it.

"Come," said Martha, shadows beneath her eyes prominent on her white skin. "Supper should be nearly ready."

But when faced with the spread of food on the dining table, I found I had no appetite at all. Following grace, Hector served me a giant portion of venison, a large heap of hominy and three biscuits on a plate of fine china.

"It's called *food*, Abigail."

I bit the insides of my cheeks. "Thank you."

"I must say, thought never to see you again," he said, spooning some hominy onto his plate. "I suppose there was always the chance that we'd run into you in Nags Head, if we'd perchance ventured there for a holiday. But we'd never go there now. The place has really declined since its heyday, I've heard."

"Has it?" I asked, pushing some meat around in the sauce with a heavy fork.

"It's not frequented nearly so much as it was by *our* acquaintances. The mountains and the hot springs are the fashion now."

"I live on Roanoke Island, so I couldn't really say."

"No more houses going up by the sea, I gather," he said. "Your father was convinced it was a brilliant idea. And who was I to contradict him? But I always thought a house by the ocean was the height of foolishness. And I see I was right in the end."

Hector began to tell a story about one of the day's patients, a dock laborer who'd grown bloody, crusty patches of skin on his face from too much time in the sun.

"There's nothing I can do in those kinds of cases but cut the offending skin off and hope the disease doesn't appear again." He sliced an imaginary scalpel across the back of hand. "I scolded him for waiting so long to visit a doctor. I tell you, the man left my office looking as if a bobcat attacked him."

Martha closed her eyes tightly and said, "Darling, not at the table."

He shrugged and smiled at Martha. "I apologize, darling," he said. "I thought your sister might want to hear that particular story. That fair skin and that island sun…"

Martha picked up her fork, but neglected to apply it to the untouched food on her plate.

"Asha wrote to me of a man who recently paid a visit to the school," Martha said, without looking at me. "She said he is writing a book on integrated schools?"

"Yes," I said. My shoulders relaxed slightly, recalling Mr. Wharton's friendly face. "He represents the Peabody Foundation. He told me of a normal school in Nashville. He thought I should…pay it a visit."

"Oh. Whatever for?" asked Martha.

He called my teaching 'revolutionary', I thought. "He offered me a job as an assistant professor."

Martha at last turned to face me, and Hector snorted. "Women faculty! The man must be a Yankee," he said. "With their notions of higher education for women and Negroes. Next you know, they'll be advocating for the education of horses."

"If I didn't know you better, I'd take offense to that," I said.

Hector just shrugged. "Women should be in the home."

"Indeed," said Martha. She then told Hector stories of her day with Sarah, and I thought I'd never seen Hector look so interested in a topic other than himself. She'd left out the thornier details of the baby's feedings and fussing, of course. Sarah didn't make an appearance during supper, though I could hear her crying upstairs.

I went to bed thinking Martha had changed her mind about allowing me to see her. I was almost asleep when I saw Martha, standing in a white night-dress in the darkened doorway. She held Sarah in her arms, blankets trailing to her knees.

I sat up, and she stepped over to the bed and handed the baby to me without a word. I could hardly see Sarah's face, it was so smudged with shadows, but as my eyes adjusted a bit, I made out dark hair beneath her cap and dark eyebrows and lashes. Her fair skin glowed in the moonlight.

"She's so beautiful," I whispered.

"She is." She sat down on the edge of the bed next to me, and we both gazed at the slumbering Sarah. She smelled like a ripe melon and was as heavy as a pan of biscuit dough.

"Everyone says she favors Hector," said Martha, running a finger over a tiny eyebrow. "But I think she has the Sinclair fire in her belly."

"God help her."

She smiled. "Daddy always appreciated your spirit."

"He disowned me. He despised my spirit, through and through."

She danced her finger from the eyebrow to an ear. "For a while, he did. But around the time that mama died, he started to speak of you again."

"Oh?" I found it hard to believe.

"There was a certain…respect he had for you. Your stubbornness, your independence. I think he thought you'd come crawling back to him someday, apologizing for your behavior."

"I never would."

The baby stirred in her wrappings, and we both quieted, watching her. I willed her to stay asleep; I could have dwelled in the moment for the rest of my days.

"It was sad, what happened to daddy," Martha said after a while. "The debt he'd accumulated during and after the war was impossible for him to shake. Daddy was the last of the lordly planters."

"He was a tyrant."

"Is that how you remember him?" She seemed genuinely puzzled.

I could tell her about daddy now, I thought. "I remember how he was never home," I said instead. "He was always off hunting, or fishing, or traveling. He left Uncle Jack to tend to the plantation more often than not."

"I suppose. I can hardly remember. I can't even recall Uncle Jack very well. I do remember how terribly you took it when he died. Do you still miss him?"

"Of course."

"I don't think daddy ever got over losing him, and losing mama and his dogs and his horses," she said. "And you."

"There I am, right after the dogs and horses."

"He was happy to leave Edenton, in the end. He'd lost touch with many of his friends. He'd become so unhappy, disoriented. Texas is a wonderful place, he tells me in his letters. He bought some land and some cattle, built a house that Charlie swears resembles the Nags Head cottage. He's even dabbling a little in politics. And Charlie is doing well in the local school. He has a good many friends, from the sound of it."

"I'm glad. He was always a bright boy, maybe too much so sometimes." I suddenly yearned for the chance just to see his face again. "Do you have his daguerreotype?"

She shook her head, apology in the gentleness of it.

"I was sorry to hear about the loss of your babies," said Martha, so low I hardly heard her.

I pulled Sarah close to my face, kissed the velvet down of her head.

If that sad and lonely Christmas morning on Leo's skiff was winter, then Sarah Capehart Newman was summer. I clung to her, to her warm and vigorous life; I could hardly bear to hand her back.

CHAPTER FOURTEEN

JANUARY 19, 1876
ELIZA DICKENS

*Heaven have mercy on us all—Presbyterians and Pagans
alike—for we are all somehow dreadfully cracked about
the head, and sadly need mending.*

—ISHMAEL, MOBY-DICK

"TWO WOMEN, WITH A HOME OF THEIR OWN," SAID IOLA.
"I still can't feature it."

"The house's for the caretaker," I said for the
hundredth time.

"And that's you."

"I know that." I dipped a crust of cornbread into
a jar of blackberry preserves.

"And the caretaker's best friend is the cook and
housekeep," she said. "She's got to have someplace
to stay too."

The news from the Yanks had lifted Iola's spirits tenfold in the last two weeks, so that she talked about how the mourning dress had somehow shrunk on her and it might be time for a new one with some color. But I didn't see Iola living in the caretaker's house with me. I only saw me and Ben there, us and our younguns. Some critters too. We could spend our lives guiding for the men and never have to part from that house.

All a sudden the cabin door flew open. I thought it was the wind done it, but there stood a man, blocking out the sunlight with his body. I saw it was the big fisherman who'd called Ben out for taking the barrel.

Iola sat up straight on her tick and smoothed her long yellow hair, still unpinned.

"There you are," he said to the cabin. He took off his hat, and his red hair sprung out from his head. "I been looking for you."

"You know how to knock?" I got to my feet and fetched up my gun.

"It's just you two here."

He grinned like a cat, though his queer white eyes were jumpy. He stepped right on inside, ducking his head as he came. I saw he'd trimmed his beard and washed since the last time we'd seen him.

"Just what do you think you're doing?"

He shrugged his ox shoulders. "I came for Iola."

"Came for her?" I put the gun to my shoulder.

"I thought we'd go a-sailing." He looked at my gun like it was nothing more than a youngun's toy. "I *should* be mending our busted skiff, but I only have one thought in my head these days. Iola."

He turned his hat about in a circle over his manhood.

"It don't surprise me you have only one thought in your head," I said. "But you don't even *know* Iola here. And she don't know you. What makes you think she's gonna go anywhere with the likes of you?"

He walked to Iola and took her hand in one of his. "You want to? I got me a row boat out there at the docks."

She nodded her head, simple as that, like he'd asked her if she wanted salt in her stew. He pulled her to her feet, and Iola tied her hair up and grabbed her bonnet and coat.

"Just a minute now. How'd you find us?"

"Oh, folks know all about you two ladies. You ain't hard to find a-tall."

Iola tittered, and they walked right on out the door with nary a look back. I put down my gun and walked to the door to watch them go. Iola had her arm in his elbow, looking like a twig hanging onto a big old oak tree for dear life.

The day dripped along slow as cold syrup. I made my way to the clubhouse and cleaned up. I worked a bit in Abner's book but couldn't keep my mind on it. Then I worked in the garden so I could keep a eye to the docks. It was getting dark by the time I locked up and made my way back to the cabin with some pork chops and collard greens I'd cooked up.

The moon was full up when they at last walked in, easy as you please.

"There's supper," I said to Iola.

She took one look at the food, setting cold on the table that Amos had made, and turned away, disgusted. "I'm not hungry."

She handed the plate to the fisherman. "You have it."

"Don't mind if I do." He picked up the chop with his bare hands and ate it standing there 'til he was left with naught but bone. He stepped to the door and tossed it out to the night.

"You raised by wild dogs?" I asked. He wiped his mouth with the back of a greasy hand as an answer.

"Leave Jonas alone," said Iola. "Strong men need their sustenance."

"I don't doubt it," I said. "I'm surprised he stopped at the bone."

He watched me as he scooped collard greens into his mouth with his hand.

I made a face at him. "When you planning on leaving?" I asked. "It's getting late."

He looked over to Iola, and she cocked her chin at me. "I told Jonas he might could sleep in the clubhouse tonight."

"And I'll tell you right now that's a flat-out no."

Iola put her hands on her hips. "He'll have to sail back north a ways, and it's awful cold out."

"That's his own fault, ain't it?"

"You're so uppity these days. You and me use the clubhouse all the time. Abner too, for your learning."

"Yeah, fair's fair," said Jonas. He stepped over and put his great arm around Iola's shoulders.

"You keep out of it. What do you know about a thing?"

"You'd be surprised." He winked down at Iola.

"I doubt that," I said. "I know your kind. You figure you can take the advantage of Iola here, a widow still in mourning who just happens to be the best friend of the caretaker of a empty crack club. Well, the men that pay me wouldn't care for me letting some no-account squatter sleep in their fine abode."

"I could stretch out in here with you gals," he said. "Would you like that better?"

I looked to Iola, hoping to catch her eye, but she only had eyes for Jonas.

"That won't work neither."

He guffawed loud then. "Alright," he said. "I can see when I'm beat. You know, it's a wonder you're not hitched, Elsie. Your nature is sweet as sugar."

"It's Eliza, you oaf. And I'll thank you to keep your opinions to yourself."

I guessed Iola had told him pretty much everything there was to know about us and the change in our fortune. I reckoned this man wouldn't be gone by tomorrow, if ever.

"How's Ben doing these days?"

"You still think he took your all-fired barrel?"

"Oh, he's got it," he said. "And I reckoned *you* might have an ideer of it yourself. Being friends like you are."

I snorted. "I have a clubhouse to run now. I don't have the time to worry over a lost barrel, no matter what's on the inside of it. And if I *did* know where it was, I wouldn't tell the likes of you."

A fit of anger flashed over his face, but he pushed it away.

"Ben is a good man. He'd never take something didn't belong rightly to him. I know that's a trait you might find strange, but it's the truth."

"I don't believe you know him good as you think you do. You know what was in that barrel?"

"This a guessing game now? How am I supposed to know?"

He looked about left and right as if checking for eavesdroppers. "It's full of ambergris. Fifty pounds at the least."

Iola wheezed. But me, well, I saw Ben heading down to Nags Head in *Tessa* with a barrel, trying hard to put any kind of space between us.

"Ain't no man can turn from all that. Not even Ben," said Jonas.

"I want you to leave him alone."

"I might," he said. "For now. But what are you able to do for me?"

I felt as old as my granny. "You see what kind of a man this is?" I asked Iola.

"It's none of my business," she said, folding her arms across her chest. "I told you to keep away from Ben but you wouldn't listen. You're blind to him and his ways, always have been, even when he left you."

Jonas winked at me.

"Fine, you sleep in that clubhouse for *one night*. But not in their beds, you hear me? And don't you touch a thing with those paws of yours."

"I knew you could find it in your heart to help me out."

"One night," I said. "Then you best find your way home."

"We'll see."

"He might need me to walk him over," said Iola, her eyes shifty. "See to it he knows where everything is."

"Yeah, I reckon I'll need some help. Looks dark over there."

"Iola, can we talk?" I asked. "Alone?"

"I'll be waitin'." Jonas walked out the cabin, leaving the door hanging wide. I banged it shut.

"Consarn you, Iola! You're giving him the wrong kind of notions."

"No, I'm not. Now leave us be."

"I won't, neither. Him and his familiar ways. You don't even seem to care that he wants Ben's head on a plate. The man's a beast."

She threw her arms up into the air. "We're just different, you and me, I guess," she said. "I want a man beside me. I'm lonesome!"

"You think I don't want a man beside me too?"

"Seems to me you're happy to pine away for a man you ain't never gonna have. You're gonna be a old maid if you don't start giving other men a chance."

"I *might* have him one day."

Iola rolled her eyes.

"Listen now. Things are bad between him and his wife. He told me so." I counted on my fingers for her. "He's working the surfman job up here. His wife is all set to leave for Nashville for some teaching school. And he put his arm around me Christmas Eve, whispered into my ear and just about kissed me. You can't tell me he ain't thinking there might still be a chance for us."

Iola didn't even grin. "I feel sorry for Abby Whimble, I really do."

I cut my eyes at her. "I thought you were *my* friend, Iola."

"I am. But I know what it's like to have gals sniffing round your man all the time," she said. "I been married before, you know."

"You're like to be hitched *again* afore too long."

"That's the plan."

I cocked my head at her. "You got a plan now?"

She looked down at her belly and rubbed it with both hands. "You guess I had a Jack in the cellar yet?"

And just like that, Iola looked a stranger to me, and I'd known her forever. "No," I breathed. I looked down at her belly but couldn't yet see a lump.

"I figured as much. I ain't put on any weight yet." Her face looked happy and sad both. "It's Amos's baby."

"Oh."

"Took me a while to figure. I wasn't gettin' my monthlies. I just reckoned it was on account of being so down and out."

I went over to hug on her, my mind filled with a hundred different notions. I pictured Iola with her nasty dolly Ermaline, how she carried her around in the crook of her arm all the time and fed her bits of stewed leaves for food. She used to say she couldn't wait to have a baby of her own, that she was gonna name it Ermaline, boy or girl. I pictured her and Amos the day of their hitching, how happy she was when she looked way, way up into Amos's face.

"And you think this fisherman is gonna take care of you and your baby, knowing it for another man's? It's too late for you to act like it's his, if that's what you're about."

"He might favor a youngun," she said. "I got a nose for such men."

"Your nose is broke, if that's the case," I said. "He don't want a baby, Iola. He ain't much more'n a baby his own self."

There was a knock on the door this time. Iola sucked in her belly and went to open it.

"You about done in here?" The man had the gall to sound puckered.

"We sure are," she said, and stole out into the night, not even bothering to take along the dirty plates and cutlery.

I waited all night for Iola to come back to the cabin, but she never did. I slept hardly a wink, thinking on that man with his fish-stink hands all over Iola and Amos's baby.

Next morning I marched myself over to find Iola in the kitchen house in her black mourning dress half buttoned and hair a-tangle.

"Where is he?"

"On one of the beds I made up," she said. "And don't have yourself a conniption fit, neither. Where else was he gonna sleep, the parlor floor?"

"Good enough for the likes of him," I said. "I told him not to sleep in the beds."

Iola's face changed from mad to sweet in one second. "He looks like a little boy when he's asleep. Sweet as pie. You should go peek on him."

I snorted. "I reckon feather beds do take a load off a body. Iola, I can't rightly believe you spent the night with him. Man like that."

She turned to face me then, face ablaze and hot mitt waving in the air. "Don't judge *me*, Eliza Dickens," she said.

She doubled over then and made like she was going to retch, but nothing came out.

"Here, sit yourself down and I'll finish up the food." I took the spoon and the mitt from her and led her to the chair.

"Can't stand the smell of food," she said. "'Specially them eggs."

"You fixed enough," I said. Must have cracked at least a dozen.

"He has a big appetite," she said, and started to titter. At the look on my face, she said, "I like him. And I don't care if you do or not. You ain't the one who's marrying him."

"You already getting hitched?"

"Just a matter of time." She bent over to retch again.

Jonas hung about all day, watching Iola cook and clean without lifting a finger. His laziness soon lay over everything, so that we all sat rocking on the porch when Abner came poling up to the clubhouse docks. He limped up to land, mailbag slung over his shoulder, and Jonas said, "Who's the cripple?"

Iola shushed him. "We've known Abner forever, from growing up in Nags Head. He's the post man out this way. And he's in love with Eliza."

Jonas guffawed. "That'd be a happy coupling if I ever saw one."

I stood quick and shooed Abner into the house.

"Who's he?" he said, cutting his eyes in the direction of the porch.

"Don't ask," I said. "He's got his eye on Iola."

"Oh," he said, breathing out. "I thought mayhaps….it was *you* he was courtin'. You know, on account Iola's in mourning."

"She should be."

He whistled low. "She likes 'em strapping, don't she?"

I shrugged. "Jonas may be big, but his brains are just like a couple of chestnuts rolling round his skull."

At the table I picked up the pen, dipped it in ink and wrote all the words I knew on a piece of paper. I counted 25, my favorites to write being *duck, butter, pup, squash, oak* and *raccoon*. Then we spent the next half hour working through some more pages of the book.

"You been practicing."

"I been pulling some of the books in the library out. Giving 'em a look-see. I don't get very far, but some of the pictures are right good. They got some good ones on wildfowl I look at."

"Mayhaps I could borrow one from you sometime?"

I snorted. "Course I'm not gonna loan you out one of their nice books, you setting on a boat in the weather all day."

Those Yankee books had the look of something good to them, better even than the cabinet full of china. Some folks just didn't cotton to that.

"You're right, Eliza. I shouldn't have thought it." He stood up. "I should get on. Got to head up to the lighthouse docks. Lots of post to hand out."

"I'll pour you some yaupon afore you go. Only take a minute."

"Alright. That's kindly of you, Eliza," he said, like I'd never done him a good deed. I watched him go out the door, heard him start in on the weather with Jonas and Iola.

I pulled the mailbag out from under the table and yanked letters from it. But nary a single one was made out to Ben Whimble.

CHAPTER FIFTEEN

JANUARY 30, 1875
ABIGAIL WHIMBLE

It is not down on any map; true places never are.

–*ISHMAEL*, **MOBY-DICK**

I WAS INVITED TO STAY WITH MARTHA AND HECTOR through January. The days were spent caring for Sarah—rocking, singing, changing, bathing. The amount of laundry that she generated would have possibly flabbergasted even Asha; curdled milk and diaper droppings stained much harder than scuppernong wine, I found. I realized that even with help both in the kitchen and in the nursery, caring for a baby was a desperate undertaking.

Martha and I treated one another cautiously, like new neighbors. Baby Sarah filled the awkward spaces between us, and we lived only in the circle of time that enveloped her, the past and the future irrelevant.

This morning a delivery was made during a particularly difficult hour. Sarah wouldn't stop her fretting, and all of the women in the household were as miserable as my niece. But when Hettie came to the nursery to tell us that a delivery from the seamstress's had been made, Martha jumped up and hurried to the door. When she returned to the nursery, she beckoned me into her dressing room.

She pulled off her spit-up stained dress and stepped into a stiff silk gown. "Help me with the buttons?" she asked me, turning her back to me.

"Maddie Buckley is throwing her annual ball tomorrow evening," she said, turning about for me in the tightly drawn blue-and-gold dress. "Not a thing in my wardrobe fits, so I had to have a new gown made."

"Maddie *Adams* Buckley?" I asked. I hadn't seen Maddie since 1868, when we'd dined with her family at the Nags Head Hotel. I'd stormed away from the dining table in anger, and Maddie had grinned at my spectacle. I'd heard bits and pieces about her from Martha's early letters, so I knew that she'd married the son of a wealthy Edenton merchant not too long after I married Ben.

"Yes," she said. "Talbot is a state senator now, did you know?"

"I heard," I said. "How is Maddie faring these days?"

"Just wonderfully, it would seem," she said. "She's the perfect senator's wife, always hosting parties and

Bible studies and coordinating service projects. She and Talbot have three daughters, all under the age of five. And they each look just like their mother."

"Mercy," I said, picturing three curly-headed blondes running wild through the house. "That's a lot of Maddies. One is more than enough."

She turned to examine her torso in the mirror. "I'm sure Maddie would love to see you."

"No," I said. "I'd be the laughing stock of Edenton."

But the following afternoon, I found myself standing before the mirror dressed in my ivory wedding gown, which Asha had insisted on altering before I'd left for Edenton for just such an occasion. It now gathered flat across my waist into a bustle in back, made with the extra inches she'd removed from the fullness of the skirt. The net sleeves and chemisette had been removed, so that the short-sleeved gown now hung off my shoulders, offering a fair show of my bosom.

A fashionable young woman, vaguely recognizable, stared out at me from the gilded looking-glass. Fortunately, Martha's long white gloves hid the bronze of my hands and lower arms, and the creaminess of the silk caused my face and neck to appear pleasantly flushed. Martha stood behind me to latch a strand of pearls around my neck, then knelt to slip a pair of fine silk shoes on my feet. Hettie curled my waist-length hair and pinned it so that it hung in ringlets down my back. Before we ventured from the dressing room, Martha draped a white-velvet dolman around my shoulders.

As we started down the stairs in our finery, a top-hatted-and-tailed Hector eyed my wedding gown and chuckled. Then he said to Martha, "My stars, my wife will be the loveliest one at the ball."

He pulled an embroidered evening cloak over her shoulders and helped her into the carriage.

"I see my wife's lent you her dolman and gloves," he said, grasping my hand. "You should know, those were gifts from me, when I was courting her."

I glanced down at the exquisite embroidery and beadwork that ran the length of the gloves.

"I'd be very disappointed if they were returned *soiled*," he said.

"What do you imagine she's going to do in them? Garden?" Martha asked.

"My dear, I'm not sure *what* your sister does these days. And I'm very attached to those particular gloves," he said. He lowered his voice. "Remember when I gave them to you? That evening on the piazza?"

"How could I forget?" she said shyly.

Hector winked at her before he climbed onto the seat in front of us and took up the reins of the carriage horses.

"Are you looking forward to seeing your old friends at the ball?" Martha asked me. "I daresay there will be many that you'll recall. Red Taylor, he's a prominent attorney now, and Alice Monroe and George Wakefield married a few years ago. George is a business partner of Talbot Buckley."

I ran a finger along a pink vine on the glove. "I'm not entirely sure that I am."

She put her hand over both of mine and squeezed. It was the first deliberate touch since my arrival. "You were never afraid of anything."

I started to shake my head, to say that I wasn't afraid in the least, but the thought snagged in my throat. I *was* afraid now; I lived my life in constant fear—fear of loss and death, fear of pain and blood.

My belly was full of fat flies when I caught sight of Maddie's home on the rise of a hill, an enormous, white plantation house on the outskirts of town, not too far from where I grew up. As our carriage pulled up the long drive to the house, Martha told me that Talbot had bought the plantation from the Osborns, who'd owned the land for almost seventy-five years but had gone into debt after the war. From the rumors to which Martha had been privy, they'd gotten it pretty cheaply, and now made a half-hearted attempt at tobacco farming.

Maddie was the first person I saw, perched near the entrance with an empty champagne flute in her hand. She was wearing a low-cut purple gown with a flowering bustle and frolicking rows of ruffles. Around her ivory neck dangled a thick emerald and gold necklace, and her gloved wrists glittered with opal and diamond bracelets. Her blonde hair was put up in a fashion similar to mine, I saw, and I smelled her strong perfume from three feet away.

When she turned to me, a gloved hand flew to her throat. "Bless my eyes," she breathed. "If it isn't Abigail Sinclair, standing right in front me."

"It's Abigail Whimble," I said. "Remember Ben?"

"Of course," she said, greedy eyes traveling up and down my gown. "I could never forget a fisherman as handsome as he. Never! I'm still hurt you didn't invite me to the wedding! Pray tell, where *is* he?"

"He's working," I said. "On the Outer Banks."

"My, my. What a pity." She turned to Martha and grasped her gloved hand. "Martha, my dear. You put me up for quite the surprise, didn't you?"

"I apologize, Maddie," she said. "But I knew you'd like to see Abigail while she's in town."

"Well, you *know* I love surprises, and this one takes the cake," she said, looking me over from head to toe.

"You do look ravishing, Abigail. As always." She leaned in to stage-whisper to me. "Though your skin does appear a trifle *tanned?*"

"Thank you, Maddie. And you're splendid as well." I leaned in to whisper back to her. "For a woman who's had three children in five years. My, you must have been determined to have it all done with."

I straightened up, while Maddie ran her hands down the belly of her gown while eyeing my own tightly cinched waist.

When she smiled, I saw teeth as yellowing as old newsprint. "What do you think of my plantation home?" she asked, waving a chubby arm about the air. "It's no Sinclair House, to be sure, but then there *is* no more Sinclair House now, is there?"

Hector sniffed, a cross between a laugh and a reprimand.

"I well know how you always coveted our home as a child. And I agree, this one doesn't quite compare," I said. "But I will say it's a perfect home for a politician."

Maddie furrowed her brow at me. The receiving line was growing behind us; I heard whispering and laughter.

"I hear your girls favor you. Will I be able to catch a glimpse of them tonight?"

"Oh, I daresay they'll be running underfoot." She rolled her big blue eyes and waved at the people directly behind us.

"Ya'll have a good time, now, and Abby, don't forget to *eat* something, for God's sake."

"You're off to a grand start, aren't you?" whispered Martha as we crossed the threshold. "I see your social graces haven't lost any of their charm over the years. Do try to calm yourself, sister."

The rooms—lit everywhere with tall candelabras—were already crowded with elegant Edentonians, and I heard the mingling of violins and flutes deep in the house. As Martha led our way through the front parlor, I saw heads turn to take us in, but they were faces I no longer recognized. In the dining room, chattering people milled about, eating and drinking. There was so much food on the long table and accompanying sideboards, I figured the spread could feed the entire Outer Banks for a month. I fought the sudden desire to pluck the apple from the pig's mouth.

Hector was summoned to a group of men, so Martha and I took glasses of champagne from a server and went to stand by the hearth to take in the sumptuous surroundings: the room dripped with crystal, tassels, fringes, velvet.

"The wallpaper makes me cross-eyed," I said, taking in the repetitive scenes of horses and hounds chasing foxes through the brush.

"I'm sure it cost Talbot a fortune," said Martha, sipping her champagne. "Maddie makes sure she has the best of everything."

"She probably set forth from her mama's womb calling for a silken receiving blanket," I said. "That silver platter underneath the roasted pig costs more than Ben could earn in five years."

Martha turned to me. "Truly?"

I sighed. "We don't do much entertaining, anyway," I said. "It would get as much use as this champagne glass."

Taking the measure of my poverty led me to thoughts of Mr. Wharton and the promise of the Peabody Normal School. I'd found myself thinking of the school more and more in the days I'd been in Edenton; it had become an oasis of civilization in a sea of uncultured sand.

I took a large mouthful of champagne and blinked at tears as bubbles burst on the back of my throat.

Hector appeared at Martha's side, a stubby glass full of golden liquid in hand. "It seems your sister is somewhat infamous, my dear," he said. "You both are wanted in the parlor."

We followed him to a group of men and women, who turned as one at our approach, much as a school of fish would. Yet their eyes weren't dull and empty, but full of curiosity. Martha knew them, and the men—one of whom wore a Confederate Army uniform—took turns kissing her gloved hand. The women stared at me with pursed lips.

"May I present my sister, Mrs. Abigail Sinclair Whimble," Martha said. And she introduced the two couples as Mr. and Mrs. Matthew Huntley and Major and Mrs. Tyler Howell. We all bowed and curtsied stiffly.

"We told old Hector here, we just had to get acquainted with Martha's sister while she was in town," said Major Howell. He reminded me of the men that daddy used to hunt with—sun-bronzed face and hands, and a shade to the rugged, even when dressed in uniform. "I can see there's a family resemblance, no surprise. I knew your mama, and that woman would never have birthed ugly daughters."

"I've heard you live in Nags Head," said Mr. Huntley, a slickly handsome man with an easy smile.

"Roanoke Island," I said. "With my husband."

"And where is he this evening?"

"He's working as a surfman at the Jones's Hill Lifesaving Station in Whales Head, on the Outer Banks."

The two wives eyed one another, but Mr. Huntley raised his glass in a toast. "That's honest work. He must be quite the seaman. I've never heard of Whales Head though. Is it near Nags Head?"

"It's quite a trip north, a full day by sail if the weather is fine," I said, recalling Leo's miasmal breath blowing in the lamplight. "But it's only a four-month shift. He'll return home in March."

The two women stepped closer to me, crowding out the men.

"My, my, such dangerous work," said Mrs. Huntley, a petite blonde with dimples in her cheeks. "And four months can pass quite slowly, especially when one's husband is away. I don't suppose you're frightfully worried about him?"

"He's very good at what he does."

"Well, I'm sure. But what in God's name are you doing with yourself, waiting on him to come home?" asked Mrs. Howell, her tiny fox-teeth bared in a grin.

"I'm a teacher," I said. "At a school on Roanoke Island."

"A teacher?" she asked, as if she'd never heard of the occupation before.

"Yes. A teacher at an integrated school."

They stared at me with white faces of fear and confusion. I wanted to tell them that teaching was my only reason for rising each morning. That the Negroes of Roanoke Island were as good as family to me. But I knew they would never understand.

"I just can't fathom…I gather you don't have children, Mrs. Whimble," said Mrs. Huntley, lips gone thin and blue. "To be able to conduct yourself such."

I tilted my champagne to my mouth, only to find that my glass was empty. I was having trouble taking deep breaths, and I wished Martha hadn't cinched my corset so tightly.

"Mrs. Whimble, tell us," said Mrs. Huntley, taking one final step closer to me. "How did you come to marry? There was talk, back in the day, that you turned quite rebellious the summer your poor daddy built that cottage on the beach. Tale of the town, I recall."

My eyes strayed to the wallpaper; the foxes and hounds fuzzed as thoughts from that summer filled my head. It *had* been rebellion, what I'd chosen to do. I'd been offered a different life, unconditional love, and I'd taken it all, with no thought to the consequences. Like a fish I'd landed and threw back into the sea, I'd taken my Edenton life, my only family, and cast it all aside. And Ben, he'd rebelled against his life as well, marrying an outsider. Perhaps Eliza should have been his choice all along.

"Let's eat some of the Buckley's fine fare, shall we?" said Martha from my side. "This champagne is going straight to my head. Ladies, if you'll excuse us."

"Those women are terrible gossips," said Martha, once we stood safely at the dining table. "Pay them no mind. Your name…well, I'll allow it took me quite a while to live it down. And when women like Mrs. Howell and Mrs. Huntley come face-to-face with such a name, they're inspired to recklessness."

Yet before I could even pick up a plate, Talbot Buckley appeared before me, bowing a greeting.

"Abigail, how wonderful to see you again."

"Senator Buckley. It's been a long time, hasn't it?"

"Indeed. Too long."

The band struck up a waltz in the next room, and he held out a white-gloved hand. "Shall we take a turn about the floor?"

His beige waistcoat was embroidered with peacock feathers, waving about as I stared. "I shouldn't."

Martha clucked. "I do apologize for my sister, Talbot. The Outer Banks has eroded a good portion of her charm. Abigail, you mustn't deny the host a dance."

I sighed and took his levitating hand. "Watch out for your toes."

It seemed odd that I could still remember the steps, but even if I hadn't, the smooth and unruffled Talbot would have led me. I recalled teaching Ben how to waltz during the first year of our marriage. Suffice it to say, he was a much quicker study at reading. Yet I recalled how strong and broad his bare shoulder had felt beneath my hand, how his eyes were closed in concentration, how his lips whispered the beats as we moved barefoot across the sand. He'd ground sand into my feet until I couldn't take it anymore.

"I think you should stick with fishing," I'd said, but had regretted it when I saw the disappointment in his face.

The music picked up tempo, and couples spun faster. Talbot twirled me about the floor, and my body relaxed into the brace of his arm. My cheeks flushed with heat, and the skirts of my wedding dress bounced about my feet, bringing to mind Asha's wind-blown laundry.

I ground my teeth, unwilling to imagine life outside this warm and gilded home, of Asha and her cold little cabin, of the dreary schoolhouse, of the empty Nags Head house, of Ben and Eliza and the icy sea. I only wanted to dance, to drink champagne, to recall nothing. Faceless spectators appeared around us, shots of color and shadows of black and white.

"You're still a stunning woman, Abigail," he said, now slightly breathless. "But I wonder, do you still have that fiery spirit?"

"I'm afraid not. As my dear sister so kindly mentioned, the Outer Banks has a habit of erosion."

"And yet, here you are," he laughed. "I don't think the fire has been *completely* extinguished."

He spun me around the meandering Howells. "You sound as if the place has lost its charm for you. Madeline's family recently sold their cottage on the sound. Her father hasn't been well, you know. But from what I saw of the place, it's not a suitable place to live one's life. Quite desolate, isn't it?"

The tempo of the waltz increased, so that further conversation was impossible. Light from the chandelier shone in the goblets, the wall sconces, the jewels, the skin of the ladies' arched necks. Silk and taffeta whipped around me, patterns of wallpaper and hothouse roses blurred as one.

And it occurred to me that I didn't belong here. With these people. With these things. I was just as provisional, aging as surely as the silver. Time sped on, a chaotic waltz. What would I be—and who would I have—when it came to an end?

My vision blacked, and I slumped against Talbot. He pulled me to a chair and snapped for a servant. The music dwindled and the dancers were sneaking glances in our direction.

I sipped water as slowly as I could manage, my sight narrowed as if through a skinny spyglass. Talbot's shiny shoes still stood next to me. Three little Maddies trounced into my tunnel in matching blue dresses.

"Daddy, dance with me!" the tallest girl begged.

"No, with me! Me!" screeched the smallest one.

"Evangeline always gets to dance with you. It's not fair. It's my turn," said the other.

He laughed. "Only if Mrs. Whimble is feeling better," he said. He laid a gloved hand on my back. The girls stared at me with round blue eyes as assessing as Maddie's.

"I am," I said. "Thank you."

"The pleasure was mine," he said. He flashed a political smile.

"Daddy, now!"

The girls swarmed about his legs like puppies. As Talbot shepherded them toward the dance floor, I heard the girl called Evangeline say, "Daddy, where did Mrs. Whimble come from?"

"From right here in Edenton."

"Well, she looks like a foreigner."

"She's not a foreigner, my dear. She just doesn't live here anymore."

The sun was ascending when we finally left the ball. The beat of the thoroughbred's hooves on the dirt road were canon fire in the sleepy silence of the carriage. Martha and I huddled together under the blankets, our breath carving diamonds in the cold air.

Acres and acres of land rolled by, pictures of my previous life I hadn't been privy to in the darkness of night. The frost on the stubby brown fields twinkled with the day.

"It's close, isn't it?"

Martha raised her head from my shoulder. "It is," she said. "Do you want to see it?"

Did I? The notion filled me with an odd mixture of anticipation and dread. I couldn't answer her, and the land continued to pass beside us. Soon we'd reach the city of Edenton.

"Yes," I said. "Yes, I think I do."

"Hector, darling," called Martha. "We'd like to see Sinclair House."

In a few minutes we were shuttling down the familiar long lane that led to the house itself. I held my breath when I saw myself—a small child—running down the lane next to us, ribbons flying in long red hair and shoes caked with mud.

There was the massive magnolia tree where I'd hidden with mama's book-in-progress. Mama had sent Asha to locate me, and of course she'd found me immediately among the thick, leafy branches where I'd crouched, trying to hide my booty beneath a handful of glossy leaves. She'd told mama that I'd disappeared, no trace of me. I'd waited for her in the kitchen, where she'd given me some warm bread with butter. Then she'd told me to fetch one of my picture books to read to her while she started on supper. Mama's habitual neglect had soon been forgotten.

I saw Ace of Spades, as fast as a train, galloping down the lane with Uncle Jack bending in the saddle. I even saw daddy atop one of his many hunting horses, following his tired hound dogs home across the lawn.

And then, there was the house. Magnificent, proportioned, solid, aged—it was a home like no other, and thinking of the girl that used to live there was like remembering a character in a novel instead of myself.

Had I really been born in the upstairs bedroom? Had I taken Asha's fresh-baked biscuits, apple pie, cherry tarts and smuggled them all out to my waiting Uncle Jack? Had I played graces and marbles here with a precocious young girl named Maddie, been a big sister to Martha and Charlie, watched slaves work the land from my bedroom window?

It all seemed like a jumbled-up dream now. Yet the ache in my heart told me that it had all happened, I just hadn't had the courage to remember it anymore. I'd buried my roots down in the sand drifts inside me, left them to wither and choke.

"The land is worked by freedmen sharecroppers," said Martha. "Daddy could never bring himself around to that arrangement."

"Who owns it?"

"Mr. Stephan Waller," said Hector. "A Yankee interested in trying to turn the land into a peanut farm."

"I'm getting out," I said, and pushed open the carriage door before either Martha or Hector could voice resistance.

Ivory skirts in hand, I walked slowly, eventually finding myself in the back gardens, its air always laden with opopanax, violets, jasmine, crab apple blossoms, roses. Now weeds and sticks littered the garden's ground, its bushes grown wild and confused.

The gardens still offered a perfect view of the acres and acres of farmland. I'd grown up watching them throughout the seasons, glorious in their constant need to change and evolve. I saw the barn and the horse stables and sharecroppers' cabins, a few Negroes milling about in the early morning. They wouldn't know me, wouldn't know that I had claimed the land as mine for almost 18 years.

Beside the garden was the little graveyard where Uncle Jack rested, now home to the bones of my mother and baby sister. Their headstones were smaller than the others, but an engraver had carved roses into the tops of the stones, one in full bloom, the other a closed bud.

I turned to the house once more, feeling older and heavier than stone.

The land, the house, the graveyard, the people, the city I'd called home before Ben—these things were a part of me, as much as the Outer Banks was a part of him. I'd tried to forget, to blot, to be someone better than I was, better than my daddy. I had an urge to lay down in the weeds at my feet, dig my whole body into the soil and rest, rest until I remembered myself.

I took a last, long look at the house and turned for the waiting carriage.

I fell atop the bed when we returned, and before I knew it, I'd fallen asleep fully dressed. My mind began to drift, passing through ball room scenes and childhood memories with equal ease. And then I held a baby, my arms flexing hard with the wealth of the treasure. We stared into one another's eyes for what seemed to be a long time, and when I wept with a joy I'd never before known, the babe reached for a tear sliding down my cheek.

I gasped aloud and sat up in the bright sunlight of the bedroom. I stared about, trying to slow my breath to the tempo of the napping household. Somehow I heard the rolling of the sea, like the rhythm of God's own breath, the way it would sound on an Outer Banks summer evening.

I lay back once more, felt the sunlight warm my wet face. I pictured the salt from the air I'd breathed for the last seven years coating the insides of my body like old diamonds. In the next dream I stood on the bow of the schooner, the sunrise in my face and the skirts of my wedding gown belling about my legs.

CHAPTER SIXTEEN

FEBRUARY 4, 1876
BENJAMIN WHIMBLE

Therefore, the tormented spirit that glared out of the bodily eyes, when what seemed Ahab rushed from his room, was for the time but a vacated thing, a formless somnambulistic being, a ray of living light, to be sure, but without an object to colour, and therefore a blankness in itself. God help thee, old man, thy thoughts have created a creature in thee; and he whose intense thinking thus makes him a Prometheus; a vulture feeds upon that heart for ever, that vulture the very creature he creates.

–ISHMAEL ON CAPTAIN AHAB, **MOBY-DICK**

THE COUGH IN MY LUNGS WAS A PART OF ME NOW, AS NATURAL as the heart in my chest and just as useless. I couldn't feature a day in time when I'd be able to take in the air without bending over double with a hacking that sounded more hound than human. It kept me from my sleep, and most others too, so I'd taken up quarters in the equipment room amid half a dozen blankets.

But I still wouldn't give up on the job at hand, that of a surfman at the Jones's Hill Lifesaving Station. I welcomed the pain that reading *Moby-Dick* and writing Abby brought me, but the whole thing left me aching in my bones even more than my work. Making sure the ocean was empty of peril put me in mind of myself again, and I took to it any chance I got.

Now I'd grown out my beard, I didn't feel the cold on my face the way I used to. And my legs were strong, even if the rest of me wasn't. I figured I could walk for days, maybe weeks, without sleep nor sustenance nor lantern light. The empty beach always stretched out ahead of me, a comfort of sorts. I wasn't even on patrol this dark, early morning. I was just out to see the sun rise up from the sea.

It was still dark as tar, and I'd walked miles north already, further than I'd ever walked before. Much further and I'd hit Virginia when the sun at last rose. But even in the dark I'd learned the feel of every kind of sand in the world. Some sand was hard as walking on a street of bricks. Some sand was so soft felt like strolling through piles of feathers. Some was naught but rocks and shell that crunched like bird bones under my boots. I tried to aim for the hard-packed sand nearest the sea, but my path went wayward into the stumbling kind of sand more often than not.

I hadn't got word from Abby since Christmas Eve. I hadn't expected to neither, but I'd written her a letter a day since then, amounting to no less than 38 letters. I pictured all my letters lined up like flapping pelicans, cruising the strands from Whales Head to Roanoke Island on orders a good bit more important than finding fish.

I never knew I'd have so much to say to her. It was like a dam had cracked inside me and let loose a flood of words. I wrote it all down and then some. If I forgot to tell her something in a letter, then I told it to her in my sleep. If I had need of paper or stamps or envelopes or ink, I'd fetch them on the mainland, for the men had been sending me on the marketing trips since I'd come down sick. I reckoned they felt sorry for me, but they also shied from me the way they might from a rabid coon. They'd quit their jesting with me, and never asked me to play a hand at cards.

I'd woke up in my cot the morning after Jonas'd tried to drown me, and Eliza had been sitting right next to me on a stool, *Moby-Dick* on her lap. She was staring at the words so hard her eyeballs were fixing to pop.

When she saw I was up, she closed the book. "If you'd slept any longer, the words would have started making some sense."

I'd tried to sit up, but every part of my body hurt. "What am I doing here?"

"Spencer found you sprawled out on the sand last night, almost froze to death. You're lucky he tripped right over you, for your lantern was gone and you looked more flotsam than man."

Then it had all come back to me.

"You want to tell me what happened?" She sounded to be scolding me, but underneath it I heard the fear. And I saw the darkness under her eyes, the stray hairs coming from her knot.

I rubbed at the pull of tightness in my chest. "I got caught by a bad wave," I said. "Took me down."

"Uh huh. Course you did. Happens all the time."

She chewed her thumbnail for a time. "Spruels came by while you been sleeping. Captain Gale let 'em search the station house for the barrel."

"They find anything?"

She just rolled her eyes. "You feel like taking some food?"

When I gave no answer, she said, "You need to keep your strength up. Men want you to work a shift tonight. How about a biscuit with milk? That always used to do you right, I recall."

My belly had felt like a closed fist. I reached out for the book, sitting on her lap, and we both took note of the ink still staining my thumb and forefinger, proof of my love for Abby. She put the book into my hand and then left me there to read. I hadn't done much else since then.

Just yesterday I'd finished up chapter 92, which gave me gooseflesh from the get-go for it was called *Ambergris*. In the chapter previous, first mate Stubb found himself some ambergris in the belly of a dead and stinking whale. He stuck both his hands inside what Melville called "rich mottled old cheese," the colors of yellow and ash. He pulled out six handfuls of the stuff before Ahab told him to get on board the ship or he'd leave him there, and leave the ambergris too, for he didn't give two bone buttons for a thing but Moby Dick.

See, Ahab only cared about one thing, and that was chasing the white whale. Didn't take a man of learning to see that when Moby Dick took Ahab's leg, he took his reason too. When they fitted him with the ivory leg—carved from the jaw of a sperm whale—they strapped his blood lust to him as well. Ahab chased a thing he shouldn't, but where others might scorn him for his wayward ambitions, I found a soft spot in my heart for him.

The book was building at the exact pace of a overfed heifer on a summer's day. I figured Melville had in mind a meeting of the captain and the angry whale. And in my experience, big, angry whales usually had the upper hand. Men were only men, after all.

Now the sun crowned its head over the horizon to my right, and I stopped to watch the birthing. Just that small amount of sunshine had a warmth to it, though I knew it was all in my head. Once the sun turned into a ball of yellow, it rose until it cast its golden shadow upon the sea. The light reached straight for me across the cold waves like a oar reaching for the stranded.

I started walking back the way I'd just come, fitting my boots into the foot holes I'd just made before the wash wiped 'em away.

Back at the station Eliza was back and forth with the breakfast dishes. Somehow she'd worked it so that she was the full-time farmhand, cook and housekeep; she was at the station house for hours of a day, seemed she was always underfoot.

She grinned her downwards grin when she saw me make my way to the table where Jerry and Lemuel sat.

"I just recruited these two," she said, putting a plate full of slapjacks and ham doings in front of me.

"What for?" The food had no smell to it, though the melted butter on the slapjacks said otherwise.

"To help me build up my keeper's quarters," she said. "I'm getting a crew together. We start up in May."

Lemuel and Jerry nodded their heads while they forked food into their mouths.

"You should come on over too," she said. "You always were good with wood."

I shook my head. "I'm heading back south in March. I told you."

She chewed her lip like she was chewing on words she wanted to say to me.

"Now Ben, I know you're hungry on account you haven't eaten a decent bite in over three weeks."

She stepped close to me and speared a big chunk of slapjack on the tines. She waved it in front of my face in big circles.

"I can feed myself," I said, taking the fork from her hand.

"I'm not so sure about that."

She grabbed for the fork again, but I put it into my mouth before she could. I managed to chew and swallow. The food tasted just like I reckoned a leaf of writing paper would.

"One bite ain't gonna sustain you, all the work you do." She grabbed for my fork yet again, her black eyes lit up. In between their own bites, the men watched us like we were two wild boars a-bickering too close for comfort.

I stood up quick. "Leave me be."

I watched her fork-hand drop down and her eyes dim. Then I made for the bedroom upstairs, where I read *Moby-Dick* 'til my lookout shift. I bent to pull my boots back on when I heard loud steps in the doorway. I knew it was Eliza before I even looked up.

"What's puckering you today?"

I shoved *Moby-Dick* under the cot and said not a word. I wouldn't even know where to start.

She came over and sat herself on the cot. She bent down and pulled out *Moby-Dick*, and I fought the urge to take it from her.

"How's the book?" She thumbed the pages to where I marked it with the letter I was writing to Abby. She fingered the paper with a rough thumb.

"Not bad."

"But not good neither?"

"It's just hard to read is all," I said. "There are good parts in it though. Funny parts."

She ran a rough hand over the blue cover. "Like what?"

I sighed. "None of it would make a lick of sense to you. I'd have to read you the whole book. Look now, I got to work my shift."

I reached out to take the book back, but she held it away from me. She was of a mood to take things from me today.

I couldn't fight her any longer. I never really could. I headed up the steps to the lookout tower, and a little ways up, I heard *Moby Dick* land on the bedroom floor, sounded like a rifle going off. I flinched from the blow the rest of lookout.

I went to church service the next day, and Eliza was there again. She held a Bible in her hands, even opened it up to try to read the words. She moved so close to me that our elbows touched.

She said, "It's filling up good."

And it was a big a crowd as any I'd seen at church. Soon we wouldn't fit inside the parlor. The reverend would have to raise up the windows so folks could hear him outside.

When the service ended, I could feel Eliza following me out the door, down into the sand, standing beside me. She started in on the chicken dinner she was fixing to bring. Folks watched us out the corners of their eyes, whispered behind their hands. I was never so happy to see Della and Jennie Blount walking toward me.

"Well go on, girl," said Della, squeezing on her shoulders. "Mr. Whimble doesn't have all day."

"Mama, I said I wanted to talk to him by myself," said Jennie. I saw she'd likely grown of recent, for the sleeves on her dress were a couple inches too short, and she had a thin, knobby look her to, like her flesh hadn't yet caught up to her bones.

Della nodded her head inside her threadbare bonnet. "Don't be long. We got dinner to fix."

She hollered at her boys—playing tag and spraying sand—and started marching toward the sound. Yet still Jennie kept her mouth shut. She looked over to Eliza, who rolled her eyes, cussed under her breath, and stomped over to the hitching post.

Jennie took a big breath. "You know that boy you tried to save back in November? The one that died?"

I bit the insides of my cheeks. "Livy Spruel?"

She nodded and looked up at me with those plummy eyes. "He was my friend."

"I did hear of that," I said, then started up coughing so that I reckoned I'd never stop.

She screwed up her rosy lips in a terrible twist. "He died in front of you, I heard."

"That's true," I gasped. "He'd fallen from the boat. Died from the cold."

She tapped gently at a eye with the back of her white hand, but her voice was rough when next she spoke. "Folks are also saying that Livy had a barrel on his boat."

Seemed the whole world spun around on the axis of the barrel. I narrowed my eyes. "What folks?"

"You know. Spruels, mostly."

Who else? "Uh huh. Well, I already told the Spruels I didn't see any barrel on the boat that night."

"I know there was a *barrel* though. I seen it before. Livy showed me. And if his family can't find it, it seems to reason he had it with him that night. I figured to ask you about it."

I rubbed my fingers through my beard. "You know what was in it?"

She looked down. "I seen it, but wasn't sure what it was."

"Well, could you tell me what it looked like?"

"You ain't gonna believe me," she said, shaking her head side to side.

"Why wouldn't I?"

She sighed. "It was a rock."

"A rock?"

"You see? It sounds crazy."

"Just a rock? You think the Spruels are all-fired to get a *rock* back?"

"I do, Mr. Whimble. There was something magic about it."

I shook my head, made like her notions really were foolish. "Jennie, I really got to get on now. I can't be dilly-dallying over magic rocks."

I started going backwards away from her. "You see, I got patrol duty today. Drills to do."

"I know that." She was fixing to cry.

"I'm sorry, Jennie," I said. I truly was. "I wish… things turned out different."

Next day I had a hard time even picking up a pen, much less reading *Moby-Dick*. In my mind the whale-boat looked just like Livy Spruel's skiff, and Ishmael looked like just Livy. I had grown to feel that I too was stuck on a ship in the wide open sea with only my shipmates for company, my home and people long gone from me. At times I too felt I was on a collision

course with a unknown and evil force, yet I was pow-
erless as Ishmael to stop it.

And every time I looked up from reading, I saw
Jennie Blount's face.

That afternoon I asked Captain Gale if he
knew where the Blounts lived, and he said, "Follow
the Jones's Hill dune southwest, you can't miss it.
Ramshackle old place."

I traded my shifts and made out walking along
the edges of the dune toward the sound, Jennie's
blue scarf wrapped about my neck. The dune
shaped itself like a giant wave toward the water,
and at the point where the sand was meeting with
the little village I found their old clapboard abode,
sitting right in the skirts of the dune. A mountain
of sand ate at the edges of it like a herd of hungry cows. Any day now, I thought, and the house
would be in the belly of the dune, bunch of forgotten boards rattling round in the grains. They'd
be coming home to nothing but sand. Sand for a
door, sand for windows, sand for a bed and sand
for a kettle.

Della's mama sat on a rocker, wrapped in about
a dozen blankets. A snuff paddle stuck from her
mouth, but it didn't stop her from giving me a toothless smile. I gave her a little wave. As I stood there
before her, wondering what to say and how loud to
say it, a face popped up in a window.

Jennie came out the door pulling a shawl about
her shoulders. Like she'd been expecting me to call.

"Hey there Jennie," I said. "I though mayhaps we
could finish our talk."

She stood there quiet, the late afternoon sun turning her blonde hair into flames. Then she turned to look up at the low porch roof.

"This house is over 200 years old. Parts, anyways."

The house did indeed have the telltale look of willy-nilly growth, wood of all kinds, all colors and shapes.

"Now the sand blows right through the cracks of the boards. Blocks out the light. We eat more sand than food, most days. The dune ate up the barn and boneyard a few years back."

I could tell she had more to say about the dilemma, but the wind picked up and blew some of the sand at us, proof of her claims. We put our hands over our eyes, but the grit made its way into my ears instead. Della's mama got up, shook the sand from the blankets and hobbled inside on her stick.

Jennie wiped her mouth and eyes with a sleeve, looking to the dune for answers. "You hungry?" she said at last.

I shrugged. I didn't want to take food from the family, but the smell of meat stewing had my belly rolling like a undertow.

"You could stay for supper, if you are," she said, stepping down to the sand. "It ain't much but the critters my little brothers trapped yesterday. Livy used to bring me some of his barrel sauce to use in our cooking, but now...things taste pretty plain."

I couldn't help myself. "Barrel sauce?"

"From the rock I told you about. Ground up. It had a sugary-fish taste one day, then the next day tasted like salt."

"Jennie, how did Livy come by this rock?"

"Found it in his net a few months back," she said. "Rolled a fish barrel over one night for me to see. Said he hadn't caught much that day but a great rock, and he opened the barrel up to show me. We poked at it and licked on it, on account it smelled right good for a rock. But when Livy showed it to his family, his pap and brothers and uncles started up how rich they were gonna be on account of it. They were all in a tizzy."

"So they just figured they'd take it from him?"

She shrugged. "They're kin."

She wrapped her hands in her skirts, troubled-like. "You know the Spruels?"

I thought of the boodle of red-headed folks in the station house, their pale faces and hungry eyes. I heard them on the dark beach, voices mean and ugly. "Only a bit."

"They're lazy as all get-out. The men especially. But they're treasure hunters of the worst kind. Any time they hear of earning a easy penny, well they'll follow it through. They hunt pirate treasure on naught but a hunch. They try to guide for the Yanks what come here to hunt and fish, but they just end up cheating 'em, taking 'em out on boats with no intention of helping 'em do nothing yet charging them two dollars a day for the time. They're…not gonna rest without finding that barrel."

Sand blew over our boots, clearly of a mind to bury us where we stood. It put you in mind of the nature of living, and how we were all dying, a little bit at a time, day after day.

I shook the sand off my boots with two angry kicks. "What do you reckon Livy wanted done with this rock?"

"At first he'd thought to keep it. But then, knowing it for something of value, he wanted to give it to Reverend Washburn."

I cleared my throat once, twice. "Come again?"

"He thought if he gave it to the reverend, then he could stop the dune from moving."

I almost grinned. "He figured the reverend to have some influence over God?"

She shrugged her bony shoulders. "Enough for Him to stop moving the sand."

I didn't think God would bother with such a childish task as blowing heaps of sand at houses. Might as well pelt us with cow chips and persimmons.

"Livy reckoned the reverend could do just about anything," she said. "His kin poked fun at his ideer of giving it to the reverend. They wanted to up and move to the mainland. Buy a big house and turpentine distillery and whatnot. All the things that money can buy."

"Livy didn't want any of that?"

Her purple eyes filled with tears. "No sir. He was happy here."

The wind picked up again, and we bowed our heads.

"One thing I could never figure," I said. "Why would he take that boat out all by himself? At night, and in that storm?"

She shrugged as she wiped her eyes with both hands, sand stuck in her tears. "All I can reckon is his kin were after him," she said. "He'd never do something so addle-brained if he was thinking straight. That's why I figure he had the barrel with him. He was taking it to the reverend. Or maybe… to me."

She lowered her head then, started to fiddling with her skirts. And I saw how it was then. They really had loved one another. And he'd wanted to help their family, save Jennie. I saw clear he'd tried to do anything he could to keep Jennie nearby and safe. And he'd lost his life for it.

I felt myself split in two then, the way the sand of the Outer Banks gets carved by the Atlantic to make a inlet. I could feel the cold water rushing thought me, crying its victory.

"I have a wife. Her name is Abby. She's all I live for in this world."

My words came out thick as wet sand, but Jennie reached out and gave the scarf she'd knit a little pull.

I'd never laid eyes on Mr. Blount. It was always Della and Jennie and her brothers at church service. But there he sat smoking a pipe by the hearth where pine knots smoldered and popped. Jennie told me he'd hurt his back a few months ago and couldn't be moved from the chair without a good amount of pain, even to piss.

I stepped to greet him, and he shook my arm with a hard grip. But I saw in his face the downtrodden look of a man on the hardest of times.

"Jimmy Blount," he said.

Jennie called from the back. "He's the man pulled Livy Spruel from the sea. The lifesaver."

I tried not to shake my head no. "I'm sorry I couldn't do more for him. Jennie…she came to me after church service, wanted to talk it over, me being the one to find him and all."

He took a big puff of his pipe. "Jennie took his passing hard," he said, smoke from the pipe circling slow and sad. "I told her, the sea don't have mercy for no one."

"No sir."

He drew deep on his pipe once more. "Every one of my ancestors was a fisherman," he said. "Blounts been here for two hundred years."

"Yessir, that's a long time. Same with the Whimbles."

He looked at me through the smoke. "Now those dunes are set to take it all away from me."

He leaned back with a little groan and shut his eyes, still holding tight to the pipe.

Granny Blount waved me over from the rocker next to a window. She reached into her apron and pulled out a corked bottle of something thick and greenish.

"Swaller a dram of this every morning. Help ease that cough of yourn."

I took the bottle from her and held it to the little window light making its way past the sand dunes outside. "I thank you, ma'am."

Except for Jimmy Blount, who had his supper brought to him in a bowl, we all sat down to eat at a little table crowded to bursting with plates and cups but no cutlery.

"Ain't got but one fork and two knives," said Jennie. She handed me the lone pair, then commenced with the blessing.

"God watch over us, and keep the sand away from the house and the garden. And mend my daddy's back so he can fish and shoot again. Make Bert and Digby mind my mama and me. And keep Livy Spruel in your loving care until I meet him again in heaven. Amen."

The supper was a thin stew, coon and squirrel most like, and the meal was quiet save for the slurping of stew from upended bowls. In no time at all Granny Blount had rolled out an accordion about the size of a barrel churn.

Jennie looked wary. "Now Granny, you don't have to trouble yourself tonight."

But Granny Blount might have been a bit hard of hearing, for she commenced to play "In the Sweet By and By" with a look of rapture on her face. And it was a good thing she kept her eyes shut, for she would have seen the boys with their hands over their ears and their tongues hanging from their mouths. I've never heard anything more off-key in my life, for it seemed like some of the machine's best parts were busted. It sounded the equal to demon music, and I figured even the angels in heaven were squirming in their gold seats. To pile on the agony, the dog hid under the table but yapped and yipped along. Jennie's ma and pa sang like nothing was amiss.

"We shall meet on that beautiful shore," they sang. I hoped it would be soon.

It was dark when I gave my goodbyes and Jennie walked me outside. "I got a thing to show you," she said.

She walked through the piles of sand around to the side of the house and lugged out a crate from underneath. "This was Livy's collection. He kept it in the boneyard in a busted coffin. When I found out he passed, I went and fetched it."

Inside the crate were all kinds of flotsam: mismatched socks and shoes, jewelry, dead timepieces, busted suspenders, fishing hooks, broken dishes, a doll, wine bottles, silver cutlery, old coinage, bits of cracked up china, a lady's comb, and spy glass.

But scattered among all of it were seashells of all kinds.

"He had a knack for finding things," she said. "Every time we walked along the ocean, he'd find something. I used to poke fun at him, but he said he'd never stop looking, even if he got to be a old man and couldn't bend over."

"My ma liked to find things on the shores too, so I've heard. Said the sea had a way of providing things, it was up to you to figure what they were for."

"His fingers were always mucky," she said, looking down at her own. "But he held these treasures like… like they were something special."

"My wife…she liked looking for shells too. She could tell you their names, where they likely came from. All sorts of things you never even wanted to know."

"I bet they'd have been friends then."

I touched a wrist bauble with red stones all along its length. "He ever want to sell any of it?"

"No sir. Never."

"What are you going to do with it all? You planning on giving it to his kin?"

"He wouldn't want that," she said. "I'll just keep adding to it all, I reckon."

Jennie looked over her shoulder at the sand dune, looming up behind us like a tidal wave in the night. The house moaned beside us; it was dying, used up, done. Jennie reached down and drew a gilded mirror from the crate, not even cracked from its time in the waves. She looked down into it.

"Livy and me, we used to like to wonder where all of it came from. All different parts of the world. We just liked to lay back and watch the sky and think about how big it all is. It was scary to think on. But exciting too at times."

Jennie looked up from the mirror at me. "You ever think about leaving here?"

I shook my head no, but then I remembered. "It was when I was about your age," I said. "All those soldiers come down here during the war. I heard all kinds of tales about where they came from, what folks were like. I used to think it might be fun to visit some different places just to see. But I never wanted to leave the Banks. Got friends and family here, you know."

She sighed real deep. "Same here."

"Thanks for the supper, Jennie. It was real good, even without the sauce," I said. "And listen, I'll fetch over some fish for you all real soon. I'd like to hear some more of your granny's accordion."

She laughed, and the sound of it reminded me of somebody I'd lost.

CHAPTER SEVENTEEN

FEBRUARY 2, 1876
ABIGAIL SINCLAIR

Now then, thou not only wantest to go a-whaling, to find out by experience what whaling is, but ye also want to go in order to see the world? Was not that what ye said? I thought so. Well then, just step forward there, and take a peep over the weather-bow, and then back to me and tell me what ye see there?

–CAPTAIN PELEG TO ISHMAEL, **MOBY-DICK**

"DID I GET ANY POST WHILE I WAS GONE?" I CLOSED THE trunk on my starched and folded wedding gown.

Asha turned to me with a stiff neck, afraid the new spectacles from Martha were going to fall from her face. "Oh, I should say you did."

"What do you mean by that?"

"Fetch up that basket."

In the basket there were a least three dozen envelopes, and on each envelope I saw Ben's blocky handwriting. I sifted through them, some letters as thick as planks.

"Seem like he got some things to say to you," said Asha.

I imagined that the letters were full of apology, reasons for his secrecy, his betrayal. Undoubtedly some comments on the weather, his surfman activity. I set the basket on the floor and stood up.

"I don't care to read them just now."

"There's one might not trouble you too much," she said. "It ain't from Ben."

I sifted through the letters and found one near the bottom of the basket in what I knew to be Mr. Wharton's handwriting. I opened the letter at once.

Greetings Mrs. Whimble,

I hope this letter finds you and your students healthy and prosperous and as warm in the schoolhouse as can be possible. I am writing from the president's rather small and untidy office in College Hall, University of Nashville, to the happy and industrious sound of instruction. I am pleased to report that on 1st of December, classes at the Peabody Normal School officially began. We had just 13 students present for the inaugural ceremony, primarily an effort to gain public recognition for the school. President Stearns keynoted by telling of difficulties encountered in starting America's first normal schools in Massachusetts. He is very optimistic for Tennessee, as it already has such a noble liberal arts tradition. Very fortunately for us, we procured a donation of textbooks from A. S. Barnes Company, of New York. But alas, the surrounding lawns are still a wasteland.

The book is almost complete, and when it's published, I will be sure to send copies to both you and Ms. Owens, as promised. On a different note, I have spoken to President Stearns about taking you on as a faculty member, and I must say he was easily convinced. Perhaps a visit in the spring would be optimal, for it would provide an opportunity for you to see the instruction and meet some of the students before the summer hiatus. I'd appreciate your thoughts on curriculum development as well.

He went on to describe the housing near the University of Nashville campus, where the two other female faculty lived. Then he endeavored to describe College Hall, where most of the classes took place—"ivy-clad walls, turrets, harmonious proportions…"

I saw the place in my mind, determined and intelligent people marching in and out of the doors. I quickly located a pen and piece of paper, thoughts of Tennessee and change filling my mind. *Dear Mr. Wharton,* I wrote in my best penmanship. *I thank you for…*

I stopped, fingers quaking.

In the back yard I heard the crunch of a chicken's neck, and I put down the pen. I knew Asha would like help with the plucking and butchering, perhaps with picking some onions and cabbage from the garden.

I left the letter on the table and opened the back door.

Asha glowed in the afternoon sunlight like the goddess of poultry, the thrashing torso dangling from her arm. Ben's horse Junie turned his head to me in greeting, the pigs lolled in the sty, the cow munched a patch of weeds in the abandoned field next door.

The wind blew from the east, and I tasted salt in the air. I stepped to the dirt and took the chicken by its legs.

After supper, Asha and I stretched out on our ticks, the candle still flickering between us.

"You look like your mama more and more each day," she said, pulling the blankets up to her chin.

"How so?" I saw my yellow-haired mama in the dark cellars of my mind, stoic and glorious.

"I reckon it's the shape of your head," she said. "You done lost all the chub in your cheeks. Show off your bones underneath. Like your mama."

The fire slumbered in its grate. "Do you ever think about her?"

"*Think*?" she said, then yawned loudly. "No, she nothing but a poor old ghost now."

"I don't…that's not what I wanted to ask you."

In one of my first memories of Asha, or Winnifred as she'd been called, I'd been wearing shoes for the first time in my life, and they'd pinched my toes so badly that I'd taken up crawling again. I remembered being pulled from the floor and stood on my feet, remembered mama's face in front of me, urging me forward. But after she'd gone, Asha had taken the shoes off and rubbed my toes as I sat on her lap. She'd sung to me, an unfamiliar tune full of guttural noise and tongue clicks. She'd let me run barefoot through the grass.

"You came to us as a wet nurse," I began. "What became of your baby?"

I heard nothing for a long while, then I heard her take a shaking breath. "He passed on."

I crawled to her tick and perched next to her. Her eyes and cheeks shone in the candlelight.

"When I came to you, I left him with a friend, had a baby of her own. After I been working for you all a few months, I got word he took sick and died."

She wasn't even there to help him, to hold him. She was nursing *me*.

"And his father?"

She was quiet for a while, staring at the yellow circle of light on the sooty ceiling. "John. Don't even know where he's at. Been gone for years and years."

"Did you ever want to…find love again?"

"Love." She said it as if she'd never uttered the word the before. "I loved you children. That's all I needed. Three children, as good as mine. You filled up my heart."

I curled into the lean curve of her body, and she pulled the blankets over us.

"I'm still waiting for him," she whispered. Then her body shuddered as her breath evened. We fell asleep and didn't wake until the sun was well risen.

We made a Sunday breakfast of the leftover chicken, then Asha left with the cart to make her laundry deliveries. With a cup of coffee warming my hands, I eyed the basket of letters. I forced myself to finish my coffee, to rinse out the cup in the washing bucket, to pin my hair up. Then I slowly moved to the basket and brought it up to the table.

I ordered the envelopes according to the dates Ben had written along the tops. I carefully opened the first envelope and extracted the letter, written on white paper as thin as cast-off snakeskin. Ink blotches covered the writing like spots of mold. It was dated December 25, Christmas Day.

My dearest wife,

I don't have to tell you how taken aback I was to see Moby-Dick on my cot. I'd forgotten all about that book and how fat it is. But even from the first page I was confounded, not knowing what all those Is and Vs and Xs were. I came to figure they were different ways to write numbers. I did the figuring, and come to find out there are 135 chapters in Moby-Dick. I didn't let the notion turn me away though. I started in reading. And right away I took to Ishmael's story, course from the get-go I started looking words up. Here's a few that stumped me in just Chapter One, called Loomings—had to look that up too. Circumambulate, pedestrian, deity, reverie, pedestrian, metaphysical, abominate, cataract, idolatrous, indignity, commonalty, consign, perdition, infliction, surveillance, urbane. I tell you, I have never heard of one of those words spoke by anyone, not even you. Why put them in a book for folks to have to scratch their heads over? Melville does make good match-ups of two different things. Like a dead whale and a snow hill. I like to make my own match-ups too, which is a thing you might not know about me. I do it all the time in my head. I've got to say Chapter 3 was the best writing I ever read. Even better than my favorite parts of Crusoe. I'll wager you're mighty surprised. If you can't quite recall, this chapter's about when Ishmael meets the black harpooner Queequeg. How Ishmael believed Queequeg to be a cannibal, and how they'd been forced to share a bed on account the inn was full. Poor Queequeg wasn't expecting a visitor to his bed when Ishmael crept in, so course Queequeg got his feathers in a fluff: Who-e debel you? You no speak-e, dam-me, I kill-e. Mr. Coffin had to break it all up before Ishmael came to see Queequeg was a decent sort of man, though he was covered in tattoos and smoked his pipe in bed. He said "Better to sleep with a sober cannibal that a drunken Christian" and I couldn't quit laughing. When I finished the chapter, I went back and read it over again. It was even funnier that time.

Well, as you can see, I'm running out of room here, so I'll end this now. But I aim to find some more paper tomorrow morning and write you another letter. Once I read Chapters 4 and 5.

He'd signed it with "Still your loving husband."

I reread the letter, a different kind of letter entirely from the correspondence I'd previously received from him. It was almost like two different men had written them. The easy yet eager tone brought to mind the man I'd met almost eight years ago. There had been no apology, no explanation about Eliza Dickens. But I could sense his sorrow, the way Ben knew a school of fish lurked just below his skiff, waiting.

When Asha returned later that morning, I asked her if she'd like to teach for me for the remainder of the winter. When I told her my plans, she'd been both thrilled and worried, but her new spectacles had seemed to hearten her.

The following week, after a visit to Jacob and Ruby's house next door, I opened Oscar Whimble's door with a bright greeting.

"We're going to move you to our house, Oscar," I said, though he was lost in open-mouthed sleep. "The house that Ben built. Until repairs can be made here."

We collected a large amount of things we'd need: all sizes of beat-up pots and pans, earthenware, the few pieces of cutlery and cookware, candles and candlesticks, a big box of kitchen matches, oil lamp, chamber pot, gardening tools, small table and two chairs, barrels for washing, wood for the hearth. We stacked it all in their wagon, then Ruby and I bundled Oscar into his coat, hat, blankets and quilts.

As Duffy yipped, we all heaved him up—he weighed much less than I thought he might—and carried him outdoors to the wagon. Duffy circled as she made to follow Oscar into the wagon. I boosted her in, her ribs and hindquarters bony in my hands. I climbed in beside Oscar, whose face was just visible beneath the layers of wool and cotton. His watering eyes stared unblinking into the blue sky.

"I'll come over and help you sometimes," said Ruby behind a hand. "Don't mind what Jacob say."

Jacob had told me that the Nags Head house was too far from their own house in the woods to help me every day, and I didn't expect them to go out of their way any more than they already had for us.

330 | DIANN DUCHARME

"It's alright," I said. "I've been watching you. I know what to do."

She shook her head. "It's a job of work for one person." She reached out and squeezed my arm. "You got to lift him up all the time, help him use the pot. Wash him, cook his food, feed him, change his clothes, wash his linens."

The wagon had reached the edge of the woods, and the sand-laden wind met us in the clearing. I pulled up an edge of blanket to block Oscar's face from the onslaught.

"What you got to eat?" she asked. "You ain't no fishwife, ain't even got a patch. And all your stock is yonder on the island."

"I brought some food in that basket," I said. "Some eggs, a loaf of bread, a rasher of bacon, and some cornmeal and lard. Some chicken broth for soup. Cabbage, carrots and beets from Asha's garden."

"How long that gonna last you?"

I shrugged. "Neither of us eat much."

"Like I said, I'll come by time to time."

At the house, Jacob jumped down from the seat and made his way up the steps to the porch while I unlatched the back of the wagon and slid out. When I climbed up the steps with Oscar's tick, I saw Jacob working the nails from the planks over the door with a hammer.

"The boards are nailed back," I said.

He turned to me, hammer in hand.

"I removed them a few months ago when I stayed the night here," I began, but didn't want to admit that I'd neglected to nail them back up. I had emptied the shelves of their shells and departed in haste. "Did *you* nail them back up?"

He shook his head, pulling hard at an embedded nail. "They sure is nailed on tight *now.*"

Wiping his forehead with a sleeve, he pulled off the last board and pushed the door open. When he stepped into the darkness of the house, he bumped into something inside the doorway and grunted.

"What you got here, now?"

I peered into the cold gloom and spotted what looked to be a barrel.

"It's a barrel," I said.

"I can see that," he said. "*You* leave it here?"

I shook my head, recalling how hard the nails had been pounded into the planks. "It must have been Ben?"

"Come all the way down to put a barrel in the house?"

I shrugged.

Jacob took it in both hands and rocked it from side to side. "Got some weight to it."

We both contemplated the barrel for a moment, before Jacob slid it into the corner. "I'm just gonna leave it here. You open it up when you see fit."

Once we'd carried Oscar into the house and lay him on his tick, Duffy finally followed us up the steps. But on her way inside she was distracted by the barrel, and crouching low, she circled the barrel three times before barking at it.

Ruby and I made several trips to the wagon to fetch the household goods while Jacob went around the house prying the boards from the windows and pumping water from the well into a bucket. By the time they were ready to leave, the house was bathed in afternoon sunlight, and Oscar was cocooned in wool.

Ruby wrung her hands in her skirts, looking about the little room like it was a prison cell. "This ain't no good. Jacob, we can't leave 'em here. Not even a fire to cook supper by."

"I can light matches, you know," I said.

I struck the long, wooden match against the edge of the box and held it to the wood. We all watched in silence as the flame finally caught the wood and began to lick along the length. They made a slow departure, Ruby fussing over Oscar's heading and pushing a broom across the bare floor boards, and Jacob running a rag over the grimy window panes and arranging the rain barrels under the eaves.

Only when I heard the wagon creak away west through the sand did I truly feel the enormity of what awaited me. I turned to Oscar, surprised to find his eyes fastened on me. Duffy was sound asleep.

"At least the roof doesn't leak," I said. "I can't promise we won't have any rats though."

I hung the pot of chicken broth from a hook over the fire and stirred the pot of broth with a wooden spoon. I tied a rag around Oscar's chin, the back of his stubbled neck tickling my fingers.

The sunset gilded the room as decadently as Maddie's chandeliers; the ocean fizzed to the sand just few a hundred yards away. Time had slowed to a tortoise's pace.

Oscar's eyes still watched me, and his mouth crept up on one side in a kind of grin. I reached out to touch his gnarled hand.

I spooned up some warm broth from a bowl, and Oscar opened his mouth enough for me to slide in the spoon. Some of the broth dribbled from the corners, but he swallowed the rest. It took another half an hour to feed him the rest of the broth, and he grew drowsy soon after. His animation ebbed, leaving only the crooked mask of affliction.

The sun had been snuffed by the douter of night, but I still had the firelight. I ate at the table, tracing pocks and scars on its stained surface with the tip of my forefinger. Ben had dined at this table with Oscar for many years, two men belching and carving and chewing in silence, a long day of work to contemplate.

After I heated water in the cauldron and washed the dishes in the bucket, I banked the fire, struggled into my nightdress, and wrapped up in blankets on Ben's old tick. I curled toward the dwindling warmth of the hearth. My mind drifted with the sea, here and then there but never settling. At the height of a swell, I was full of purpose. But when the swell met land, I turned fearful and uncertain. I didn't want to ruminate over a future with Ben, but instead recollected the long summer days I'd sat with him on the porch of my family's cottage, reading and teaching and talking.

Dog and man snored three feet away, and I drifted off to the memory of Ben's hands, sweaty and rough, the sun in his eyes.

When the dawn came, the room trembled with early light. The window showed the silver sea through the swaying live oaks and cedar pine.

I turned to set another log onto the grate and poked the fire into life. Duffy raised herself up with a popping stretch and creaked over to the door, so I let her out to wander into the brisk morning, watching from the doorway as she trotted down to the ocean and then along the edge of the surf line, muzzle snuffing the sand.

The fire grew, so I stirred the remaining broth in the pot, then cracked eggs and fried bacon on the skillet. The smells of food must have made their way to the beach, for I soon heard Duffy's long toenails rake down the door. I fed her a strip of bacon before she stepped over to lick Oscar's cheeks with a greasy tongue. His eyes opened and looked to the hearth to the door to the windows, where the white sun blasted through each of the panes.

"Good morning, Oscar," I said. "I'm Abigail, your daughter-in-law. You're with me now, in the house that your son Ben built. I hope you're hungry."

Once he was upright and bibbed, I fed him a bowl of broth. I'd guessed he'd be sleepy afterward, but he blinked at me, wide awake. I rummaged through my bag for the book that I'd taken from the schoolhouse shelf the last day I'd taught. I couldn't have said why I'd brought it along, but when I pulled it from the bag, I kissed its frayed cover and inhaled its scent, vaguely salty.

"I think you'll enjoy this book, because Ben did. It's called *Robinson Crusoe*."

I started to read aloud.

I glanced up occasionally to find Oscar's eyes—Ben's eyes—still fixed on me. He remained upright for the first 10 pages before his head began to sag and his eyelids droop. I settled him back on his tick and set about gathering the dirty dishes and cookware. I pumped water into the bucket at the well and drank a dipperful while standing in the sand. It tasted of spring.

While Oscar slept, I read the remainder of Ben's letters. When I folded the last one into its envelope, a loneliness descended, as if a good friend had just left the house. He had never once mentioned Eliza and only occasionally touched on his job as a surfman. But it was as if he'd shed the seven long years we'd been together, as if he'd become once more the man I'd first met. The words in his letters were spaced together so closely that at times it seemed one long word, full of fever.

That evening, I sat at the table with ink and several sheets of paper. My heart beat against its bone cage; the candle flame beckoned as I dipped the pen. Thoughts of *Moby-Dick* stirred, mingling with the words in Ben's letters. I began to move the pen over the paper in the cumbersome print that Ben could read, as answers and comments and memories came to mind, continuing the dialogue between us. The more I wrote, the more I felt to be reaching back through time, picking up the thread of words that we'd lost. The ocean rushed and retreated nearby, and forgiveness seeped into my hand, into my fingers that held the pen.

Toward the end, I added, "I'm living at the Nags Head house so that I can care for your daddy. The roof of the old house was leaking badly, and rats were getting quite comfortable there, despite Duffy's best efforts. Jacob and Ruby helped me load a wagon with supplies and get us settled. He is doing quite well, given the change. Asha is teaching for me while I'm gone."

I folded the papers and was stuffing them into an envelope when Duffy crept over to sniff at the barrel. Around and around she went before she started to bark again. I tried to pull her away from it, but she skirted my grasping hands every time.

"What is it, Duffy?" I asked. "What do you smell?"

She yipped at me, her eyes wide and tail swinging with canine excitement. I rummaged through the pile of old tools I'd brought from Oscar's home and found a dented crowbar. I worked the edge under the lid of the barrel as Duffy urged me on with a dripping tongue. When at last I managed to pry off the lid, the terrible stench of old fish overwhelmed me. Duffy jumped as high as her back legs could manage to sniff at the opening. I held my nose and leaned to peer inside.

A large, whitish-gray rock rested in the confines of the barrel. I rocked the barrel back and forth, and the rock nudged softly against the wood, as if porous. I sniffed once more, and there below the fish stink was a piquant odor—earthy, and pleasant, like soil and freshly fallen leaves. Beneath the island aroma lingered the exact scent of my old home.

Duffy whined and tried once more to jump.

"It's just a rock," I said, but it didn't sound quite like the truth. I hammered the lid back on the barrel, then grabbed Duffy by her scruff and pulled her over to Oscar's tick. "It's not food, girl. I promise."

I sat down, unfolded the letter to Ben, and scrawled out a postscript, asking about the barrel and the white rock and if he'd been the one to leave it here.

Then I stuffed the stack of paper into an envelope and lay down on my tick, but I wasn't tired, even after the long day of work. The moon was too bright in the darkness surrounding it, as bright as the sun in a blue sky. There was no escape in this little house by the sea.

As I was drifting to sleep, I remembered Mr. Wharton's letter, all he'd offered to me. I still hadn't responded.

It was a crisp winter's day, with the ocean and sky melded into a marble of deep blue, the whitecaps a mirror image of the rocky clouds overhead. After breakfast and washing, I propped Oscar's head with a roll of heading, so that he had a good view of the ocean through the live oaks. Then I settled into the chair near the fire to read *Robinson Crusoe* to him.

Duffy had gone out this morning to explore and hadn't yet returned. At what I took for her ascent up the steps, I rose to let her in. But on my way to the door, a hard knocking began. I unlatched the door to find three women standing before me. They all wore

heavy woolen bonnets and shawls over their homespun, and all carried baskets covered with cloths.
Two of the women hung back a bit. But the woman
closest to me was white-haired and brown-faced, with
a bosom that hung to her waist. She held a walking
stick of smoothed driftwood.

"How's he faring?" she asked me, eyes darting to
the room behind me.

"Who?"

"T.W.!" she crackled. "That's him, ain't it?"

Word had traveled surprisingly fast. "Oh, yes."
His cheeks looked pink in the morning sun shining
through the doorway. "He's a little better, I believe."

She looked me up and down. "You don't know
me. But I'm a friend of Ben's momma's. Long time
ago. Loretta Weeks. I didn't come to your hitching."

"Oh. I… that's alright."

She turned to the women behind her. "These here
are my girls. That's Alice, and that there's Ida." They
too had lines on their brown faces, but the strands
that peeked from their withered bonnets were still a
greasy brown.

"Please, come inside," I said, and I held the door
open as the two women helped Loretta over the
threshold. I offered them the two chairs, and Mrs.
Weeks sat, but Alice and Ida stood. The smells of fish
stew and cornbread emanated from the basket.

"Hey there, T.W.," Mrs. Weeks hollered at Oscar.
"It's me, Loretta."

Oscar stared at her, his mouth twisted into a
rictus.

Alice leaned toward me then. "Me and Ida and some others been helping out Jacob and Ruby, taking care of T.W. since his fit."

"Yes, I knew that some of…you…were helping us," I said. "I thank you. It was so hard for us to get over here from the island."

They all glanced at one another. "You're a schoolmarm," said Alice. "Or so I heard."

"Yes."

"You teach the darkies?"

"And a few white children as well."

"Do tell," she said. "Well, I reckon you should start up a school here in Nags Head some time. My younguns…they ain't got much learning to speak of."

"To be truthful, I've quit teaching for a while, so that I can care for…T.W."

"Oh, we know. And you did right," said Loretta, and reached over to pat my cheek with a softly calloused hand. "Ain't got but one family in this world."

We stared at Oscar as if he was late in delivering a keynote address.

"Mama, tell her about the food," said Ida.

Loretta looked to the hearth, blinked at the small basket of food and buckets of water nearby. "Ain't no way you can fix food and care for T.W. proper, all on your own. The women got together and agreed to bring you some food, trade the job around."

"What women?"

"Nags Headers, o' course."

I had the urge to laugh and cry at the same time. "That's very kind of you. I don't…know what to say."

She grinned at me, displaying slick gums with a handful of teeth. "Just a little sustenance. Nothing of the quality, you know. Don't be expecting nothing fancy, now."

"I wouldn't."

CHAPTER EIGHTEEN

FEBRUARY 19, 1876
ELIZA DICKENS

*Human madness is oftentimes a cunning and most feline
thing. When you think it fled, it may have but become trans-
figured into still subtler form. Ahab's full lunacy subsided
not, but deepeningly contracted…*

–*ISHMAEL*, **MOBY-DICK**

WASN'T SO BLASTED COLD, SO ME AND ABNER SAT ON THE
crack club porch. I held the learning book in my
hands. Abner took his finger and ran it under the
words I read. Like I couldn't do that for my own self.
I swatted his finger away.

"Come with me, Ann, and see the man with the
black hat on his head," I read. "The fat hen has left
the nest. Run, Nat, and get the eggs."

Abner hooted. "Nary a wobble! I swear, you're reading better than me."

I snorted. "Fat hens forsooth. What good is reading this nonsense gonna do me?"

He just grinned. "Time comes, you'll be doffing your hat to Ann and Nat."

We rocked for a while, watching the fowl fly about the sound. I reckoned there weren't but one or two better feelings than having the sun warm you up in winter time.

"We should have ourselves a little outing today," Abner said. "Like Iola and Jonas do."

I quit rocking to look at him. "What are you spouting off about now?"

"A outing of sorts. Supper on the skiff mayhaps. We could pack a blanket and watch the moon rise." His fist rose up into the air to show me something round. His good leg jiggled antsy while he watched me.

Ben had come day before with some bluefish for us, at long last. I was so glad to see him I tried to hug on him, but he held me at arms' length. Like I was a muddy dog aiming to sniff his crotch. Since then I'd been on pins and needles.

I smoothed out the learning book on my lap. "Care to fetch me some cider from the barrel out back? Pour some for yourself too."

When he went behind the house I grabbed up his mail bag and started to pulling out letters. Didn't take me long to find a letter for Ben. The envelope was thick, stuffed to bursting with folded paper and covered all over with nice and straight print, nary a ink splotch to be seen. *"Ben Whimble, Jones's Hill Lifesaving Station,"* it said.

I heard Abner side-stepping around the clubhouse, so I quick raised my skirts and slid it inside the waistband of my stockings. I shoved the other letters back inside the bag and pulled it shut.

Abner hopped slow into view, his good eye on the tin cups of cider. He handed me one of the cups, sticky already with spilt juice.

"Drink that down and come around back with me," he said.

"Why?"

"Just come on. I got something to show you."

We drank the cider down, then walked around back. At the steps near the barrel he got down on his hands and knees, joints cracking and leg stuck out like a broom handle. He reached under the bottom step and pulled out his hands real slow. They held a tiny ball of fur, spotted in shades of brown and black. Eyelids shut tight as jars, they were so young.

"There looks to be around five of 'em," he said. "Spaniel, mayhaps some setter."

I felt that same old hook-snag on my heart when I lay eyes on such helpless critters. He handed the pup to me real careful, and I held it to my chest. It curled up soft in my hand, no heavier than a bit of dandelion fluff.

"I don't see their mama in there. Bunch of marsh grass for a birthing nest though," he said. "She might be around, looking for food. You seen a hound about?"

I shook my head. I didn't want to talk or even breathe. It was like a spell of magic, holding something like this. I could feel Abner watching me with soft, wet eyes, like I'd just done birthed our own baby.

"You're gonna care for 'em, ain't you?" he said, running a finger down the pup's back. "If their mama doesn't come back."

"You know I will," I said, and I hardly knew my own voice it was so high and soft.

"Yeah, I know," he said, sounding sad. "You always were a soft heart for the strays. I always wished you'd take care of me too, Eliza."

I clutched the pup harder to my chest. "I can't."

"Why not?" He sounded like he really couldn't work it out.

"I'm spoken for."

"That so." He huffed and puffed himself to his feet, then dipped himself some more cider from the barrel.

"I knew what was gonna happen to you when you saw Ben at Amos's funeral," he said. He wiped his mouth with a sleeve.

I buried my face in the pup's fur. It smelled like brackish water and blood.

"Those two, they got something. I ain't sure what it is, but they got it."

"Not anymore."

He blew air from his mouth, then banged his cup down on the step. He walked back into the house so fast it was like his bad leg was working just fine. I heard him fetch his mailbag, then watched him stump down the docks to his skiff.

I sat on the back step with the pup sleeping in my skirts for a long time. I wished Iola were around, but she was off with Jonas every day now.

Canada geese flew over the sound, so queer in their quiet.

I bent under the steps to put the pup back with his kin. I almost bawled when I saw him raise up his head to sniff hungry at another's belly and snuggle up, paws scrabbling. *Just like Ben and me. Us against the world.* When I went inside, I saw that Abner'd taken the learning book with him, the book he'd had me write my name in. I figured I wouldn't be seeing Abner again, save for when he poled by with his mail.

I didn't know what to do with the letter that night. I pulled it out from my waistband where it'd already scraped me raw. I just looked at it, all hard and thick in my hands. I wondered what-all Abigail'd told him. I thought of the book Ben was reading and his own long letters.

I shoved the thing under my tick. But I had a hard time falling asleep with that mound of paper right under me, felt like it was burning a hole in my back. I rolled onto one side, then the other, thinking of things like *Moby Dick, unborn babies, newborn pups, caretaker's house.* I couldn't settle on any notion, other than Ben's whisperings at the Christmas party, how his breath went through my ear straight to my heart.

I knew things were done between Ben and Abigail. They were just having a hard time with the notion. One letter wasn't gonna make a difference.

What's fair is fair, I thought. I'd had Ben taken from me. I wasn't about to just let him loose again.

I fetched up a blanket and started walking south-west 'til I saw the lookout tower of the station house. Then I hid myself behind the shed. The lighthouse light blinked on and off for me, making the sand around me go red, then white, red then white. I saw Ben's face in my mind the night we saw the tower get lit, recalled how happy he was with me beside him.

After a while I heard some talking amongst men and saw one set out north and one south. I squinted at them hard in their lantern light, and I saw it was only Jerry and Spencer. I curled up into my blanket. It was gonna be a long night waiting but it didn't bother me none.

Few hours later and Jerry made his way back to the station house a bit slower then when he'd started out. Soon enough Spencer came back too. Then two men waiting on them took the lanterns and set out north and south. One of the men made nothing but noise, hee-hawing and calling back to Spencer. *Lewis,* I thought. But the other man was quiet as the grave, and I just knew he had to be Ben. Sure enough, I saw his beard in the lantern light.

I did what I had to do, biting my cheeks against the cold, and draped the blanket about me once more. Then I ran to catch him up. I followed in his steps for a time, but he didn't even turn. It was dark everywhere but where the lantern swung. There was nothing to hear over the ocean noise.

"Ben," I said when I judged the time to be right. He flinched bad and stopped walking. He turned about quick and swung the lantern up so he could see my face.

"Good God, Eliza." He didn't smile, nothing even close. "What in the hell? I took you for Jonas Spruel, come to gut me at last."

I didn't say a word. I just let the blanket slide down my body, let the cold air have its way on my skin.

He moved the lantern down a bit and saw that I was naked. I walked up to him and put my limbs around him. I buried my face into the neck of his coat and breathed in his smell, the salty-sweet I'd known for so long. I rubbed my breasts on him, ground my woman parts on him.

I heard the lantern drop down to the sand, and then felt his hands on my back. I burned hot until I felt him use those hands to push me down off him. But I couldn't be pried away that easy. I clung to him with all I had. The bones of my fingers dug into the back of the coat, my toes dug into the tops of his boots.

"No," I said into his neck, my teeth gritted hard. "No."

I didn't want to let go, but there was something wrong with my body. Like I was made of summer jelly, no bones in me a-tall. He got me down to the sand. He grabbed the blanket, wrapped it twice around me.

"I still love my wife." He said it like he was so sure of it.

I tried to shake my head no, but started to shivering bad enough to shake the skin off.

"Look at you," he said. He reached down and plucked me from the sand. He started carrying me back from where we'd come, lantern swinging squeaky from a hand.

"You can't keep doing this." His breath smelled of apple butter. I tried to kiss him on the mouth, but my neck had gone stiff as a corpse. I gave it all up and leaned my head on his arm, felt the hard muscle of it holding my weight.

Didn't take him long to haul me back. He tried to lay me down in the cook house where the warmth still hung on, but I started clinging on him again. He had to use his knee to wedge inside the both of us and push me away. I fell down hard to the floor, but I didn't feel a thing.

"Where'd you put your clothes?"

I wriggled from the blanket and stood there naked again. Now he could see me. Mayhaps now he could hear me.

"Here I am, Ben." I turned about for him. "Just me. Just…everything you need. No clothes, no books, no damned letters, younguns galore. It can be this easy, Benny. Just like it used to be."

He shaded his eyes like the sun was shining. "Please, now, put that blanket back on."

My lips were numb, but the fire inside me melted the cold away. "You look at me, Ben Whimble!"

He put a finger to his lips, but it wasn't a circumstance who heard me.

"You know you want it. I saw your pecker poking through your pantaloons when you were cuddling up with me Christmas Eve. You can't deny it!"

He clapped his hands over his mouth and shut his eyes.

I stepped closer to him. "I been waiting on you to stake your claim ever since then. But you can't be bothered with nothing but reading that blasted book and writing letters all day!"

"I know," he said. "I should have told you what was going on with me. I should have. I'm sorry I didn't. I just felt…bad about…"

I reached up to stroke his golden beard, but he quick moved his head away.

"Shhh." I reached with my other hand to rub his ear and felt his skittishness, the way I felt an animal's. I could always calm such a animal. I spoke soft, like he was a bird with a broken wing. "Don't fret. Lyzee's here now. I won't ever leave you."

He grabbed my fingers tight. "Eliza, I told you. I still love Abby. More than I can say. Being with you…" he said, and let go my hand.

"Go on." Tears warmed my cheeks as they washed down.

"I don't…" His voice shook like a wind was blowing in his throat. "When I came here to Whales Head, I thought I was gonna lose her. We had a rough patch for a while there, and things between us were just…I don't know, just…broke. I was lonesome, see, when I met up with you again. But even when I was with you, I thought of Abby all the time. I wanted her back so bad."

My fingernails dug into the skin of my hands hard, listening to his sad, sad voice tell of how much he loved another woman.

"You ain't meant for each other," I said stern, like my mama would.

"You may be right." Now he sounded like he might cry. "She ain't even written me back one letter, after all the letters I sent her. And I don't blame her! She doesn't deserve the likes of me, I sure know that."

"Maybe that's why she ain't writing," I said, real soft. "She's moving on. That teacher school…"

He shook his head hard, then said, "I reckon so."

"Maybe it's too hard, being with her. You *need* a Banker. Someone that knows how hard it is, living out here. Someone that's strong enough to take it. She's too soft and high-falutin'."

Quick as a cat, he reached down and took up the blanket and flung it over me. He pushed me up against the cook stove and put his face right next to mine so I had to look into his eyes. And those eyes, those same eyes I'd seen bright with happy and full with love, were burning with hate. I couldn't look away, much as I wanted. They were Ben's eyes.

"Just stop it," he said, spitting with his words. "You don't have a notion what you're speaking of."

I didn't feel the skittish in him then. I knew there was a fire in his belly, the same way I knew to get the hell out of a rabid coon's way. He let go my shoulders, and I went down hard.

"Where'd you put your clothes?"

"Out," I tried to say, but sound came out as a thin as a kitten's whisker. I tried once more. "Out back… behind the shed."

He went out the door and came back with my clothes and shoes. He just about threw them down in front of me.

He picked up the lantern and made to leave me there, then stopped. "You gonna need someone to help you get back to the crack club?"

I looked at my hands, not a bit of feeling to 'em. "No."

"Alright then."

The cold air rushed in with a vengeance when he opened the cook house door. It was just a small sliver of the night, but it was enough for him to disappear into.

I woke up with a jump in the black of the cabin. I tried to make myself breathe.

My blankets were down at my feet and I shivered like I had the ague. I saw the light coming through the cracks of the logs, saw the tore-up envelope with Abby's letter pages messed about on the floor. It was morning already, but I knew I'd only just gone to sleep.

The cabin creaked and spit, angry like me. I grabbed up the pages and stuffed 'em back in the envelope. I dressed quick, my hair all atangle, and stomped over to the clubhouse with my gun on my shoulder. Up the steps I went. I heard the pups whining underneath, but I didn't peek to see if their mama was there. Life was gonna chew their flesh and spit out their bones, either way.

No surprise, Iola and Jonas were there like they owned the place, setting at the dining table eating vittles off the good china and drinking coffee from the tea cups. Jonas eyed my tangled hair and britches and army coat.

"You look god-awful," he said. "More than usual, is what I mean."

He held a match to Mr. Parrish's pipe.

"You sure know how to make yourself at home," I said.

Out came a mouthful of the fanciest tobacco smoke. "I got a taste for the fine things in life."

He winked at Iola.

"I'm heading down to Nags Head today. Gonna visit with mama," I said.

"You are?"

"High time for a visit. I won't be able to, come the spring."

"Well, I reckon that'll do you a whole world of good. Get some rest."

"You can handle everything here, I take it."

"Oh we sure can," said Jonas. "Don't you worry about a thing now. You have yourself a nice, long visit."

I almost choked on my eggs, but I ate up and grabbed my gun.

The house Ben built for Abby still came unbid to my mind sometimes, clear as day. The bulls-eye of my shame. I'd often thought of burning it to the ground. I'd let it stand, tried to smudge it from my mind's eye. But now it was high time for a reckoning. I almost *wanted* to see the house again.

That letter of Abigail's was a job of work to read, but I read every word of it. And I came to see that the things she'd put in that letter were things that didn't matter at all. Book words, they were. Gloppy thoughts, like a pig's breakfast all over the paper. A hundred times worse than Nat and Ann's plodding. The world would go on turning, hard and steady, and the things that were in that letter would fly up in the sky with the littlest wind, gone forever.

A person shouldn't have to think about such things, let alone read and write about them. And if there was one thing I knew, it was Ben's love of all things simple. He wanted the ease of water, the hardness of muscle and bone, the warm sun and fish to eat. Ambergris was simple too. Gold from the sea. Course he wanted it for himself. I'd seen him that day, the barrel in *Tessa*'s bow, heard the lies in his mouth as he spurted them out. Things stopped being simple right there. Cheating around, like he did when he first met Abigail, going against his nature. She'd soured him, led him astray from who he was. Ambergris might as well be a lump of coal for all the good it was gonna do him and his wife. Anybody with two eyes could see *that*.

I took out Abigail's letter and ripped it up into about a hundred little pieces, then threw 'em into the water behind me. Looked like chum afloating, which to my mind wasn't near as foul as all those book words.

It was late in the night, time I pulled up to the Nags Head pier and tied up the skiff. The lantern showed me the faded lines of what I knew was there: the two empty hotels, the house on stilts where

Loretta Weeks lived, mama's market. Mama didn't live far, only a little ways into the woods, but my feet took me straight to the ocean side.

In no time I saw the house through clumps of crooked trees. I picked my way through dead branches and went right up to the windows. But all was dark in the house, fire gone down low.

I held the gun tight in my hands and went up the porch steps. I knocked on the door with the end of my boot, heard Duffy bark in the house. The hard in my jaw bone softened up a bit. I'd forgot about Duffy. I'd loved that dog as my own once.

"Who's there?" she called, all sleepy.

"It's me," I spat.

"Loretta?"

"No, it ain't Loretta. It's me. Eliza Dickens."

Took a while, but I heard the door unlatch, watched it crack open a inch. I pushed it wide with the end of the gun and stepped inside, saw Abigail's white face in the light of her candle.

Duffy knew me, started to squealing and bumping all around my legs, but I just swung the lantern up and looked about the little room. House really was a lot smaller than I ever gave it credit for. Saw a few things in the shadows—what must be T.W. sleeping on a tick, baskets of food and dirty linens, the barrel in the corner.

"What do you want?" she asked. She had the gall to sound mad with me.

I stepped over to the barrel, wedged up the butt of my rifle under the lid and popped it open. I leaned into it and took a powerful sniff. The smell of the rotted fish and whatever it was ambergris smelled of clouded up my whole head like a fog.

I turned to Abigail, standing there cold in her nightdress with her long hair and eyes gone big in the candlelight.

"Don't you know it's gold settin' here in your own house? You must be some kind of stupid."

She raised her chin up. "What are you talking about?"

"I reckon Ben doesn't tell you much now anyhow, so I guess I'll have to be the one to do it. It's ambergris in this barrel. You ever heard of that?"

"I have."

She had to step close to me to get to the barrel, but she kept her head high. She bent to give a uppity sniff.

"I should have known," she said, like it was a game we played at.

"Oh, I reckon you know all about it. So damned smart, ain't you."

"I've read about it. I've never smelled it."

"Course you *read* about it. But you know, you can't learn all you need to know by reading. Like the fact that we fell back in love up there this winter. He tell you about us?"

"No." But her eyes told me she knew anyways.

"We had a grand time, carrying on behind your back, 'til he started reading that *Moby-Dick* book and writing you those damnable letters."

At last my jumping eyes found the letters, stuffed in a basket under the table. I stepped over and dumped them all out onto the floor.

"These bits of paper don't mean a thing, in the grand scheme of things. Bunch of horse shit." I ground my boots all over the paper, heard them tear. "That letter you last wrote to him. I took it. Read it too. I learned me to read, see. I'm moving up in this world, got a job better'n yours I'll wager. Figured Ben would like me better. But it turns out that hope was for naught. Reading still did me some good, for it told of the barrel setting here. It's in high demand, up there in Whales Head, and no one knows it's here but me. And Ben, o' course."

Abigail put her candle down slow and turned to put a log on the hearth. When she turned back to me, she said, "Is it yours?"

"It is now. It used to be Livy Spruel's, then Ben aimed to own it. And he took it upon himself to hide it here.

He's a liar, you know. Fair and square. And he deserves me taking this ambergris out from under him. Thing is, I just can't feature what he was going to spend the money on. Buy you some pretty dresses like you like. Nice shiny ear baubles or some such. But I figure a woman like you doesn't need any more help. You've had your fine time. It's time for others to have a shot at life."

"I don't want it," she said, but I didn't really hear her.

"I'll have you know, you hoodwinked Ben, once upon a time. But you ain't never fooled me. I always knew you for a outsider. You just lookin' in on folks from the outside all the time, and wondering '*How is it up your way?*' and trying hard to cut yourself in another pattern but never knowing you weren't meant to *be* on the inside. You'll *always* be an outsider. I know it, and Ben knows it now too. No matter where you go, you'll always be lost. And that's a sorry place to be. Might as well be dead."

I slammed the lid back on the barrel and banged it shut with the gun. I made to open the door when I heard T.W. say a word or two. My heart churned butter in my chest. I turned my head to where he lay on the tick, saw Abigail squatting over him with a tin cup.

I stepped over and bent down to look into his old face. Hardly looked the same man. Skin like tanned hide. Thin, white lips a-muttering, eyeballs skidding under the flaps. I'd loved him like he was my own daddy. It should've been *me* caring for him, *me* living in this house. I grabbed the tin cup of water from Abigail's hand, spilled a little on the floor.

"Hey there, T.W. It's Lyzee." I sounded to be choking on a chicken bone. "Remember me?"

I held the cup to his cracked lips, but he didn't want any drink. Tears stung bad at my eyes, but I rubbed 'em away. He always hated crying, even if blood was pouring from your skin. I kissed him on his cheek, gritty as a sandy sail. Patted on his skinny shoulder, tried not to recall how strong he used to be, how he could lift me into a boat easy as blowing on a dandelion.

I got up, took the lid off the barrel once more, and dumped out the ambergris. Then I chopped a chunk off the soft rock of ambergris with my knife.

My arm burned to throw it, but I set the rock down soft on a shelf.

"You tell him it's from me," I said. "You hear?"

I heaved the rock back inside the barrel and rolled it out the door.

I never grinned so much as I did on the trip back to Whales Head. I mostly thought on what Ben's face might look like when he found out I'd paid his wife a visit, took his barrel of ambergris too. Spoiled his designs, no doubt, the way he'd spoiled mine, over and over again.

My own pap was better'n Ben, and let me tell you, that is saying something. The old coot took out his hate with the world by beating his women with fists. By liquoring too much and cutting up everywhere he went. Made me the way I am today—skittish as a cat, can't even look men in their eyes. There was a time when I thought pap the worst man alive. But he ain't got nothing on Ben.

It takes a low-down, soulless kind of man to get a person's hopes up just to exflunticate 'em. At least pap let us know where we stood with him. We knew we were more useless to him than the hens that ran pecking and shitting about the house. We never hoped for more.

But Ben made me believe I meant something to him, that I was something special. There was a part of me that still held to that, when I started in seeing him this winter. But he took my soft heart and put it to the hot sun, left it out to harden and die. Now I was walking around with a brick heart in my chest.

Folks better just watch out, they see me comin', for I'll do to them same thing I did to Ben and Abigail, just reach out and take what I want.

I saw Abigail, standing in that little house with her arms crossed about her and teeth chittering. Looking like a sack of flour a-standing there, nothing more. *Ben could have her*, I thought, and laughed just about all the way back to Whales Head.

But when I poled the skiff up to the Yankee docks, I started to cussing fit to bust. There were about six dories and dugouts tied up, crowding the pier, and I had a good notion whose they were. I got out and pulled the skiff to land and hid it inside the deepest of the marsh grasses, sail draped across the barrel.

Britches dripping wet, I walked up to the house with my gun and peeked in the side window. There sat Jonas, head of the damned table crowded to bursting with his kin. They all had slices of Iola's pork loins set atop the china and laughing fit to bust. Likely had corn liquor in the good china tea cups. Iola was up and serving folks buns off a tray, face whiter than Abigail's.

I was so huffed I didn't even go back to the cabin to change out of my britches. I stomped my way inside and showed myself gun first. But they were so beat down by life and liquor that they barely turned their heads from their meals.

"By the horn spoons, if it ain't the Spruel family," I said, teeth grinding.

Iola almost dropped the bun tray. "Eliza! You're back! I...I wasn't expecting you for at...at least a couple more days. You sure were quick about visiting!"

"Well, mama didn't like it that I'd left the club-house alone, figuring it was ripe for the hornswogglers. You know mama," I said with a wink, "always right."

I looked about at the mudsill, forks and knives held tight in their fists. "What brings such a fine family as yours to our humble little crack club?"

Jonas opened his mouth to talk, but not quick enough for me.

"I swear, old Jonas here sure has made himself right at home. What's that you're drinking there, some of the Yanks' best whiskey? Smoking from the Yanks' pipe? Eating off their pork loin? Course he is. He fancies himself a huckleberry above most folk's persimmons. Which he sure ain't."

"Watch your mouth, Eliza," said Jonas. He kept his face loose, but I did see as how he eyed my gun. His kin—eight redheads of all different ages—watched me and Jonas with lazy eyes. They were used to his cutting up, I saw. Likely wouldn't have been a circumstance to see him gut me with the butter knife, then sit down and slather a roll with it.

Iola said, "Now Eliza, why don't you set yourself down and eat? You've had a long trip, and I can see you're tired." She handed me a roll with a sorry smile on her face. "How's your mama?"

A boy with dirt on his forehead took up a silver spoon and turned it about before his face. Then he started to smacking it on the table. I bent to snatch it from his grubby hand.

"I don't think I will sit with the likes of these folks, manners fit to fill a thimble. I'd rather take a meal with the horses in the barn."

The Spruels didn't even flinch, just kept up with their shecoonery. I went through the kitchen house and was on my way outside when I thought of the ambergris, setting all alone in my skiff with Spruels running loose. I must've lost my mind. I made myself put my gun up. Then I went to stand in the dining room doorway, gave the monkey his spoon back.

"I...Iola's hit the nail on the head. I'm tired. I am. And I do want to excuse myself for acting so surly."

The two younguns guffawed, showing chompers like molded cheese. Their mamas watched me with blue cat-eyes. An old woman spat over her shoulder on the nice rug.

Jonas stabbed a bite of pork with his knife and pointed it at me. "My granny don't like you."

"Like I said, I'm...sorry. To make it up, you all could stay the night, if you don't want to head back after supper."

Jonas eyed me suspicious while he chewed the meat. "You feeling poorly or something?"

I shrugged. Come to think, I *was* feeling poorly. Poorly enough to gut every single Spruel where they sat.

"We'll stay the night. And not on account of you. We were planning to anyways."

I swallowed down my bitter words and acted like I was hungry for the food Iola put in my hands. The younguns skedaddled when the platters emptied, but I stood there watching Jonas pour bottle after bottle of the Yanks' liquor into fine crystal glasses. Seemed their rundown bodies took the quality of the drink hard, for they soon called it a night. Iola led 'em like sheep up the stairs to the bedrooms, where I'm sure she'd done up the feather beds in the good linens. I started to clearing up the dishes when I heard a ruckus in the library.

Come to find, the younguns had found the ink and pens and paper and dripped it all over tarnation: the rug, the wood, the leather. They'd taken Mr. Parrish's books from the shelves and ripped out pages to draw on. I stood there staring for a long while, a powerful anger rising up in me, like they'd shat all over my very own books. I grabbed 'em by their ears and towed them hollering up the stairs.

I found their mamas in Mr. Sexton's bedroom, already laid flat. "You gonna mind your younguns?"

"Get your hands offa them," they clucked.

I let go of their ears and they ran for their lives. "Dumb crackers don't know how to act. They've been on a spree same as if two ruttin' boars got loose."

"Ain't you the housekeep?" said one mama. "Clean it up."

I thought of the ambergris again, to settle myself. I closed the door and went back down to help Iola in the kitchen, but she wasn't there. I chewed snuff for a while in the torn-up library, keeping watch for the younguns. At last the clubhouse got quiet, and I made my way to the docks in the moonlit dark. I waded through the marsh to where the old sail lay atop the barrel, then started to rolling it toward land.

I pushed open the door of the game barn, still full of barrels of feathers and smelling of musk and oils. One more barrel wasn't gonna make a difference. I slid it into the back corner when a voice in the dark said, "I knew you were up to something, girl."

My mind started to pump with stories and lies, just like when I was a youngun.

"Consarn you. You scared me to death."

I heard Jonas's boots step toward me in the dark. "I meant to," he said. I could only see the stuff of his hair in the shadows. "What you got there?"

"Nothing that concerns you."

He took two steps closer, so that I smelled the pork loin on his beard. "That so?"

I backed up against the wall of the barn. "Uh-huh. Just something I found."

"Where at? Some place Ben put it, most like. I *knew* you knew where it was."

"No, you listen to me now. I found it, out hunting the other day. Half-buried in the mud of Long John Pond. Had to use my pole to fish it out, and I just barely got the job done without losing my life in that mud. Whoever did put it there knew it would be a devil of a time getting out. But I figured it was your precious barrel, so I thought to help you out. Fact is, you should be thanking me."

It was too dark to see his hand come up to slap me across my head. I went down on my knees, and he stepped around me to take up a tool of some sort and pry open the barrel. He took a big whiff of the inside of it, then sneezed.

"You smelled it yet?"

I smelled old cow dung, dried seaweed, wet driftwood, the sun, tobacco. Things I smelled every day, but all mixed up in a potion I'd never before smelled. I shook my head no.

"Smells like money."

"I *was* planning on telling you, once I got it hid away."

"I should kill you where you lay," he said, but his voice was giddy as a boy's.

"Iola won't like it if you do," I said. I saw Iola's pretty face in my mind, recalled how sad she was when we put Amos in the ground. She'd be sad again, most like, but it was the only way.

"She tell you she's with child yet?"

He glared at me. "You shut your mouth."

"You ain't seen the way her belly's growing?"

Sure he had. He rubbed his face with big hands. Bent over at the middle.

"It ain't yours. It's her dead husband's. And she's never gonna love you like she loved Amos. Never gonna love you like she's gonna love his baby."

He shuffled his feet about, huffed and puffed. "Shitfire, shitfire."

He shook himself all over like a wet dog. "There was a blasted baby in her belly, and us carrying on like that…why'd she have to go and do this? Trick me like that."

"I know. You should just cut your losses and ske-daddle while you can. You don't seem like you're ready to be a pap."

"Hell no. I'm to be a rich man soon!" He reached over to pat the barrel. "Get me a woman without all that baggage."

"Start fresh."

"That's what I'll do, damn it to hell." He walked to the door, looked out into the night.

"You tell her? Tell her I couldn't live with a woman and another man's baby and she ought to've fessed up at the get-go?"

"I'll be glad to."

He started in rolling the barrel out the door. He hooted at me, still sitting on the floor. "Easy come, easy go. Ain't that right?"

"That is what they say."

"Better work a little harder to fool Jonas next time."

But the fact was, I'd already done cut another chunk of ambergris off, stashed it in a bucket on the skiff. It was small enough that Jonas wouldn't cotton to the missing of it, but big enough to make a difference in the lives of folks I cared about. Mama didn't raise me up simple, you know.

CHAPTER NINETEEN

MARCH 1, 1876
BEN WHIMBLE

Book! You lie there; the fact is, you books must know your places. You'll do to give us the bare words and facts, but we come in to supply the thoughts.

– ISHMAEL, MOBY-DICK

I SPENT THE MORNING ON THE SHORE WITH THE SURFMEN, taking it in turns to throw a line from a heaving stick as far as we could into the windy sea. I reckon we'd all lost some of our strength in the long months of our employ, for that heaving stick could hardly be made to clear the nearest breakers. Eliza had stopped coming by with food, but it seemed the men were fine to forego full bellies to have her gone.

Captain Gale found me hunched over and coughing on the way back to the equipment room. Even so, he ran down a list of provisions he had going in his head. Being the best man on a boat, I was the only one he sent to the mainland for supplies any more. In truth I looked forward to the job on account it broke up the days of walking with a trip on the waters of the Currituck Sound.

I missed the sound, but it seemed she'd grown angry at my absence. Her waters were peaked as mountains, and the shoals were covered in only a few inches of water on account of the wind. I pulled up the anchor on the station's own skiff and poled hard out of the shallows heading west to the mainland. The wind pushed at my back, and I soon raised the spritsails. I bounced in and out of the peaks so hard I bit my tongue. It was looking to be a hard four miles.

The bow's tumble sprayed water into my eyes, and I coughed so hard I saw nothing but black before me. The closer I got to the shores of the mainland, the higher the water rose. When I tried to put oars in to steer her, the left row-lock broke, and I cursed and hollered, made to use only one oar. I washed up into a tangle of brush nowhere near the port. I pulled the boat to land over the flooding marsh grasses and started out for the village of Tulls Creek.

"Don't tell me. You need some paper and stamps," said Lionel Tatum when at last I stepped into the store. Business must've been slow, for he sat behind the counter carving what looked to be his fifth duck decoy.

I shook my head no. "You can't fix a row-lock, can you?"

"Yours busted? I ain't surprised, with that wind a-screeching."

"Boat's down south a ways."

"I'll have to fetch Wick Hazlett for you. The blacksmith out here. It may take some time to rout him out. Why don't you pick out what you need, and I'll head on to his place."

I piled up the provisions next to the ducks: sacks of cornmeal and grits and coal, a tub of lard, crate of sweet potatoes, sundry items for cleaning. Then I drifted to the writing supplies. Just looking at the sheaves of paper, the lines of ink bottles, made me limp.

I made myself pick up a bottle of ink, turn it about in my cold hands. I was worn down by the black, oily stuff, by the cold, white paper. I'd started to see how my own mind was filled with other men's words, words that had taken the place of my own. I put the ink down on the shelf, hoping I'd never have cause to purchase one more bottle of the stuff. Writing, well, the habit was meant for a kind of person I wasn't.

I turned my back on the writing supplies and went out front to see if I could spot Lionel, but nothing was moving on the road save the dirt in the wind. A boy and a girl sat on the steps of one of the only abodes in Tulls Creek, tossing a pine cone in the air. They eyed me for the empty-souled stranger that I was.

I walked down to the sound, at a safe enough distance to marvel at the size of the swells. I couldn't even make out the Banks across the wild waters. A "V" of Canada geese flew over the land, likely looking for the safety of a cove. It was about time for them to start heading for the icy Canada north, their true homes, where they bred and birthed their young. I watched them soar, their brown wings beating against the wind. I'd seen tiny wrinkles and little gray hairs on some of the birds, proof of their long lives. I'd seen them fly hundreds of yards with bullets in their bellies, seen them fly 'til they were dead. Hungry for life, they were. I worried over them for the better part of my life. They'd given me a thing to long for, a hole in my chest that never filled. I wished them safe flight as the tail ends of the "V" flew out of sight.

A while later I heard Lionel's boots come up behind me. "Had to rouse him from his bed."

Lionel helped me pull the skiff to the workshop on a wagon, just in time to see Wick coming out the door of his cabin. I reckoned the man to be about 100 years old. He walked with a stick, and a gray beard tickled his belly. His whole body creaked. But he perked up when he eyed the busted row-lock and bent to his work.

Even so, I had to stay the night atop a pile of old sails in Lionel's storehouse. The cold wind wormed through the half-rotten boards, and I curled up so tight under the moth-eaten blanket that I breathed onto my knee caps. I reckoned sleep wouldn't come, but when I closed my eyes I saw those geese on the wing. With every flip of their wings the cold, dark sky took me over. Heading home.

It was after noon the next day when I pulled a cart loaded with the provisions across the sand to the

370 | DIANN DUCHARME

station. On my way into the day-room I heard men's voices upstairs. It took me a while to figure they weren't the voices I knew. And what's more, they were talking in a language I never heard.

I ran up the stairs two at a time. In the bedroom four dark-haired men lay on our cots. Two were out cold, but the others were trying to talk to Della and Jennie Blount, who were tending them. Jennie held a spoonful of broth to a man's mouth, and Della was bent over a bloody bandage wrapped about a foot. They eyed me when I stepped into the room but didn't stop their work.

"You better go on out there," said Jennie.

"Out where?" I said. "What's happened?"

Though I already knew.

I ran back down the stairs and into the boat room, its big door wide open to the heavy northeast wind. The surf boat was gone, yet the life belts still hung dry on their pegs. I ran down the boat ramp to the sand, and a few hundred yards south I saw a bunch of folks standing close to the apparatus cart.

There wasn't a wreck to be seen, but big chunks of wood were scattered about the sea. I ran down the beach, and the folks turned to point and call to me. The surfboat sat like a dead cooter in the dunes, bottom-up and with the oars scattered about, and the mortar lay cock-eyed, its vent clogged with sand.

I saw nary a surfman, but the crowd—all of the lighthouse crew, plus a couple of men and keeper Willis Partridge from the Caffey's Inlet Lifesaving Station—closed in on me, faces grum yet iron-eyed.

Then I saw the row of bodies laid out on the sand, too many to count in one glance. *At least ten,* I thought wild.

A old woman I recalled from church service glared at me. "You're too late," she said. "Where in tarnation you been?"

"Where are they?" I tried to keep from hollering.

"They've all perished!" cried the woman. "Can't you see? Where you been?"

I turned to the row of bodies lay side by side. And I did see. I saw them all, the men I'd worked with and joked and eaten and slept with for the past four months. The woman went to fall at the men's feet, then started to crying and praying.

I turned away from the sight, toward the invisible shipwreck in the sea. I looked and looked and didn't see. It was all gone.

H. T. Halstead stepped over to me. "It was right after dusk last night Captain Gale spotted the ship from the station house, not two hundred yards from shore," he said. "Jerry Munden came a-running to the village, hollering to wake the dead. I rounded up as many folks as I could and headed over."

"Gale said they were short a man, gone for supplies," said J. W. Lewis. "Reckoned he'd be back shortly. But turned out Caffey's Inlet men showed up before you even got back from Tulls Creek."

H.T. said, "I tried to help. Sat right in the boat with 'em. But Captain Gale picked George Wilson to take your place. Said he was younger'n me."

He looked over at the row of bodies. The cold wind tore at us.

"They took a lantern with 'em. But it soon went out. Then we heard a scream. A god-awful one. I reckoned the boat capsized. The oars came ashore soon after. Then along came their boat, bottom-up."

"Then came Malachi," said J.W.

I bent over, couldn't breathe.

"We waited all through the night for a sign from them. It was the longest night I ever seen. We shot up 41 rockets to raise their spirits, you know. But John Gale came ashore dead, then Lemuel, Lewis, George, and five of the crew."

I heard him, I know I did. But the words slid off my ears, down to the blowing sand. I couldn't catch 'em. They scurried off blind.

"Dawn came, and she was still standing, masts up and sails afurl. A few men on her deck all standing together."

"Jerry and Spencer."

He nodded. "We spotted them on the ship with what was left of the crew."

"They must've been within range of the mortar," I said, my words tearing through the fog.

H.T. rubbed a hand down his beard. "You can see we tried to fire it out," he said. He shook his head. "It jammed up bad. Exhausted all the shot. No one knew how to use it proper."

"Four of the crew rode in on a piece of the wreck," he said. "Busted up bad and not a lick of English. Spaniards, or French mayhaps. But they're alive."

"And…Spencer? Jerry?"

He shook his head slow. "Came ashore a while ago."

I watched Captain Partridge step over to the mortar, try to gouge out sand from its vent with a finger. He soon stood up and kicked the mortar with a boot heel.

"What about their life belts?" I couldn't help but holler now. "They're still at the station!"

"They didn't mess with the life belts," said J.W. "They just took the boat out."

"If they'd have worn the vests, they wouldn't have drowned!"

They all looked at me, doubt in their worn faces. Captain Gale stood forth in the bow of my mind, steering oar in his hands and shouting to the crew. He likely did as he felt comfortable with, no thought to wasting time with the life car nor even the belts. He just wanted to help, to get there fast. It was the first and last shipwreck of their lives.

I squared myself to the sea, my friend and foe since the day I was born. I tried to pray for the souls of the surfmen, for George Wilson, for their families, but words boiled about in the soup of my head.

I was numb with cold and misery when I gathered them all in my arms, the weeping kin of my fellow surfmen. But I couldn't offer them words that might tell how they'd come to face their worst fears, how I'd slipped the hook of fate. I just helped them how I could, with muscles grown queerly powerful with the need to help and the will to forget. I couldn't look at their faces. I helped them load the surfmen's bodies into wagons, then rode with them to the soundside docks to help them carry the bodies to their skiffs.

That night I pretended to sleep, curled up like a sow in the corner of the cook house, dreading to climb the stairs to the room where I'd slept with the surfmen, where four strangers now rested instead. The cook house was warm, for the Blount women had lit the oven to boil water and cook food—cornbread and chicken broth by the smell of it. I heard them walking in and out during the night, whispering to each other, the soft clang of the kettle on the stove, the squeak of the oven door. I heard them say my name sometimes, then late in the night I felt a blanket being laid tender atop my body. I yanked it off when they left. When I saw grey light through the floorboard cracks, I stood up and went outside to the shed where I fetched a shovel.

CHAPTER TWENTY

MARCH 4, 1876
ABIGAIL WHIMBLE

Consider them both, the sea and the land; and do you not find a strange analogy to something in yourself? For as this appalling ocean surrounds the verdant land, so in the soul of man there lies one insular Tahiti, full of peace and joy, but encompassed by all the horrors of the half known life. God keep thee! Push not off from that isle, thou canst never return!

--ISHMAEL, **MOBY-DICK**

"YOU BEST SIT DOWN," SAID LORETTA. IDA AND ALICE STOOD on the threshold at either side of their mama, faces shadowed beneath grey scarves tied tightly under their chins.

I saw Ben as I'd seen him once before, face-down in the cold sand. I hadn't received a letter from him in two weeks. I couldn't sit down.

"What's happened?"

"Now look, before you start to frettin', Benny is alright."

I exhaled, a hand on my concaved chest. The memory of Ben rolled onto his knees and coughed up sea water.

"It's the rest of his crew that ain't so good," said Loretta, grabbing for my hands. "They perished in their duties. 'Twas a shipwreck, you see. Few days past."

My heart beat in the balls of my eyes. "All of them?"

"Even a local man, I heard tell. Took the place of Benny on the boat."

There was very little air in my chest. I used it to exhale, "Where was Ben?"

"Seems he was off fetching supplies from the mainland. Missed the trouble."

A *marketing trip*? What a backwards blessing of fate, to escape death in such a mundane way. My mouth wrestled with senseless words.

"How do you know this?"

The women stepped inside and closed the door. Loretta lowered herself into the chair, knees cracking. "Heard it from Roy. Alice's man. Was up there trading, you see, and heard the news. 'Twas all over the village."

Ida passed me a bottle she'd brought in the basket of food. "Ben is alive, Abigail. Roy saw him with his own two eyes, digging graves for the foreigners who perished in the wreck. Real broke up, he was."

I pulled out the cork and took a pull of the corn liquor. It oozed down my throat like a lit candle. I passed it back to Ida, who drank it as easily as water. They helped me with Oscar, then handed me a plate of cold, gray fish and crumbling cornbread.

"I'm not hungry," I said.

Loretta scratched at the bristly white hairs along her chin as her eyes roamed my length.

"A baby won't take hold if you're too skinny."

It seemed wrong to speak of babies after hearing the news of so many dead, yet Alice and Ida nodded their heads knowingly.

Loretta fiddled with her snuff box and paddle with unsteady fingers. Ida reached to help, but Loretta shooed her off. Once her paddle was firmly tucked between her gums, she declared, "It's a sad day. I know it is. But in my time I've seen a good bit more life than death. Tended to the births of 300 babies since I was but a girl."

"I didn't know you were a midwife."

"I was the one birthed Benny," she said. "I reckoned he'd come fetch me for the birthing of your own babe while back."

"Some of the island women tended me," I said. "It was a…hard labor."

"I heard. Benny should have fetched me over at the get-go. Most folks here figured 'twas on account you didn't want a thing to do with us." She spat a gob of dark juice to the dusty floor. "Scared Benny off from his own kind."

My jaw unhinged. "Not at all. You never…I never felt welcome here."

"You never tried fitting in."

Alice and Ida looked up from the housework, a mixture of guilt and amusement on their faces. Loretta reached a gnarled hand out to pat my knee.

"Now, now. We can see you're a good woman—a schoolmarm, don't you know! We see why Benny cares for you like he does. But back then all we know is Benny's getting hitched with a stranger, stole him right from Eliza Dickens to boot. Took it all bad, she did, thought for sure they'd marry. And we all knowed and loved Eliza since she was borned. By my hands too, I might say, smack in the middle of a storm. Tiny little dark thing, squalling and kicking in time to the thunder. Life ain't been easy for her since, but she fights anyways. I do believe you two have that trait in common."

I saw Eliza as she'd been in this very house not quite two weeks ago. Trembling from chin to ankles with righteousness. I'd tried not to show my fear, or my own latent anger, but the room smelled of spoiled eggs afterward. I glanced to the shelf at the rock of ambergris, its jagged edges.

Loretta passed the plate of food to me again.

"A woman needs a bit of fat on her," she said. "Eat up."

The tin plate rested heavily in my hands.

"Perhaps I'll never have a child." Saying it aloud didn't sound as terrible as I'd hoped.

She shrugged and shifted the paddle to the other side of her mouth. "I reckon life will keep on, either way. But you still got to eat."

Despite the storm that settled on the Banks the next day, Duffy and I left the house to struggle along the eroded shoreline. I'd stewed on the tragic deaths of the surfmen until the entire seascape about me snarled with threat. The house had picked up on the mood as well, hissing and snapping in the wind and rain.

On the narrow beach, shells blinked from their burial grounds. Hungry sea birds fought to fly, searching for wayward prey. With the unfamiliar exercise, however, the thoughts of despair were soon wiped from my head. I worried over each step through the pulling sand as my weakened limbs shook beneath me. Duffy's paws slogged slow and silent in my uneven wake. It seemed the island itself was hungry for our beating hearts and tried mightily to suck us down, devour us, spit out our bones to rest with the driftwood. The faster I tried to walk, the slower I progressed, and I panicked, afraid of being lost here on these treacherous strands. I picked up my skirts and ran stumbling, all the way back to the house.

I woke the next day to find that the storm had tumbled away, revealing the forgotten blue sky. It was as if a great iron had lifted from the linen of the world, and the day fluttered open with renewed hope.

With Oscar somewhat fed and tucked into blankets, I donned my damp coat and bonnet and began to walk north toward Nags Head Woods. I passed the gristmill, the shingle factory, some small farms. When I came to the sandy mountains of Run Hill, I picked up my skirts and loped its inclines to the top.

With my blood warmed at last, I searched for the tree I'd loved since my first summer in Nags Head. Ben had pointed it out to me with the pride of a doting father, encouraging me to look twice at it. The dunes, he'd explained, had crept to the edges of the woods in the steady onslaught of the northeast Atlantic winds and were now devouring trees as easily as cannon fire cuts down soldiers. Most of the trees on the northern edges of the dunes had looked quite dead, but this particular loblolly pine had held a tinge of greenness in its needles, showed the strength of its life in the way the thick vines had crawled greedily over its branches.

We hadn't visited the tree in many years, yet my thoughts had often come to it in the thickets of my mind. It stood before me now, crooked in the mound of sand that had long ago covered its trunk. I wiped my face of sand and perspiration with my coat sleeve and approached it through the silken sand.

It was a corpse of a tree, shrunken and rattling, with bare sticks outstretched in a final plea. The entire mass was dry and brown, with strips and patches of white. Brittle vines snaked across the crusty limbs. No green, no breath, no spirit.

Yet the wind had revealed a small space beneath the branches and vines, a space large enough for a pair of curious lovers. I crawled into the crevice and sat amongst the brown needles, thinking of all I had lost since I'd come here. Two babies, a mother, a baby sister, a father, a sister and a brother, numerous students. Perhaps a marriage. And while I had been struggling, this tree had been foundering as well.

There had been nothing I could do to save it, save any of it.

Birds twittered among the branches above me, the condition of the tree irrelevant.

"Shoo!" I yelled, and they took flight at once, leaving me to the tree's skeletal silence. I said a prayer for the perished surfmen, their families.

After a time, I crawled from the hole and stood up to face the Roanoke Sound and the midday sun.

I was stirring some fouled linens in a boiling pot in the last of the daylight when I caught sight of Asha making her way through the trees. Happiness tugged at my downtrodden heart, and I threw my arms about her before she could say a word.

"I came soon as I could," she mumbled into my hair. I'd written to her about the shipwreck, but I hadn't expected to see her. "Would've come sooner, but you know I couldn't come here without killing a chicken."

Fried chicken mingled with the steam of the laundry pot, and an unfamiliar appetite pricked its ears and sniffed. Asha helped me wring out the linens and hang them to dry before we went inside for supper. The chicken tasted as if it had been laced with ambergris.

After tending to Oscar, I stoked the fire, and Asha and I sat before the hearth, watching the flames lick lazily along the driftwood. The food and the warmth of the fire had brought on an undeniable lethargy, and I closed my eyes, so that I didn't see Asha pull from her bag a package wrapped in brown paper.

"This came for us t'other day," she said, and I opened my eyes reluctantly. Her brown eyes spangled in the low light as she handed the package to me. I recognized Mr. Wharton's handwriting on the paper; it was addressed to Asha Owens and Abigail Whimble.

Sleep suspended, I cut the twine that bound it with a knife. Wrapped securely within were two copies of his book; *The State of Integrated Education in the South* smelled of fresh paper and ink, the smell of promise. There was an unopened letter too, addressed to me.

I handed her a book. "Find the chapter about you," I said. "I know that's what you've been waiting to do."

"No, I ain't," she scolded. But she donned her spectacles and flipped the book open to the table of contents to locate the chapter he wrote specifically about her. With episodic interjections from Asha, I read Mr. Wharton's letter.

Then I read it a second time, more slowly.

The school had been awarded money from the Peabody Foundation, an amount that would buy new supplies, desks and books for a hundred students at least, as well as pay for a teacher. He then went on at length about the Peabody Normal School and the progress that had been made in the last few months. He wondered if I'd considered the position of assistant professor and when I could come to Nashville, if only for a visit.

Possibility broke before me like an early morning swell, rushed and bubbled to my feet with surprising speed. I put a hand over my mouth to hide my jaw-cracking smile, but Asha looked up from the book anyway.

"Good news?"

I let out a breath. "Yes."

Asha and I talked and read late into the night with a candlestick traded back and forth, squeezed beside one another on my tick. As the night wore thin, and conversation ebbed, I told her of Eliza and the ambergris. I showed her the rock she'd left for Oscar; she claimed it smelled of John, of squalling babies, of mother's milk.

"What you fixin' to do?"

"I don't know," I said. "I'm still not sure I'm qualified to be a professor. And you…you could give up the laundry business now. Become the official teacher."

"I meant 'bout your man."

"Oh."

I blew the candle out.

She chuckled a bit. "Barrel full of ambergris. Lord have mercy. He always holdin' on too tight. Afraid to let go," she said. "All those letters he done wrote this winter. Never seen so many letters. Must've spent all his money on stamps, the fool."

I'd thought of the letters, now nothing more than hearth fodder from Eliza's stomping wrath. They'd been echoes of a time long past—of the sun's rays, of aquamarine breakers, of longing. In the safety of the pages, we'd assumed the roles that we'd navigated when we first fell in love on the porch of my family's cottage. Teacher and student, student and teacher.

But Ben's letters had been overlaid with fuming clouds of desperation. He'd endeavored to say more, stretch his mind further than he ever had, and he'd succeeded. But I hadn't been able to escape the feeling that it was the last conversation we'd ever have about a book. The letters were his final masterpiece, resounding proof of his love and force of will. I'd dreaded the last of them, while simultaneously searching for the release.

Though I doubted the conclusion would ever come.

I could feel the shift that had taken place within him. It was in the sands of Run Hill, the quick-moving coastal clouds, the tide lines of the coast. It was bound to happen; the barrier islands that comprised the Outer Banks were long, and stubborn in their way, but at their heart they were thin and fragile, opening and closing.

I shook my head. "I don't think he's afraid anymore."

Asha reached over to stroke my cheek with a rough fingertip.

"You got to go on to that school. You do it for me, and Luella, and Ruth, and all of us. That school in Nashville…that's where you meant to be. It ain't gonna wait for you, neither. Ben, well…he can write you some more letters."

CHAPTER TWENTY ONE

MARCH 20, 1876
BEN WHIMBLE

*I survived myself; my death and burial were locked up
in my chest.*

—*ISHMAEL*, **MOBY-DICK**

WEEKS AFTER DIGGING THOSE SAILOR'S GRAVES, MY HANDS
still chafed raw. I'd left off wearing my gloves on
my patrols. The salty air stung 'em but after a while
served as balm.

I stepped inside the station, my footsteps loud
and ugly on the day-room floorboards. The sound
was about the worst one I ever heard, so I took my
boots off and walked sock-footed up the steps to the
bedroom. Dark room full of cots empty of blankets
and pillows and men. I lay back on the one with the
spread-up quilts.

Jennie and Della still came around to see to me, but I couldn't feature why. I'd never done a good turn for them. Fact, I'd lied to Jennie, then turned about and taken supper from her family.

I took up *Moby-Dick* and started in on chapter 129 in the light of a candle.

Nothing good was coming at the end of the book. Corpses and funerals and other ship's smashed up whaleboats, all on account of the white whale. But Ahab was on the beast's trail now and wouldn't give it up for nothing, taking up the post of lookout himself. The reading came easy for me now, so that the dictionary grew dust on the floor beside me. I thought to still be reading when I fell into sleep. I woke with the sun, *Moby-Dick* open on my belly and the candle burned to a lump.

"Mr. Whimble?" It was Jennie, hollering from the day-room.

"Yeah," I said, voicebox gone rusty.

"Got some cornbread and eggs here for your breakfast," she called up the staircase. I heard Della's voice too and the clatter of dishes.

"Thank you."

"Come on down now."

But I found I didn't want to see Jennie or Della right now. I picked up *Moby-Dick* once more and set in reading. I wasn't sure how long I read, but I soon heard footsteps to the bottom of the staircase.

"You ain't coming down?" called Jennie. She waited a bit. "Mr. Whimble? You alright?"

I sighed and lay the book on the floor. I came down in my socks, trying to smooth my crusty hair and beard.

"Mercy. You look a mess," said Della. She pushed the plate of food toward me.

"Mama," Jennie scolded.

"You been reading that book again?" she asked me.

"I have." I picked up the fork, and the two women hovered about.

"You should close this place up. Like the government men told you," said Della. "You don't need to be here no more. Go home."

"I can't. Someone's got to stay on."

Della sat down, her forehead folded into worry. "You done gave those government men good advice. You done your duty."

I snorted. *My duty, she says.*

Me and the lifesaving government men talked for nigh on a day about what went down that night. Nary a batted eye with regards to my broken row-lock and list of provisions. They just wondered over the mistakes of Captain Gale. *Why, for God's sakes, had he used the surfboat instead of the beach apparatus, for the wreck was in easy range of the mortar and the cart was full of line and shot? Why did he forego the lifebelts? Why did he let the foreigners jump into the surfboat, likely making it capsize?* But in the end, there was no getting away from the deaths of the crew and most of the sailors on the bark.

By way of help, I'd told the men my notions on bettering the service, starting with hiring men with more experience on the sea, mayhaps even more men at each station. I said they needed to build more stations on the Outer Banks on account there was too much sand between one station and another. They needed to have longer active seasons, not just a trifling four months of a year, and changes needed to be made with the drilling schedule, 'specially with the capsize drills. While they were at it, they should buy horses to help the men pull the apparatus cart; a telegraph machine in all the stations; uniforms for the crews; houses close to the surfmen, so folks wouldn't have to travel and fret so much, so the surfmen would have more help, more comfort, less lonesomeness in their lives.

The men, they'd scribbled it all down, fast as they could. I'd felt a little better in saying my peace. Yet my grief caught me up soon enough.

"You got any planking left from the wreck?" asked Della. I'd forgot she was sitting there.

"A bit," I said, poking the cold eggs with my fork like I meant to eat them.

"Sand busted through the kitchen window last night. It's all over the place, hardly fit for living."

I drew myself up straight. "I'm sorry to hear it. I'll come round to help you fix it up this afternoon."

She sighed. "Ain't gonna do much good for the long haul."

It wouldn't. That dune was fixing to eat that house, one way or the other. "Still. I'll come by."

Rain started in early that afternoon, drops dark and thick as goose droppings that slopped their way down the bedroom windows. I read on by the candle light, hardly hearing the wind pound the panes. My only thoughts were of Ahab, what he was doing to his crew with his crazy notions. I hated the sight of his name on the page, couldn't feature how I'd ever had a soft spot in my heart for him. He'd forgotten his duty, forgotten who he was. I told him, *nothing good ever comes from fixing too hard on a thing you can't have.*

I read clean through the last chase, the sinking of the Pequod, the death of Captain Ahab, the senseless survival of Ishmael. There was no stopping me. I plum forgot about going over to the Blounts to fix the window, forgot to piss. Forgot even what Roy had told me, that Abby was living in the Nags Head house and caring for pap. Forgot the look on his face when he saw I didn't even know the triflingest facts about my own family.

I was in the ocean, going down with the crew, no God or Jesus or Bible to save us now. The ocean ruled us over, as ever it did.

I let them come then, the ghosts of the crew. Jerry's low voice called for help. Lewis screamed my name. Captain Gale tumbled into the sea, the steering oar flying from his hand. Spencer muttered prayers for his wife, his children, his unborn child. Malachi, Lemuel, George, they swam about in the cold water, too senseless to even think. All the prayers I'd learned from church service filled my head, and I said them to myself, least 10 times over.

At last I put the book down, eyeballs burning and head spinning. I knew what I had to do.

CHAPTER TWENTY TWO

APRIL 1, 1876
ABIGAIL WHIMBLE

He lives on the sea, as prairie cocks in their prairie; he hides among the waves, he climbs them as chamois hunters climb the Alps. For years he knows not the land; so that when he comes to it at last, it smells like another world, more strangely than the moon would to an Earthsman.

–ISHMAEL, **MOBY-DICK**

A MEMORY OF SPRING AWOKE WHEN I OPENED THE DOOR for Duffy. The air had lost its early morning bite, and the sunrise over the sea dripped with oily color.

After chores, I sat barefoot on the porch, a letter to Martha atop Mr. Wharton's book in my lap. We'd written regularly since my visit, and her letters were both informative and heartfelt, describing in great detail Sarah's emerging character and quickly growing body. The more she opened up to me about her life, the more I wanted to share with her about mine—about Ben, and Eliza, the ambergris, the Peabody Normal School. But I knew that I would have to begin with the loss of my babies, an almost impossible starting point.

I wriggled my cold, white toes in the patch of sunlight. I figured I should get up and don a pair of stockings, for it was still too brisk for bare skin.

I sighed and raised my head from the paper, then jerked to see a man standing at the bottom of the steps. I saw it was Ben, but he'd grown a thick beard and gazed out at the world with eyes of a dimmer blue. He was thin, and his clothing, though clean and mended with patches at the knees and elbows, bagged on his frame.

"Abby," he said.

I stood up, the letter and book slipping from my hands to the porch. As if in a dream, my mouth wouldn't formulate sounds, my body wouldn't budge.

He was home.

I wanted to embrace him, but he seemed a man of sand and sea water and sky, a coastal apparition. Duffy was under no such illusions, hobbling down the steps to him with a keen in her throat. Ben spent some time rubbing her displayed belly, murmuring apologies for his long absence. With a final pat on her head, he climbed the steps. And it seemed the porch was a gallows and I was the executioner, for all of the joy in his homecoming.

392 | DIANN DUCHARME

"I can't quite get over you living here," he said, with an attempt at a smile. "With pap no less. But here you are. What in tarnation came over you?"

I shrugged. There had been no true explanation, no reasoning. "I wanted to help," I said, then added, "To say my peace."

He turned his head just slightly in the direction of the gravestone and nodded slowly.

"Pap's faring alright?"

"Yes, but he sleeps most of the time. Doesn't have much of an appetite either."

Ben's arm reached tentatively through the viscous space between us; he took my hand and kissed it with arid lips. "Thank you, Abby. You're a good woman."

He dropped my hand and peered into the dim house. "You mind if I go in and see him?"

"It's your house too." The words were meant to be light, but once uttered, hung sad and heavy in the air.

I followed him in, and watched him as he crouched by Oscar's side.

"Pap," he said firmly. "It's Ben. I've come back."

Oscar's sluggish eyelids fought with the man's will to awaken, at last cracking apart to take in the sight of his only child's face. Father and son regarded one another for a moment, their long years together, their regard for one another, quite audible in their unsaid words.

Ben told him the story of the shipwreck, the names of the surfmen, their wives and children. He told him they were good men, honorable and strong, and that he never should have doubted them, that he should have done more to help them. His daddy had heard enough after awhile—he listened much longer than I thought he would—and drifted into sleep.

Ben watched him breathe for a while, then stood up and looked about the house. "I guess you seen a barrel setting in here?"

"I have," I said. "But it's gone now."

Expectation turned to alarm. "It's gone? Where to?"

"Eliza Dickens came for it a few weeks ago."

"Eliza Dickens. Came here for the barrel." He enunciated each word. "What did she say? She know what was in it?"

"Ambergris." I said it softly; even the way Americans said the French word—*amber-grease*—sounded beautiful.

"I'll be damned," he said, making Duffy growl in her sleep. He paced to the window, his fingers moving restlessly through his beard. "I can't feature how she knew about it. How she knew it was here."

I looked away from him then. "She somehow found the most recent letter I'd written to you. Read it well enough to learn that I'd asked about the barrel. Seems she'd known already what was in it."

"Where'd she find this letter?"

"She didn't say. But she said she was taking the ambergris to hurt you. She was very angry."

His eyes flicked left and right, as if working a puzzle. "It doesn't hurt *me* none. I was fixing to give it to a family in need, up in Whales Head. Jennie Blount."

"The knitter," I said, nodding. "Well, Eliza did leave a bit of it. For your daddy."

I pointed to the shelf, where it still rested, safe from Duffy's slaver.

An upside-down grin distorted his mouth. "She always did have a soft spot for him."

He picked up the little rock and worked it between his hands. "What else was in your letter?" he asked after a time.

"Nothing much."

He nodded thoughtfully, a little smile on his lips, and took a deep pull of the rock's aroma. Then he placed it carefully back on the shelf and turned to face me.

"At first, I wanted the ambergris for us. To give us a better life," he said. "I figured we deserved it, all we've been through."

"Was it even yours?"

He sighed, and walked over to the hearth to peer into the simmering pot of broth on the hook. He took up the wooden spoon and began to stir.

"I was on patrol, one night in November, when a boy washed up near dead on the beach. His boat was up the shore apace, all cracked up. But there was a barrel in it, tied down tight. The boy—Livy Spruel was his name—he told me to keep it safe. Seems he was trying hard to keep it from his no-account kin. Wanted to give it to the reverend up there, so he could help out his girl's family. Jennie's family."

He banged the spoon hard on the edge of the pot. "And then…he died. Right in front of me. I hid the barrel away in the dunes. 'Til I opened it up one day."

He stood, still evading my eyes. "I didn't know what to do, Abby. I wanted to fix us somehow. I got to thinking. And hoping. The Spruels were after it for a time, figured I'd took it. But the more I thought on it, the more I figured the Blounts should have it. Their house is about to cave in from the sand dunes, and their pap can't work for a bad back. I was planning to give it to them, mayhaps help 'em sell it up north. I reckon Livy would have wanted it like that."

So much had happened in his absence, so much that he'd kept from me. "You could have told me."

He stepped to the window where chains of white linked unbroken across the blue. "I should have told you a lot of things I didn't."

"You wrote about *Moby-Dick* instead."

"Yeah, it felt good while I was doing it. To be talking to you again. In our way, you know."

"They were impressive letters. I should have let you read *Moby-Dick* a long time ago."

He shook his head. "I wasn't ready then."

He looked about the little house he'd built, regret and sadness in the cant of his head. Then he held out his arm for me, suggesting a walk. I took it, and we stepped out the door and down into the sand. With Duffy trotting ahead, we headed to the ocean, then turned south, but I soon noticed Ben's long strides were outpacing me; I was almost running to keep up with him, dodging shards of shells and clumps of dry seaweed in my bare feet while still gripping his arm.

At last he seemed to feel the dead weight of me and slowed his pace. "Sorry, this is just how I walk these days. I didn't do much else these last few months."

He came to a stop and looked about us at the desolate stretch of beach, the ocean scattered with fishing boats and attendant seabirds. He shrugged, as if I'd asked him a question for which he didn't have an answer. He held my face hard with his hands and searched my eyes, the way he used to when the world wasn't so burdensome.

"I want you to let me go now, Abby. It's time."

My racing heart collapsed and fell silent.

He stepped away from me, too close to the sea, so that the ocean washed over the tops of his boots and wet the ends of his britches. He watched the boats drag their nets. I dug my toes into the cold sand, my heart screeching with the gulls.

At last he turned, but kept the sea in his sights. "I'm to be a fisherman again. Just a fisherman. The way pap meant me to be, who I was raised to be. I never should have…I just got the wrong notions into my head. About a lot of things."

He cocked his head to the boats. "Fishermen… live hard. We know life can turn with the changing of the tides or the coming of a storm. Hardship rides along in the skiff with us, eats our meals with us, pisses over the edge with us. It ain't very high up, but we know where we stand in life. And it's a comfort."

He reached into his coat pocket and pulled out *Moby-Dick*. He tried to put it into my hands, but I didn't take it. I took a few steps back from him.

He looked down at the big book. "Some fish are too keen, too hard to land. We've got to let them go. Do you see?"

I shook my head. He'd finished the book, I realized, and had concluded that the hunt for the white whale had been too perilous, the cost too great.

He grabbed one of my calloused hands and turned it palm up. "You ain't made for working with your hands."

He pushed the appendage to my side, as if it offended him.

"Now, I know you can do it. Dear God, you're a strong and smart woman, and you can do whatever you put your mind to. But you ain't *made* for house work, or yard work, or caregiving neither. This life I've given you, it's all wrong. You're made for the workings of the mind. To go to that fancy school and teach and learn. And that's all."

I saw in my mind the old dream of our baby in Ben's arms, a softly rocking skiff beneath them. The hues of the sky, the sea, the baby's white blanket, were so bright, I looked away.

"What about caring for a child? Becoming a mother?" I asked, a mildew of sadness fuzzing my throat. "Am I not made for that?"

His face sagged, the fire gone from his eyes. "Mayhaps," he said softly. "In time."

He turned back to the ocean. "Abby, there's a world out there that's better for you. It's waiting for you. I reckon I knew it all along. I wrote that letter, you know."

I was suddenly tired of letters, of their inability to ameliorate, to illuminate. "Which letter?"

"The letter to the Peabody Foundation, about the Elijah Africa School. And its teacher. I wrote it."

A wave could have overtaken me then, carried me out to sea. "The anonymous author was you?"

"I wanted to help you. I didn't reckon on a job in Tennessee, but I figured writing to the foundation could only get you and the school some of what you deserved. And sure enough, it did."

He shoved the book into my surprised hands.

"Abby, I want you to go to that school. We need to get on with our lives."

He started back toward the house. I watched him trudge until I felt the loss of him, a missing of eyes, and ears, and limbs. I ran after him until the Nags Head house crept into view, cracked and grey.

"Ben!" I hollered. *No, no. I'm not ready to lose him.* The words echoed in my head with every stride, the only words I knew. "Wait!"

He bounded up the steps to the porch and yanked up his bag. I made my way to the bottom of the steps, and his face, when he turned to me, was pinched as a cabbage head.

"I'm coming back," I breathed. "To the school house. Someday. Luella."

And when I said her name, a vision of the Peabody Normal School grew large in my mind. A brick building with numerous windows and hard, stable land in every direction. Eliza was wrong; I hadn't been lost at all. Here on the Outer Banks, I'd been found.

Ben sighed, his blue eyes reflecting indifference, though they brimmed with unshed tears.

"The house…" I said, and had to pause for the crush of my chest. "The way the sunrise and the sunset and the shadows of the trees fill the windows. And the stubborn strength of its wood when the wind blows. And the smell of live oak and smoke and salt. Living here…it's been a good house."

He nodded, and turned to regard it. "It was meant to be."

CHAPTER TWENTY THREE

SEPTEMBER 10, 1876
ELIZA DICKENS

"Close! Stand close to me, Starbuck; let me look into a human eye; it is better than to gaze into sea or sky; better than to gaze upon God. By the green land, by the bright hearth-stone! This is the magic glass, man; I see my wife and my child in thine eye."

–CAPTAIN AHAB, **MOBY-DICK**

ME AND IOLA ROCKED ON THE PORCH, WATCHING THE sun roll toward the west over the sound. The frogs and dogs and gallnippers made such a racket I couldn't hear Iola's baby boy sucking at the teat right next to me.

The Yanks had sent down the wood for the new caretaker's house back in May, and the men I found to put up the house came eager to work. They put it up in only a few weeks, it being so small. But it was big for all we were used to. It had three rooms, so I didn't have to wake every time Willy hollered in the night for his sustenance. The Yanks even sent down a coal cook stove for it, plus two narrow feather beds, a table, two chairs and a chest of drawers.

Needn't say, we hadn't spent much of the money the Yanks had paid us. Iola's mama brought up her old cradle, and the Nags Head women knitted a grist of swaddling clothes, blankets, booties, caps, anything the babe might need. Iola hadn't a notion, but the ambergris was wrapped and buried in the sandy dirt beneath our house, in case Iola and Willy ever had need of it. One never did know, when it came to Yankees.

And Willy was doing just fine, with me and Iola to tend him. We could already tell he was Amos's boy, hands down. He's the biggest, jolliest newborn babe I ever did see. Iola hasn't said Jonas Spruel's name since the day Willy was born. She didn't seem to care if she ever saw him again. She only had eyes for Willy. We planned to raise him up right here in the house, bring him to the clubhouse when Iola had to cook and clean. Us two women would learn him all there was to know about being a man on the Banks.

I couldn't have told why or how I'd come to the awful pass I'd found myself at this past winter. The whole of the season was nothing more than a grease smear in my mind. I hadn't thought of Ben so much neither the past few months. And it was queer how he was just…gone. Like my soul recalled what it was like,

Ben being gone from it, and settled down, at peace again. Didn't even chirk me to hear that him and Abigail were really done too, her gone to Tennessee and Ben living with T.W. in their old abode.

I didn't much care what happened to those two no more. I swear.

I did stew on Abner though, more'n more with every day. When I swept the house out, or hung sheets to dry, or spread up the new coverings on my new bedstead, I saw his face in my mind, like I was doing it all for him. I'd felt bad about taking that letter all those months ago. I'd put him in a bad spot, for what if he'd been brought to answer for the loss of it? Course, no one ever missed that letter. Bunch of claptrap, that's all it was.

Abner still came by the clubhouse every other week or so with letters from the Yanks. He wasn't one to quit a job, once he'd started it. 'Twas like it was his God-given duty coming here. He'd help me read their convoluted script and write out my own letter, then head back on his way. He even took our black-berries with him to sell for us on the mainland, never asked a cent for it. I wanted to cry watching him head north on his skiff, for I recalled the days when he'd waved goodbye to me and just about broke his arm off in doing it. Now he gave me a good look at the back of his head.

But I kept myself busy. I was training the five pups we found to fetch fowl shot from the sky. I worked all day at it, and they were getting to be right good retriev-ers. I'd keep two or three for the Yanks—'specially

Virginia. I planned to sell off the others at my own profit. If I could bring myself to.

I was out knee-deep in the sound with the dogs when Abner came poling up to the docks. I clapped twice to release 'em, and they started splashing and playing just like younguns on the first warm day of spring. I stumped over in wet britches to the caretaker house to meet up with him, loping along with his mailbag bumping his hip. My hand still recalled what it felt like to reach round on the rough inside of it, feel all the cold envelopes, their corners poking my wrist and fingertips.

On the porch he wiped sweat from his brow with a torn shirt sleeve. Then he reached into his coat pocket and pulled out the old learning book. It was good to see it again.

"It's yours," he said. He showed me where he'd written my name on the inside of it. "I shouldn't have took it from you."

Book in hand, I felt my brick heart soften up a bit.

"Got a letter for you." He sat down on the top step and took the letter from his bag. But I didn't move to sit beside him.

"You don't need to help me no more."

That gave him pause. "I don't?"

"I can read script and write on my own good enough to suit the Yanks. They know I'm no schoolmarm."

His one good eye was full of doubt. "It's no skin off my back, coming here."

We looked at one another for a long time, likely the longest I ever looked at another person afore in my life, even Ben. Saw he had a pair of pretty green eyes I never knew he had. A nice straight nose between 'em. He handed me the letter, real slow, and then got up to go.

"You like oyster stew?"

He cocked his head at me. "Is that your notion of a invitation for supper?"

"Mayhaps." I called into the house through the window crack. "You make enough for three?"

Iola raised the window and poked her red face out. She grinned at Abner. "You staying for supper?"

"If Amos Junior says it's alright."

"He could use a man around here. But ain't you got the post to carry?"

"There's always post to carry. There ain't always food to eat."

The dogs smelled the stew and came hightailing it over. Abner's face lit up as he rubbed all of their muzzles.

"I never had me a dog," he said. He stroked Colonel's forehead slow and tender. "I've seen you working with 'em. You do have a knack."

"It takes a grist of patience. But I've had the time to do it."

"Mama said that raising me was all she could handle."

"Pshaw. You're not as hard as all that."

He took his cap off and stepped inside. He looked about at all the Yanks had provided, then turned to me and winked his good eye. And that was all.

We ate supper in the warm quiet, then Abner helped me with the dishes while Iola nursed Willy. It felt right good having him in the house with me. Right natural.

We sat out on the porch in the dark, no candles or lamps to draw the gallnippers.

"How was Nags Head this summer? I ain't been there in a coon's age."

"Busy," he said. "Couple more houses going up on the ocean side. And that Blount family is staying in Ben and Abby's oceanside house for a spell 'til they can take down the wood of their diggings and move it someplace the sand won't get at it. Jennie's got all her knick-knacks lined up on shelves. All kinds of things she's found on the beaches. Some real pretty seashells too."

I could tell he turned his head to look at me. "I reckon you heard Abby and Ben are over. You were right, they really were up on hard times."

I just grunted. I didn't want to talk about Ben, or think about Ben, a day more in my life. I put my hand on the thigh of Abner's bad leg. The warmth of it made me feel the grit I knew him to have, the good heart he had, the love he felt for all kinds of folks, not just me. I'd known Abner almost my whole life, but I didn't truly know him 'til now.

"Can you feel this?" I gave the leg a squeeze.

"Uh-huh," he said. "It's not dead meat."

There was a smile in his words. I moved my hand a good ways further up, felt life perk up beneath my hand. I stood up and went to straddle his lap. Afore he could say a word I leaned in to kiss him. His tongue was soft as Virginia's ears. He groaned a bit and wrapped his arms about me, long and strong. I didn't even think of Ben. Well, maybe just a little. But not much.

"I been wanting to kiss you in those britches for a long time," he said.

He pulled a hand up to touch my cheek. His other hand ran up and down my back, stopping just at the top of my hind parts. My insides turned about, caught up in the wash.

"You should know by now I ain't the quickest learner."

He snorted. "You don't fool me."

I kissed him again. I felt I could sit there kissing him for the rest of my life, if I hadn't of wondered what it might feel like to have him inside me instead. I took him by the hand and led him to my new bed. I pulled back the quilt, and we lay down. And let me just say this. If his leg was half as strong as his pecker he'd be walking pretty good indeed.

I took Abner and the dogs out shooting early season widgeon next morning. I'd been watching their feeding ground for a few days, so we crept in and scared 'em into the sky, them being too skittish to shoot on the water. Abner took slow and careful aim at a hen and took her down easy. He took another shot, then another, and I raised my hand for the dogs to set about their job.

But my own shotgun hung off my arm as I stood there watching the ducks fly for their lives. And I grinned to myself. They scrawled words in a script only I could read.

AUTHOR'S NOTE

Jones's Hill Lifesaving Station was one of the original seven lifesaving stations established on the Outer Banks in 1874 by the United States Lifesaving Service. On the evening of March 1, the Italian bark Nuova Ottavia ran aground on a bar just north of the station. Five of keeper John Gale's crew—Spencer Gray, Lemuel Griggs, Lewis White, Malachi Brumsey and Jerry Munden—and local volunteer George Wilson went to the aid of the shipwrecked crew. Nine of the bark's crew perished, and not one of the surfmen made it back to shore alive.

The sixth surfman—John G. Chappel—was procuring provisions at the time of the rescue attempt.

ACKNOWLEDGEMENTS

This book would not have been possible without my "patron," Sean Ducharme. Breadwinner supreme, father of my three offspring, "beta dog," carpool assistant, light bulb, engine oil, and air filter changer, beach cart packer, middle-aged basketball star, and fellow wine enthusiast, he encourages me in my writing with his steadfast husbandly strength, allowing me the time to pursue an often mentally exhausting and isolating hobby.

Thank you also to my agent, Byrd Leavell, who continued to appreciate the potential of this book.

Thank you to my friends and family who've been especially good cheerleaders—Suzanne and Jeff Gore, Jean and Shep Hanner, Colin and Jamie Ducharme, Lori Jerden, Liz Scioscia, and longtime dinner clubbers Karen and Randy Williamson, Steve and Angela Richter, and Tom and Mary York: Food, drink and friends are the greatest of inspirations. To Eliza Bosworth, thank you dearly for the Nags Head photos, cover sketches, and glorious wine-and-cheese beach weekends, not to mention your unwavering support and cutting-edge style. Thank also to the book club women and bookstore owners I've had the pleasure and honor to meet these past few years; without readers, books would be pretty useless. Thank you for reading mine.

And to my kids, thanks for your pride and constant support, and for reminding me that I can—occasionally—do two things pretty well, but usually not at the same time.

To my late parents, Norman and Patricia Schnell, thank you for fostering my love of books and learning, and for allowing my imagination to grow much bigger than it probably should have. Our time together was far too short, but our love of the Outer Banks lives on.

ABOUT THE AUTHOR

Diann Ducharme grew up in Newport News, Virginia. She majored in English literature at the University of Virginia, and received a Master of Teaching degree from Virginia Commonwealth University.

The Outer Banks House was published in 2010. Her second novel, *Chasing Eternity*, was published in 2012.

Married to Sean Ducharme in Duck, North Carolina on the Outer Banks, she has three beach-loving children and one vivacious border collie. The family lives in Manakin-Sabot, Virginia.

Printed in the USA
CPSIA information can be obtained
at www.ICGtesting.com
LVHW041947040824
787332LV00003B/200